"The Lo[...]itt Reid,
The Gre[...]d, The
Lone Ra[...]inspired
both the[...]ed writers
within these pages will tell you where the story goes
next. Sounds pretty damned exciting to me!"
—Walter Koenig, actor and writer

"It's no surprise that The Green Hornet has survived the
decades in the memories of diehard fans: the concept
of Britt Reid and his alter ego is still intriguing, as the
stories in this anthology clearly prove. And some things
never change: criminals still feel the weight of the law by
the sting of The Green Hornet!"
—Leonard Maltin, movie historian and critic

ACKNOWLEDGEMENTS

You hold this book in your hands through the
support, patience, and assistance of:

David Grace of Loeb & Loeb, LLP representing
The Green Hornet, Inc.

Glen Orbik (www.orbikart.com)

Jeff Butler (www.jeff-butler.com)

Karl Kirchner (www.theblackbeauty.com)

Dennis Rau

John Haig

Lisa Eckert

Jeanne Schanberger

... and Green Hornet fans everywhere.

D1598347

THE GREEN HORNET CHRONICLES

EDITED BY
JOE GENTILE
AND
WIN SCOTT ECKERT

Joe Gentile and Win Scott Eckert
Co-Editors

Rubén Procopio
Art Direction & Story Illustrations

Rich Harvey, Publication Design

"Green Hornet" logo
rebuilt by Tracy Mark Lee

Green Hornet Direct Market PB
(cover by Rubén Procopio)
ISBN: 978-1933076-72-0

Green Hornet Book Market PB
(Cover by Glen Orbik)
ISBN: 978-1-933076-73-7

Green Hornet HC
(cover by Glen Orbik)
ISBN: 978-1933076-74-4

Green Hornet Slipcase HC
(cover by Rubén Procopio)
ISBN: 978-1933076-75-1

Published by
Moonstone Entertainment, Inc.
582 Torrence Ave.,
Calumet City, IL 60409
www.moonstonebooks.com

Direct Market softcover and slip-case hardcover edition cover art: Rubén Procopio

Book Market softcover and hard-cover edition cover art: Glen Orbik

CONTENTS

REFLECTIONS ON THE GREEN HORNET

by Van Williams

My first connection with the TV Green Hornet was when my agent, William Morris, called me and said William Dozier wanted to see me regarding a new TV show called *The Green Hornet*. I was a bit puzzled because a pilot that I had done that year, *Pursue and Destroy*, for Four Star Productions, was on the schedule for the Fall of 1966. To make a long story short, that show was pulled off the schedule because ABC was moving away from single-sponsor shows, and Alcoa was the only interested party, so that show didn't go forward, freeing me up to play The Hornet.

I had always been a great fan of *The Green Hornet* radio show and had followed it for years. When I met with William Dozier, the Executive Producer for the TV show, I told him that I wasn't interested in taking the role if the show's direction was for The Green Hornet character to be campy as had been done with the Batman character on that show. Dozier said that his vision was to follow the approach that the radio show had taken, that is, playing it straight.

Bruce Lee was perfectly cast as Kato and we ended up being very good friends. He and I had a great deal of fun shooting the series together, despite the toll that the long hours and physical effort involved in the fight scenes took on both of us. Even though it was by far the hardest show I had ever done, I enjoyed every minute of it.

I had some concerns about playing the lead as a costumed, masked hero because of the potential of being forever typecast. In some ways this has turned out to be the case, but what a great character to be closely identified with! I must say I am still proud of what I did with the character and I hope that the people that watched the show appreciated and enjoyed how I portrayed him. It's now a big part of my legacy to have played The Green Hornet in the 1966 version of the TV *Green Hornet*.

Flash forward now more than 40 years later, it's wonderful to see The Green Hornet back in the limelight, or should I say green-light? I hope you'll enjoy reading a new set of his adventures, those of his aide Kato, and their rolling arsenal The Black Beauty, in this book of great stories imagined by these talented writers, keeping alive the lore of this unique character.

"...and now, to protect the rights and lives of decent citizens, rides The Green Hornet!"

Sincerely,
Van Williams
"The Green Hornet"

THE NIGHT CAR

by Will Murray

As he stepped off the elevator, Britt Reid could hear the arguing—three male voices blending in a cat-and-dog alley fight.

Mike Axford was shouting, "I tell you, this story is my kind of meat, and don't tell me it isn't!"

"Now see here, Axford. It's right up my alley and you know it." Those were the steady tones of the *Daily Sentinel*'s star reporter, Ed Lowery.

"Both of you settle down!" came the booming basso of Gunnigan. "As City Editor, I make the decisions around here. And I say—"

"Say it more quietly, Gunnigan," inserted Reid in a tired voice. "I was up half the night."

The trio spun around to plead their cases, their voices tangling up like unspooling magnetic tape.

"One at a time," Reid said. "Ed?"

"Mr. Reid, there's this computer expert who says he's got a sure-fire line on The Green Hornet."

"Is that so?" Reid waved him to follow.

The three accompanied their boss into his spacious office. Reid claimed his seat behind the executive desk facing a brooding portrait of his father.

"As police reporter, The Green Hornet is my beat!" exploded Axford, pounding the desktop with a red, calloused fist.

"It's a science story, Mr. Reid," Lowery interjected.

"It's both, from the sound of it," said Reid. "Gunnigan?"

"I want to cover it from the science angle, Mr. Reid. This fella says his newfangled computer can track The Green Hornet back to his nest."

Reid considered briefly. "Sounds right to me. Then it's settled."

"Settled!" Axford fumed, face turning the color of a cooking apple. "If you send Lowery, he'll softpedal The Hornet angle. You know he has a weak spot for that emerald devil."

"And you," said Reid, leveling a finger at the aging ex-cop, "are out of your depth interviewing a man like—"

"Russell Law," supplied Gunnigan and Lowery together.

"Never heard of him," said Reid.

Lowery supplied, "Fresh out of MIT. Computer whiz. Sure to reach the top of his field some day."

"Good. Go to it. The rest of you—scatter! We have a paper to get out."

The trio departed as Reid's secretary, Lenore Case, slipped in, looking fetching with her auburn hair piled high, humor dancing in her brown eyes.

"Break up another family fight?" she asked, smiling.

"There's a Russell Law who is an up and comer in the world of computers, Casey. Ed's going to interview him." Britt Reid's level gray eyes met those of his secretary. "He is supposed to have a foolproof way to track The Green Hornet, no less."

"Oh. Do you want me to fetch his file from our morgue?"

"Discreetly."

"The way I see it," Russell Law was saying, "is that the authorities have taken the wrong approach to The Green Hornet from the start."

Behind him, a tall computer sat quietly like a black filing cabinet equipped with status lights and magnetic tape reels behind a glass panel. In the center, an oscilloscope glowed a phosphorecent green.

"How so?" asked Lowery, stabbing shorthand on a notepad.

Law pushed his slipping glasses back off the bridge of his narrow nose. "Since he started terrorizing this city, every effort has been made to unmask him. But he's proven to be a phantom—positively untraceable."

"He's slick," Lowery agreed.

"No crime lord like him exists anywhere else. He's masked, obviously sophisticated by underworld standards, yet no one knows what his racket is. And he's ruthless."

"No murder has ever been pinned on The Hornet. Not definitely."

"But he's suspected of dozens," Law pointed out. "And every time a lesser player sticks his head out, The Hornet obliterates him—one way or the other."

"More oxygen for him. But how do you propose to unmask The Hornet?"

"By focusing not on the riddle on The Green Hornet's actual identity. That has proven to be a dead end. Commissioner Higgins is on record as admitting that the police are no closer to identifying him than the day he first buzzed through town."

Law gestured toward the silent computer bank behind him.

"Mentor will track The Hornet by finding that custom-built thugmobile he drives," he said firmly.

Lowery raised an eyebrow sharply. "The mystery supercar?"

"I prefer to call it his night car. For obviously he owns a day car and a night car. That logically points to a two-car garage."

Lowery frowned. "Or a chop shop."

"Either way, every night The Hornet puts on his mask and by day he takes it off. Masks leave no marks on a face. But an automobile leaves tire tracks. Especially one as unique as The Hornet's."

"Go on," prompted Lowery, scribbling furiously.

"I don't propose to track the night car by its tire tread—although that may be useful too," Law explained. "But whenever The Hornet is walking around in broad daylight, unmasked, his vehicle is garaged somewhere, probably in the same place each day."

"I think you're on to something..."

"I know I am. The police have never tracked the night car successfully. It's like a ghost. And since The Hornet is a criminal going about a criminal's business, he follows no predictable routes. Except one."

Lowery looked up from his pad, saying, "When he exits and enters his secret garage."

"Exactly! I intend to set up a hotline, taking tips from the citizenry, then feed all sightings of the night car into Mentor here. Out of that data, a pattern will emerge. Wherever the movements cluster, that will point to a definite area where the Hornet car logically and inescapably must be hidden."

"I'm sure the *Daily Sentinel* will be happy to publicize your Hornet hot line, Mr. Law."

Britt Reid read the story in galley proofs in the privacy of his office.

"Are you going to kill the story, Mr. Reid?" asked Casey anxiously.

"And have a rival paper scoop me? Not a chance!"

"But, what if Mr. Law can do what he claims he can do?"

"That, Miss Case, is a problem for The Green Hornet..."

"But you—"

Reid lifted an admonishing finger. "No gossiping on duty."

Casey stiffened. "Yes, Mr. Reid. Anything else?"

"Yes, you may return Mr. Law's file to the *Sentinel* morgue. It made very impressive reading."

After the afternoon editions had hit the streets, Britt Reid started to leave for the day.

"Going home already?" grumbled Mike Axford. "If your father kept bankers' hours like you do—"

"Leave my father out of this, Mike. What did you think of Ed's story?"

Axford made an impatient swiping gesture. "Ah, it's a bunch of malarkey. No electronic brain will ever nail The Green Hornet. Old-fashioned legwork will crack that nut. Mark my words."

"Good-night, Mike."

Claiming his white Chrysler 300 convertible from his personal parking space, Britt Reid sent it shooting out into rush hour traffic. At a light, he paused to take an old-time gold pocket watch out of the glove compartment. He depressed a rim button at 1:50. A slender antenna jutted out.

Nothing seemed to happen, but across town in the District Attorney's office, Frank P. Scanlon had to remove his horn-rimmed eyeglasses to shut off the insistent buzz piercing his ears.

"Miss Hewitt, I'm leaving for the day," he told his secretary.

Britt Reid coasted his convertible into his West Side townhouse garage, automatic doors sealing behind him.

Attired in his crisp white valet outfit, Kato met him with a fresh cup of coffee and a folded newspaper.

"I read Mr. Lowery's story," he said.

Reid nodded. "Pour another cup, Hayashi. I expect company."

Kato's eyes seemed to smile. Whenever his employer called him by his first name, action was in the offing.

A strange chime alerted them. Reid actuated a hidden mechanism by pulling down three cased books on their hidden hinges.

The fieldstone fireplace lifted, and down from the exposed open-cage elevator stepped the district attorney, looking grim.

"What is it this time?" Scanlon asked.

Kato handed him his coffee while Britt Reid pointed a remote at the console TV.

"Good timing, Frank. This will explain everything."

Over DSTV came a televised interview with Russell Law. Behind him, Mentor was alive with blinking lights. Its radar scope-style glass eye stared from its otherwise blank face, a baleful green.

Law was saying, "Against an electronic brain, The Green Hornet is outclassed. It's only matter of time before Mentor fixes his coordinates."

"I see," mused Scanlon. "Do you take this seriously?"

"Seriously enough that The Green Hornet is going to roll on Russell Law and his Mentor computer."

Scanlon grimaced. "He's breaking no laws, you know."

"No, but he's challenged The Green Hornet. It doesn't seem to have occurred to him that The Hornet might pay him a social call."

Kato suppressed a tight smile of anticipation.

"No rough stuff," Scanlon warned.

Reid continued. "Frank, The Green Hornet has done more good for this city than the police and the *Sentinel* combined."

"Ouch."

"Hear me out, Frank. The Green Hornet is too important to be compromised by anyone—including a well-meaning computer expert. If Law does have a scientific way of tracking Black Beauty, I want to know about it."

Scanlon nodded. "What do you need from me?"

"He's depending on tips on The Hornet's movements. I may want you to run interference for me."

"You mean for The Hornet? Okay, let me know what you need, and when you need it." The DA climbed into the elevator to go. "Well, you have one thing in your favor."

"What's that?"

"He's looking for a two-car garage."

The elevator lifted the D.A. from sight, the fireplace dropped back into place and Britt Reid turned to his most trusted friend.

"We roll at midnight, Kato. If you didn't catch up on last night's lost sleep, now is the time."

At midnight, Britt Reid and Kato finished changing into fresh clothes. Reid wore a midnight green overcoat with a black velvet collar and all the other accoutrements of a high-level gangland figure—black gloves, white muffler and dark green homburg.

Kato was elegant in a black chauffeur's uniform and smart driver's cap.

Both men drew on hard masks that moulded to the contours of their faces.

Stepping through a secret door to the garage, they went to a cork pegboard and Kato gave a ratchet wrench a twirl. This exposed a control panel. Buttons were pressed in sequence. Green overhead lights came on.

Then a series of actions caused clamps to take hold of steel bars that jutted out from the four corners of the convertible. Kato pressed a final button.

To the whine of servo motors, the concrete floor began revolving and the white convertible slipped from view. In its place appeared a sleek ebony town car, painted a flat matte finish—the Black Beauty!

Both left-side doors opened automatically. Britt slid into the rear compartment. Kato slipped behind the wheel.

They checked their weapons methodically. Then the Black Beauty eased toward the blank rear wall. It rolled up, opening into an alley. At the terminus, a brick wall parted, and they slid out into a quiet back street behind Reid's home.

Garish green headlights glaring, the Black Beauty ran silent as a shark toward its destination on the other side of town.

Kato steered a zigzag course through the rain-washed city streets, knowing that the police were always on the prowl for The Green Hornet. At intervals, he doused the headlights, and brought up the polarized sets of lights, observing all through the dropdown windshield filter. It was part of his ever-changing evasive driving pattern that perpetually confounded police pursuit.

"Slow up," The Hornet directed from the rear as Kato turned the final corner before the Law lab came into sight.

Kato eased Black Beauty to a crawl. Both men peered through the infra-green light. An unusual black car was parked outside the lab. It had a jutting front end like the chrome-fanged mouth of a wild boar and a tunneled rear window

The Hornet said, "That doesn't look like any car a self-respecting scientist would drive."

"It's not," returned Kato crisply. "That's a Lincoln Mercury Marauder. Just off the production line. It's a big black brute of a muscle car."

"Cruise past it, Kato."

"Right."

Kato slid by the other machine. Head pivoting, the driver spotted them and hit his horn. It blared like a wounded animal.

"Eddie Imbruglia, Kato!"

Kato nodded. "Royal Musto's right arm."

"And my money says Royal himself is inside with his muscle men," bit out The Hornet. "Let's lead them on a chase."

Kato peeled out, making as much noise as possible.

Behind them, excited men spilled out from the Law lab. They piled into the Marauder. It left the curb on smoking tires.

From there on, it was a test of high-performance machines in the city's mazelike streets.

Kato took the next corner on slithering tires. Swerving, the Marauder fell in right behind them.

"How do you size us up against them?" The Hornet asked, peering back through the slit of a rear window.

"They have eight cylinders to our twelve, so we've got the edge. But that's a luxury sports car, therefore more nimble."

"Outrun them if you can. We'll double back to look into Law."

"Right, Boss."

Kato made for the nearest artery and poured on the gas, the Marauder careening after them like a wild animal.

"Sloppy driving," The Hornet said.

"The Marauder tends to shimmy on the hard turns," Kato supplied. "Rear wheels have trouble holding the road."

"Exploit that weakness any way you can."

But the Musto mob had something else up its sleeve.

Abruptly, the Marauder cut across traffic, and disappeared down side streets.

Kato called back, "Orders?"

"Backtrack!"

"Will do."

Leaning into the wheel, Kato pushed Black Beauty back onto residential streets, keeping a vigilant eye for police patrol cars.

Slipping through narrow lanes, Black Beauty picked its way back to the block where the tree-shaded street with the Law lab stood.

All was quiet. Until—

Out from a side street lunged a black monster of a car. It cut them off. Doors opened on both vehicles simultaneously.

Kato came out throwing darts with uncanny speed. The Hornet had his gas gun in hand.

The first hood took a dart on the shoulder and the shock of it spilled a .38 from his numbing paw. The second dodged a squirt of green vapor jetting from the Hornet gun, backed up, and collapsed into the open Marauder door.

Kato moved in. Flashing fists and kicks pummeled another hood into submission. He collapsed like a folding chair.

That was when an arresting sight changed the name of the game.

Royal Musto himself emerged, cradling an old-fashioned Thompson sub-machine gun of forty years vintage, judging by the fat ammo drum. Baring his teeth, he leaned on the firing lever.

It started stuttering and smoking, making his black hair vibrate in sympathy.

The Hornet and Kato retreated to the armored protection of Black Beauty. There was nothing else to do. Their weapons were all non-lethal. Only the Hornet Sting might have worked, but several seconds were required to train its ultrasonic beam on a target to produce results.

For nearly a minute, Black Beauty took a ferocious pounding. Then Kato jockeyed the ebony town car back, then forward, trying to point the front rocket pods at the Marauder.

The approaching caterwaul of a police car ruined that strategy.

Tommy gun smoking, Musto ducked back into his vehicle. Casualties were collected and doors snapped shut. The Marauder backed up and roared away, leaving the stink of burnt rubber in its wake.

"Home, Kato."

Kato hesitated, repressed fury on his masked face.

"Home!" The Hornet repeated.

Reluctantly, Kato sent Black Beauty slinking away.

"We can still catch them!" he insisted.

"We can't chance that our tires haven't collected a few .45 slugs."

"They're bullet-proof."

"Against small caliber lead, yes. So drive carefully."

Kato drove in studied silence, but under his black mask his face was burning.

"We will settle scores with those goons another time," he said tightly.

"You can count on it," The Hornet promised, settling back in his black leather cushions.

That night, they laid their plans.

"Royal Musto knows that he's high on The Green Hornet's list," Britt Reid was saying as he paced his living room.

"So naturally he wants an edge."

"Exactly. And Law's Mentor computer might give him that edge."

"I get it. He wants to track The Green Hornet down for himself, not for Russell Law—or the law."

"Exactly. My guess is that the Musto mob intends to grab Russell Law."

"Which means that we have to stop them—or go to his rescue."

"It's the only way to protect our secrets, Hayashi."

Kato was silent. He fumed.

"You want another crack at them, I know," Reid said.

"So bad I can taste it!"

"You'll get your crack. We both will. But I'm thinking beyond the Musto Mob."

"How so?"

"Law's Mentor computer is useless without its inventor, correct?"

"Correct. They don't dare harm him." Kato's dark eyes narrowed like those of a cat. "Are you saying—"

Britt Reid said, "I'm thinking that it might be to our advantage if Royal Musto does snatch Russell Law and Mentor...."

"You mean, to the advantage of The Green Hornet?"

"That's exactly what I mean, Kato."

Russell Law picked up his lab office telephone three days later to find an increasingly familiar voice asking, "Has the hotline been set up yet?"

"Yes, Mr. Musto."

"Call me Royal. We're friends now. We share the same goal—to crush The Hornet."

"I still can't believe that I am in league with you," Russell Law said, his voice on the verge of cracking.

"You make me sound like the very Devil," purred Royal Musto.

"You are a wanted criminal...."

"Who saved you from being kidnapped or killed by The Hornet. And will keep you safe until The Hornet is finished. Now that you're all set to go, I'll send a few of my boys around to watch over you."

"I suppose there is no way around that," Law said unhappily.

"Not if you want to live. People who cross The Green Hornet have a way of disappearing. And as long as he's alive, you and I have big green bull's eyes on our backs."

"Yes, I realize that now. Well, I must inform the press that the hotline is operational."

"See you around, Law."

The line went dead and Russell Law turned to face Mentor. "You will either kill me, or save me," he muttered. "I see no third alternative."

He picked up the phone again. "Mr. Lowery, please. Russell Law calling..."

Mike Axford barged into Britt Reid's office, interrupting his boss and Ed Lowery in earnest conversation.

Reid looked up. "What it is, Mike?"

"I just seen the afternoon edition. Now that Law has his hotline working, I want a piece of this story."

Ed Lowery began to protest. Reid cut him off.

"What's your angle?" asked Reid of Axford.

"The Hornet! What other angle is there!"

"Mike, if you find an angle that doesn't tread on Ed's toes, I won't rein you in."

"Thanks, Boss! See ya later, Lowery."

Axford was out the *Sentinel* building like a shot.

"This could get mighty complicated, Mr. Reid," Lowery warned.

"More complicated than you think," agreed Britt Reid thoughtfully.

That night, Black Beauty stormed the streets like a black banshee. Emerging from her hidden lair, she ranged the city, harried the police and led the city's finest on a series of daring wild goose chases.

Sliding often into dim back alleys, retreating to rabbit warren side streets, Kato avoided numerous police traps. In the back seat, The Hornet opened up a console and launched the Hornet Scanner, which flew out of the trunk trapdoors and orbited the city skyline, transmitting television images of police movements. Only when the coast was clear, did Black Beauty venture back into night traffic.

Long beyond midnight, all pursuit shaken off or foiled, Kato slipped back into Britt Reid's garage. As the floor turntable swallowed the armored dreadnaught, The Hornet began doffing overcoat and mask.

"Let's see how good Mentor is, Kato."

"I defy any mechancal brain to make sense of our movements tonight," Kato said crisply.

When they awoke the next morning, the news was not good. DSTV was broadcasting an electronic pattern map of Mentor's findings. It showed green blips on the computer's radar-screen eye, signifying where citizens had reported sightings of the mystery car.

"Pretty solid data," Reid admitted.

"But not perfect." Kato shot out a finger. "Look at that. We were never in that sector."

Reid took notice. "Isn't that where Law has his lab?"

"Yes, and there's another false cluster over there."

The broadcast cut to Russell Law, looking nervous, explaining his findings.

"This is a promising start for the Mentor program. I urge all citizens to help find that master criminal known as The Green Hornet by calling this number…"

Reid switched off the set. "I didn't get a good look, but I think that other cluster is the neigborhood where Russell Law lives."

Kato frowned. "What could that mean?"

"I don't know, Hayashi. But it suggests Mentor isn't perfect. And we'll need to exploit every weakness in its electronic brain to stay out of peril."

"Not to mention prison," Kato said.

The day at the *Sentinel* was uneventful until Mike Axford burst in, saying, "There's something fishy over at Law lab!"

Reid looked concerned. "Fishy how?"

"I seen a couple of Royal Musto's goons coming out of that Russell Law's place."

"Mike, are you sure?"

"Sure I'm sure! I'd know those mugs anywhere. And what's more, another pair showed up not long after. So I hung around and watched. And what do you know—"

"Spill it, Mike!" Reid said impatiently.

"They were coming and going all day and half the night like they was factory workers changing shifts!"

Britt Reid's brow gathered darkly. "Now what would Royal Musto have in common with—"

"Don't kid me! They're both out to get The Hornet, and after that green thug tried to snatch Law the other night—"

"Hold on, Mike! That's not necessarily so."

"Well, he wasn't paying the professor any social call, now was he?"

Reid relented. "You have a point. Stay on it. But don't get too close. Where Royal Musto's hoods congregate, lead has a way of flying."

"Ah, I've been dodging lead since they were calling police vans black Marias and prowl cars blue beetles. I can handle myself."

"You obey orders, Mike. Or I'll dock you a week's pay for every slug the doctors have to extract from your stubborn Irish hide."

Turning on his heel, the veteran crime reporter almost bowled over Casey in his rush to get back on the streets.

"What's got into him?" Lenore Case asked wonderingly.

"Mike is on to something. It looks like Royal Musto has taken an interest in Russell Law."

Casey frowned. "Which is not good news for Mr. Law."

"True. But he may not know it just yet. He's more afraid of The Green Hornet."

Casey shut the door with her back.

"Mr. Reid, I'm worried about this thing," she undertoned.

"I am too. But that's The Hornet's problem."

Lenore Case stared at her boss, her feline eyes narrowing, "It will be everybody's problem if he goes to jail—or worse. I think I will make some calls to that hotline tonight. Just to confuse matters."

"Not yet. I need to know just how good Mentor is before we start throwing chaff into its radar."

"Well, the sooner the better, if you ask me."

That night, Britt Reid found Kato glued to the house TV set, oblivious to his daily duties. He looked like he was wearing yesterday's house coat, too. It was uncharacteristically in need of pressing.

"Any new word?" Reid asked.

"No, Mr. Reid," said Kato, keeping up the pretense of a faithful man servant addressing his employer. "But I have been watching repeats of that computer oscilloscope image."

"You're trying to figure out why Mentor showed Black Beauty in two spots she wasn't near last night?"

"Precisely."

"Hold that thought. Mike Axford tells me that Royal Musto's men have been coming in and out of Law's lab all day. That can mean only one thing. Instead of kidnapping Law, the Musto Mob is providing him protection."

Kato jumped up. "Against The Green Hornet!"

"Exactly. We figured wrong. Musto is smarter than I thought."

Kato's jaw tightened. "Smart but not smart enough. We can take him."

"And we will. But first we need to figure out why Mentor is seeing two Black Beautys."

Kato smiled thinly. "Then let's roll, Mr. Reid."

"After you, Mr. Kato."

Black Beauty slithered out into the street long after the sun went down. The Green Hornet and Kato were full of hot coffee and cold determination.

"Kato, let's investigate Law's home neighborhood first."

"Indirect route?" asked Kato.

"Drive like an eel."

The city appeared to be up late, if all the illuminated residential windows were any indication. They spotted shadowy heads leaning out of upper floor windows, binoculars handy.

"Law has the entire city hunting Black Beauty," said Kato grimly.

The Hornet nodded. "This will be a better test than last night. Publicity has excited the armchair hunters."

Black Beauty took corners on barking tires, left rubber tread marks along straightaways and once tangled with an overeager motorcycle cop. A squirt of fresh oil out of the retractable rear-deck nozzle left cycle and rider sliding on their sides to a harmless scraping stop.

Cruising down the sleepy residential streets where Russell Law lived, The Hornet sent the Scanner into the sky. It beamed a crisp video image to a small TV in the back-seat rear console, showing no house lights were on.

"He's sure to be holed up at the lab, anyway," Kato remarked.

Reid recalled the Scanner back into its trunk launch platform, and the assembly retracted silently.

The Hornet's rough voice said, "Take the long way to the lab, Kato."

Black Beauty whirled in a widening circuit of the city. They encountered no trouble. It was as if Kato, by some uncanny sixth sense, could anticipate where prowl cars lurked.

Sliding up the road to the Russell Law lab, they both spotted a familiar machine, back at its familiar stand.

"Marauder," Kato hissed. "Squatting like a big black watchdog."

"Kato, I think I just solved one puzzle. That black bruiser looks a little like Black Beauty around the edges."

Kato grunted. "Looks more like Black Ugly to me."

"To an untrained eye, it might be mistaken for The Hornet's town car."

"It might, at that," Kato conceded. "So that's why Mentor was confused...."

"It's a flaw in the hotline reporting system that I intend to exploit. And we can start now. Let's roust Mr. Imbruglia from his nap."

Kato sent Black Beauty surging ahead. He hit the horn. A gigantic buzzing as of a ferocious Hornet sounded.

The driver snapped awake. He spotted Black Beauty drawing up.

Kato rolled down the passenger side window and gave Eddie Imbruglia a challenging sneer. He revved the engine three times, loudly, then gunned away.

Black Beauty shot into the night like an obsidian javelin.

The black Marauder leapt in hot pursuit, Eddie Imbruglia cursing behind the wheel.

"Shake him, Boss?" Kato asked confidently.

"No. Give him a run for his mileage. Confuse him. Keep him off balance and guessing. The more places he's spotted, the better it is for us."

Kato led the black muscle car on a merry chase. They snaked through Chinatown, Little Italy—even past several precinct houses.

The similarity of two threatening looking black cars confused the police as well. Twice the Marauder was pulled over and twice Black Beauty came around to taunt it into taking up the chase again—once the police had departed, frustrated.

Exhausted, running low on gas, the Marauder finally coasted to a slow stop.

Black Beauty slowed, backed up, and drew alongside again. Kato lowered the passenger side window.

"I win," he said. Then peeling out on screaming tires, he left his defeated foe to suck in a lungful of burning rubber smell.

As Kato began to jockey Black Beauty for a run to the alley where they could vanish from view, The Hornet said, "Keep going."

Unquestioning, Kato obeyed. They shot past the brick wall with its faded mint candy advertisement of two lovers kissing.

"Pedestrian with binoculars," The Hornet advised. "Too dangerous to return home just yet."

"This is getting hairy," Kato said grimly.

"Cat and mouse always is..."

Three times, Black Beauty attempted to return to base. And each time, watchful eyes made that simple maneuver too risky to undertake.

As dawn approached, Kato asked warily, "What do we do now?"

"Head for my country home. We can garage her there."

"Inconvenient."

"Prison is much more inconvenient, my friend," said The Green Hornet, sounding worried.

That morning they rose late. DSTV was reporting Mentor's second-night results. Russell Law, looking as sleepy as Britt Reid and Kato felt, was saying, "Patterns are beginning to emerge. If you look at that screen, the green blips are all individual reports of The Hornet's night car. But once I press this button, Mentor will illuminate in red the area most likely to be The Hornet's base of operations."

The screen changed and certain clusters sprang out like warning lights.

Britt Reid and Kato grunted in unison.

Three areas were outlined phosphorescent red. One was the neighborhood in which they lived.

Grimly, Reid said, "Necessity may be the mother of invention, but it may also have saved our bacon. We'll have to operate out of Ann Arbor for a while."

"Country roads in and out of the city are harder to operate on," Kato pointed out.

"We don't dare garage Black Beauty as usual. Not as long as Mentor can plot our course."

Britt Reid called in sick and then slept late, building up a reservoir of strength for the battle ahead. That afternoon, they laid plans.

"We should pick off Royal Musto and his boys first," Kato suggested.

"Normally I would agree. But Mentor is our biggest problem right now," Reid said seriously.

"We can split up. You tackle Law and I'll make mincemeat of that Marauder."

"Simmer down, Hayashi. Only a cool head will win this night."

But Kato did not simmer down. If anything, he burned even more fiercely. It was in his cheeks and his eyes like hot coals.

Perhaps it was that which led to their first run of bad luck in the battle of wits with the Mentor tracking computer. Or perhaps it was only the odds narrowing in a normal way.

After dusk, with the moon low but climbing in the night sky, Black Beauty eased out of the two-car garage of Britt Reid's country home.

Runing silent, polarized headlights shooting phantom beams of illumination ahead, Black Beauty raced for the city limits. Kato had dropped the steel brooms that whisked tell-tale tread marks off the dirt roads.

Cars whipped past them. But the drivers could hardly pull over and report via phone booths. No such booths this far out of the city.

Luck was not with them. They hit a speed trap, of all things.

A State Police car flung out from behind a roadside billboard, and took up pursuit, lights whirling.

Kato got busy flicking switches on his driver's-side control console. The rear license plate revolved, showing a new number. A small gesture, but it had helped confuse police pursuit in the past. Oil sprayed from the retractable rear-deck nozzle, but after swerving wildly, the Trooper held the road.

"He's stubborn, Boss," Kato reported.

"Shake him any way you can!" The Hornet ordered.

Kato sent the speedometer crawling beyond the red line. He pulled away, Black Beauty's powerful engine leaving the pursing vehicle far behind.

But two miles further along, the flashing lights were behind them again.

"Must know a shortcut we don't," The Hornet fumed. "If you can't shake him, Kato, shake him up."

"Right, Boss."

Suddenly, Kato applied the brakes, swerved and came around, accelerating. He held the road, pointing the black juggernaut at the unsuspecting State Police car.

In the dark, without the benefit of visible oncoming headlights, the Trooper saw nothing—until his own headlights painted the Black Beauty's gleaming grille.

Abruptly, Kato hit the button that dropped the green-tinted double headlights into view. They snapped on with blinding emerald intensity.

Caught unprepared, the Trooper yanked his wheel hard, and was forced onto the soft shoulder of the road. The car careened, then flipped over.

Kato muscled Black Beauty around, and shot past the scene. In the rear, The Hornet's masked eyes appraised the situation.

"He's hurt!"

Kato braked instinctively, backed up.

The Hornet jumped out of the rear seat, went to the Trooper's side. They pulled him out before the engine caught fire.

Together, they loaded the unconscious Trooper into the back seat.

"City hospital, Kato."

"We in a tight spot now," Kato warned, hitting the gas pedal.

"Can't risk the death of a State Trooper on The Hornet's rap sheet."

Driving with expert speed combined with caution, Kato got Black Beauty as far as the city hospital emergency room.

The Hornet carried the Trooper in, Kato hovering around him like a menacing angel of protection. A security guard stepped in, and Kato gave him a restrained taste of Gung Fu. The guard wilted, his weapon unfired.

"This man needs help," The Hornet told the hospital staff, laying him on a waiting room couch.

Then they were gone, melting into the shadows.

Black Beauty negotiated the city's streets with difficulty after that.

An all-points bulletin was out for them. Police from adjoining counties, not to mention angry State Troopers, poured into the city.

They gave The Hornet and Kato a hot time.

"Boss! We have to break for home!"

"Too dangerous! Keep evading!"

But the cordon grew tighter and tighter, until in the end, The Hornet had to recognize the wisdom of his wheel man.

"Home, Kato!"

The brick wall parted, then closed, swallowing the most wanted car and occupants since the days of John Dillinger.

They shucked off their form-fitting masks, betraying clothes and equipment while still in the car. Then they locked all incriminating accouterments in Black Beauty and sent her revolving into her subterranean hideaway.

Dressed in casual attire, Britt Reid and Kato returned to the living room with its comforting fieldstone fireplace.

"That was a close shave," Kato breathed.

"Too close," Reid said thinly. "Mentor may have a fix on us now."

The phone rang. It was Scanlon. "Britt, you're playing with fire."

"The Trooper was an accident, Frank," Reid explained.

"I know it was. And I've been calling in false Hornet sightings, but I'm not sure it's doing any good. I think you'd better lay low for a while."

"We're in too deep to back off now, Frank."

There was nothing more to say. They hung up.

The late evening newscast confirmed their worst suspicions. DSTV was reporting Russell Law's announcement that The Hornet hotline was proving to be a great success.

The local anchor broke in. "According to the computer expert, Mentor has narrowed The Green Hornet's base of operations down to a six-block area on the west side of the city. Tomorrow, Law is promising to reveal the location where he believes the night car is secretly garaged. Further bulletins as they break. This is DSTV."

"No chance Mentor fouled up," Kato said angrily.

"The police, not to mention the public, will swarm all over this neighborhood once Mentor's findings are revealed. And Frank's right. Black Beauty is too hot to travel now."

"Maybe it's time to smash that computer!" Kato said tightly.

"Law may be willing to wait until morning to announce his findings, but the police won't—and neither will Musto. I have a hunch a battle royale may break out at Law's lab tonight."

Kato paced like a caged tiger, "And we're stuck here without wheels."

"We have wheels, Kato. We just need a plan…"

The hour was just shy of midnight. The city was simmering down. But the streets were full of pacing police vehicles like black and white bulldogs on the hunt.

The black Maurauder was again parked outside of Russell Law's lab, Eddie Imbruglia behind the wheel—not napping this time.

Inside, flanked by two of his boys, Royal Musto confronted Law.

"Fork over the results, Professor!"

"This is my data. I intend to release it to the proper authorities."

"Do you think The Hornet will let you live that long?"

"He has not shown his masked face since that first night," Law countered.

"Because he's afraid to, thanks to my boys. But now he's a cornered tiger, and a cornered tiger knows no fear. Mark me, he'll be here any minute."

Law protested, "You promised to protect me."

Royal Musto smiled with suave insincerity. "And here I am—in person. If that doesn't show good faith, what will?"

Law hesitated. "Very well. I will let you see Mentor's findings."

He went over to Mentor and pressed a button. The oscilloscope style glass screen was illuminated. Magnetic tape reels twitched and jerked as data was scanned and processed.

Soon, individual green blips began appearing, forming clusters. One cluster grew larger than the other. Then it flared up red.

"There," said Russell Law proudly, "is where The Hornet parks his night car. Look for two-car garage."

"Alden Park," a Musto mobsman muttered. "Swanky neighborhood."

"Yeah! Well, we're about to tear it apart. Let's go, boys!"

Law gulped, "Wait! What about me?"

"That's right," said Royal Musto, drawing a heavy automatic. He lifted it, aimed the cold muzzle at the cowering computer expert. At the point of pulling the trigger, his hand shifted suddenly.

Three bullets volleyed into Mentor's glowing oscilloscope eye.

Smoke and sparks curled out. The tape reels jerked to a halt. The odor of burning wires filled the room.

And Russell Law collapsed in a corner, shaking in every limb.

Outside, a slim man on a motorcycle drew up alongside the parked Marauder. Attired in a black leather jacket and goggles, the rider shook a green dart decorated with insect wings from one sleeve.

He used to it score a silver line down the car's ebony flank, making a screeching noise that brought the driver popping out from behind the wheel.

Eddie Imbruglia took one look at the motorcycle rider and a flash of recognition warped his angry face.

"Score two for me," said Kato, taking off.

Imbruglia slammed back behind the wheel and took off after his tormentor.

From the lab, Royal Musto came out yelling, "Where the hell are you going?"

A white Chrysler convertible, idling up the street, doused its lights and a tall figure moved away from it, going from bush to bush, picking his way toward the spot where Royal Musto and two tight-coated cohorts were stamping impatient circles in the pavement.

Soundlessly, the stealthy figure emerged from the darkness and sent a roundhouse right at one of the mobsters, striking him behind the ear.

The hood hit the pavement like a side of beef and stayed there.

Musto whirled, a gun suddenly in his hairy fist.

He spied a shadowy figure in an ordinary gray topcoat, wearing a black surgical-style mask with a green hornet enblazoned over the mouth area. Cold eyes bored at him under a dark green homburg.

"You!"

"In the flesh," said The Hornet, giving the mob boss a squirt of billowing green vapor.

Musto and his confederate took it full in the face. Their eyes rolled up in their heads. Knees buckling, they started to collapse into a pile.

The Hornet caught Musto before he hit concrete, pulling him into the bushes.

There, he threw him over his shoulder and hustled him to his idling convertible. The top was down and into the back seat went Royal Musto like a stylish sack of potatoes. Reid hastily stuffed something long and green into the man's empty shoulder holster.

Slamming the door after him, The Hornet slipped behind the wheel. He raised the convertible's roof and locked it into place. The white car took off. Lifting his Hornet watch to his masked lips, Britt Reid asked Kato, "Where are you?"

"Having some fun with this muscle head."

"Where?"

"Crossing Archdale Street."

"Lead him to Woodlawn and Murat Avenue."

"Woodlawn and Murat. Got it."

The Hornet reached the rendezvous first. He hunkered down behind the wheel, not daring to remove his mask in public, and not wanting to be spotted. He was wearing a paper Hornet mask reserved for emergencies. It had the added quality of being gas proof, thanks to a chemical mouth filter.

The sound of Kato's approaching motorcycle brought the Hornet up in his seat finally.

Kato flew by. The Hornet lunged ahead, blocking the intersection with the convertable.

The pursuing Marauder slewed to a squealing stop. Out popped the door, and from it a very angry Eddie Imbruglia. He waved a .38 revolver in the air. His mistake. He should have aimed it.

The Hornet stepped in, his black-gloved fists striking right, then left, then right again.

Staggering and punch drunk, Imbruglia lost his pistol and all attention at exactly the same instant.

The Hornet shoved him into the passenger seat, and transferred the unconscious Royal Musto from one back seat to the other. Reid eased into the Marauder's bucket seat. Backing up, the Hornet grabbed the wheel and the U-shaped shift, and sent the Marauder roaring into the night.

Kato came around, abandoned his motorcycle, and claimed Britt Reid's convertible. He drove at a decorous pace, his goggles going into the glove compartment. A thin smile of satisfaction made his almond face glow.

Over the watch radio, the voices of The Hornet and his chauffuer crackled back and forth.

"All that's left is to stash this thing," The Hornet was saying.

"How does it handle?" Kato asked, curious.

"Corners like the rear deck is trying to shake loose. But I can manage it."

Britt Reid eased into his own neighborhood, slowing. No sense risking police suspicion now, he thought.

But he failed to allow for one thing. Russell Law's hotline.

The neighborhood was alive with prowl cars! They began popping up like swarming soldier ants.

"Kato," Reid said urgently. "Scrap the plan."

"Now?"

"Now!"

"I can run interference," Kato insisted.

"And drag Britt Reid into this? Not a chance!"

"What about your captives?"

"That will have to wait, too."

But it couldn't wait. The Marauder had been spotted, and its resemblance to the mysterious Black Beauty was too marked to ignore.

Sirens wailing, prowl cars began converging on the area like baying hounds.

"Kato, the net is closing. We'll have to improvise."

Anxiously, Kato asked, "How can I help?"

"You can't. Wait! Meet me at Melrose and Clay Street."

"That's in your block!"

"It's the only shot we have. Hurry!"

Using the speed knob attached to the steering wheel, The Hornet flung the Marauder into a wild screeching spin. Tires smoking, he regained control and sped for home. It was a desperate chance. But it was the only manuver remaining.

Careening wildly, the Marauder fought its way through a closing cordon of patrol cars. The Hornet sideswiped two, made sure the drivers saw his masked face, and gunned the V-8 engine hard.

At the prearranged intersection, Reid spotted his convertable approaching. "Kato," he shouted into his watch. "Brace yourself!"

"Brace—?"

The Maruader pounced. Kato swerved to avoid it. But without a clearer warning, he was caught by off guard. The black car hit the convertible broadside.

With a frightening crunch of metal, the two vehicles tangled.

Bouncing away from one another, the convertable went up on the sidewalk, while the Marauder struck a light pole, snapping it in two.

For a long moment, Britt Reid sat behind the wheel, shaken. Then he pulled himself together. Striking a match, he tore off his paper mask and set it alight. It flared up in a sudden burst of flame. Flash paper. He next doffed his hat and flung it into the back seat, where Royal Musto sprawled oblivious to everything. Reid slid out of the battered Marauder, moving low.

Kato was in the act of pushing open the convertible door when a husky voice snapped, "Shove over!"

Britt Reid slipped behind the wheel and urged, "Act dazed."

Both men went into a feigned slump just as the police vehicles surrounded the spot. Doors disgorged men in blue. Flashlights blazed in the headlight glare.

Britt Reid shook his head and looked into the lights splashing into his bewildered face.

"What—what happened, officer?" he said groggily.

"Out of the car, sir. *Now!*"

Carefully, Reid obeyed. Kato came out at the other side, hands lifting.

"I nabbed two of them, sergeant," the patrolman called out.

An answering voice came back. "There's one over here. Looks like he was driving, but the impact threw him into the passenger seat."

A thick excited voice cried, "Where is he? Where's The Hornet? I heard it all over the police band! Now give out!" It was a voice Britt Reid knew well.

The cop with the flashlight in Britt Reid's face said, "This one is wearing a topcoat, sarge."

The familar voice demanded, "Is it green? Tell me! Is it green?"

"No, it's gray."

Mike Axford shoved into view, red face eager. He blinked in the glare, and then his eyes came to rest on the pained features in the flashlight glow.

He burst out, "What! I can't believe it!"

"Believe what?" asked the patrolman.

"That's Mr. Reid!"

"Who?"

"You fool! That's Britt Reid, publisher of the *Sentinel*. My boss. He's no more The Green Hornet than you are!"

More lights came up. Then they began lowering as Britt Reid's driver's license was offered and inspected.

"What happened, Mr. Reid?" asked Axford.

Reid lowered his arms and adjusted his topcoat. "We were driving home and a strange black car came out of nowhere and slammed into us."

Axford yelped, "Saints! The Green Hornet himself almost killed you! For that must be his infernal car."

Other officers were inspecting the battered black vehicle. The driver's door lay open. Light played about the interior. A cop called out, "There's a body in back!"

"Let me see," said Axford, rushing to the scene. Reid and Kato followed, faces serious.

They all gathered around the open door. A back window had shattered in the impact and they got a good look at a man's head, covered by an askew green hat.

An officer reached in and removed the hat, exposing a heavy face.

"That's Royal Musto, head of the Musto Mob!" Axford exploded.

"Is he—is he The Green Hornet?" Britt asked in a shaky voice.

"Naw, he ain't."

But police hands going through the unconscious Musto's pockets brought forth a special pistol. It was as green as a fresh lime.

Axford whistled. "The Hornet's very gas gun! Be careful with that, boys. One whiff will knock you out—maybe you won't ever wake up again, either."

"So," mused Britt Reid. "Royal Musto is The Green Hornet."

"Is?" crowed Axford. "You mean—was. He's going straight to the clink. He'll sting this town no more, mark my words. I tell you, Britt, I've waited many a long year for this day!"

"That means," offered Kato blandly, "this driver is his accomplice."

The police sergeant took the driver by the hair and lifted his slack face into view. "That's Eddie Imbruglia, Musto's chief enforcer."

"And the meanest confederate since Baby Face Nelson!" Axford insisted. "The Hornet's wheel man, nailed at last."

"What happened, Mike?" Reid demanded.

"Well, that Law fellow called it in. Seems Royal Musto—I mean the Hornet—showed up, big as life and demanded what information he had on Hornet's getaway car, and then shot his computer to flinders once he got it. Then The Hornet—I mean Musto—took it on the lam."

"Looks like he was headed for his secret lair," Reid suggested.

Mike nodded eagerly. "Exactly. Law says it's right around here somewhere. We just have to uncover it. According to the professor, it's a two-car garage, at least."

Reid sighed. "Well, that lets out my street. Everyone has a single-car garage—including me."

A general search was conducted. A converted warehouse was discovered with signs that it had once housed a car. Discarded tools and oil drippings indicated that. But no trace of its owner was discovered—or would be discovered. It proved to be a dead end. For it had been rented by Britt Reid through a blind. It was the garage where Black Beauty was originally built.

Dawn had broken by the time it was all out in the open.

"So this is The Hornet's lair!" Axford was muttering. "It looks like it was a horse stable back in the old days."

"What better place to hide a wanted and notorious hood car?" Britt

Reid asked.

Ed Lowery was on the scene by now. He and Axford were fighting over the story, as usual.

"It's my scoop!" Axford said hotly. "And I was Johnny on the spot. Don't you deny it!"

"Russell Law is my interview subject," Lowery countered. "I broke the story."

"Tell you what," Britt Reid said wearily. "Why don't you two split the difference for once? Axford, you handle the scene here. Lowery, you get Russell Law's statement. I want both stories breaking large on the front page tomorrow morning. Side by side. Is that clear?"

"I'm on it," said Lowery.

"Okay by me," grumbled Axford. "There's just one thing."

"What's that?" asked Britt Reid, ready for another argument.

"It's already morning."

Reid turned to Kato. "Get hold of Gunnigan. Have him hold page one. Tell him we're on our way in. Axford—Lowery! You two have stories to write. Headline: Green Hornet Caught. Notorious masked mobster apprehended at last."

"I got a better one, Boss," said Axford.

"What's that?" demanded Reid.

Mike Axford spread his hands as if envisioning the scarehead.

"Green Hornet No Longer at Large!"

Britt Reid gave his crime reporter a shove. "Go with that! Now get cracking. We have paper to put out!"

Behind him, unnoticed in the chaos of the crime scene, Kato repressed a satisfied smile. He knew that The Green Hornet would have to lay low for awhile. But once the heat was off, they would be back in business… the family business.

I HAD THE GREEN HORNET'S LOVE CHILD

by Greg Cox

The headline blared from the front page of the *Daily Torch*, Detroit's sleaziest tabloid. An accompanying photo depicted a sultry blonde cradling a plump infant in her lap. It was surely not a coincidence that the baby had been posed so as not to obscure the blonde's impressive décolletage. In a creative touch, a facsimile of The Green Hornet's trademark mask was superimposed over the baby's face. Pudgy fingers gripped a miniature toy pistol. Smaller headlines, still above the fold, promised:

"Sizzling Excerpts from Flossi's Private
Diaries! Exclusive to the *Torch*!"

Britt Reid scowled at the lurid come-ons. He tossed the tabloid onto his desk, offended in more ways than one. Autumn sunlight flooded the offices of the *Daily Sentinel*. "Is this a joke?"

"Probably," Gunnigan replied. "The *Torch* is a rag, a scandal sheet. You know that." The cantankerous city editor sneered at the rival newspaper in disdain. "No reputable paper would touch a fabricated story like this. It's all hearsay and innuendo."

"Maybe," Mike Axford said. "But, holy crow, it's selling like hotcakes. This Flossi O'Meara dame is already the talk of the town." The veteran crime reporter usually had an ink-stained finger on the pulse of the city. "People can't wait for the next installment of her diaries. It's a sensation!"

"More like sensationalism," Reid said. The dapper young publisher wore a tailored gray suit. He contemplated the not-so-demure madonna in the photo. "Who is this O'Meara woman anyway?"

"An ex-showgirl," Axford supplied. "Used to dance at the Egyptian." The ritzy nightclub was a notorious mob hangout. "That's supposed to be where she caught The Hornet's eye."

Is that so? Reid thought dubiously. He knew for a fact that underworld tips and scuttlebutt were all The Green Hornet had ever picked up at the Egyptian. The woman's face and name meant nothing to him. He couldn't have picked her out of a lineup. *Quite a looker, though.* The black-and-white photo looked more like a glamour shot than a news photo. For a moment, he almost regretted that the seamy allegations were false.

Almost.

He deposited the tabloid in the trash, where it belonged. "I'll tell you this, gentlemen. As long I'm publisher of this newspaper, the *Sentinel* will not wallow in uncorroborated gossip. We have more important stories to cover, like those reports that The Green Hornet is muscling in Salvatore Carlino's numbers racket."

Carlino, an old-school Cosa Nostra type, was The Hornet's latest target. His grubby hands were all over everything from drugs to racketeering. Reid hoped to see him put out of business soon.

"I figured as much," Gunnigan said. "Just thought you ought to see how low the competition is sinking."

"Yeah, they're sinking all right," Axford grumbled. "All the way to the bank."

"Thank you for keeping me informed." Reid gestured toward the door. "Now if you don't mind, Miss Case and I have some dictation to catch up with."

"Sure thing, Boss." Axford joined Gunnigan on his way out. "See ya later."

The men departed Reid's office, closing the door behind them. He looked for his secretary, only to find Lenore Case curled up on a leather couch, engrossed in her own copy of the *Torch*. She flipped the pages eagerly.

"*Et tu*, Miss Case?"

Chestnut eyes looked up from the paper. She grinned impishly. "Anything you want to share?"

"No, and you know it." He was in no mood to be teased. "I can't believe you're actually reading that hogwash."

She shrugged. "Fictitious or not, these 'diaries' are pretty hot stuff." Despite the air-conditioning, she fanned herself appreciatively. "Miss O'Meara has quite a ... vivid ... imagination."

"One that could land her in hot water," Reid said gravely. All joking aside, this was a serious matter. "She's playing a dangerous game. The Green Hornet has plenty of enemies, on the wrong side of the law, who would like nothing better than to strike back at him via his 'child.'" He regarded the masked infant on the front page. "What's the baby's name?"

Casey scanned the text. "Danny. Danny O'Meara."

Poor kid, Reid thought. *Only a few weeks old and already in the soup.* He paced across the office. "I need to nip this story in the bud—pronto."

Casey put down the paper. "I suppose a blood test is out of the question?"

"Not an option," he agreed. "And The Green Hornet can't exactly sue for libel. One of the drawbacks to being a masked criminal." He came to a decision. "I think The Hornet is going to have to call on Flossi directly. Get her to retract the story for her own safety's sake—and that of her innocent child."

Casey gave him a worried look. "You're not going to be too rough on her? She *is* a mother, you know."

"Just rough enough," he assured her. "Hopefully, The Hornet's ruthless reputation will suffice to make her see the error of her ways." He smirked at his own spurious villainy. "That's the *advantage* of being an infamous underworld figure...."

"So they tell me." Casey got up from couch, unfolding her supple limbs. She scrutinized Reid's handsome features. "You know, little Danny does kind of have your eyes...."

"Just find out where she's staying," he said crisply. "And cancel my appointments for this evening."

The Continental was one of the swankiest hotels downtown. The *Torch* had to be doing well if they could afford to set up Flossi O'Meara in a penthouse suite while she "edited" her memoirs. It seemed that crime wasn't the only thing that paid in Detroit these days. Slander and scandal was booming, too.

But not if I have anything to say about it.

An ominous figure crept across the hotel's moonlit rooftop. A midnight green trenchcoat flapped in the cool night breeze. The brim of a green fedora shaded his features. A stylized rendering of an angry hornet was emblazoned on the brow of a mask feared by criminals and law-abiding citizens alike. Beneath the half-mask, a chiseled jaw was set in grim determination. His stealthy tread was drowned out by the muffled whirr of spinning ventilators. Cars honked and sirens blared in the streets below. A nearby clock tower tolled the hour. Ten o'clock.

Flossi was about to meet The Green Hornet—for real.

A glow from a skylight suggested that the creative diarist had not yet retired for the evening. *Good*, The Hornet thought. *I won't have to wake her.*

Kato waited for him in the Black Beauty, which was discreetly parked in a nearby alley. The Hornet doubted that he needed an accomplice to intimidate an overly imaginative showgirl. With any luck, this wouldn't take long.

He darted across the tar-papered rooftop to the edge of the skylight. He peered down through the glass.

The alleged mother of his love child was indeed burning the midnight oil. Clad in a silky pink peignoir, Floss was seated in front of a spanking new Smith-Corona typewriter, pounding out yet another steamy excerpt from her "diaries." A pair of horn-rimmed glasses, which had been conspicuously absent from her portrait in the paper, rested on her pert nose. Platinum curls tumbled onto her shapely shoulders. A pencil was tucked behind one ear. The tip of her tongue protruded from the corner of her mouth as she concentrated on her literary efforts. A steaming cup of black coffee rested by her elbow.

The Green Hornet admired her industry, if nothing else. Still, if he had his way, this latest "exposé" would never see print.

Cool gray-blue eyes surveyed the scene below, cautiously evaluating the situation before making his move. Little Danny was nowhere in sight; The Hornet guessed that the baby was sleeping in one of the adjoining rooms. No boyfriends or bodyguards, either. He nodded in satisfaction. That made things easier.

He inspected the clasp on the skylight, which was locked from the inside. No problem. He extracted the Hornet Sting from the pocket of his trenchcoat. A snap of the wrist caused the foot-long metal baton to telescope out to its full length. He set the sonic device to its lowest setting. *That ought to be enough to shatter the clasp.*

Before he could zap the lock, however, a knock at the door disturbed Flossi's nocturnal typing. A gruff voice called from the hallway outside. "Room service!"

"Keep your voice down!" she shot back in a hushed tone. Her husky voice held a hint of Little Dublin. "You wanna wake the baby?" Drawing the front of her nightgown shut, she scurried to the door. Vanity drove her to tuck the unflattering glasses into her cleavage. "Thank God," she whispered loud enough for The Hornet to hear. "I'm so famished I could eat a kangaroo!"

She squinted through a peephole for safety's sake, then unbolted the door. It swung open. "Thanks, guys. Just put it over by the—"

Three toughs in white livery pushed past her into the room. One of them grabbed Flossi, placing a hand over her mouth and an arm around her waist. A second thug checked the hallway to see if anyone was watching, then kicked the door shut behind him. The third goon put down the tray he was carrying and started searching the suite. "Make it snappy!" Flossi's captor snarled. "Let's snatch the kid and get outta here!"

Damn, The Green Hornet thought. Just as he'd feared, the bad guys were after little Danny. *And they're not wasting any time.*

Neither was he. Throwing subtlety to the wind, he switched the Sting to full power and shattered the skylight with a high-frequency blast. Broken glass rained down on the penthouse below, missing Flossi and her captors by the door. The Green Hornet leaped through the smashed window, drawing his Hornet Gun as he did so. The customized pistol was already poised and ready as he landed nimbly on the plush shag carpet. Glass fragments crunched beneath the soles of his feet.

His dramatic entrance caught the disguised hoods by surprise. They froze in shock. "Holy Toledo!" the thug holding Flossi exclaimed. "It's The Green Hornet!"

The goon by the door reached inside his vest, going for his gun, but The Hornet was too fast for him. A cloud of swirling green vapor jetted from the muzzle of the pistol, right into the face of the trigger-happy crook. The knockout gas had an immediate effect. The goon's eyes rolled up until only the whites were visible and he slumped unconscious to the floor. Limp fingers fell away from his concealed weapon.

That's one down, The Green Hornet thought. He whirled around to confront the acne-scarred bruiser holding Flossi. Well-versed in Detroit's mob scene, he recognized the would-be kidnapper as Johnny "Pizza-face" DeVito, a made man working for Salvatore Carlino. No doubt Carlino had ordered the grab on little Danny, to get The Green Hornet to back off. Anger flared in The Hornet's heart at the thought of an innocent child being used as a bargaining chip in a gangland turf war. He glared at DeVito and his wide-eyed hostage, who wriggled frantically in the crook's grasp. "Let her go, Johnny!"

"S-stay back, Hornet!" the mobster warned. A tremor in his voice betrayed the fear beneath his bravado; nobody had ever gotten the better of The Green Hornet before. He tightened his grip on Flossi, squeezing her so hard she let out a muffled squeal. "Or your kid's an orphan!"

The Hornet finger hesitated on the finger of his gun. The sleeping gas was potent stuff. He didn't want to knock out Flossi, too. He heard a baby cry out in a bedroom behind him, all too aware that the third hoodlum was unaccounted for. This was taking too long. Both Danny and his mother were still in danger.

Looks like I should have brought Kato along after all.

"You think I care?" The Green Hornet sneered at the captive blonde. "This tramp means nothing to me. She's nothing but a lying floozie who should have known better than to throw my name around." Flossi flinched at his harsh words, yet he couldn't worry about that now. "But she's my business, not yours. Clear out ... and take your buddies with you."

"Oh, yeah?" DeVito blustered. "I don't take orders from you."

Just as The Hornet was contemplating his next move, Flossi took matters into her own hands. She bit down hard on DeVito's palm, drawing blood, while simultaneously kicking him in the shin with her bare heel. He hopped backwards, yelping in pain.

"Putana!" Cursing in Sicilian, he shoved Flossi away from him. She tumbled to the floor, her glasses spilling from her cleavage. The Hornet took advantage of the distraction to lunge at DeVito. He swung the Sting like a baton, smacking the crook in the temple. DeVito toppled over like an unbalanced stack of empty pizza boxes. The Hornet gave him a lungful of gas to make sure he wouldn't be getting up again anytime soon.

Two down, he thought. *But where is Danny?*

He checked on Flossi, who was sprawled on the carpet several feet away. "Miss O'Meara?"

"Forget about me!" She gestured frantically at the open bedroom door. Her naked panic struck him as genuine, even if her story wasn't. "Don't let them get my baby!"

He wasn't planning on it. Leaving her alone with the anesthetized gangsters, he burst into the bedroom only to discover that he was already too late. His heart sank at the sight of an empty cradle next to the queen-sized bed. Curtains fluttered in an open window. Racing footsteps pounded down the fire escape outside. He heard a baby crying.

I was afraid of this, The Hornet thought. He had taken too long to dispatch the other two thugs. Rushing to the window, he spotted another of Carlino's men, Lonnie Gallo, nearing the bottom of the fire escape with the crying baby in his arms. A getaway car was parked at the curb nearby. Another mobster called out to Gallo from the driver's seat:

"Get a move on! The boss wants that brat now!"

The Green Hornet realized he couldn't catch Gallo in time; the fleeing thug had too much of a head start. There was no way Kato could intercept him either. Gallo had already dropped onto the sidewalk and was dashing for his ride.

This was going to be a chase.

The Hornet raised his fist. A jade signet ring gleamed upon his finger. "Kato!" he barked into the ring. The miniature transmitter hidden beneath the gemstone had recently been upgraded to carry voice communications as well as a homing signal. "Can you read me?"

"Loud and clear, Boss." His aide's voice emanated from the ring. A slight accent tinged his words. "What's up?"

"We're too late," The Hornet said tersely. "Carlino's men are absconding with the baby in a silver hardtop Cadillac DeVille. Launch the Scanner, pronto. We can't lose that car!"

"Roger that," Kato answered. "You coming down?"

Definitely, The Hornet thought. "Fire up the Beauty. I'll be right with you!"

He cut short the transmission. With no time to lose, he scrambled out of the window onto the fire escape. Before he got too far, however, silk rustled inside the penthouse. He glanced back to see Flossi framed in the bedroom door. Tears streaked her face, smearing her mascara. "Please, get my baby back." Sobs shook her svelte figure. She wrung her hands in dismay. "We both know he's not really yours, but ..."

"That doesn't matter now," he said curtly.

There was no time to comfort her further. Gallo and his precious bundle had already piled into the waiting Cadillac, which was pulling away from the curb. "Call the police to pick up those hoods," he ordered before racing down the fire escape, taking the steps two a time. The cast-iron scaffolding clattered beneath him, waking The Continental's other guests. Startled voices blurted inside the hotel. Darkened windows lit up as he rushed past them. A curious older gentlemen poked his head out the window, only to yank it back in at the sight of the forbidding green apparition descending the stairs. "Ohmigod, it's The Green Hornet!" the alarmed senior citizen shouted to a companion. "Call the cops!"

You do that, the Hornet thought. *I'll be long gone by the time they get here.*

Motor buzzing, the Black Beauty met him at the bottom of the fire escape. He slid into the back seat of the sleek Chrysler Crown Imperial. Its ebony exterior blended in with the night. Glowing green headlights cast emerald shadows on the blacktop ahead. Kato nodded at him from behind the wheel. A black domino mask matched his impeccably-pressed chauffeur's cap and uniform. The Green Hornet slammed the car door shut behind him.

"Let's roll," he said.

Kato hit the gas. The Black Beauty peeled out onto the city streets. Brakes squealed and horns honked as other vehicles got out of the way. Traffic was light this time of night, but there were still plenty of taxis, trucks, and private automobiles cruising downtown Detroit. Steering as deftly as a professional race car driver, Kato wove through the traffic in pursuit of the escaping Cadillac. They quickly left The Continental behind.

The Hornet quickly brought Kato up to speed. "Did you deploy the Scanner?"

"You bet," the driver replied. "It's keeping an eye on that Caddy, just like you wanted."

The Scanner was a remote-operated aerial surveillance drone, which could be launched from the trunk of the Black Beauty. The Hornet switched on a miniature TV screen built into back of the seat in front of him. A bird's-eye view of the speeding Cadillac appeared before his eyes. The flying camera kept pace with the getaway car.

"They're heading northeast along the waterfront," he informed Kato. "Probably heading for Carlino's casino out by the Gold Coast."

"Got it," Kato said. He swerved right toward the docks. The speedometer climbed towards ninety. The Chrysler's powerful engine buzzed furiously.

Police sirens sounded behind him. The cops were no doubt responding to the commotion at The Continental. The Hornet scowled. He didn't have time to play fox-and-hound with the law tonight.

"Silent running," he instructed. "And dark."

"Good idea." Keeping one hand on the wheel, Kato flipped open a control panel next to the gear shift. The press of a button muted the buzzing of the engine, rendering the Black Beauty virtually silent. Infra-green headlights allowed to Kato to navigate the city streets even as the ebony Chrysler appeared totally dark from the outside. Its glossy black exterior practically absorbed the city lights. The cops would need eyes like owls to spot them now.

The Black Beauty sped along the sleeping waterfront. Wharves and warehouses zipped past its tinted windows. Immense steel cranes loomed over the piers. Moonlight rippled atop the surface of the mighty Detroit River. Its deep currents had disposed of many an unlucky mob victim.

How many rivals had Carlino fed to the fishes?

Thanks to the Scanner, and Kato's skills at the wheel, the Black Beauty quickly caught up with the silver Caddy. While they noiselessly tailed the getaway car, The Hornet tried to figure out the safest way to extract little Danny from the gangster's clutches.

That wasn't going to be easy.

"Uh-oh," Kato blurted. A well-lit intersection briefly exposed the Chrysler to view. "I think they've made us."

Sure enough, Gallo leaned out of one of the Caddy's passenger side windows. Spotting the Black Beauty behind him, he opened fire on his pursuers with a loaded Beretta. Flying lead sparked off the Beauty's armored body and bulletproof windshield.

Kato fingered the Beauty's own weapon controls, ready to retaliate. "Rockets or gas cannons?"

"Neither," The Hornet said. "Not with the baby aboard."

"Right," Kato said, sounding slightly abashed that he hadn't thought of that himself. They couldn't risk crashing the Cadillac with little Danny inside. "So now what?"

The Hornet wished he knew. He leaned forward tensely, grateful that Danny wasn't really his own flesh-and-blood. Worrying about the safety of another's baby was nerve-wracking enough. He could only imagine what Flossi O'Meara was going through right now.

The Scanner scoped out the route ahead. Blue-gray eyes widened behind The Hornet's mask as he spied a low bridge crossing one of the many tributaries feeding into the river. The Cadillac was speeding towards the bridge at this very minute. Inspiration struck with the force of the Hornet Sting. The timing was going to be tricky, but it just might work ...

"The Hornet Mortar!" he barked. "Maximum elevation!"

"Of course!" Years of teamwork paid off as Kato instantly grasped what his partner had in mind. Unlike their ordinary rockets, the mortar tubes could be angled to fire at a much higher elevation. He hit the firing controls. "Here goes!"

A blazing missile rocketed from the Scanner launcher in the trunk. It arced above the Caddy to strike the bridge instead. A fiery explosion lit up the waterfront, blowing the bridge to kingdom come. Shattered steel and concrete splashed down into the stream below, sinking deep beneath the frothing surface of the water. The Hornet winced slightly at the property damage. He made a mental note to have Britt Reid make a substantial donation to the city's public works department.

The bomb had done the trick, though. A smoking chasm blocked the Caddy's path, cutting off their escape. It skidded abruptly to a halt. The Black Beauty hit the brakes right behind them, trapping the kidnappers between the Chrysler and the mangled remains of the bridge. The Green Hornet and Kato exited the car from opposite sides, taking cover behind the bulletproof side doors. Bright green headlights caught the cornered Caddy in their glare. Kato hit the horn to get the crooks' attention. A loud buzz sounded in the night—like a swarm of angry hornets.

"End of the road, Gallo!" The Hornet shouted. "You're not going anywhere with that baby!"

The gangster burst from the back seat, gun blazing. He clutched the squirming baby to his chest while firing at The Hornet, who ducked behind the armored car door. Kato whipped a hornet-shaped throwing dart from his sleeve and flung it at Gallo with pinpoint accuracy. The winged dart nailed Gallo in the wrist, causing the hoodlum's gun to go flying from his fingers. It flew over the edge of the pier and splashed down into the river.

Gallo swore out loud. Baby Danny wailed like a banshee. The driver of the getaway car tried to make a break for it, but a second dart struck the Caddy's side-view mirror, only inches from the driver's nose. Kato wagged a warning finger.

The driver retreated back into the car.

That left only Gallo to deal with. The Green Hornet advanced on the disarmed thug, who backed up against the edge of the pier. "It's over, Gallo." He held out his arms. "Give me that child."

Gallo's neanderthal features flushed purple. "You want this screaming brat?" Spittle sprayed from his lips. "Tough!"

Without warning, he hurled Danny over the guardrail into the river.

"No!"

The Green Hornet dived headfirst off the dock. The sudden immersion into cold water came as a shock to the system, but the chilly wetness was the last thing on his mind. The sodden trenchcoat weighed him down, so he hastily wriggled out of it, then kicked off his polished Italian leather shoes. His fedora floated away from his head.

Where? he thought urgently. *Where is Danny?*

Holding his breath, he searched the murky water for the missing baby. At first, he didn't see anything but bubbles and drifting sludge, but...wait, what was that over there? Just when he was on the verge of running out of air, he glimpsed a flailing pink form sinking deeper beneath the river.

Danny!

Powerful kicks propelled him after the baby. He reached out desperately...and felt his hands grab onto a pudgy waist.

Got him!

Lungs burning, he kicked to the surface. His head and shoulders erupted from the river. Holding the baby above the water, while padding to stay afloat, he gasped for breath. Detroit's smoggy air had never tasted so sweet. Water streamed from his soaked brown hair.

But what about Danny? The baby, who had been raising a ruckus in Gallo's arms only minutes before, had fallen worryingly silent. His damp flesh was cool to the touch. The Hornet prayed that he had not been too late again. He slapped the baby on the back.

Cold water gushed from Danny's lips. The baby coughed and sputtered before letting loose with an ear-piercing screech.

"Atta, boy!" A rare smile cracked the fearsome visage of The Green Hornet. The heartfelt wail was like music to his ears. He couldn't have been prouder of little Danny if the boy had been an actual chip off his block. "You've got plenty of lung power, haven't you?"

A life preserver hit the water a few feet away. The Hornet looked up to see Kato gazing down at him from atop the pier. There was no sign of Gallo or his driver. The Hornet guessed that Kato had already taken care of the two mobsters with his customary efficiency. Chances were, Gallo and his accomplice were sleeping off a couple of well-placed karate chops.

The Hornet paddled toward the floating ring.

"All right, Danny boy, let's get you back to your mom."

"Thank God!"

Back at the penthouse, Flossi hugged her baby like she was never going to let go of him again. A pair of police bodyguards, freshly assigned to Flossi in the wake of the kidnapping, snored on the carpet by the door. The Green Hornet had found it necessary to gas them in order to get a few moments alone with the reunited mother and child. The cops would be fine—in an hour or two.

Eyes wet with tears, Flossi looked at The Hornet. She had changed out of the filmy nightgown into a cashmere sweater and snug Capri pants. "Thank you so much! There's no way I can ever repay you for bringing my Danny back to me."

"Just tell the truth," he said brusquely. Although secretly moved by the touching tableau before him, he had to maintain The Green Hornet's nefarious reputation. "That will be better for all of us. I don't need this kind of attention ... or complications."

Guilt contorted the showgirl's lovely face. "I swear, I didn't mean any harm. I just wanted to provide for my baby, after Danny's *real* father left us high and dry." Her husky voice took on a bitter edge. "He was a low-life hood who swept me off my feet, then made tracks as soon as he got me preggers. Claimed he worked for you, actually, but, too late, I wised up that he was just a big, fat liar. Still, that's where I got the idea for this scam." She glanced over at the Smith-Corona. "I always wanted to be a writer ..."

"Words have consequences," The Hornet admonished her. "Never underestimate them."

"I see that now." She wiped her tears away with her sleeve. "Don't worry. I'll go to the papers tomorrow. Tell them I made the whole story up." Violet eyes gazed wistfully around the palatial suite. "Even if it means giving up these ritzy digs."

Despite the trouble she had caused him, The Hornet found himself warming to the struggling single mom, who was proving more likable than he had anticipated. He recalled Casey's appreciative response to Flossi's bogus diary. An idea occurred to him.

"You play ball," he proposed, "maybe we can find another way for you to support your kid."

Hope returned to Flossi's face. "How?"

"Leave it to me," The Green Hornet said. "I have connections in this town."

"Miss Case?"

The distracted secretary looked up from her desk outside Reid's office. She sheepishly put down the brand-new hardcover novel she had been caught reading. A blush of embarrassment tinted her cheeks. "Sorry, Boss. I didn't hear you get back from lunch." She shrugged. "I just can't stop reading this darn thing."

Reid glanced at the book in question. A racy dust jacket displayed the embossed silhouette of a curvy nude being menaced by a large symbolic wasp ... or hornet. Blood-red type identified the book as *Passion's Deadly Sting*.

By Flossi O'Meara.

Reid chuckled to himself. Flossi's first book, a spicy detective novel, had just hit the bestseller lists, months after little Danny's close call with the kidnappers. Reid, in response to a supposed threat from The Green Hornet, had used his professional contacts to introduce Flossi to a colleague at a big New York publishing house. Now properly marketed as fiction, Flossi's literary efforts were finding a big audience, guaranteeing her and her baby a secure future.

"A real page-turner is it?"

"And then some!" Casey raved. "This is even hotter than those phony diaries she was peddling last year. No wonder it's flying off the shelves."

Reid nodded sagely. "And I imagine the scandal surrounding that Green Hornet hoax hasn't exactly hurt sales." The *Torch* had been forced to eat crow, after the *Sentinel* broke the story of how Flossi had pulled the wool over their eyes. "You can't buy that kind of publicity."

Maybe I should send Salvatore Carlino a copy, he mused. The mob boss was currently serving a life sentence in a federal penitentiary, thanks to evidence turned up by The Green Hornet. Carlino had plenty of time on his hands these days. He and his whole gang.

Casey snuck another peek at Flossi's red-hot prose. "I'm almost finished," she volunteered. "You want to borrow it when I'm done?"

"No need," he assured her. "I already have an autographed copy."

Dedicated to The Green Hornet, of course.

WEAKNESS

by C.J. Henderson

Britt Reid sat at his table in the little known Esquire Room of one of Detroit's finer restaurants, The Scotch Brigade. The Brigade had been the city's most exclusive night spot forty years earlier. The twenties had been good to it, and Detroit in general. But time had passed, as it always did. Now, in the bustling, modern sixties, the Brigade was not the "place to be seen" it once was, but it had good food and clean tables. It had survived.

Such attributes were good enough for Reid.

Truth be told, he was also not interested that particular afternoon in being seen. Or at least, in being seen together with his expected luncheon companion. As the owner and publisher of the *Daily Sentinel*, Reid knew something of how to avoid being noticed by the hovering eyes of the city's society columnists desperate for this or that juicy bon mot to drop into their daily list of insinuations. Most of them would not bother with the Brigade anymore. Those that would did not have the pull to get past the doors of the Esquire Room.

Reid glanced at his watch. 12:19. Still eleven minutes early.

"I suppose," he thought, "that's what comes from having the best driver in town."

Time was precious to a man in Reid's position. A commodity he did not care to waste, he turned his attention to the two newspapers he had brought with him. Every day his secretary picked up copies of the *Sentinel's* main competitors, the *Daily Torch* and the *Daily Express*. He did not read them cover to cover, of course. Some days he could not find the time to open a single one of them. But, he liked to keep an eye on the competition, see what they were up to. Had anyone come up with any bold new ideas about lay-out? Had any new advertisers hit the scene? Was a story building somewhere about which the *Sentinel* did not know?

Not caring in which order he looked at them, Reid pulled one of the papers out of his attaché case. Unfolding it, he scanned the headline.

TIME TO SQUASH
THE HORNET

"Double bar banner," the publisher said under his breath, his tone one of quiet pride at the amount of ink his alter-ego had captured. And then, as he glanced over the first column of the accompanying front page article, his lips curled into a smile. He could not help himself.

The headline was a quote given to the paper by Norman "Bud" Peters, Detroit's representative in the Michigan statehouse. Reading with some interest, Reid took in the fact that Peters had suddenly taken an extremely tough "hard on crime" position, and that he had his aim focused on The Green Hornet as the main cause of their fair city's woes. Indeed, so hostile was the level of invective the representative had used, the interview seemed more than the usual politician-filling-the-trough-with-what-the-people-want-to-hear. Peters seemed as if he were out for blood. As if his attitude over The Hornet was more than that of a defender of the people denouncing a threat. To those who could read between the lines, the representative's vitriol sounded brutally personal.

Which was why Reid was smiling.

"So where is this son'va bitch?"

"Please, Mr. Peters, you must control yourself. You mustn't allow this hooligan to upset you. That's how his type gains the upper-hand in a situation."

"*Gains* the upper-hand?" Norman Peters spat the words, choking with disbelief. "Where the hell have you been? He's *got* the goddamned upper-hand and he's using it to squeeze my balls. How is that not clear to you, Nolan?"

As one might suspect, the scenario being played out that evening was as clear as the waters of the Bahamas to Benjamin L. Nolan. He was a fixer, one who had been a behind-the-scenes figure trolling the underbelly of Michigan politics for decades. Stumbling, foolish Norman Peters was a blustering, petty dignitary who thought the rules did not apply to him. He was not the first that the party had called Nolan in to save.

"And luckily," the tall soft-spoken man thought, rolling his eyes in a private, mocking gesture, "job security-wise, he certainly won't be the last, either."

The pair were waiting in a nicely appointed apartment on the twenty-third floor of the very exclusive Randell Arms. It was a comfortably furnished place, one with a rather spectacular view. From its panoramic balcony, one could see both Lakes Erie and Huron, as well as lower Ontario. To obtain such a magnificent perspective one had to achieve a certain height, and when renting this particular suite Peters had spared no expense. He wanted a place that over-looked the water with no other buildings in close proximity.

He had his reasons.

"Everything is clear to me, Mr. Peters," the fixer announced. Masking his exasperation with his client, he added, "At least of that little which I have been told. But, as you know, I have yet to be told very much. If I'm going to be able to help you through this evening, then you are going to have to stop merely shouting and start giving me some information. Now, all I know is you have been caught in an indiscretion, and that you are being blackmailed."

"You're damn right—"

"*Mr. Peters,*" Nolan snapped the politician's name at him like a whip, concerned over ever capturing the representative's full attention. "Listen to me. The rendezvous about which you are so worried is to happen in less than a half an hour. If you do not stop posturing and start telling me what happened, then I can be of no service to you. If it is the case that I actually can be of no service to you, then tell me so that I might leave. You aren't the only fool who needs help in this state, you know."

Norman Peters' usually caustic side began to make an immediate retort, but the calmer aspect of his nature, the part that enabled him to win elections—to smile when embracing his opponents—rushed forward, demanding he stop alienating the only person that might possibly be able to extract him from the situation into which he had flung himself.

"I'm sorry," he said. The words rang of insincerity, but the convenience of them was enough to get the representative to the point where he might cease being his own worst enemy. As he began to fumble for more words of apology, Nolan raised his hand, adding;

"Forget it. You're scared. You've been backed into a corner by some bastard over what I'm certain is some *idiotically* minor indiscretion. Something that wouldn't mean much to any ordinary dullard walking the streets, but which could mean the end for someone in your position."

"You got that right," agreed Peters bitterly. "Ever since JFK left the back of his head in Dallas, the press has started closing in. Used to be you could get a pass on this sort of thing. Look't Kennedy, for Christ sake. The president of the United States, and yet he used to bag every loose piece of quail that wandered by. Everybody knew it, but they kept their mouths shut. Just a couple of years ago, but it seems like forever. People had some respect then, you know?"

Peters sighed heavily at that point, the anger within him crumbling. With no hope in sight and his back to the wall, the representative finally relented, admitting that Nolan was right about his situation. He had been trapped—his back forced to the wall. Knowing no time remained for him to further indulge his need for self-pity, Norman Peters finally came to the point. He had been maneuvered into a corner, all right, one of the oldest ones to be found in the ancient architecture of blackmail.

Slowly, quietly, Norman Peters began to tell his story.

It had begun only a handful of weeks earlier. The representative had noticed a girl working one of the desks in his campaign headquarters. She was a sweet thing, a down home type, a good Michigan girl who came to the big city with both dreams and needs. For years folks had urged her to be a model. She had resisted throughout high school, wanted to go to college, make something of herself.

But, then her father had taken ill. Cancer. His company had let him go, not wanting to bother with the expense of his insurance. His medical bills had been coming close to swallowing up everything the family had. In desperation his daughter had postponed her dreams of college and come to Detroit to follow a lead for a modeling job.

The lead had not panned out. It had only been a huckster's come on, a lure to trap the naive and foolish. The girl had escaped the trap, but not her problems. Her parents still needed money, were still counting on her. With nowhere to turn, she had taken one thankless job after another. Two, three at a time. Her wholesome, but dazzling looks had gotten her part-time work as a greeter in Peters' campaign headquarters. She had been there three weeks when she met the representative.

Norman Peters was not much in the way of a loyal husband. But, he was a canny politician. Carefully arranged trysts, secure, paid-for assignations were at the top of the list in his play book. The representative was a rogue, but he was a careful one—not the type to put himself or his career in harms way. But, Miss Karen Pierce had been different. Not looking to him for anything. Sweet. Vulnerable. Alone.

Helpless.

Before a week had passed after their meeting Peters was seeing her privately. In less than two weeks she succumbed to his charms, giving herself over to him. In only another week she was living on the twenty-third floor of the Randell Arms in an apartment to which both she and the representative had the key. For another three weeks, Norman Peters felt himself the luckiest man in the world. His marriage, as most suspected, was merely a convenience. He had never had any real feelings for his wife—their union had always been for him nothing more than a career-advancing formality.

But, with the arrival of Karen Pierce into his life, his beautiful Karen who worried over him, and cared for him—who put all of his needs first, who was so dutiful and understanding and caring—the representative believed that at last he had been blessed as had so many lesser men. That finally, he had found love.

And then, the envelope had arrived.

It had been sent to Peters' home, marked personal and confidential. Inside it had held three things. The first was a set of photographs of himself with Karen, there in the apartment. Most of them without any traces of either clothing or restraint. The second was a note suggesting he be present there on the twenty-third floor that night with a down-payment of fifty-thousand dollars. In cash. In unmarked bills.

These were, of course, upsetting things to find. But they were manageable. Peters had been indiscrete—had not been careful. Or at least, not careful enough. Still, extortion was something any politician could comprehend. Those putting the squeeze on others were the kinds of people he could understand. What had him so upset was the third thing in the envelope. A single small circle of laminated cardboard. One containing the image of a green hornet.

The calling card of the most feared man in Detroit.

The Green Hornet was feared because he fit no easily understood category. The police could find links from him to almost every major racket in town, but could not find any actual evidence that he controlled any of them. He terrorized the gangs, shaking them down, stealing from them, leaving their members scared, bleeding and broken for reasons known only by himself.

Anyone inside the game, on either side of the law, knew there was something not right about The Green Hornet. Yes, he bled the rackets, demanding tribute, stealing their cash, ruthlessly destroying their operations. It was obvious to all he desired wealth. That was a given. But none could comprehend his master strategy. Yes, he had powerful weapons. Yes, his enforcer was an unstoppable mayhem machine. Some thought his odd methods and unpredictability were simply part of his overall game plan, his way of keeping his rivals and victims off-balance. Unprepared.

Many had tried to eliminate him.

So far, all had failed.

And now, now he had leverage on Peters.

"What," the representative had wondered. "What could he want with me?" Peters was many undesirable things, but he was no fool. He knew a figure like The Green Hornet did not bother with petty blackmail. Even the demand of a fifty thousand dollar first payment—*first* payment—an exorbitant sum for most, was as nothing for such a criminal.

No, Peters was certain The Hornet was after something bigger. That this was merely the opening move in a much larger gambit. But, what could that bigger picture entail? Just what could The Green Hornet possibly be after?

Really be after?

The representative had briefly entertained the notion of ambushing The Hornet—filling the apartment with hand-picked police officers, those willing to shoot without question. He had quickly dismissed the idea, however, as more than foolish—as practically suicidal. Obviously The Hornet knew what went on there on the twenty-third floor. He could see inside. Take pictures through its very walls.

No, Peters realized, one whiff of betrayal and his secret would be out. His wife would have grounds for divorce. She would get everything. And she would get it in a loud and splashy way that would guarantee the end of his career.

As distasteful as the thought was, he simply had to meet with The Hornet, find out what he wanted, and then just give it to him.

"Yes," Nolan agreed, "sadly, at least for now, that is the only sensible thing you can do."

"What do you mean, 'for now?'"

"I'm saying until we see this fellow up close, hear him out, find out what he's willing to say he wants, we don't have any other viable choice. Maybe, once we've established contact, gotten a feel for this man, then perhaps some other avenue of forward motion will avail itself to us. But for now, you've got to sit on your hands and politely keep your mouth shut."

Peters glared, but Nolan simply returned his glare, snapping;

"And for Gods sake, man, don't get your back up at me now. I'm right and you know it. If I wasn't, you wouldn't have sent for me in the first place. Do we understand each other?"

"Yes, damn you."

"Hurl all the invective you like at me," answered the fixer. "Just do yourself a favor and contain your more colorful side when our guest arrives."

And, as if on cue in one of the more standard, unimaginative television dramas, it was at that moment that the sound of a key turning in the lock of the front door was heard. Peters looked at his watch, feeling a cold sweat breaking out on his palms, his forehead, the back of his neck.

11:00.

Right on schedule.

The Green Hornet had arrived.

Peters could not believe what he was seeing. The first to enter the room was The Hornet's man, the one who drove his car, the one who moved like a snake, the one who killed men with a touch from his palm. They said he could walk through walls. That he could fly. That he could punch his way through a man's body or forged steel. The representative had dismissed much of what he had heard about the being standing before him dressed in black, but now, there in his presence, he was not so certain.

The fellow was not overly tall, but his body, the way it moved, even his most casual motions ... Peters did not know how to describe the masked man. The silent, unblinking man taking measure of the room, of Nolan. Of himself.

His tongue feeling dry, Peters tried to lick his lips. He found them dehydrated as well. Five seconds in the presence of the short man in the black mask and his mouth had lost all of its moisture. The fellow had stared at him for two of those seconds, and the representative had gone weak, his shoulders sagging, his forearms feeling so heavy he honestly believed he might not be able to lift them.

"Jesus Christ," thought Peters, "what the hell's wrong with me. He's just a man. He's just ..."

And then, after a total of eight seconds in the presence of the servant, the master entered, and for the first time in his life, Norman Peters knew true and utter terror.

The Green Hornet came into the apartment in much the same manner as his enforcer. Silently, his every movement calculated—tight. Compact. Peters found himself actually gulping as the criminal master walked forward. The representative lowered his head as The Hornet drew closer, unable to force himself to make eye contact with the masked man. Peters' mind cursed him for the weakness, for feeling such fear simply because a person had approached him, but he kept his mouth shut, further frightened by anything he might say—by the depths of terror he might reveal to this man who already knew far too much about him.

Nolan, not completely composed by any means, either, but knowing why he was being paid to be present, debated within his mind whether or not to take a forward step when he spoke. He knew the action would send a subconscious signal of strength—of confidence. But, the back of his mind whispered, what would it signal if he were to stumble, to trip on the rug, drag his feet? The fixer had met the most ruthless men in the state, and numerous other states as well. He had dined, played cards, gone drinking with murderers and monsters of every stripe. Always he had been able to count on his own inner hardness to carry him through.

But ... this man ... this Hornet person ...

Deciding against risking a faltering step, Nolan remained standing where he was, swallowing carefully to keep his voice from cracking when he said;

"So, The Green Hornet, I presume?"

"Benjamin Nolan," countered the criminal. Holding his hands behind his back, the masked man said cordially, "The party must think as highly of Peters as I do, to send someone with your reputation to protect him tonight."

The fixer felt his jaw quiver. He had not expected to be known to The Hornet. Although he was recognized in a vague manner throughout the world of Michigan politics, his actual purpose was known to only those behind the most closed of doors, and then only at the highest levels. His lower jaw threatening to shake uncontrollably, Nolan clamped his teeth shut, covering his lack of response by merely tilting his head. As he did so, he caught the slightest upturn of one end of The Hornet's mouth.

The masked man was smiling at Nolan's discomfort. Laughing at him. The fixer felt the fingers of one hand beginning to curl into a fist. Then, suddenly, as he realized his emotions were on the rise, Nolan felt an equal surge of panic. In the days to come he would tell himself he allowed his fingers to return to a relaxed position so as not to arouse The Hornet's suspicions, to reveal that he was more in control than the gangster might think. In that moment, however, Nolan knew the truth.

He was frightened.

Filled with a weakening fear by a man who had done nothing more than compliment him. And smile.

"Gentlemen," said The Hornet, his voice low, hard but concise, "can we get down to business."

Despite the wording, or the casualness of his voice, The Hornet had not asked a question. Standing in the center of the room, his eyes fixed on the pair of politicians, it was clear he was waiting for something. Both knew what it was. Placing his hand gently on Peters' shoulder, signalling him to remained both seated and quiet, Nolan reached behind the chair in which the representative was seated. Pulling forth an innocent looking leather satchel, he held it out before him.

Without any signal either man could see, The Hornet's man stepped forward and took the bag. Again, his movements struck both Peters and Nolan. Had not the enforcer been across the room? How had he crossed so quickly? It seemed as if he had taken but a single step, and yet, given his height and the distance, such seemed impossible.

It was such a minor concern, thought Nolan, and yet the answer to it might possibly explain so much. The stories he had heard about The Hornet and his man—his terribly dangerous man—many swore The Hornet's enforcer could not be merely human. There were rumors of satanic rites, barbaric sacrifices made to dark gods so that the fellow might reap supernatural benefits. Some said he was a vampire. Or robot. The fixer had always laughed at such wild, impossible notions.

He was not laughing any more.

Silently Nolan watched the enforcer snap open the bag he had been handed. He could not follow the movement of the man's hands—his gloved hands. The fixer had found the bag's clasp troublesome, and yet this fellow opened the satchel with the barest touch. One moment it was closed in his hand. The next, it was empty, the money that had been inside stacked on a nearby table, the bag discarded. After that, the enforcer pulled a cloth, string-draw bag from somewhere on his person and slid the cash inside it. Drawing the bag tight, he slung it over his shoulder in a simple motion and then went back to his original defensive position.

Peters and Nolan could do nothing but stare. The entire transfer had taken The Hornet's man no more than ten seconds. Less. Time they might have taken to plan a strategy, to work out what they would say next— might have, if they had been dealing with anyone else.

"All right," said The Hornet, his voice catching the pair of politicians off guard, shocking them, reminding them that their evening was far from over, "let's get this over with."

"But, the money ..." said Peters weakly, "you ... you didn't count it."

"Did I need to?"

The sudden shift in The Hornet's tone filled the representative with terror. He was used to dealing with all manner of men in his world, but even when necessity forced him to consort with society's less desirable elements, never had he ever found himself in the presence of one so utterly strong-willed, so overpoweringly self-assured.

Despite his slightly higher level of self-control, Nolan felt much the same way as his charge for the evening. Before the arrival of the masked pair, the fixer had been thinking of possible strategies he might follow, certain standard snares he might set during the conversation he would engineer that might help give him a stronger bargaining position. But, having been in the presence of The Green Hornet for less than a minute, he had already been forced to admit within the privacy of his mind that he had no idea with what he was dealing.

"If you would like to end things," Nolan offered, desperately hoping to keep his voice from breaking, "you're going to have to direct us. After all, you said be here, have money—we were. We did. So now, tell us—what next?"

Again The Hornet's enforcer crossed the room faster than either Nolan or Peters could register. Somehow his previously empty hand now held a sealed envelope. Nolan bit at his lower lip unconsciously. He had thought his question would bring forth a response from their adversary, give him some further information, along with some much needed time, with which he might puzzle the man out a bit. But such was not the case.

"What's this," he asked, accepting the envelope.

"Read it."

The pair of words were spit at him by the enforcer. The man's voice had an Asian tone to it, but the accent was too gruff, too Americanized for him to try and identify the man's nationality.

"Stop trying to be clever, Ben," a cautious voice from inside his mind whispered. "Study. Learn—survive the night. Settle for simply living to see tomorrow."

As the fixer considered his own advice, he tore open the envelope, extracting the single sheet of paper within. Unfolding it, he found a typed list of conditions beyond the initial payment made that evening—assignments, tasks, demands—which The Hornet apparently required. Nolan read the eight points on the list quickly, then again more slowly. Having absorbed their essence, he passed the sheet to Peters, instructing him to read it as well. He made it to the seventh point before commenting.

"What is this crap?"

"A problem, Mr. Peters?"

"You're goddamned right there's a problem. What do you mean with this shit?"

"These are things you gentlemen will arrange. There is nothing difficult here, not for the two of you, working together."

"But ..."

"If you'd rather I go to the papers—"

"But the things on this list, they ... they don't make any sense."

"They don't make any sense to you, Mr. Peters."

So far The Hornet had remained standing in the center of the room, roughly three yards away from the still seated representative. Now, he took a step forward. His hands still behind his back, his voice still sharp and low, he said;

"I'm not in the habit of explaining myself, but I'll make an exception here. This time. We're going into business together, Mr. Peters. Or should I say, I'm coming into your business. As, shall we say, a silent partner."

Peters began to speak, began to rise, but Nolan put his hand firmly on the representative's shoulder and kept him in his chair. Nodding sharply, his eyes an unblinking warning, the fixer glared his client into silence. Pretending not to notice the exchange, The Hornet continued, saying;

"That you don't understand my requirements of you is a good thing. The less you know, the less trouble you'll be, and the less trouble you'll be able to cause. Especially for yourself."

"But ..."

"Everything on that list is something I need done. You will see that they are done. It's as simple as that. I need certain men moved from one position to another. I need several districts rezoned. The why of any of it is not important for you to understand."

"You're telling me to divorce my wife!"

"Is that a problem, Mr. Peters?"

The representative froze, holding himself in check. The Hornet's voice had dropped to a frighteningly sinister whisper. The man had taken two more steps toward him. Towering over Peters, the masked man said;

"I asked you a question."

"A, a divorce ... that's the end of a political career. If I file, when everything comes out ... what would be the difference if you send your pictures to the papers or not?"

"Have I gotten my facts wrong? Is there something I don't understand? Are you telling me that you actually love your wife?"

"No, not really. She's just, well you know, convenient. A good politician's wife. Good family. Clean past. Knows how to keep her mouth shut ..."

"Does she know you're a cheat?"

Again Peters hesitated. Then, thinking he was getting a sense of what was happening, he admitted;

"She's not a stupid woman. She probably suspects."

"Then she probably wouldn't mind being rid of you, would she?"

Peters' mind churned. Things were changing, he knew that was true. People did get divorced without media fanfare. And, he knew The Hornet was correct. Peters' wife was desperate to be shed of him. So desperate, if he gave her the option to leave quietly, she would jump at the chance.

"What's in all this for me?"

"Besides getting to keep your seat at the statehouse?"

"Look," snapped the representative, feeling some slight control over the situation returning to him, "I—"

"What Mr. Peters means," interrupted Nolan, seizing control of the conversation, "I believe, is that he simply wants to understand the parameters of our situation. You have the money. We have your list. If all eight of your points are met, what comes after that? Where will we stand?"

"You, Bud," The Hornet smiled again as he paused after using Peters nickname, "will be the shining knight, fighting for the rights of the people. Alone in the world—your wife off doing whatever feminists do when they leave their noble, long-suffering husbands—you will throw yourself into the protection of the innocent. You will fight for a system that cracks down on the corrupt and thieving. You will become Michigan's Batman, her Dick Tracy, Shadow, whatever you like."

"So that's it," growled Peters. Nolan placed his hand on the representative's shoulder once more, but Peters shrugged it off. Angry enough to throw caution along with common sense out the window, he actually rose from his chair, snarling;

"I'm just supposed to become your puppet. Your stooge. And just how long is this going to go on? What's the use of such a life to me?"

"I don't bleed people, Mr. Peters," answered The Hornet in an almost paternal voice. "It's ultimately useless because it breeds hopelessness. You want to know what happens next, I'll tell you. I walk out the door with your money. You perform the tasks on your list. After that, you bark about crime and the need for reform, and we never see each other again."

"And why should I bother?"

"Because," added The Hornet as he turned his back and walked for the door, "you probably want to see Karen Pierce once more. Alive."

Peters' eyes went wide, his spine cold, his soul numb. In his self-concerned fear, he had not even stopped to wonder about her whereabouts. He had noticed that she was not there when he arrived, of course, but he had been so wrapped up in his own problems he had not thought about her. His Karen. His precious love. In the hands of the animal walking away from him, the monster laughing at him. The Green Hornet.

"You son'va bitch," screamed Peters. Without thought the representative launched himself forward—for several inches. Then, he slammed into the waiting palm of The Hornet's enforcer. The masked man, almost forgotten, had moved with his terrifying swiftness, placing himself in between the his criminal master and Peters. The representative bounced off the man's open palm, stumbling backward, arms flailing, breath knocked from his lungs. As Nolan caught Peters before he fell, The Hornet turned, smiling as he said;

"Well, good to see you have at least some guts. Just do as you've been told, Mr. Peters, and everything just might be fine."

And then, The Green Hornet passed through the apartment's front door and disappeared out onto the twenty-third floor. As his enforcer vanished behind him, Peters shrugged his way out of Nolan's grasp. Shaking his fist at the closing door, he shouted;

"This isn't over. I'll get you, Hornet. You'll see. I'll wipe that smile off your face."

His adrenaline rush subsiding, reality seeping once more toward the front of his mind, the representative began to realize the extent to which he had fractured his life. Turning toward Nolan, he stared directly into the man's eyes. Seeing his own weakness reflected therein, Norman Peters stumbled off to a chair where he could simply collapse and lose himself in his tears.

Britt Reid continued to hold his newspaper, there at his table in the Esquire Room, but he was no longer reading. His mind was lost in thought over Peters and what he had done to the man. He wondered if the representative would ever put together how Kato had simply come down from the roof to the twenty-third floor of the Randell Arms to take his pictures. Of course, his ability to enter the penthouse silently had been greatly facilitated by the fact the door to the balcony had been left unlocked by Peters' paramour.

Karen Pierce was not the woman's name, nor was she any helpless innocent. She was a prostitute, one well paid for her services. The woman was given the assignment to lure and seduce the representative, and to be ready to leave town forever when told to do so. Given both her cash payment of fifty thousand dollars, and the fear she held for The Green Hornet, she had been on a train headed for Los Angeles fifty-five minutes after she had received the cloth, string-draw bag Kato brought to her that same evening.

The list Peters had received from The Hornet had for the most part been a blind, false alleys to confuse and dumbfound the representative into doing the two things he actually wished the man to do. First, he wanted Peters angry at The Green Hornet. His was a dangerous game, striking at the mobs from within. If he wanted people to believe he actually was a criminal, he did have to commit some crimes once in a while.

Reid believed, quite rightly, that what he had done to Peters would keep the pot stirred for quite some time.

As he saw his luncheon companion being escorted to his table, he folded his newspaper, waiting to hear if he had worked things so he might get the second thing he was after.

"Britt," said the woman, allowing the waiter to pull out her seat, "it's been ages. Too long."

"Well, you know me, always running around up to something."

"I don't care," she answered, her smile beaming at him, "your timing couldn't be more perfect. I have the most wonderful news."

The woman was a striking brunette, one whose face showed a one-time loveliness worn dull by stress and tension. She was buoyant and lively at that moment, however, enough so that one could tell much of whatever had marred her former beauty had been eliminated from her life.

"Are you confirming the rumors we've all been hearing?"

"Yes I am." Her smile widening, the woman tilted her head as she suddenly began to giggle, and then simply laugh out loud. Rapidly the details surrounding her joy spilled forth. After years of being trapped in a loveless marriage, she was finally getting a divorce from her husband. It was something she had never expected. He needed her on his arm for the crowd. Her social position and good breeding had been an asset to him during his climb to the State House. But now, for some reason unknown to her, he had suggested that a quiet, amicable separation might be the best thing for them.

"I don't know what's come over him, letting me go free, this new anti-crime crusade of his, and frankly Britt, I don't care." Reaching across the table, in the manner of a friend only, she squeezed Reid's hand, adding;

"I just thank my lucky stars for whatever saint thought it was my turn to be blessed with a miracle."

For the next several minutes, the soon-to-be ex-Mrs. Norman Peters let spill her excitement over her future. She was, she had just begun to realize, still young enough to do many of the things she had always wanted to do. Dreamed of doing. She was already in the process of putting most of her belongings into storage.

"I've already booked a flight to France," she announced, her eyes focused not so much upon her luncheon companion as they were some point in the future. "I'm going to be living in Paris for at least the next year."

"That sounds exciting."

"I hope it is, but you know, I don't care if it's exciting. As long as it's different. As long as I never again feel the way I've felt the last eleven years." Taking a sip from her water glass, the woman licked her lips, then added;

"I'm going to live, Britt. I'm going to throw myself out into the world, and *live!* And God help any fool who gets in my way this time."

Then, the woman laughed. And as she did so, Reid realized it was the first time he had heard his old friend do so in a very long time. It was not a harsh or vindictive noise, or a thing laced with self-pity. No, it was a wild, cleansing thing—more the sound a person makes who somehow staggers out of a plane wreck unscathed. Who flies through a windshield without taking a cut. Who falls from a rooftop and barely scrapes a knee. Who beats a cancer.

Or lives through a suicide.

It was the laughter of those who never expected to laugh again. And it was a music that soothed a man's soul in the way that nothing else could. Britt Reid watched his friend feel joy once more, and the feeling of it made him smile as well. Especially when he remembered her husband's parting words to him;

"I'll get you, Hornet. You'll see. I'll wipe that smile off your face."

"Well, maybe you will at that, Bud," thought Reid. Grateful as he was for the boost Peters' anti-crime campaign was giving his criminal reputation, still he knew making a personal enemy in the State House was a dangerous move.

"But then," he added, knowing that in the end, the only thing that mattered was that he had done what was right—

"Maybe not."

TOPSY-TURVY
by James Chambers

The hippie in the tie-dyed shirt wore brass knuckles.

He had an angry face and a long reach, but he was clumsy and slow.

The Green Hornet blocked the tie-dyed man's punch to his jaw, feeling the weight of the brass weapon as he brushed it aside, and then landed a devastating left against the man's right ear. He continued with two quick jabs to the man's left kidney, blocked another awkward shot, and then finished with a tight, fast uppercut to his opponent's chin. The blow sent the tie-dyed man sprawling backward onto the alley's wet floor.

Footsteps slapped the ground.

The Hornet spun.

A man in a peace shirt rushed him, but The Hornet responded with a roundhouse kick that jolted his attacker against the alley's brick wall.

Nearby a bearded man swinging a motorcycle chain slashed the air around Kato, who twisted and danced to evade it. Kato darted under the chain and jabbed his foe's legs with sharp, open-handed blows until the man lost balance. Then he leapt above the lashing weapon, spun, and struck with a jackhammer kick to the bearded man's face, putting him down in a jumbled mess with his chain wrapped around him. Kato landed, facing The Green Hornet with a tight smile on his face.

It faded fast.

"Boss!" he shouted.

Reacting on instinct, The Hornet dropped to a crouch, and then reached up and back to grab the man in the peace shirt, who was attacking him from behind. He grabbed onto him, then thrust upward, and launched him across the alley. Peace shirt spiraled downward, fell across the bearded man, groaned, and didn't get up.

"Maybe next time they'll give peace a chance," said The Green Hornet.

"Don't count on it," Kato said.

"Let's see what they're hauling."

The Hornet walked to the back of a delivery truck parked at the mouth of the alley and raised the rear door.

Faint whispering sounds came from the dark cargo space. The Hornet took a flashlight from his belt and lit up the inside. Sacks of seed were stacked against the walls, and tied and gagged between them squatted three terrified teenagers: two girls and a boy. They blinked against the light with dazed, glassy eyes.

"Get them out of there," The Hornet told Kato. Then he walked back to the tie-dyed man, who was stirring, and flipped him face up.

"Who do you work for?" said The Hornet.

The man spat out a blob of blood. "Get...lost...."

The Hornet dragged the man upright and slammed him against the wall. He punched him twice in the gut.

"Where were you taking those kids? You think I'm going to let drug monkeys like you cut in on my action?"

The Hornet jerked the man by his shirt, cracking his head against the brick wall.

"Tell me who you work for!"

"Boss," Kato said.

The warning tone in Kato's voice cut through The Hornet's rage. He dropped the tie-dyed man to the ground.

"It's pretty clear who's running this show," said Kato. "There are boxes of these in the truck."

Kato handed The Hornet a comic book.

"*Topsy-Turvy,* 'The Adventures of the Man Who Lived an Upside-Down Life,'" The Hornet read from the cover. The art showed a trippy caricature of a man, dressed in a red coat with his hair floating around him like a halo. The Hornet flipped through the pages, skimming the psychedelic drawings. "Raja Ben, Detroit's homegrown Donovan. Looks like the rumors are true. Find anything else?"

"In the sacks are about 500 pounds of rye seed. What could that be for?"

The Hornet didn't answer. He watched the three teens climb down from the back of the truck. They looked disoriented and high, but their fear kept them focused.

"How did you wind up here?" The Hornet asked them.

One of the girls stepped forward and said, "We won't tell the cops you were here, okay, man? Just...don't hurt us. Please."

"I won't, if you answer my question."

"We were at a concert at the Live Flyer club. Someone invited us backstage to drop acid, except it wasn't acid. Stuff got really strange. It was like the music was rubbing against our skin, then everything went black, and then ... then, we woke up in this truck."

"What concert?"

"That guy." The girl pointed to the comic in The Hornet's hand. "Raja Ben."

Britt Reid looked through the open door into a hospital room painted gold with morning sunlight. Lenore Case, his personal secretary, sat at the bedside of her cousin, a young woman named Lana. An intravenous drip fed medicine into the sleeping girl. Lenore looked as if she hadn't slept all night.

Britt knocked on the door. "Casey," he said.

Lenore's eyes lit up when she saw Britt. She jumped up and hugged him tight. "It's so good to see you. It's been such an awful night."

"I'm sorry I wasn't here sooner."

"It's all right. You're here now."

"How is she?"

"The doctors flushed the drugs out of her, and she's going to recover, but..."

"But what?"

"She's going to be fine physically, but they're not sure about psychologically. They won't know what she was on until they get test results back, but whatever she took was potent. She's always been such a sweet girl, but when I got to her at the club, you should have heard the things she said, rambling about living an upside-down life and turning the world inside out, and all the garbage from that comic book I told you about."

Lenore picked up her handbag, pulled out a rolled-up comic book, and handed it to Britt. It was *Topsy Turvy*, a different issue than the one he'd seen last night. It showed Raja Ben and three young people floating over the Detroit skyline, except the city was upside down at the top of the page, and the Raja and his followers were positioned so that they looked right-side up on the cover.

"*Topsy-Turvy*."

"Not exactly *Little Lulu*," said Lenore. "She wouldn't let go of it until they sedated her."

"You're sure she was at the Raja Ben concert?"

"I saw him on stage. A lot of the kids there were like Lana. This Raja guy is some kind of pied piper filling their heads with nonsense. Lana wasn't supposed to be there. My Aunt Gladys is adamant about that sort of thing, but she snuck out with her friends. One of them called me when she saw how weird Lana was acting. Someone at the club must have slipped her the drug."

Britt thought of the three teens he'd rescued. After getting Lenore's call about Lana in the middle of the night, he'd decided to investigate as The Green Hornet. He had been monitoring Raja Ben as a player on the Detroit drug scene for weeks, and he thought he might catch a break. He and Kato had arrived at the Live Flyer club in time to spy the three men loading a truck by the back exit, and then they tailed them to the alley where they confronted them. Britt shuddered to think of what might have been in store for those kids if not for him and Kato, of what might have happened to Lana if Lenore had not gone to get her.

"She got lucky. It could've been much worse."

"What do you mean?" said Lenore.

"It's a good thing you were there for her. That's all. Listen, Casey, whatever the doctors need to do for Lana, tell them to spare no expense. The *Sentinel* will cover the costs."

"Thank you." Lenore hugged Britt again and kissed him. "Sometimes it's not so bad having a media mogul for a boss. I owe you a night out."

"No argument from me," said Britt, smiling. "I'll call you later to see how Lana's doing."

The Asian man dressed like a square in a neat, black suit looked entirely out of place in the cramped head shop. The store's shelves were jammed with little statues and imaginatively carved pipes and bongs, and on the walls hung black-light posters and tie-dyed sheets. There were shelves of record albums, a spinner rack full of comic books, like *Zap Comix* and *Topsy-Turvy*, and a display of underground newspapers and magazines. Incense smoldered by the cash register, filling the air with an earthy aroma. The head shop was one of several owned by Raja Ben.

The pale man behind the counter wore sunglasses with small, round lenses and a stained Jimi Hendrix t-shirt.

"Peace, bro," he said. "Give you a hand with anything?"

"Perhaps," said Kato. He took a copy of *Topsy-turvy* from the rack and set it on the counter. "I'm a pop art collector. I'd like to meet the man who draws this. It's Raja Ben, right?"

"The Raja only publishes it. Guy named High Waters draws it. But he lives in Frisco, so you won't meet him around here. If you're interested in the Raja, he plays a gig two or three nights a week over at the Live Flyer. He's playing tonight. I hear he's got some of the original art. Maybe he'd show it to you."

"That would be most generous of him."

"Yeah, man, he's into that whole groove about uniting the world through art. He's cool."

"Very cool. How much?"

"Like it says on the cover, fifteen cents."

"One of these, too."

Kato took one of Raja Ben's albums from the display. The cover featured a photo of the Raja in a flowing, red coat, holding a white cane, his long hair tucked beneath a Westernized turban. He was smiling, but it was a joyless, toothy grin. Kato put money on the counter then left the store. He walked around the corner, where he slid into the passenger seat of Britt Reid's white Chrysler convertible.

He handed the album and comic book to Britt.

"Well, Hayashi?"

"One man behind the cash register. I heard others in back, at least three. At the other shops there was only the cashier. A truck like the one we saw last night is parked a few stores down."

"Maybe it will happen here tonight."

"It seems likely. Raja Ben is performing again."

Britt started the engine and pulled away from the curb. "Let's circle the block, get the lay of the land."

"We have two more of Raja Ben's shops to visit," Kato said.

"We will. Then we're going to take in a concert. I want to see the Raja in person. He's dealing marijuana and LSD, definitely, and heroin, probably, and now we know he's kidnapping young people. A friend in the Windsor land records department tells me the Raja has property outside the city there, but he couldn't get the address."

"Ontario. Could be they're taking those kids across the border?"

"There's more happening here than we've uncovered. The Raja isn't what he seems. He calls himself the Motor City mystic, but Raja Ben's real name is Ben Rogers. He's from Ann Arbor, and he has a degree in chemistry. We have to find his place in Windsor and see what his real game is."

"What do you suggest?"

"What would you say if I asked you to take a dive next time we face the Raja's men? Then let them pack you off with the kids, except you'll be wearing this." Britt handed Kato a green jade signet ring identical to the one he wore as The Green Hornet. Inside the stone was a transmitter. "I'll track you, and you'll be on the inside when we take them down. You game?"

"I'm in," said Kato. "Only one problem. Who's going to believe one of those guys could take me?"

"They're not too bright. Make it look like a lucky shot. They'll buy it."

Kato parked the Black Beauty behind a Dumpster down a deserted alley one block away from the Live Flyer club. The Green Hornet swapped his costume for a plain black suit, and then he walked to the club and entered as Britt Reid. Twenty minutes later Kato followed him, also dressed in ordinary clothes. Inside the club the two acted as if they didn't know each other. Kato found a space at the bar, and Britt hung back in the smoky shadows toward the rear. They were older than most of the people there and they didn't blend in, but it didn't matter. The crowd was too preoccupied with the music and atmosphere to worry about a couple of squares who didn't look like cops.

The club was decorated in a psychedelic aviation motif with cartoon airplanes trailing rainbow clouds painted on the walls. Strange creatures danced on the colorful swirls. Miniature, tie-dyed parachutes hung from the ceiling, each one dangling a peace symbol from its strings.

Some of the young people on the dance floor moved to the jukebox music, waiting for the concert to begin. Most others stood around talking, drinking, and smoking. A few had the same glassy-eyed look Britt had seen on the teens he and Kato had rescued. At least, Britt thought, it seemed Lana would be all right. Lenore had called him that afternoon to say the doctors had determined that she'd ingested an attenuated type of ergot, a fungus that grew on rye plants and from which LSD was synthesized. With some therapy, Lana would recover, but Britt wondered how things might have gone if the drug had stayed in her system. Raja Ben's expertise in chemistry would enable him to cook rye-produced ergot into a dangerous, custom drug. He wondered how many other kids had fallen prey to Raja Ben's scheme and if there'd ever be any recovery for them. Drugs were pervasive on the street these days. It was an insidious, deadly evil The Green Hornet couldn't confront directly; he wondered if it was a battle that could ever be won.

The jukebox music faded. The house lights dimmed.

The room plunged into darkness, and a tambourine began to jangle a short, fast rhythm. A bass guitar joined in, popping and rolling deep notes through the club, and then came a quick, punchy drum beat, followed by lazy chords played on an acoustic guitar in counterpoint to the other instruments.

The lights flashed bright.

At center stage stood Raja Ben in a flowing red coat and a sleek, blue turban. He strummed a Martin acoustic and stared at the crowd with an intensity that surprised Britt. Behind him a band played. The music was powerful, alluring, and when the Raja began to sing, his rich voice filled the club. It got inside Britt's head and drew him into the song. The lyrics told of a man who lived an upside-down life and learned to change the world through love by bringing everyone together in the great topsy-turvy. Britt felt his mind start to empty, his eyes drawn to the colors flashing around the room. He shook off the feeling and focused on three men moving through the crowd.

They were the same three he and Kato had fought last night, now bruised and bandaged. They were choosing glassy-eyed teens and ushering them backstage. They gathered four: two boys and two girls.

That was all Britt needed to see. He left the club, knowing Kato would soon follow.

Back in the Black Beauty, The Green Hornet fitted his mask on his face and donned his hat to complete his costume. He checked all his equipment, and Kato, now also wearing a mask, did the same. The Black Beauty had been well hidden down the alley. Kato started the engine and drove into position to watch the rear exit of the Live Flyer club. A Volkswagen bus was parked there.

The Green Hornet and Kato waited.

More than an hour passed before the door opened.

The tie-dyed man emerged, followed by the bearded man, with his motorcycle chain looped across his chest. The four teenagers came next. The men ushered them into the Volkswagen and slammed the doors shut. The third man appeared, sporting a shirt with a stylized hand flashing the peace sign in red, white, and blue.

The three men got into the bus and drove away.

Kato nudged the gas and followed them.

The Black Beauty rolled in silence, its "infra-green" headlight array activated to prevent the Raja's men from spotting it. With the special lenses fitted into their masks, The Hornet and Kato could see by "infra-green" as if it were daylight, while no one else would even notice the faint, emerald glow emitted by the car's headlights. It was one of the many inventive modifications The Green Hornet and Kato had built into the car.

They drove a meandering route that suggested the Raja's men were being more cautious after their encounter with The Green Hornet, but eventually the Volkswagen turned down a street to one of the Raja's head shops. The delivery truck Kato had spotted that afternoon was still parked there. The Volkswagen stopped, and the three men hopped out. The bearded man raised the truck's cargo door, while his two partners led the four dazed teens out of the bus.

Down the street The Green Hornet and Kato slipped from the Black Beauty and crept through the shadows, waiting until they were within ten yards of the truck before dashing across the remaining distance. Their footfalls alerted the Raja's men. Two of them began to shove the teens up into the truck, while the bearded man un-looped his motorcycle chain and ran forward to fight.

He swung the chain in a deadly arc.

Kato dropped to his knees and slid under it, passing the bearded man and jabbing him in the side as he went. Then he was up and running toward the truck. There he traded blows with the tie-dyed man, but the man's long reach and brass knuckles held Kato back. The man in the peace shirt had disappeared with the teens into the cargo space.

The bearded man turned to go after Kato, but The Green Hornet stepped into his path.

"Ready for you tonight," the bearded man said.

"Glad to know we made an impression," said The Hornet. "I can still see it there where my friend kicked your chin."

The bearded man swung the chain over his head and flicked the end toward The Hornet.

"Same weapon, same fighting technique," said The Hornet. "The only thing you're ready for is bed."

The man scowled and moved to attack, but The Hornet drew a strange, sleek gun from his hip and sent a stream of green gas into the bearded man's face. The man's eyes fluttered, and then he crumpled to the street, asleep. His chain cascaded down around him.

"Hurry it up, Marko!" shouted the tie-dyed man. "The Green Hornet gassed Charger!"

The man in the peace shirt reappeared. With a series of furious blows, the tie-dyed man drove Kato toward the Volkswagen, and then he turned and leapt into the truck. The Hornet raced forward with his gun raised. Marko lifted a metal ball in one hand, yanked something away from it, and then tossed it to the street. He reached up and pulled the truck door shut. The metal ball rolled on the pavement.

"Boss, it's a grenade!" Kato yelled.

The Hornet saw Kato rush forward from the other side of the Volkswagen toward the explosive, and then a flash of light blinded him and a shockwave slammed into his body like a hundred brick fists.

The Green Hornet felt a fleeting sense of falling ...

... the world went dark and silent before he came down....

The Volkswagen shielded Kato, but the shock of the explosion still knocked him off his feet. Afterward a shrill ringing filled his head. The truck door rolled up, eerily soundless to his blasted ears. He saw The Hornet motionless on the sidewalk.

Marko and the tie-dyed man scrambled down, grabbed The Hornet, and hustled him into the truck. They turned toward Kato, but he was already on his feet in a fighting stance despite how shaken he was. The world spun around him, and his head throbbed. His legs felt like hollow sticks. If the men attacked him now, he wasn't sure he could take them, but the sight of him put fear in their eyes. Instead of fighting, Marko jumped into the back of the truck and slammed down the door. The tie-dyed man raced to the driver's side of the cab and got in. The truck engine roared to life. Kato watched the vehicle rumble away, and then the moment his legs felt steady, he ran back to Black Beauty, and followed.

Running silent behind the "infra-green" array, Kato guided Black Beauty through the dark city. The Raja's truck was miles ahead, but he could track its progress by the transmitter in The Hornet's signet ring, identical to the one he'd given Kato; a receiver in the dashboard beeped and flashed to tell Kato how far away the truck was.

They hadn't counted on a concussion grenade.

Kato didn't think The Green Hornet had taken a dive.

He'd gone down hard and sudden, and Kato hoped he wasn't seriously hurt.

Or worse.

A lucky shot, he thought. *Why is it, Boss, you always take things to extremes? It was supposed to be me playing possum.*

Kato turned down a road that led to the tunnel beneath the Detroit River into Windsor. The signal stopped. Kato slowed the car and waited, trying not to consider that the Raja's men might have found the transmitter. His head still ached from the blast.

Minutes passed.

A lucky shot.

Kato was nearing the tunnel entrance. The signal had been dead so long he was almost certain the Raja's men had found the transmitter, destroyed it, and turned off for another part of the city.

They could've taken the Boss anywhere.

Where do I go?

Black Beauty rolled almost to a stop, and then the light on the dashboard lit up again and the beeping resumed. The truck had emerged from the other end of the tunnel. Kato floored the gas and raced after it.

The Green Hornet played dead.

It wasn't difficult; the grenade blast had walloped him. It took a long time for his hearing to return, and he guessed by then that the truck was already across the border. He dared a glance around. Only Marko was guarding him and the four teens. He could've taken him, but it was better to wait and rest for now.

The terrain changed. The truck jolted and shook. The Green Hornet guessed they'd turned down an unpaved road.

Fifteen minutes later, the truck stopped.

The Hornet lay still, waiting while the men brought the teens inside. A steady ache pounded in his head and neck. Wind whistled, and somewhere nearby, a pack of dogs barked. The Hornet looked out the open back of the truck and saw the corner of an old farmhouse. Beyond it a barbed-wire fence ran along the edge of the property, and in between was a field of rye, dipping and swaying in the wind. The Hornet wondered if it was tainted with the raw material for the Raja's poison.

The men returned, lifted The Hornet by his arms and legs, and carried him onto the house's creaky porch. The motion sent rails of pain through The Hornet's body.

"Why are we keeping this guy alive?" asked Marko.

"The Raja wants to bring him into the fold, use his resources for the topsy-turvy," the tie-dyed man said.

"He'd think twice if he knew how hard this guy hits."

The sound of barking got louder, closing fast.

"Shut up and open the door already. The dogs are out."

Inside the house voices and music filled the air.

The Hornet smelled incense mingled with cigarette and marijuana smoke and the odor of stale sweat. He was carried further inside. The voices faded, and there were footsteps shuffling in every part of the room, moving closer. The Hornet sensed people gathering around him. Marko and the tie-dyed man dropped him on a sofa.

The Green Hornet opened his eyes.

He was surrounded by teenagers.

All of them wore vibrant, flashy clothing, and they stared at The Hornet like he was a strange specimen pinned to a corkboard. The room was lit by candles and small lamps draped with red and orange silks. The walls showed a riot of color; a dozen different paints were spattered and splashed helter-skelter over the plaster, decorated with crude drawings of flowers, peace symbols, comets, and stars. It wasn't enough to hide the rundown shabbiness of the place, and the clothes and music did little to conceal how tired and frightened the teens were. Many of them had the glassy-eyed stare The Hornet had come to despise.

"Why make so much trouble, man?"

The Hornet recognized the voice.

Raja Ben stepped into view, still dressed in his stage clothes and clutching his white cane. His stare was intense and manic, and The Hornet guessed he was high on something, or maybe simply out of his mind. In one hand he held a wooden cup.

"Peace is so much better. Life should be about music and art and love. But you and your friend keep beating on my guys and bringing us down. Drink this, and we'll love you like a brother." The Raja extended the cup. "Then you can be part of the topsy-turvy when we turn Detroit upside down. Peace and music will rule the streets after that."

"You're holding these kids prisoner. How does that work into Ben Rogers' idea of peace and love?" said The Green Hornet.

The Raja looked shaken. "Who? Ben who?"

"Ben Rogers." The Hornet sat up, ignoring the throbbing in his head, and looked around at the teens. "He calls himself Raja Ben and claims he has wisdom from the east. It's a lie. His name is Ben Rogers. He's from Ann Arbor."

"Liar!" shouted the Raja. He smacked his cane against The Hornet's shoulder. "You're lying. You're the one hiding behind a mask."

"I didn't lie to these kids and kidnap them. What do you do with them? Put them to work making your drugs?"

The Raja swung his cane again, but The Hornet caught it and yanked it away. He leapt to his feet.

"He doesn't care about you," The Hornet told the teens. "He doesn't care about peace. He only wants to deal his poison in the streets. That's why he's got you all here, working his farm, growing rye to produce ergot, so he can synthesize his drugs. You think you're doing the work of peace here? You're only slaves."

"Kill him!" the Raja screamed.

He hurled the cup at The Hornet. It bounced off his arm and spilled its contents onto the sofa. Marko and the tie-dyed man attacked, but The Hornet clipped each one in the face with the Raja's cane then dropped into a boxer's stance.

"Free yourselves," The Hornet said to the kids. "There are only three of them. We can stop them. You may never get another chance."

Marko swung at The Hornet, missed, and then reeled back as The Hornet smashed his nose with a powerful blow. The tie-dyed man slipped his brass knuckles around his fingers.

The Hornet felt his strength fading, his head spinning, and he realized he must have sustained a concussion in the grenade blast. He couldn't fight for long.

"Peace only comes through freedom," he said. "Set yourselves free."

Then the tie-dyed man was on him, angry, hell-bent on payback, and The Hornet was struggling to defend himself. Everything whirled around him; every move he made drove a spike of pain deeper into his head. Still The Hornet landed several solid hits, until the tie-dyed man slammed his brass knuckles into The Hornet's shoulder, driving him to his knees under a wave of pain.

The Green Hornet tried to rise. He couldn't.

"Don't let him steal your lives," he said.

The tie-dyed man kicked him, ramming him against the sofa. The Raja drew a gun.

"Peace at the end of a gun. That's what Ben Rogers is all about," said The Hornet. "Money, drugs, and power. Hypocrite."

"Shut up," said the Raja. "I'd hoped we could be friends, that your organization and mine would make the topsy-turvy a reality. But I'll do it alone, and you won't be around to see it."

A strange noise ripped the air.

It sounded like a mad insect swarm, buzzing and rattling through the night.

"What the hell is that?" said the Raja.

The Hornet laughed.

The sound grew louder and more intense. It thrummed in the wood of the house as if it were right on top of it. The dogs launched into a fury of barking for several seconds, and then all at once they stopped, silenced.

"What is it?" said the Raja.

Marko looked out the front window. "Nothing's there."

A black-gloved fist smashed through the glass and into Marko's already bloody face, knocking him down and out. A moment later the front door blasted inward. The Hornet lunged and grabbed the gun from the Raja's hand. The tie-dyed man turned and hit him once, but then Kato was through the door, twisting like a cyclone shadow as he crossed the room and reduced the tie-dyed man to a stupor with a lightning fast series of blows.

Terrified, the Raja turned to flee through the back of the house. A wall of confused teenagers blocked him. They'd seen the gun and heard The Hornet's words, and their drug haze was clearing.

"Get back," said the Raja. "Let me through. Don't listen to what this... *criminal* says. We'll all live together in peace. I promise!"

Kato helped The Hornet to his feet.

The teenagers surrounded Raja Ben.

"I swear! Once the topsy-turvy comes—"

The teens' glassy stares flared to life with hot anger, and then the Raja disappeared beneath them as they grabbed and kicked and punched him. They tore his clothes and drove him to the floor. For awhile he screamed for help, but soon his deep voice shrank to whimpers. The Hornet and Kato waded in then and broke up the mob. They dragged the Raja clear. With his costume destroyed, he looked thin and comical.

"The only place the topsy-turvy ever existed was in your upside-down mind," The Hornet told him.

Kato found a phone and called the police, and then he and The Hornet tied up the Raja and his men.

Afterward The Green Hornet stared at the teenagers for a long time without speaking, studying the awful mix of innocence and anger he saw within them, thinking about how easy it was to lead them astray, and how the place where their hopes and ideals clashed with reality was fertile ground to be exploited by evil men. He hoped they would all go on to better lives, but he didn't expect it. He felt certain there were some among them who might cross paths with him in the future. Although he had saved them all for tonight, some would fall again. He stared at them until they became uncomfortable and looked away, until their admiration for him turned to cold fear.

He and Kato left then.

A far-off siren lanced the night. In his speeding, near-silent car, The Green Hornet was long gone before it reached the farmhouse.

NOTHING GOLD CAN STAY

An origin story of Kato

by Richard Dean Starr

So Eden sank to grief,
so dawn goes down to day.
— Robert Frost

Although Kato had been born a half a world away, in a verdant land that could not have been more different from the hard gray streets of Detroit, he still considered the sprawling metropolis to be his only real home.

In truth, Kato could remember little of his homeland. Just fragments, really, a kaleidoscope of fractured images distorted by the lens of time.

When he slept, however, that did not prevent him from dreaming of the life he might have led had he remained in that faraway place—had he not gone back in search of his own roots and eventually met his lifelong friend, Britt Reid. What kind of man would he have become? Would he have married? Been a father?

His sleep was occasionally plagued by such questions, and it was not uncommon for him to awake, disquieted, in the middle of the night.

It was during those times that Kato most often thought of his mother. Over the years, however, he had come to believe that it served no purpose to dwell on such things. Rather than try to sort through his turbulent emotions he would often slip away from his apartment in Britt Reid's spacious home and take to the streets.

Tonight, however, was different.

He was not escaping unpleasant dreams or decades-old memories that remained tantalizingly vague. Instead he was doing something he enjoyed immensely:

Driving.

And not just any car, but the Black Beauty, the infamous trademark vehicle of his boss' alter-ego, The Green Hornet.

As he cruised along streets slick with half-melted ice from an earlier rain, Kato was in a fine mood. The car was performing extraordinarily well, which he found pleasing if not particularly surprising. He was, after all, the one responsible for its upkeep as well as the remarkable array of special features that made the heavily-modified Chrysler one of the most versatile—and lethal—vehicles on the road.

Detroit's array of fine automobiles, he thought with a slight smile, *had nothing on the Black Beauty.*

That was too bad for them, really.

His smile widened into a grin and he pushed down on the accelerator. The Black Beauty responded with a throaty roar, a sound that could be silenced or replaced by the menacing sound of a hornet at the touch of a button. The car surged forward, pressing him back against the ebony leather seat.

Kato glanced at the various status lights along the dashboard and noted that the car's complex systems were all operating properly and ready for deployment. He was especially satisfied because this included a recent addition to the onboard arsenal, an oil-dispensing device designed to send a pursuing vehicle spinning out of control.

That was the theory, anyway. He'd yet to test it, which was one of his goals during tonight's trip around the city. Britt Reid had been in Chicago for the past three days attending a publisher's convention, which meant that Kato was free to do as he liked until tomorrow morning, when his friend returned home.

The first item on Kato's agenda was trying out the new oil slick device. The second was to push the Black Beauty's limits on wet, icy road conditions using his latest innovation: a mechanism that slowed the engine rpm's while modulating the individual speed of the tires during acceleration.

Technically, this should keep the car from locking into a slide under the most adverse road conditions.

Again, that was the theory.

Kato was abruptly stricken by the realization that this night was too full of theories. Now was the time to prove their worth through practical application.

As he turned onto Lafayette Boulevard he glanced to his right. An enormous building with four numbers displayed prominently along the roof dominated the skyline. At thirty stories high, 1300 Lafayette East was one of Detroit's newer luxury apartment complexes and a prominent symbol of affluence for the power elite that called it home.

Britt Reid owned two units in the building but did not live there himself.

Kato had visited the building with his boss but found the steel, concrete, and glass too cold for his taste. Even with its spectacular views of the city and the Detroit River just a few blocks away, it was not the kind of place Kato would have chosen to live.

He turned his gaze back to the road in front of him—

—and nearly ran down the woman and young girl who had appeared in the middle of the street as if conjured there.

Only his cat-quick reflexes prevented a horrific accident. He spun the wheel hard and caught a momentary glimpse of their faces, pale white tinged green by the Black Beauty's headlights, and then he was past them.

For a moment Kato thought the tires would find dry pavement and that he would be able to regain control. Then he felt the car slide onto a patch of ice. Free of friction, it spun with reckless grace across the road and toward a telephone pole that suddenly seemed as big as 1300 Lafayette East.

He pressed down on the brake pedal and turned into the slide. To his mild surprise, the new braking system performed exactly as he had theorized and he was able to steer away from the pole. It missed the edge of the trunk by inches, which was a relief. Still, the Black Beauty ran off the road and into a small field.

Spinning the wheel again, Kato brought the car to a halt, frozen stalks of dead grass crunching like breaking bones beneath the specially-made tires. Pausing just long enough to take a deep breath, he started up the car again and then drove back onto the street. He parked along the shoulder, threw open the door, and stepped out onto the pavement.

The woman was still standing in the street as if paralyzed, her face stiff with shock. He could see that she was slender, with glamorous, medium-length blonde hair. She was wearing an expensive, stylish pantsuit that seemed jarringly out of place in such a dark and lonely place.

When she saw him emerge from the Black Beauty her expression transformed from shock to terror to resignation, all in the blink of an eye. It took Kato a moment to realize that she was probably reacting to the sight of his black uniform and mask.

"Please," he said, holding up his hands to show that he was unarmed. "I mean you no harm."

"You're with him," she said, her voice flat. "You must be. Why else would you be dressed like that?"

He could hear defeat in her voice, but also a defiant edge.

The girl holding her hand was no older than twelve, but Kato could see nothing but fear in her eyes.

"A mask does not necessarily conceal evil," Kato said. "Again, I mean you no harm."

She looked back over her shoulder to the darkened streets and alleys of the industrial neighborhoods that stretched from Lafayette Avenue all the way to the banks of the Detroit River.

"He's coming," she said. "So if you're one of them do us both a favor and kill us now." She stared directly into his eyes. "Death would be preferable to what he'll do to us."

Kato frowned. "No one is going to be killed tonight."

Just then, he heard a high-pitched sound and a small breeze brushed his face, ruffling a stray lock of jet-black hair that poked out from beneath the edge of his short-billed cap. His frown deepened. There was something very familiar about that sound. Again, the breeze gusted against his face. Then suddenly he was no longer wearing his hat.

Kato might have died where he stood had the second gunshot not struck the armored side of the Black Beauty and ricocheted away with a shrill scream. In a single, seamless movement, he dropped to one knee, snatched up his hat, and then rolled toward the woman and the girl.

Rising to his feet, Kato pushed them both toward the open door of the Black Beauty. Sparks jumped from the pavement where they had been standing, marking the passage of multiple bullets.

Death comes on the wings of doves, Kato though grimly. Clearly, their assailants were using silencers.

They reached the Black Beauty in just a few steps. Kato pushed them both inside and then jumped behind the wheel, pulling the door shut behind him.

Just then, a group of men burst from the entrance of a nearby alley, their muted pistols and sub-machine guns spitting fire. Bullets struck the car, tracked up the side, and then marched along the windows like furious ants, each of their impacts like powerful, ineffectual bites.

The bulletproof glass fractured slightly but did not shatter, exactly as it had been designed to do. It would need to be replaced before Reid returned, Kato knew, but all things considered, it was preferable to being dead.

Kato pressed the ignition button and the Black Beauty roared to life. Stomping the accelerator, he fishtailed off of the shoulder and back onto the blacktop. A fusillade of flying lead thumped into the trunk, but since they were now a moving target, more missed than made contact.

In just a few moments the street curved a bit and their attackers fell out of sight. Kato took a deep breath and then exhaled, relieved that they had gotten away with only some cracked windows.

Because the Black Beauty's body panels were constructed of a special color-saturated alloy, the car was invulnerable to most ammunition as well as the occasional dents and scratches. Unfortunately, current technology limited the alloy's color to black. One day he would take the time to develop another shade. Maybe purple? Or perhaps he'd just add some red trim along the sides.

Kato dismissed that train of thought as quickly as it had come and glanced over at the woman. He was mildly irritated to see that she was huddled against the passenger door, as far from him as she could possibly get without actually getting out of the car. Her arms were wrapped protectively around the young girl as if he might snatch her up at any moment.

He sighed. "Look, I told you, I do not work for whoever it is that's after you. I am trying to help, so you don't need to be afraid of me."

She didn't respond, just stared back at him. The defiance was still there, to be sure. Then, to his surprise, a tear tracked slowly down the right side of her face, marring her perfectly applied makeup.

For some reason the sight of that single, solitary tear jolted him, summoning a lost memory so vivid that he was unable to comprehend how he could have ever forgotten it...

The ocean of stars is what Kato believes he will remember forever.

Even at only six years old he knows that the anchors of his life have been torn away and that he and his mother have been cast adrift in a sea of teeming humanity. He is also instinctively aware that she is the one thing preventing him from being submerged beneath the tide of panicked villagers. So he clings to her hand with the strength of the fearful child that he has suddenly become, yet barely understands.

Overhead, the stars Kato loves are a multitude of distant mooring lamps, and he imagines they promise a safer harbor far away from this place of fear and despair.

Still clutching her fingers with his much smaller hand, he shuffles along in her wake, his six year-old heart jumping in his chest like a tiny cricket. He keeps his gaze on the clear and peaceful night sky. Bright and true, the stars help to calm him as they have for as long as he can remember.

Then there is the sound of squealing brakes. The dull beams of yellow headlights slice through the crowd, ragged blades of light that make Kato squint. A truck has cut across the villager's path, preventing the flow of refugees from continuing further down the narrow dirt road. The people shuffle restlessly. Behind them are the remains of their burning homes; on the other side, the great river; and opposite that, a dense forest. They know they are trapped and Kato senses their mounting alarm.

A voice shouts. A rifle fires. Then another, followed by screams. In moments, the cries blend together into a cacophony of discordant sound that carries the unmistakable tenor of absolute terror.

The herd of villagers erupts in panic, turning with the dizzying force of a tsunami. His mother staggers as she is buffeted about by her fellow villagers and nearly goes down, taking Kato with her.

He leans into her body, keeping her upright just long enough for them to spot a narrow opening to the forest. His mother does not hesitate, and they push out from between the stifling bodies and run toward the concealing foliage.

Behind them a soldier spots them and shouts words in a language that Kato cannot understand. Then they are among the trees, and the screams of the villagers fall away...

Still shocked by this sudden onslaught of a memory he'd thought lost, Kato turned his gaze away from his terrified passengers and back to the road. Ahead were two pairs of headlights, side by side and blocking the highway. Tapping the brakes, Kato slowed the Black Beauty and considered his options.

Before he could give their situation much thought, however, more headlights filled the rearview mirror, coming up fast behind them at a high rate of speed.

It seemed that they were trapped, much like he and his mother had been so long ago.

Kato felt a slow anger begin to build in his chest, a burning sense of injustice that he knew would overcome him if he failed to maintain his self-control.

Who were these people that would kill a woman and a child without hesitation? What kind of men would do such a thing?

His mouth tightened into a grim line. Unfortunately, that was a question he was uniquely qualified to answer. It seemed that such individuals were as common today, in this place he called home, as they had once been in the land of his birth.

This time, however, it would be different.

The type of men might be the same, but he was no longer a helpless boy. The pursuers of the woman and the girl would soon discover this, to their detriment.

Twisting the wheel, Kato turned the Black Beauty down a narrow side street that led toward the riverfront. Once again, he found himself fleeing for his life along a river, only now there was a forest of concrete and steel rather than one of wood and bark and leaves.

Indeed, some things have changed, Kato though grimly, *yet others remain very much the same.*

He glanced at the mirror and saw two sedans careen around the corner in fevered pursuit. Lacking the Black Beauty's sophisticated handling ability, both vehicles jumped the curb, hitting some aluminum trash cans and sending them flying. As one of the sedans lurched back onto the pavement it struck a parked station wagon, throwing up bright sparks like a magic trick in some darkened theater.

Kato shook his head in wonder. Their pursuers were reckless to the point of being suicidal. He looked over at the woman and smiled encouragingly.

"You don't need to be afraid. They haven't caught us yet."

"It doesn't matter," the woman said, her voice rich and almost melodious. "No matter what you do he'll find us and then we'll all be dead."

Spinning the wheel a second time, Kato turned down a narrow alley only to see another pair of headlights heading toward them, tearing through piles of garbage with all the finesse of a mad bull.

"You need not fear death just yet," Kato said. "I will keep us safe." He smiled encouragingly. "What is your name?"

"I'm Joanna," she said. "And this is my daughter, Melissa."

One of the pursuing sedans entered the alleyway behind them and a thug leaned out of the passenger window, firing his sub-machine gun. Bullets struck the back window, probing and testing the limits of the special glass. In the blink of an eye, Kato's clear view became a shattered skein of light and shadow.

There was one final chance for them to escape, a street that led even closer to the river and the many new buildings being constructed there. It could be the ideal place to lose their pursuers and plan their next move.

The only problem was the two sedans that were about to box them in. Kato accelerated, pushing the Black Beauty to its limit. They entered the intersection of alley and street just seconds ahead of the onrushing sedan and cut hard to the left. The Black Beauty turned, started to spin, and then lifted onto its two right tires.

For a moment, Kato was sure they were going to flip over, and that would have been the end of that.

Then all four tires hit the ground and found traction. Within moments they were away from the intersection, and after a few more evasive maneuvers, they parked behind a small lumber yard just out of sight from the main road. Kato hit the lights and the engine button and immediately they were surrounded by the cold winter darkness.

Sensing that they were at least temporarily safe, the young girl spoke for the first time. "Mommy, she said, her voice so faint that Kato could barely hear it. "What's going to happen to us? Why are those men trying to hurt you?"

The woman smiled gently and smoothed the girl's hair, which Kato noticed was almost the same shade of blonde as hers. "It's going to be okay," she whispered. "They can't see us here, honey. Just stay quiet and we'll be all right."

Their silhouettes, barely visible by the light of the distant stars, touched Kato with a degree of poignancy that he wouldn't have thought possible just a few hours ago.

He wasn't surprised, then, when another memory swept over him, taking him back to those faraway woods so long, long ago...

The forest is dark and filled with dense foliage, and it takes just a few moments for Kato and his mother to become scratched and abraded by the stubborn brush.

Picking an especially dense clump of bushes, his mother forces them both down inside its concealing branches as two soldiers emerge from the nearby trees.

A stick is lodged painfully against Kato's ribs and he longs to cry out. When he tries to shift it aside, he accidentally breaks it instead, and the sound is like one of the gunshots they can hear along the distant riverbank.

His mother stiffens and her hand tightens on his arm, warning him not to move any further. The two soldiers move toward them and then stop. For a moment, nothing happens. Then one of the mean speaks in Kato's native language, surprising him so much that he nearly bolts from their hiding place.

"Come out now, little rabbits," the soldier says softly. "We won't hurt you if you don't resist."

Although the man's words are meant to soothe, his rough accent, which Kato does not recognize, only makes the boy more frightened. Fear also radiates from his mother, yet the hand on his arm never trembles.

"Come now," the soldier says, sounding more impatient. "Don't make us come in there. If you do I promise it will not be pleasant."

Another voice, strangely familiar, echoes through the woods in English, a language that Kato already understands much of from his bible study.

"Why are you two men loafing here when there is so much business to take care of by the river, eh?"

Kato cannot remember where he has heard the voice before, but he knows that he has.

"We saw two of them run into the woods, sir," the first soldier replies. "We were just going to get them out and take them back with the rest of the villagers."

"And I can see you're doing a fine job of it," the second man says. "They're probably long gone by now. You are to go back to the river and report to *Rikugun Shōi* Morioka!"

"Hai!"

The two soldiers turn and hurry away between the trees, heading back toward the sound of gunshots and the hoarse screams and shouts of Kato's people.

After they have gone, the man speaks again. "You must come out," he says. "I watched you both run into the woods and I shouted, but you did not hear me."

To Kato's astonishment, his mother stands and climbs out of the bushes, pulling him along with her. Waiting in the moonlight is a soldier wearing the uniform that, in a very short time, Kato and his people have come to fear more than anything else on earth.

"Mother!" he says, horrified. "Come, we must run now!"

She looks down at him and smiles sadly. "Do not be frightened, my son. We are not in danger."

"But he is...but..."

Kato struggles to articulate what he *feels* as much as he *knows*—that this man is the enemy, and that they are both in mortal danger.

"He is not what you think," his mother says, kneeling beside him and holding his arm to prevent him from running. "My son, please—"

The soldier crouches beside his mother and places a hand on Kato's shoulder. Repelled, Kato tries to pull away but his mother shakes him roughly.

"You must listen, my son!" she says. "We have very little time!"

The soldier sighs. "You know that I cannot spirit you both away," he says to Kato's mother, "as much as I might want to. *Rikugun Shōsa* Mukai hates your people with a passion I do not fully understand. The boy, however, I can manage. I am so very sorry, Chunhua."

Kato's mother begins to weep, and Kato finds himself nearly overcome with sudden terror. Who is this soldier, this enemy that his mother seems to know so well? And why is she crying?

What the soldier says next, however, shocks Kato so badly that all feeling seems to drain from his legs and he nearly falls to the ground.

"Hayashi, you must come with me. There is no time to explain, but we must go now."

"That is not my name!" Kato shouts, jerking away from the man. "My name is Kato, not Hayashi!"

He is screaming now, and tears he cannot control are streaming down his cheeks. A face he had forgotten comes back to him as clearly as if he had seen it just the day before...and it is the face of the man before him.

"You must be silent, boy!" the soldier scolds, glancing worriedly toward the river. "I am sorry, Chunhua, but if I am to save our son, I must do this now."

Kato barely registers the meaning of the soldier's words before something strikes him painfully hard alongside the head. Blackness surrounds him as he cries out one final time, a soul-wrenching grief that will take a lifetime for him to comprehend...

When the lights flashed on behind them, flooding the rearview mirror with a brilliant schism of indistinct images, Kato knew they were in trouble. Again.

Already, the memories of that face he'd forgotten since childhood were beginning to slide away from him like a crocodile returning to the muddy depths of a river.

He would have preferred to spend more time trying to remember something about the man, but it seemed that their pursuers had once again managed to locate them. This was confirmed when more headlights appeared, this time in front of them and speeding in their direction.

Kato hit the starter and threw the Black Beauty into gear. "These people, they are at least consistent. Why do they wish to harm you?"

As they sped down the narrow alley and screeched left onto another street that led even closer to the new construction along the waterfront, Joanna sighed.

"Oh, they don't want to 'harm' me," she said. "Not the way you mean it. If they did, it wouldn't go well for them."

"What?" Kato turned his head so quickly that he nearly lost control of the Black Beauty. "If they are not trying to harm *you*, then who *are* they after?"

She grimaced. "You, I'd imagine."

"Me?" Kato was astonished. "What did *I* do?"

"Interfered. They were coming to retrieve me and you made it complicated." She glanced down at her daughter, who was tucked against her lap with her eyes tightly closed, and smiled tenderly. "You saved me anyway, and my daughter, and I'm more grateful for that than I can say."

"I did not save you from much," Kato said, trying not to sound grumpy, "if they were not actually going to harm you."

"*They* wouldn't have," she explained, "but as I told you before, what *he* will do when he catches us is worse than anything his henchman could ever conceive of."

"He?"

"My husband, of course," she said, and this time it was Kato's turn to grimace.

The Black Beauty crested a small rise in the road topped by railroad tracks, and for a moment the ice-choked expanse of the river seemed to stretch out ahead of them, glistening like a field of rough diamonds in the moonlight. Then, with timing so precise it could have been choreographed, two of their pursuers roared out of perpendicular streets and hurtled down the road toward them.

"Your husband is a very determined man," Kato said, watching the blur of approaching lights in the rearview mirror. "You will please assure me that this is more than some simple domestic argument?"

She almost laughed, but choked it off with what Kato thought sounded like a near-sob. "Not hardly," she said at last. "My husband is insane, and when he catches us, he will kill you first—slowly—and then he'll do the same to us."

"It has always been my preference to experience death with the quickness of lightning," Kato said, not pressing down on the accelerator. "I would not be patient enough to wait long for that great unknown mystery."

When the approaching sedans were less than fifty feet from the back of the Black Beauty, he leaned casually across the seat and flipped a small switch on the dashboard. One of the green status lights flashed and then turned blue.

Somewhere inside the Black Beauty, powerful hydraulics began to work followed by the sound of liquid, thick and heavy, passing through a network of pipes under enormous pressure.

Although he couldn't see it due to the damaged back window, Kato assumed that twin sheets of oil had been ejected from the special jet tubes concealed beneath the bumper of the Black Beauty, and that the road was now coated with a dangerously slippery surface.

They would know in a moment.

Just then, the first set of headlights reached the oil and spun away as the sedan they were attached to slid perilously across the pavement.

Kato stepped on the gas and the Black Beauty surged away from the tracks. He grinned when he heard the shriek of tortured metal and the tinkle of breaking glass as the second car collided with the first one.

It seemed that the oil slick's functionality—as well as its effectiveness—was no longer theoretical.

At the next intersection Kato glanced to his left. More headlights approached, two sedans running side-by-side and coming fast from less than two blocks away. They would arrive in seconds. Going back the way they had come, Kato knew, was out of the question. It would not be long before more thugs appeared who could, and would, easily circumvent the oil slick.

At this point it was obvious to him that their pursuers were using radios to coordinate the chase. Not an inexpensive proposition. He stared more directly at his passenger. Her expression was still defiant but beginning to show signs of resignation.

"You will pardon me," he said, "but I think it is far past time for me to have asked this question: who *is* this man, your husband?"

"Anthony Hale," she replied. "I thought you would have guessed by now. You wear a mask; he hides in the shadows. I figured you were both operating on the same side of the street."

Kato sighed. "You are married to one of the most notorious crime lords in the Midwest, and you did not think it important to tell me this immediately?"

"I'm sorry," she said. "But honestly, I was scared stiff and you were busy driving. And not to be flippant, but you didn't ask."

He took a deeper breath. Their options were narrowing considerably. The river was filled with ice but it was largely broken up. Even if had been frozen solid, he would have hesitated to drive a car as heavy as the Black Beauty out onto its surface.

"So we go to the right," he said quietly, and accelerated away from their pursuers.

Hoping they might find a place to hide, Kato drove straight for the shadowy, under-construction hulks of several multi-story buildings that lined the waterfront. In the pale light of the moon their half-finished skeletons loomed like undead sentinels, each one staring passively over the frigid river and the rest of Detroit.

Whether sentries or merely witnesses to what was to come, Kato knew it was unlikely that either one offered safety...or salvation...

When six-year old Kato awakens in darkness, he is at first disoriented.

A wool blanket has been wrapped loosely around his body, and it clings to his face, choking his nostrils with the nauseating stench of pig and other things he'd rather not think about. Frightened, he begins to panic and struggles against the confining folds. For a moment, he is sure that he cannot breath. Then he remembers...

His mother!

Kato redoubles his efforts, when suddenly a hand he cannot see strikes him in the shoulder and he cries out in pain and surprise.

"Be silent, Hayashi," hisses the same voice that came from the man in the forest, "or you will be the end of us both!"

"My name is not—!" Kato cries, only to have the wind knocked out of him when the same hand chops him in the solar plexus. Unable to double over because of the blanket, gasping for breath and not caring in the least that he seems to be inhaling the entire spirit of some long-departed farm animal, he tries to keep from throwing up.

"You will be quiet, boy," the voice repeats, "or I will knock you unconscious a second time. While you struggle for breath, remember that. I will tell you when you may speak. Until then, lie still!"

With pain continuing to radiate from his middle, Kato tries to remain unmoving and quiet while praying that his mother is nearby and that she is safe. After some time has passed, light flashes across the blanket and then points away from him. Kato can hear several men moving around outside wherever it is he is being held. Then, a voice:

"Is that the package?"

The voice speaks in English, which Kato only partially understands. His mother had learned the language from the priests from beyond the great river and taught him enough that he had already begun to learn from their holy book. Actually *speaking* English, however, has proven much more difficult for him to master.

"This...package—it is most precious to me, Lieutenant. I would hope you will guard hi—" The man from the forest corrects himself. "*It*, with your life. The package must arrive safely in America. My family there has been notified and will know what to do."

"I could tell you I would give my life for your package, *Rikugun*, but I would be lying. That said, you have paid me handsomely in gold, so I am confident it will make it to America without a problem."

"I am grateful."

"You *do* realize it's unlikely that we'll be able to talk again? After what happened last week, in fact, it's possible our people may not have diplomatic relations for many, many years. In fact, if my superiors knew that I was meeting with you right now it would be, as they say, my head on a platter."

"Again, Lieutenant, I am grateful for the risks that you are taking on my behalf."

"Not to sound like an opportunist, but your gold was a powerful motivator. The salary of a naval supply officer isn't exactly what I was anticipating when I graduated from the University of Chicago. I have some ambitious plans, but this conflict has, most unfortunately, postponed them."

"Then it is my sincere hope that my gold will be of help to you in achieving your goals when the conflict is over."

The man laughed. "Oh, it will, *Rikugun* Kato. I can assure you, it most certainly will..."

More convinced that ever that they were being corralled by Hale's men, Kato did his best to avoid the patrolling sedans so that their final destination might remain secret as long as possible. After several close calls, they found themselves parked beneath the unfinished mezzanine of a tall office building directly facing the Detroit River.

He parked the Black Beauty under the overhang and cut the headlights. In the sudden silence, the ice-choked water could be heard lapping lethargically against the gravel shore nearby.

His thoughts still swam with freshly recalled images from his past. Much to his frustration, many of the memories continued to fade away before he could re-establish them in the forefront of his mind.

Feeling safe, at least for the moment, he put the past behind him and stepped out of the car for some fresh air and to plan their next move. A moment later the passenger door opened and Joanna and Melissa stood shivering in the moonlit darkness.

"What do we do now?" Joanna said, her voice cracking. "There's nowhere else for us to go." She glanced at the building. "Wait, I know this place! I've been here before. My God, Tony owns it!"

Kato pursed his lips and stared at the frigid river. It appeared that Hale had managed to force them to flee to precisely where he wanted them after all.

"Why," he said at last, "does your husband wish you such grievous harm? Surely this is not merely because you have chosen to leave him?"

She stared at Kato across the roof of the Black Beauty, seeming to consider her answer carefully before she replied.

"When I met Tony," she said, "he was the kindest, most gentle man I'd ever met. His manners were impeccable and he treated me like a princess."

Kato's expression must have reflected his skepticism.

"Oh, it's a cliché, I know," she acknowledged, "but in Tony's case it was also absolutely true. I wanted for nothing, physical, mental, or emotional. At least, not at first."

Kato remained silent, waiting for her to continue. Finally, she did.

"After a while things became strained. I probably *could* have walked away then. Probably *should* have. But then Melissa was born and everything changed. And before you ask—no, not for the better."

She sighed, and the wind off the river seemed to stroke her golden hair in sympathy. By the light of the moon, it seemed as iridescent as spun gold. Kato was suddenly aware of how vulnerable—and how stunningly beautiful—she was.

"For a man to harm his only child," Kato said, thinking of the man he only barely remembered as his father, "he must either be without hope, or be an unimaginable monster."

"Or be desperate," Joanna said. "Unfortunately for my daughter and me, we both saw something we shouldn't have. Although even then I don't think he would have killed us. Oh, he had already become cold and distant, even abusive by then. But kill us? I doubt it."

"You said you saw something that caused all of this?" Kato prompted.

"Yes. Last week, Tony planned some big meeting and told us to stay in the residential wing of the house. I assumed he meant the common areas and that he would be holding the meeting in his home office. But it didn't happen that way. Melissa and I decided to go for a swim and came out into the indoor pool just in time to see him—"

Joanna choked up at the memory. When Melissa saw this, she hugged her mother even tighter. As if drawing strength from this simple act, Joanna finished, "—we saw him shoot a man in the head. He was sitting in a chair and Tony was walking behind him when he pulled a gun out of his waistband and just...just killed him."

"And Hale obviously saw you?"

She nodded. "Yes. He noticed us standing there just as he pulled the trigger."

"I'm sorry," Kato said.

Before he could say anything else, the front tire closest to Joanna and Melissa exploded, causing the Black Beauty to lurch in the air. At the same time, the sound of high-powered rifle echoed through the open mezzanine and across the icy river.

Both of the women screamed and ran around the car, trying to put something between them and the shooter. Kato pushed them down and crouched beside them, the gravel digging painfully into his right knee.

"Stay here," he said. "Although we can no longer escape in the Black Beauty, its panels are bulletproof and will protect you for now. However, we must take shelter inside this building."

What Kato didn't say was that the rifle being fired at them had to be exceptionally powerful. The Black Beauty's tires were lined with a relatively new material called Kevlar, capable of repelling most standard ammunition. For a single bullet to cause such damage meant that they were more than vulnerable: they were, as Britt would have said, "sitting ducks."

He looked around calmly, assessing their options. The elevators had not yet been installed and the emergency stairwell was blocked by a cheap two-panel plywood door. If the choices were a concrete shaft or a half-finished stairwell, it was really no choice at all.

"I will get that stairway door open," he said, pointing toward the closed-off stairwell. "When I signal, run toward me as fast as you can. Okay?"

She nodded and held her daughter closer. Both women were shivering from cold and terror. The sight of their raw, naked fear galvanized Kato into action. He sprinted toward the door that led to the unfinished stairwell...

...and that's when it exploded out of the frame and tumbled toward him like a giant playing card.

Kato ducked, leaning back at a ninety-degree angle as the door flew past his shoulder. He caught a brief, distorted glimpse of his startled expression reflected in the cheap brass doorknob and then it was past him, striking the ground and digging a deep furrow in the gravel.

At first Kato thought there had been an explosion of some kind. What he saw next, however, convinced him that a bomb would have been the preferable alternative.

An enormous man stood in the doorway, his bulk so vast that it filled the shattered frame and allowed only minimal light to escape around his shoulders and from between his trunk-like legs. He was wearing a suit that would not have seemed out of place in most corporate boardrooms—except that Kato suspected it could have actually *covered* the entire meeting, with space left over for catering.

As the man twisted his enormous body through the door, the moonlight shone on his face and Kato was startled to see that he looked like a teenager. If not for his tremendous bulk and crown of gray/brown hair, combed neatly to one side, he could have easily been mistaken for one.

The giant grinned when he saw Kato, displaying two rows of perfect white teeth that seemed twice the average size.

"Come," he said in a surprisingly ordinary voice with a slight Eastern European accent. He gestured toward Kato with an index finger the size of a pork sausage. "Do not be afraid, little man. When I tear you apart, it will only hurt for a moment, eh? You make me chase you, though, it will hurt longer."

"Philosophically," Kato said, moving carefully to one side while keeping the giant clearly in sight, "I am against pain. However, if I must experience it I would agree that less is better."

He was acutely aware that in a nearby building a gunman could very well have him at the center of his crosshairs. It was not a soothing thought. Still, despite that ever-present danger, the most pressing issue appeared to be standing in front him, fully prepared to rip him limb from limb.

"I don't know what you are babbling about, little man. You talk too much, I think."

With that, the giant charged, his face twisted in an expression of gleeful rage. He was faster than Kato expected; *much* faster.

Kato stumbled backward as the gravel shifted under his heel. Before he could get out of the way, the giant grabbed the front of his jacked and jerked him into the air. Kato dangled there for a moment, his feet almost a foot off the ground. Then the giant threw him the way a smaller man might toss a beach ball.

He tucked himself as best he could, but nonetheless hit the ground hard. Pain lanced through his shoulder, but he rolled with the impact and saved himself from what could have been a more serious injury. Springing to his feet, he had only a moment to prepare before the giant was on him again.

Using both massive fists like battering rams, the giant slammed Kato in the chest. The collision knocked the smaller man onto his back, his head hitting the ground just inches from the jagged ice lining the river's edge.

He lay there for a moment like a beached fish, trying to suck some air back into his punished lungs. The giant stomped across the beach, clearly anticipating an easy victory.

For a brief moment, Kato wondered if this was really how his life was meant to end. Would the giant simply snap his neck? Or would he take his time as he'd promised, perhaps drowning him slowly in an insignificant depth of water along the shore?

Then he was overcome by a flash of images:

His mother, crying and holding him.

Joanna trying to shelter her daughter, another young child powerless to escape her destiny.

When he was a boy Kato had been unable to rescue his mother. But he'd made a promise to himself that he would not abandon Joanna and Melissa to their fate at the hands of Anthony Hale.

It was a promise he meant to keep.

As the giant bore down on him, he felt his hands slide across a crag of ice, its spiked edge sharp against his palm. Grasping it with a strength born of desperation, he broke it off at the base. Chuckling in anticipation, the giant fell to one knee beside Kato's prostate form and reached for his neck with both hands. And that's when Kato jammed the dagger of ice into his neck with all the force he could muster.

The giant paused with a loud grunt and his face filled with almost childlike wonder. Then, groaning, his eyes rolled back in his head and he tumbled straight toward Kato.

Rolling frantically to the side, Kato tried to get out of the way and just barely succeeded. The giant's body missed him by inches, crashing face-first into the river and throwing up a small geyser of ice and water.

Kato lay on the shore for a moment, relieved to find that he was still alive. Then he remembered the gunman and pushed himself to his feet. "Get back in the car," he yelled toward Joanna. "Lock the doors and I'll be back as soon as I can!"

Joanna nodded and slipped open the driver's door. A moment later they were inside, and for the moment, out of harm's way.

Kato knew that the Black Beauty would protect them—but only up to a certain point. If the gunman kept firing eventually the bullets would breach the armored panels, but not if he found the gunman hiding in the other building first.

Unwilling to waste another moment, Kato sprinted across the parking lot, the hairs on the back of his neck prickling in anticipation of a bullet that never came.

Less than a minute later he was inside the second building. This one was even further from being completed and was little more than a concrete shell with some wood scaffolding throughout to allow access for the workers. He checked to make sure his hidden sleeve darts were still securely in place, then found the stairwell and took the steps two at a time, knowing that it was only a matter of time until the gunman began firing at the Black Beauty again.

On the second floor, Kato paused and stared out through the empty windows at the Black Beauty sitting silently beneath the skeletal mezzanine. There was no sound but the wind, noticeably stronger this high off the ground, and the right side of his face became instantly numb from the bitter cold blowing off of the river.

When the gunman fired again, Kato was surprised to hear the shots come from almost overhead, just one floor above. Down on the ground, the Black Beauty's passenger side window exploded and he could hear two women screaming.

He spun on his heel and ran for the stairwell. It took him only moments to emerge onto the third floor. Kato saw the gunman almost immediately, resting the barrel of a large rifle on one of the open windows, and was only slightly surprised when he saw that it was Anthony Hale himself, whom he recognized from various stories published in Britt's own newspaper. Hale was in the middle of reloading when he looked up and saw Kato.

To Kato's surprise, the criminal kingpin smiled but did not put down the rifle. "So," he said, "you really have become as fast as they say. I didn't think anyone could defeat Lucian, but you managed to."

"You could say he forced me to kill him in cold blood," Kato said with a humorless grin. He nodded at the rifle. "You know you will not have time to fire that again before I have you?"

"Oh, I wouldn't be too sure of that," the man said. "You might get to me first, but now that I've switched to hollow-points the next one will take out those two bitches before you even get close."

"And then what?" Kato said, trying to keep the gangster talking. He stepped from the doorway onto one of the boards that had been laid across the unfinished floor. It sagged slightly under his weight but held firm.

Beyond Hale, a space that would eventually hold floor-to-ceiling windows was open to the elements and covered only partially by a huge sheet of ripped and torn plastic. The wind shifted, gusting through the opening and piercing Kato's skin with a deep, cutting chill.

"No closer," Hale warned, slammed the half-loaded magazine into the rifle and chambered a fresh round.

Kato froze.

"Joanna told me what they saw," Kato said. "You have no chance now but to surrender."

Hale grinned, looking Kato up and down appraisingly.

"You know the funniest thing? You don't recognize me at all. Not that you would, of course."

The board beneath Kato creaked and he stepped lightly onto another one that looked slightly less warped and only marginally more stable.

"Of course I recognize you," Kato said. "We have never met, but I have seen the stories of your exploits in the newspapers."

"Oh, but we have met," Hale said. "In fact, I'm here doing my own 'dirty work,' as they say, because of you."

Kato frowned. "If we have met, I do not remember it."

Hale didn't respond for a moment. He sighted along the barrel but kept his finger off the trigger. Kato vowed silently that if Hale moved to fire again, he would throw one of his sleeve darts and kill the man before he could harm the two women.

Then Hale sighed. "You know, it's actually not that odd, our paths crossing like this. When my men reported that the Black Beauty was involved with Joanna and my daughter, I decided to kill two birds with one stone, as it were. You and The Green Hornet were on my agenda in the near future anyway. Why do you think I chose to expand my operation into Detroit? This seemed like the ideal situation to solve both problems at the same time."

"I told you," Kato said, irritated by Hale's smug banter, "I have never met you before. And I hope to never meet you again."

"Oh, we've met," Hale said absently. "Not that you'd remember it. You were quite young, I think. Six or seven, maybe?"

Kato was shocked so badly by Hale's words that he nearly lost his footing and fell between the boards. His astonishment must have shown on his face, for Hale burst out laughing.

"Not quite so cool and confident now, are you, Hayashi?" he said, still chuckling. "I followed your life for years, wondering if there was a way to capitalize off your father's influence and money a second time. And when you wound up here in Detroit, it didn't take long for me to figure out who the mysterious oriental was that worked with The Green Hornet and then put two and two together."

"But...when...how..."

Then Kato remembered, the memory brighter and more vivid than any of the ones that had come before it...

The ship that will carry Kato to his new land is docked in a harbor that the young boy does not recognize, tucked tight against a bustling wharf that teems with people from what is obviously a variety of different nations.

When Kato is released from the concealed compartment in the bed of the dark gray military truck, he is almost immediately struck by the overwhelming stench of butchered fish, the cloying salt smell of the ocean, and the odor of many human bodies forced into close contact.

"Come along, boy," says the man who has released him. He is dressed in a uniform that Kato does not recognize either, the most prominent features of which are a black and white cap with a gold medallion and a neatly tailored black jacket with gold ribbons on the sleeves.

Kato considers running, but one look around convinces him that it would be futile to try and escape. He has no idea where he is, and so far, this man is the only connection he has to his mother.

"Now listen up," the man says. "You're going to board this ship and it *will* take you to safety. Your father paid me to make that happen and that's what I'm going to do."

With a jolt, Kato realizes that the man's voice is the same one he heard while he was wrapped in the smelly blanket.

"Don't worry," the man continued, "you'll be at sea for a good long while, but when you get where you're going someone will be waiting for you."

A burly seaman approaches the man and they exchange cursory nods. Grasping him firmly by the arm, the seaman begins pulling Kato toward the gangway.

"Wait!" Kato cries. "What about my mother?"

The man in the uniform shrugs apologetically, seemingly disinterested. "Don't know what to tell you, kid. My guess is that by this time she's got a bullet in the head. Sorry."

"No!" Kato screams and begins to fight against the muscular sailor. Then, for the second time in as many days, something strikes him alongside the head and darkness caves in around him...

"You," Kato whispered. "It was *you* who helped take me away from my mother."

Hale's grin widened. "So you do remember! Good for you, Hayashi, good for you."

Kato tottered on the flimsy board, closing his eyes and trying to regain his equilibrium. Anthony Hale was the American naval officer who had spirited him away from his homeland. Perhaps Hale had not left his mother to die.

Then again, Kato would never know for certain, because she had vanished not long after he had been taken away and on more than one trip back he had been unable to locate her...

He thought of Joanna and Melissa, cowering in the Black Beauty, waiting for the bullets that would end their lives just as surely as the one that had taken his mother's, and felt a fury unlike any he'd ever known wash over him like the tides of that distant ocean so long ago.

Almost without thinking, Kato leapt towards Hale, reaching for a sleeve dart at the same time.

He took three dance-like steps across the boards. One of them gave way under his foot with a loud "thwang" and fell out of sight, clattering against the concrete on the floor below.

Kato saw Hale's eyes widen in surprise and his finger reached for the trigger. Just before he fired, Kato released a dart and saw it lodge in Hale's throat.

Gurgling, pulling at his damaged neck, Hale fell away from the window. The rifle exploded one final time, the bullet plunging away into the river, and then the large weapon fell from Hale's nerveless fingers.

Before Kato could stop him, Hale staggered toward the open window frame and tumbled after his bullet with one final, strangled cry.

The Detroit Airport was as busy as it always was, with the heavy domestic and international traffic typical of the major airline hub that it had become.

Kato glanced up from the newspaper he was pretending to read while waiting for Britt's flight to land. A Michigan National Guard pilot happened to be passing by and did a double-taken when he saw Kato, who smiled in return and nodded in friendly greeting. The Guardsman frowned and kept moving.

Although the Korean War had been over for several years, hostility in America toward those of Asian descent was not uncommon. The fact that he was not Korean, Kato thought, probably never entered the pilot's mind.

Across the terminal a woman and her daughter, both with newly-dyed brunette hair, stood at the American Airlines counter, glancing nervously around them. The woman saw Kato and her face registered no recognition, which was good. He knew that he looked much different without his distinctive cap, mask, and tunic, but still it surprised him that he was not recognized at least occasionally.

Soon, courtesy of The Green Hornet's underworld contacts, the two women—formerly Joanna and Melissa Hale, now known as Janette and Marion Jahnsen—would be bound for Los Angeles and the new life that awaited them there.

Kato's smile drifted away. The sight of the two women made him think of his own mother, now more poignantly than ever. He frowned. Less than two days ago he had believed that such memories were muddied by time and largely obscured by the experiences that had shaped him as an adult.

Now he knew it was the other way around. In reality, it was those memories that had made him the man he was today, and without them he could never be complete.

No, it was not good to live too much in the past, he concluded. Nonetheless, he was determined to remember his mother for as long as he lived, to honor her memory and the sacrifices she made on his behalf.

Not long after Joanna's plane departed, Britt Reid arrived at the same terminal carrying only a simple overnight bag and a garment case slung over one shoulder. "Hello, Hayashi-san," he said as they walked along together. "How were things while I was gone?"

"Fine," Kato said. "I went for a...long drive, I think you would call it. In the process I tested the new oil slick device, which worked exactly as planned."

"Outstanding, glad to hear it! So let's get ready to roll again, my friend, and soon."

"That may take a bit longer than anticipated," Kato said. "I've had to make a number of...repairs."

Britt stopped in the middle of the terminal, his eyes wide. "What kind of repairs?"

"It is a very long story about what was really a very short period of time," Kato said with a sigh. "I will tell you about it on the way home."

Just before the two men exited the terminal, Kato paused and looked back through the great glass windows at the open airfield and the blue sky beyond. In the distance, he imagined he could see Joanna's plane, now little more than a dot above the horizon and disappearing fast.

His smiled returned, and suddenly he felt better than he had in days. "Getting back to action sounds very good," he said. "After all, it is never the same without you, Boss."

JUST A MAN

by Thomas Brannan

Inhaling smoke.

The orange glow of the tip of a cigarette was like a smaller version of the sunrise in my hand. I held the smoke in for a beat longer than I should have, probably, and it wanted to come out, like now.

I held it some more.

Dawn was brightening the side of the warehouse I leaned against, a bright promise that couldn't possibly be fulfilled. I would be brought down by the new day—whatever came with it—just as I had by every new day before it.

My lungs were on fire.

I held it some more.

My father was bustling around inside the coffee import warehouse, hobbling along on his one good leg. The man was demented, a broken clockwork train that didn't know how to quit. I was sure that the hated four-letter word would have been scratched out of the Q section of his dictionary, had he owned one.

He didn't call me in from smoking, and the only reason I even drove a forklift at his place was because we were family. He thought I was a quitter. When I got kicked out of the Corps for medical reasons, he just snorted and walked away. Hobbled away.

Medical reasons, I thought, blowing my hot lungful of smoke out through my nose. I had to blow it through my nose, because during my first week back on Hill 55, a counter-sniper shot me in the jaw, ruining my face.

My right eye, my sighting eye, itched because it had been uncovered for too long. I pulled down the olive-drab eye patch I wore because I couldn't blink so often. I dropped the cigarette and grunted, the only sound I could make, and started in to face my disappointed father.

Every morning I did the same thing, so I could turn my back on the sunrise.

Knocking off at six in the evening meant riding home in the back of the pickup truck while Dad drove and cursed the awkwardness of his malformed leg. I used to sit in the cab with him, but one, two, three shifts into the drive, he would usually look over at me as if the design of the clutch was my fault. That, and his disgust at my ravaged face after I got back was too much for me.

So. Rather than resent the old man, I would just sit in the back. That day, the one that had started like every other, looked to end out the same way. We'd ride home and I would go on up to my room and read a book and drink and drink and drink until Dad was shaking me awake for the next day of work.

Instead, there were two men standing by the truck and in front of a white Cadillac when we walked out onto the warehouse's dirt lot. One of them was big and blunt, like a man-sized hollow-point bullet in shirtsleeves. The other was smaller and natty in a straight-cut black suit and hat. Neither of them looked like they were there for coffee grounds.

There was another car parked a little ways away. A long, black job. It looked dangerous.

"Help you gents?" my father asked, wiping his hands on the rag he kept in his back pocket.

"Actually, my good man, we're here to help you, a new businessman in a new city. Last week an associate of mine," he shook his thumb back at the black car, "came by with a business proposition, and . . . good God, son. You go around in public, looking like that?"

The big man scowled and looked at the lower half of my face as if he was going to be ill.

"Boy. I asked you a question."

My father interceded. "He can't talk none. And even if he could, he's got nothing to say to you. Neither do I, for that matter. I'll tell you the same thing I told your associate, The Hornet." Dad took a step closer to the neat man and stuck a finger in his face. "You stay away from my business, you hear? I'm not the only one on this block that'll tell you that, either. We won't put up with you hoods—"

The blunt man interrupted my dad by grabbing his head, faster than such a big guy ought to have been able to.

I moved.

The Corps had taught me how to fight dirty, so I did. I put two good left hooks into the big guy's side and one in his neck, and he let my father go. I shuffled back, ready to throw down with him. A metallic *click* stopped me.

"Mick, quit fooling around with the mute kid," the neat guy said, holding a .357 revolver out at me. "His face is messed up enough. Don't want to even guess what he'd look like once you were done with him."

Both men laughed at that.

"Keep us in mind, old timer. The Green Hornet don't like to be kept waiting," the neat man said, and walked away. They just turned their backs and walked to their waiting Caddy, no fear. A smallish Asian man in a chauffer's outfit and black mask stood outside the sleek black car. I hadn't even heard the door open or close. He nodded at me and got back in, and the black car rolled away quietly.

And my father. He just looked at me like I'd quit again.

"Out there you're going to have to become part of the jungle."

The Sergeant addressed us, the four new snipers just off the plane and shipped back to Hill 55. We'd been in-country before as regular grunts before being recommended for sniper training. We'd been back for three days already, filling in for odd jobs assigned to the sniper squad while Sarge and his spotter were out on a long patrol. He'd just got back and wanted to talk to us. I looked up to this man already, this man with the giant price on his head and known well to the Vietcong.

"We're going to have to make an impact. The rest of the Marines here, they're not sure how to take you. The men in charge aren't sure how to use you."

The barking of a dog caught the Sergeant's attention.

"Get down!" he yelled.

I never saw a flash. I never heard the report. One minute, I was looking for my bag to take it with me, the next I was looking at the sky.

The dog barked on.

The acrid smell of smoke took me out of my dream, and I stood up while the floor shifted like loose tiles under my feet.

I was still drunk.

I was still drunk, and the house was on fire.

Grunting as I tried to yell for my Dad, I staggered from the end of the hall and lurched towards his room. I pounded on the thin wood door and burned my hand when I grabbed the handle.

The fire is in there.

I took a couple of woozy steps back and rammed the door with my shoulder. It didn't give and I fell over, coughing. The smoke was getting thicker. Using the wall to steady me, I worked my way back to my feet and aimed a kick next to the doorknob. Then again.

The jamb splintered and the door flew open, flames roaring out and slapping me back. I grunted louder as I fell to my knees, frustrated that I didn't have a voice to yell with. Because I really needed to yell right then.

My father was still in bed. He was in his burning pyre.

I dragged myself from my knees and ran for the front of the house. I had to get out, get a neighbor to call the fire department for me. Not for the first time, I inwardly cursed the Vietcong ghost that put a hole in my face.

The front door wouldn't open. What? I pushed on it, using my good hand and my bruised shoulder. It wouldn't open, and I grunted, almost a howl.

I moved to the front window and peeked out. My father had splurged one day and bought a reinforced door to make my mother feel better about moving to Detroit, and it was the strongest thing in the house, probably. This strong door had a truck parked up against it.

My good eye darting around the room, I grabbed the coffee table and hurled it through the big window fronting the house. Almost as soon as it cleared, before the broken glass even bounced off the front lawn, shotgun blasts came flying into the living room.

I ran for the back door, slamming into it and turning the handle. Went nowhere. I looked through the narrow slot window next to the door and there was a car parked there, grill to door.

The same car from this afternoon, the white Cadillac.

Sons of bitches!

I staggered for the bomb shelter under the kitchen, thankful for the first time in my life that my father had been deathly afraid of the Reds.

Inhaling smoke. The orange glow of my cigarette brought back to me the sight of my father in his funeral pyre.

I dropped the cigarette and stomped it out. Nasty habit, anyway.

The rough wooden side of my neighbor's house held me up while the fire department dug through the rubble that had been my home, looking for mortal remains. The only reason that I wasn't in the pile waiting to be found was the tunnel my father had dug to the vacant lot across the street. Hard to explain to a new neighbor if anyone had bought it, but my dad wouldn't have to worry about that anymore.

Everybody was very busy, but there was no sense of urgency. Why should there be? I ambled back to the shed in the backyard, ignoring the laid-back chaos surrounding my ex-house.

A big brass lock kept me out, but a borrowed fire-ax took care of that. None of the firemen would look me in the eye when I took it back to them, and I knew. I just knew.

The police were the same way, for the most part. The only ones that even looked my way as I took my old duffel bag out of the shed were the guys with slick grins on their faces for a job poorly done. Those were the cops that were just a little bit fatter in the wallet today for taking their time last night. I doubted they even knew who was in the house, as none of them gave me a second look. The rest of them probably hadn't taken any money from that weasel-faced bastard with the white Caddy, nor had the firemen.

But they were to blame, too, weren't they?

I grabbed one other thing out of the shed and turned away, walking up the road.

The steady diet of vodka at night instead of beer had kept my middle trim, so the uniform still fit.

My eye patch was made of the same green material as my old Marine Corps rags and matched nicely. It rode up on my forehead as I sat in my father's warehouse and cleaned my rifle. Every once in a while a hacking, grunting cough would explode out of my ruined face, but I figured that would go away sooner or later.

I cleaned my rifle carefully and thought about my father's killers. Certainly, the natty man and his large associate were responsible, but who was that in the black car, pulling their strings? Both my dad and the slim guy had said, "Hornet."

The Green Hornet, according to slim guy.

As comforting as sitting in my battle clothes and cleaning my rifle was, I needed to hit a library. Ever since coming back from Vietnam, I'd avoided watching the news, reading the paper. I already knew what was happening over there. It had happened to me.

I blew out a breath and pushed the vodka bottle away from me. That wouldn't help at all; I needed to be clear-headed for this. All right. While the sun was still up, I'd go to the library and do a little homework.

When the sun went down, I'd hang out near here, maybe see why the warehouse was so important to these gangsters. Maybe I'd just shoot them.

I sat in the middle of a mountain of newspapers with a headache and a very full pad of paper. There was a wealth of information about The Green Hornet and the rackets in Detroit, but none of them were more openly damning of the masked man than the *Daily Sentinel*. Britt Reid must have had a death wish.

I liked him already. I made a note to write him a letter.

But that was it, then, wasn't it? The guys in the white Caddy had burned down my house, but they did it on the say-so of The Green Hornet. Fine. That was fine. It made Detroit what my sniper instructors called a target-rich environment.

Scribbling notes on the pad of paper, I dug around in my satchel for my ballistics tables. I would need subsonic rounds, because the small crack as the bullet broke the sound barrier would give me away. Something heavy, because I didn't want to have to fire more than once, and something I wouldn't have to send away for. Everything local.

I checked my watch, noting that the library was due to close soon. After gathering up the newspapers and putting them back, I pushed all my stuff back into my satchel and kissed my notepad.

Homework done.

On the way out of the library, I almost ran into a tall guy, brown hair. He said, "Excuse me," and pushed on past. The librarian greeted him by name.

"Good afternoon, Mr. Reid," she said, and I stood at the entrance of the library as the door swung shut behind him. Where had I seen his face? I grunted and turned away. A picture of him graced the more damning articles in the paper. I wondered about what kind of man he was.

He hadn't looked twice at my ruined face.

Two blocks down from my father's warehouse, I lay on a rooftop of a squat office building, prone under a gray blanket and looking through a pair of powerful green binoculars brought home from across the pond. I wasn't using both lenses, as my wacky eye got dry, so the patch was down. I'd also set up my .30-06 rifle with an eight-power Unertl sniper scope mounted to it. No silencer, as I couldn't find one, and couldn't mill one myself.

Earlier that evening, I'd used rubber bands to tie some bright green leaves to sign posts between where I was hidden and the warehouse. That would give me wind strength and direction. The rooftop I was on was a bit higher than everything else in the area, which would help me get a clear shot, but I hated shooting at a down angle.

Oh, well, I thought cheerily. *Maybe I'll give myself away, die, and then I won't have to worry about doing this again. See? There's always an upside.*

I was sure that I'd take at least one of these bastards with me before I bit the dust. And, I'd already written and mailed a letter to the *Daily Sentinel*, so that the world would know that The Hornet was to blame for my father's death.

An idle part of my brain was amused by the fact that everything was green now. My clothes, my binocs, the leaves I was using for windage flags. *I stole your color, Hornet.* I made a mental note to write another letter if I made it through this alive.

The white Cadillac pulled into the dirt lot next to my father's warehouse and my breath caught in my chest. Carefully, because I didn't have anyone to give me range, I swapped from the binoculars to the rifle as the two scumbags from the night before got out of the car. No sign of the long, sleek black job, but that would wait. There was a red muscle car pulling in, too, a Barracuda.

The natty guy got out first. He was jabbering away at the big fella, and they were both laughing it up. The big guy flicked a lighter a couple of times, and that was it. Forget about finding out why the warehouse was important. I did not care why they wanted to squeeze my father ... just that they'd killed him. Tried to kill me.

My breath slowed until I was almost holding it. I pulled my eye patch up onto my forehead and sighted in. The big guy swanned around in my crosshairs for a couple of seconds as a stillness came over me. I noted the leaves, and how they were moving. And then, as if God knew what I was up to and approved, the light breeze died away.

I squeezed the trigger.

Blunt man's head went wide open like a rotten melon bursting against a wall and he went down. I worked the bolt on the rifle, cursing myself. It was stupid to take a headshot, even from only a couple of blocks away. The torso moves so much less, even when people are talking.

Natty man hadn't moved, and I readied to shoot him down, when he fell over. *Hm.*

I moved the rifle and checked the other car, seeing who else I had to shoot. The red 'Cuda was kicking up a big plume of dust as it pulled back onto the road, tires screeching for purchase on the black tarmac.

The rifle shot had been loud. It was time to go, in case the guys in the other car were coming this way.

I could not believe my eyes. Eye.

The morning edition of the *Daily Sentinel* had a page-three article about a gangland slaying in the warehouse district. The police reporter was calling it a bona-fide mystery, as both men had been felled by a *single shot.*

More evidence that Someone Upstairs approved? I chose to take it that way, at least. "One shot, one kill," had been our motto and our creed.

Anything more than that was a gift from Providence.

I scanned the whole paper, front to back, and in the article on the fire at my house, there was no connection with The Hornet. My letter to the editor was curiously absent. I was about to just throw the paper away when a detail leapt out at me.

The patch came off so I could see it with both eyes, just to be sure.

I was a dead man.

Right there, in black and white, was an account of the fire at my father's house and I was listed as among the dead. Did no one really know that I had made it out? A smile folded up the ugly corners of my misshapen mouth.

Gangland couldn't track me. I was dead, and the only people that had seen my nasty face up close, really up close, were taking a dirt nap.

Matter of fact, the only person that knew I wasn't dead was Britt Reid, as I'd sent him a letter. And another thing dawned on me . . . he let the paper go out, listing me as dead. I wondered if he would put Two and Two together and come up with me as the Four that had killed the men at the warehouse?

Wait. There was The Hornet's driver, too. I held my head between my hands as I tried to put everything together in a way that would allow me to continue. The hit at the warehouse had gone so well. The guys in the other car had sure bugged out like they were scared.

Scared.

I could use that fear. I put my eye patch back on and pulled a sheet of paper to me. Another letter to the *Sentinel*, this one bound for the police writer, Mike Axford. He'd know what to do with it.

The letter, when it was put out in the evening edition, looked like this:

> *Attention, Green Hornet,*
>
> *I have taken your color. I have killed two of your men. I will work my way up the food chain until I have you in my sights, Hornet.*
>
> *And everyone else that has helped The Hornet along his way up, watch out. I'm coming for you, too.*
>
> *Signed,*
>
> *Green Viper*

I read the paper again in the dim light of my father's warehouse and made a sound that was almost a giggle. Thinking about who had helped The Hornet on the way up didn't really take long. All those newspapers I'd read painted the picture for me pretty clearly. Maybe because it was I was new to the city and hadn't been pulled along gently like a fish on a line, like everyone else, but I knew who'd been helping The Hornet.

Oh, he'd talked about The Hornet enough, and every once in a while he'd hold a press conference, promising to bring The Green Hornet down. But what had he done?

What had District Attorney Frank Scanlon really done? The accounts in the papers read like a litany of failure. That is, against The Hornet. Other rackets got shut down left and right, but not The Green Hornet.

When he woke up in the morning, Scanlon would have a package waiting for him on his front step and a very nice note from me, letting him know what was in his future.

I was looking at my stack of green paper (once I'd decided on my Green Viper device, I took it all the way) and composing the letter in my head when there came a knock at the back door of the warehouse. Quietly, I stood and walked over, wondering what this was. The slat to the left of the door gapped a little, and I peered through it.

Britt Reid stood there, hand raised to knock again, still looking just like his picture in the *Sentinel*.

Yanking the door open, I grabbed his arm and pulled him into the warehouse. He was stronger than he looked, something of a grappler, and I had to work hard to get him in a Judo hold they'd taught me in Basic. The thought crossed my mind that maybe he was letting me.

"I'm not here to make trouble," he said. His muscles under the sport coat were taut. "I'm just here to talk."

And I, of course, just grunted. But I let him go and stepped back. He turned to look at me, and as before, he didn't stare at my ruined face. Instead, he looked me in the eye.

"Now, I know you can't talk," Reid said. "Can you sign?"

I shook my head, a little startled that a newspaper and television magnate knew sign language and I, a mute, did not.

"Just as well. If you have some paper . . ."

I put up one finger and led him further into the warehouse, to where I'd been sitting and reading the *Sentinel*. He sat cross-legged on the floor across from me and smoothed his slacks over his knees as I looked for my pen. When I was ready, he started.

"There's something you need to know. I want you to understand; I'm sorry for your loss. It can't be easy to lose your loved ones . . . that way. But you have to stop what you're doing. Now."

I cocked my head the way a dog does. My eyebrows asked the question for me: *Why, Mr. Reid, whatever do you mean?*

His brows knit. "You don't have to play games with me. What kind of coincidence is it that two known gangsters are killed by sniper fire outside this warehouse? The warehouse of a man killed the day before, a man whose son was a Marine Corps sniper?"

I felt the crude smile trying to appear on my ruined face.

"Listen," he said, "this kind of thing happens here in Detroit. These criminals, they're always in some kind of war with each other, trying to take over rackets. Do you follow me?"

I nodded. He was offering me a way off the path I'd taken my first bloody steps down. But I wasn't sure I wanted off. I grabbed a sheet of paper and looked at it, tapping my pen on my forehead as I thought about how I wanted to word things.

"There are things you need to know," Reid was saying. My eyebrows came up at this, and he continued. "Frank Scanlon is a good friend of mine. We've worked together on a lot of things, and one of those things was going to be a sting at your father's warehouse. We had inside information that those criminals were planning to use the warehouse as a distribution center for Detroit's opium trade."

Inside information? I wrote.

"Yes," Reid said, nodding. "We got this information from The Green Hornet. Hear me out," he said, noting the look that crossed my face.

"The Hornet is a wanted criminal. But sometimes, he gives us things. He gives up people that would do more harm than good, for the city, for his own criminal empire. He knows what tar will do here, and he doesn't want it in 'his city'."

I heard the quotes in Britt Reid's voice.

"He knows that junkies don't earn for him, and he wants to keep business thriving. He doesn't want to lose any of his cut. The main players were the two men you shot. They were keeping this close to the vest, and that meant doing all the dirty work themselves. With them out of the way, the plan is closed down. And now The Green Hornet has nothing for us. He has no chips to bargain with, so we can turn all our attention to him. Let the police do their job. Leave The Green Hornet to the law."

I didn't know what to think of Britt Reid. He seemed so sincere. He also seemed very smart. The more I thought about it, the more I could not believe that he wouldn't know that his 'good friend' Frank Scanlon was in The Hornet's pocket. Hell, half the articles that I put that together with came from his own paper!

I needed him to believe that I was done, get him off my back until I could make up my mind. I wrote out a quick note and showed it to him.

All right. You win. No more.

He smiled and clapped my shoulder, and I managed not to grimace at his touch.

"You won't regret this," he said as we walked to the door. I nodded, kept on nodding as he left and I closed the door behind him.

I had to pack up. If I was right about Reid, the warehouse wasn't a safe hiding place for me anymore.

Two weeks later, rain soaked through the flimsy hood of my green M-85 field jacket and rivulets of water trickled down my back. My green uniform pants were wet almost to the knee and my socks were barely holding together inside my combat boots.

I'd forgotten how much "fun" it was to stalk someone.

I stood outside the home of Frank P. Scanlon and waited for the dawn. That's when I would do him. There was never anyone around, his house would be easy enough to break into, and instead of using the rifle, I was going to be up close and personal.

Following Scanlon around for a fortnight, I'd been getting his routine down. I knew when he went shopping for groceries. I knew where he liked to eat, and when. I knew that he only took his clothes to the dry cleaners when dutiful Irma was working, never slothful Edith.

From my jacket pocket I pulled my olive bandana and tied it around my face, covering the lower half. With the hood up, I was a specter in green. The weight of a .45 automatic under my arm was comforting, and I put the gun in my hand as I climbed the steps to Scanlon's back door.

A whisper of something behind me, and I turned, striking out with the butt of the gun. The man moved, ever so slightly, and I missed. I continued my turn and launched into a body tackle.

I missed again.

The black-masked chauffer from before bounced on his toes in front of me. Then a foot flashed out of the darkness and caught me in the side, doubling me over. His black-gloved fist (I almost didn't see it) crashed against my head and the night got darker.

I woke up on a bench seat, sitting in the back of a well-appointed car. The first thing I saw was an array of buttons and screens. I figured that I wasn't sitting in the back of an ambulance or squad car.

"This has been coming for some time," a voice said next to me. I turned and looked into steady eyes surrounded by a green mask, Detroit rolling by behind him.

My hand shot to my armpit. Of course my automatic wasn't there.

"You've already been given one chance to walk away from all this. This is your last chance. Do you have anything to say? If you can sign, I understand it."

I was a little startled, this time that a criminal mastermind knew sign language and I didn't. This might get to be embarrassing. I shook my head and made a mental note to go back to the library.

"That's fine," The Hornet said, swinging out a keyboard. It was laid out like a typewriter, a cable going from the back of it into the console in front of us. "Can you spell?"

I narrowed my eyes and hunched over the keyboard, hunting and pecking my answer for The Hornet. My words appeared in green on the black screen in front of us.

You killed my father.

The Green Hornet shook his head, and if I wasn't mistaken, looked a little more tired.

"Your father . . . that wasn't my doing. I would have given your father another week to think about it. Dead customers can't pay."

I lunged at him and The Hornet's fist shot out, cracking my malformed jaw and pushing me back into my seat.

"Don't be stupid. I know what you want to do. And I know where you'll end up. First you want to take me out. And then, if you do it, you think you'll be happy." The Hornet shook his head.

"All it will do is get worse. That emptiness you feel inside you, it will just grow and grow until it's all you have left. You won't be able to stop with me. You won't be able to put away The Green Viper. And all that will get you is a prison cell or an unmarked grave."

Those steady eyes bore into mine and I knew that he was speaking from experience.

"You're not immortal. You're not a force of nature. You're a man. Just a man."

The car rolled to a stop a block from the train station.

"Last chance," he said, holding out a rail ticket with my name on it. "What's it going to be?"

I snatched the ticket out of his hand and turned to type out my goodbye.

I'm just a man.

He nodded and the door on my side opened. I got out of the car and pulled the olive bandana off my face, pulled my hood down.

The black car rolled into the night. I ran from the train station.

I made the most of the time The Hornet gave me and had a busy, busy week. It came to a close with me sitting in my father's darkened warehouse, dressed out in my full Green Viper kit. My .30-06 rifle sat across my lap, another .45 automatic in my shoulder rig, and a pair of rope ends in my hands.

"I thought you were going to leave town," The Green Hornet said from the shadows of the warehouse. He stepped up, just outside the circle of light my Coleman lantern provided, and I yanked hard on the rope in my right hand.

There was a pair of loud *thumps* as heavy pallets fell in front of the main and back doors.

The Hornet stopped and looked around. With my free hand, I tossed a paper airplane to him, one made out of my green paper. He opened it up and looked it over. It read:

> *Hornet,*
>
> *I've thought a lot about what you told me, and you're right. You're one hundred percent right. If I decide to go through with it, if I open that door, I will never be able to close it again.*
>
> *I've decided, then, to wipe the color green from Detroit's palette. There's no way out of this warehouse.*

He looked at me and I saw alarm in his eyes. We both drew at the same time, I my .45, he a black collapsible baton with a gold tip. I recognized it from a description I'd read in the paper; it was the Hornet Sting.

My eyebrows beetled together. What did he think he was going to do with *that*? There really was no way out.

He raised his wrist and spoke into it. "Give me a side door, Kato."

There was a loud roar as something explosive slammed into the corner of the warehouse, opening a hole to the outside, and I pulled the second rope as hard as I could. The triggers on charges I'd set up went off at the same time, matching the angry explosion behind me. I stood and fired my .45 at the now-running Hornet, but I was off-balance from the twin explosions. Bits of the rafters started coming down at us, and flames ate at the boxes and boxes of oil-soaked rags I'd been piling in the warehouse all week.

Running, The Hornet pointed his Sting baton at me and my gun vibrated so bad that I couldn't keep hold of it. I felt my bones rattle with it as I tripped over a flaming bit of rafter and went down hard, knocking my head against a cinderblock.

Inhaling smoke. The orange glow of the burning warehouse was like an up close and personal sunrise, here for me and only me. I held the smoke in for a beat longer than I should have, probably, and it wanted to come out, like now.

I held it some more.

The dawn was brightening outside the warehouse, a bright promise of peace. Finally, some peace. I didn't get The Hornet, but I got me, and that would have to do. Dad would have to be happy with that. See that, Dad? I didn't quit.

My clothes were on fire.

My lungs were on fire.

I held it some more.

I dropped my head and grunted, the only sound I could make.

The Green Hornet and Kato stood outside the furiously burning building, The Hornet with his head down, Kato with one hand on his partner's shoulder.

"This didn't have to go this way. I could have ... I could have—"

The masked companion shook his head. "You gave him more chances than you gave anyone else. Even after he was going to kill Mr. Scanlon."

The Hornet leaned against the hood of the Black Beauty, more tired than he'd been in a long while.

"Sometimes, this is the worst job in the world."

Kato cracked his knuckles. "If you don't do it, Boss, who will?" He looked around, holding his hand up to block some light from the brightly burning fire. "We should get out of here before the fire trucks show up."

The Green Hornet looked into the fire.

"Boss?"

It was a horrible job. But it was also the only job he could do. This was who he was. He stood, straightening his shoulders and resolving to never let things go this far again.

"Let's roll, Kato."

THE COLD CASH KILL

by James Reasoner

Most guys in his shoes would have been mighty happy. It had been a nice evening so far. Dinner and a movie—some really long saga about a Russian doctor—and Phil Lockwood was walking along the street with a sweet, good-looking blonde on his arm. He was young, healthy, and had a good job as a pressman at the *Daily Sentinel*.

But even though Phil wore a smile, he was worried as hell, and more than a little scared. He knew he was doing the right thing, though. By noon tomorrow, this would all be over. Whatever happened, he would just have to live with it.

"—to Phil."

He gave a little shake of his head and looked over at the blonde. "What did you say, Clicker?"

"I said, earth to Phil. I swear, honey, you looked so far away right then, you might as well have been up in one of those space capsules, orbiting around the earth."

"I'm sorry. I've just got a lot on my mind."

"Like the fact that I finally agreed to go out with you after all those times you asked me?"

"Well...yeah," Phil admitted. Normally, that was exactly how he would have felt. Clicker Binny was a beautiful young woman, as well as one of the *Sentinel*'s top news photographers. A guy ought to be pleased to be out on a date with her. Under normal circumstances, he would have been.

It was just that his circumstances were far from normal these days.

Clicker tightened her arm around his. "Don't worry about it, Phil. I know my gorgeousness is pretty intimidating."

"Yeah, it is."

"But I promise I won't bite...unless you—"

She didn't get to finish what she was about to say. They were walking the couple of blocks from the theater to Phil's car, and as they passed another car parked along the street, a man suddenly got out from behind the wheel, leveled a gun at them, and snapped, "Hold it, you two! Don't move, or this goes off!"

Phil felt Clicker stiffen in fear, or more likely, considering her personality, a mixture of fear and anger that anybody would dare try to hold them up.

The man came closer. He wore a long coat with the collar turned up and an old-fashioned fedora with the brim pulled down so that it obscured his face. He jabbed the automatic toward Phil and demanded, "All right, hand over your wallet, buddy, and maybe that pretty little blonde won't have to watch you bleed all over the sidewalk!"

Phil's heart slugged hard in his chest. He couldn't seem to stop staring at the gun muzzle. He and Clicker had lingered in the theater lobby after the show let out, looking at the posters for movies that were being released soon, so the street had had a chance to clear out. No one was nearby, and the stores along here had closed down for the night. The dim lights that burned in their windows were enough to give Phil a good view of the gun, though.

With everything else that was going on in his life right now, he was getting himself mugged! It was almost funny. He suppressed an irrational urge to laugh.

"The wallet and your watch, now!"

"Take it easy," Phil said as he slipped his arm free from Clicker's and reached toward his back pocket. "I'm cooperating. I'll give you what you want, buddy."

He caught a glimpse of a feral smile on the man's face. "Yeah, you sure will. Me and the night will be satisfied."

Phil's breath hissed between his teeth as he drew in a sharp breath. He opened his mouth to say something, to plead for his life, maybe, but it was too late.

"Reach for a gun, will you?" the man yelled. "You damned fool!"

He fired.

Flame spurted from the gun muzzle, and Phil felt a hammerblow to his chest. The bullet's impact knocked him back a step. Clicker started to scream as the gunman blasted another round into Phil's body. Phil didn't feel this one nearly as much. He was already going numb all over.

He crashed to the sidewalk but didn't know it. He wasn't aware of much of anything except Clicker's screams and the man's shout, "He shouldn't have tried to reach for a gun! Sorry, sister!"

Then a car door slammed, an engine revved, and tires squealed, leaving Phil Lockwood lying on his back on the concrete. He was cold all over now. His vision started to blur as he looked up and saw Clicker's face. She knelt beside him, leaning over him. She put a hand on each side of his face and said, "Don't die, Phil, don't die! I'll call an ambulance! Just don't die!"

He would have liked to go along with what she wanted. But like everything else, it was out of his hands now. The last thing he heard was Clicker urging him to hang on.

"And just like that, he was gone," Clicker said. "There was nothing I could do to help him."

"You poor dear," Lenore Case murmured as she rested a consoling hand on Clicker's shoulder. The news photographer sat in a leather chair in front of the big desk belonging to Britt Reid, publisher of the *Daily Sentinel*.

"You're lucky that robber didn't shoot you, too, Clicker," Britt said from behind the desk. "Usually in a case like that, a killer doesn't want to leave any witnesses behind."

"Well, I never got a good look at his face, Boss. I guess he knew that and decided he didn't want a second murder rap hanging over his head."

Britt smiled. "I'm just glad you're alive. I'd hate to lose one of the best shutterbugs in the business."

"But you lost one of your pressmen in Phil," Clicker pointed out.

"Yes, I did," Britt agreed as he grew solemn again. Even though he was the publisher, he made it his business to know something about everyone who worked for him. "Phil didn't have much family, did he? Just a mother?"

"I think that's right. I didn't know him all that well myself yet. That was just our..." Clicker's voice caught in her throat. "Our first date."

Britt nodded. Clicker was tough, and her work had given her the sort of thick skin that most people in the news business acquired as they reported all the woes and tragedies of humankind. But being a reporter or photographer and seeing such things in your line of work was different from watching a friend being gunned down at close range. Of course Clicker was shaken up. That was why Britt had called her into his office as soon as he heard from crime reporter Mike Axford about what happened the night before. He wanted to see how Clicker was doing and tell her to take some time off if necessary.

"And it was all so senseless!" Clicker went on. "The robber thought Phil was reaching for a gun, but of course he wasn't. Phil didn't have a gun."

"That's what caused the man to fire?" Britt asked.

Clicker nodded. "That's what he yelled out just before he pulled the trigger. And then he said it again just before he jumped back in his car and drove off. I thought I was a goner for sure, Mr. Reid."

"I don't blame you for feeling that way. You didn't have to come in to work today. Why don't you go on home? Take the rest of the day off. Longer if you need it."

Clicker surprised him by responding with an emphatic shake of her head. "No, sir," she said. "I'd feel a lot better working. If I go home, I'll just think about how Phil...about how Phil looked lying there on the sidewalk . . ."

Britt knew she was right. He said, "That's fine. Axford's going to cover some sort of Treasury Department press conference at the federal building later this morning. Why don't you go with him and get some shots?"

Clicker nodded and stood up. "Will do, Boss. And, Mr. Reid... thanks."

"No thanks necessary. Go do your job."

Clicker turned toward the door, then paused. "There was one other thing that was sort of odd," she said. "Phil tried to tell the robber that he would cooperate. He said he'd give the man what he wanted. And the man said that he and the night would be satisfied. Then he shouted that about the gun and shot Phil. That's a strange thing to say, isn't it?"

"Yes, it is," Britt agreed. "But who knows how the mind of a killer like that works in the first place?"

"I suppose so. See you later, Boss. You, too, Casey."

Lenore Case smiled and nodded a farewell.

Then, when Clicker was gone, Casey turned and looked at Britt Reid, who sat behind the desk with a frown on his handsome face.

"Something bothering you, Britt?"

"It doesn't ring true. Almost, but not quite."

"And you're going to have to do something about it, aren't you? Or rather—"

He held up a hand to stop her. "The first thing I'm going to do is go see Phil Lockwood's mother. I think Britt Reid should pay his respects and convey his condolences, don't you?"

Phil Lockwood's mother lived in a small, neat house in a lower-class neighborhood. The area was beginning to deteriorate, but for now it probably wasn't a bad place to live. Until the night before, Phil had shared the house with his mother. Now she was there alone, except for some neighbors who had come over to sit with her in her grief.

"Thank you for coming, Mr. Reid," she said as she shook Britt's hand. Like the house where she lived, she was small and neat. Her hair was mostly gray, with a few darker strands left in it. "Phil always spoke highly of you. He said you weren't like most bosses who don't know and don't care about their employees."

"We thought a lot of Phil at the *Sentinel*, too," Britt assured her. "Of course, I didn't really see that much of him, what with him working in the pressroom on the late edition of the paper. That's a pretty small crew in the middle of the night like that."

"Yes, but Phil liked it," Mrs. Lockwood said with a wistful smile. "If he had been at work yesterday, instead of taking a night off, well..." She couldn't go on for a moment. "We just never know, do we, Mr. Reid?"

"No, we don't," Britt said, thinking for a second about some of the strange twists his own life had taken. He pressed on, saying, "Mrs. Lockwood, did Phil seem to you to be worried or upset about anything lately?"

"Worried?" she repeated, frowning a little. "I don't know that I'd go so far as to say that. I thought a time or two that he had more on his mind than usual. I'd catch him staring off into space, and when I asked him if something was wrong, he always said that everything was fine. I wasn't sure I believed him, but...he wasn't in some sort of trouble, was he, Mr. Reid?"

"Not that I know of."

"Because Phil was always a good boy. He was honest as the day is long, I'd swear it."

"No one believes otherwise," Britt said quickly. He hadn't come here to worry the dead man's mother, but what Mrs. Lockwood said fit in with what Clicker had mentioned about Phil being preoccupied about something.

Britt went on, "I want you to know, the *Sentinel* is going to take care of all the expenses. At least you won't have to worry about that."

"That's mighty kind of you, Mr. Reid."

Britt shook his head. "Not at all. We're like family at the *Sentinel*, and family takes care of its own."

After expressing his sympathy again, he left the Lockwood home and headed back to the office. As he reached the *Sentinel* building, Mike Axford and Clicker were just entering as well.

"Any news from that press conference, Axford?" Britt asked.

The rugged crime reporter shook his head. "No, just more empty talk about catching counterfeiters and such. Seems that there's more funny money floating around in the city than usual. The Feds say they'll be making an arrest soon." Axford snorted. "You know what that usually means. They don't have any idea where that phony dough is coming from."

Britt nodded and looked at Clicker. The blonde had more color in her cheeks and looked more like herself again. Clicker had been right. The work was good for her.

Britt had work to do, too.

But he wouldn't be doing it as a newspaper publisher.

"And why exactly are we spying on your own newspaper, Boss?" Kato asked as he sat behind the wheel of the Black Beauty.

"It's not the newspaper I'm interested in tonight," The Green Hornet answered from the rear seat of the sleek black car. "It's the men who print it. And if I'm not mistaken, there go two of them now."

The hour was well after midnight. The crimefighting duo was parked down the street from the *Sentinel* building, just around a corner in a patch of darkness where the car wasn't noticeable. But from here The Green Hornet could see the door that led up to the street from the printing plant in the basement. Two men had just emerged from that door.

"Willie Compton and Jerry Goldman," The Hornet went on. "Compton is the foreman of the late edition crew. Goldman is in charge of distribution for that edition. By now the papers are bundled and ready to be loaded on the trucks."

Kato's eyes met those of The Hornet in the rearview mirror and narrowed in puzzlement. The Hornet's partner was a highly intelligent man, but clearly he didn't understand the significance of what The Hornet was telling him.

The Green Hornet said, "Let's just follow them and see where they go."

Kato kept the Black Beauty well back of the two men as they walked along the street. After a few blocks, Compton and Goldman stopped and went down some stairs to a basement entrance in a darkened office building. They disappeared inside.

"The Cellar," The Hornet breathed as the car glided past, its powerful engine humming quietly, except for the faint buzzing sound it made. "I'm not surprised."

"That's that after-hours club, right?" Kato asked. "Lance Duncan's place?"

"That's right. The authorities turn a blind eye to it because men who work these late shifts want a place to stop in for a drink on their way home after work, and because Duncan keeps a tight lid on any trouble there. Find a place to park where we won't be seen. We're going to wait and have a talk with Compton and Goldman."

Kato smiled. "I'll bet they need another drink after a conversation with The Green Hornet."

"I'll see you tomorrow night," Willie Compton was saying to his companion an hour later as they headed toward a subway station after leaving The Cellar.

"Stop right there," a cold, hard voice commanded from behind them.

The two men jerked around. Goldman said, "Who—"

A tall figure stepped out of the shadows and pointed what looked like a long-barreled automatic at them. The stranger wore a long, midnight-green coat, and a mask of the same color covered his eyes and the upper part of his face under a dark fedora.

A startled exclamation came from Compton. "The Green Hornet!"

"That's right," The Hornet said, "and I want to know whatever you can tell me about Phil Lockwood."

"Lockwood!" Goldman said. "He's dead. Poor guy got bumped off during a robbery last night."

"Yeah," Compton put in. "And come to think of it, the guy who pulled the trigger on him was dressed something like you, Hornet, according to what Clicker Binny said! Why'd you do it, Hornet? I know you're a crook, but Phil never hurt anybody."

"I didn't kill Phil Lockwood," The Hornet said, "but I have a pretty good idea who was responsible for his death. Spill what you know, or face the consequences!"

Compton and Goldman began backing away. "We don't know anything about what happened to Phil," Compton blustered.

"We didn't have anything to do with it," Goldman added.

The Hornet took a step toward them, his face hard and implacable. The gun in his hand was more menacing than ever.

"Wait!" Goldman cried. "I'll tell you what you want to know!"

"Jerry! Shut up!" Compton said.

"Are you crazy? What does it matter to us if The Hornet muscles in and takes over? We get our cut either—"

From the mouth of a nearby alley, muzzle flame bloomed in the darkness as an automatic weapon let out a stuttering roar. The Hornet threw himself aside, but the bullets weren't intended for him. Instead, they ripped into Compton and Goldman, making them jerk around in a grotesque dance. After a moment, the hail of lead knocked the two men off their feet.

A thick plume of green gas shot from The Hornet's gas gun, aimed at the alley where the machine gunner dealt out death. The yammering weapon fell silent, but The Hornet wasn't convinced that the knockout gas invented by Kato had done the trick this time. As if to confirm that hunch, a swift rataplan of running footsteps sounded from the alley.

Kato had been waiting in the shadows in case The Hornet needed him. Now he seemed to materialize from the darkness in his mask and chauffeur's uniform and cap. "I'll go around, try to cut him off!"

The Hornet reached out to stop Kato from plunging into action. "No, it's not necessary," he told his friend. "I know where we need to go next."

They hurried back to the Black Beauty, and as soon as the doors had closed behind them, The Hornet gave Kato the address of their next destination.

"Let's roll, Kato!"

"How do you know that's the right truck, Boss?" Kato asked a short time later as he wheeled the car through the city's dark streets, a few blocks behind one of the trucks that had left the *Daily Sentinel*'s distribution center.

"The driver is Neil Bristow," The Hornet said. "He's Jerry Goldman's brother-in-law. It figures that he'd be in on the racket with them."

Anger burned in The Green Hornet's voice. As Britt Reid, he had devoted his journalistic life to the pursuit of justice through his newspaper and television station. As The Green Hornet, he had used more direct methods to smash countless criminal schemes. The Hornet had a reputation among the police and other authorities as an outlaw, but in reality he used that as a tool to help him bring down the real public enemies. It galled him to think about what had been going on practically right under his nose.

"Bristow doesn't know it yet, but I figure we're about to save his life," The Hornet went on. "I think the mastermind behind this has decided it's time to shut things down. He's going to clean house now and get rid of everybody who could tie him to the scheme. Compton and Goldman were doomed as soon as they left work tonight, and there'll be a bullet waiting for Bristow as soon as he's made his delivery, too."

The truck made several turns, but the Black Beauty, running without lights because the streets were so sparsely populated at this time of night, stuck right with it. The Hornet and Kato watched as the truck pulled up at a gate in the fence along the rear of a good-sized estate on the outskirts of the city. The gate rumbled open, activated by some mechanism, then slid closed again after the truck had rolled through.

A moment later, a pair of almost invisible figures darted through the shadows near the fence.

Two shadowy figures slipped silently through a rear window into an old carriage house that had been on the property behind the main house for a hundred years or more. A few minutes later, a truck rolled in through open double doors in the front of the building. The insides of the place had been gutted out, though, and it had been transformed into a machine shop of some sort. Several men waited there, and as the truck came to a stop, they closed the doors behind it. One of the men lifted the vehicle's rear door, climbed inside, and began tossing out bundles of newspapers tied together with twine. The other men picked up the bundles and carried them over to a long metal table.

Neil Bristow got out of the cab and grinned at the men. Judging by his expression, he had no idea his brother-in-law had been mowed down by machine-gun fire less than an hour earlier.

"All right, boys, here's this week's shipment," he said.

"Good job, Bristow," one of the waiting men told him. "Say, come on over and take a look. You've never actually seen how this set-up works, have you?"

Bristow shook his head. "Nope. All I've seen is the extra dough I get paid for making these deliveries here once a week."

The man motioned him closer. "Come on."

Bristow shrugged and walked over to the table, which had a large machine with several cutting blades attached to it mounted at one end. The men who had placed the bundles of newspapers on the table were cutting them open, then going through each paper and pulling out the classifieds. They tossed the other sections aside. Then they opened the ad section to the middle and removed the single sheet of newsprint that formed that middle.

Instead of help wanted and items for sale and personal ads, the paper was printed front and back with five, ten, and twenty dollar bills.

Bristow's eyes widened. "I never seen that much loot in one place before, even phony loot. What do you do, put the sheets through that gizmo at the end of the table?"

"That's right," the other man said. "Those blades cut it up into individual bills, then they go into another machine that sorts and bundles 'em. In a couple of hours, we'll have more than two hundred grand in counterfeit dough ready to be spread out through the city."

"But the quality can't be good enough to fool anybody for very long, can it?" Bristow asked with a frown. "I mean, it's printed on newsprint."

The other man shook his head. "Nah, we got a guy—your brother-in-law's buddy Compton—who sees to it that our special paper gets substituted for the newsprint that that particular page is supposed to be printed on. Maybe it ain't as perfect as what you'd get if you were turnin' it out on a smaller press, but our business is quantity, not quality. We're makin' a bundle, and the Treasury boys got no idea where it's comin' from."

Bristow let out a low whistle. "Yeah, that's a sweet deal. I'm glad Jerry cut me in on it."

"Yeah," the other man said as he raised a pistol behind Bristow's head. "You're a lucky guy."

Before he could pull the trigger, somebody let out a startled yell. The man with the gun whirled around in time to see one of his fellow counterfeiters go flying through the air from a high kick delivered by Kato. He and The Green Hornet attacked swiftly, almost before the counterfeiters knew what was happening.

Green gas belched from The Hornet's gas gun. A couple of the men caught one whiff of it and collapsed. Kato put some of the crooks to sleep the old-fashioned way, kicking and punching his way through them.

The Hornet headed for Bristow and the man who had been about to kill him. Before he could get there, the crook grabbed Bristow, looping an arm around his neck and jamming the barrel of the gun against his head.

"Hold it, Hornet!" the counterfeiter yelled. "You saved this guy's life a minute ago. What, is he double-crossin' us with you? Don't come any closer or I'll blow his brains out!"

The Hornet stopped and glanced around. He saw that the rest of the gang was out of the fight, rendered unconscious either by the gas from the Hornet Gun or Kato's flashing feet and fists. He looked back at Bristow and the other man and smiled coldly.

"Go ahead and pull the trigger," The Green Hornet said. "He doesn't work for me. I just want that phony cash. I don't care what happens to some petty crook."

"You...you're musclin' in?"

"It's what I do," The Hornet said.

As he spoke, a faint hum sounded as well. The noise came from a small dart shaped something like a hornet, which Kato had just thrown with amazing speed, power, and accuracy while his partner in crimefighting distracted the gunman. The sharp point buried itself in the back of the man's hand, causing his fingers to open as he cried out in pain. The gun thudded to the floor.

And a split-second later, the butt of The Green Hornet's gas gun thudded on the gunman's skull, knocking the man out. He folded up, collapsing to the floor at Bristow's feet.

Bristow's face was ashen. Beads of sweat stood out on his forehead. "I...I thought I was a dead man," he said. "I thought you were really gonna let him kill me, Hornet. But you saved me! I'll do anything you want, Hornet. I'll work for you now!"

The Green Hornet had stowed his gun away in its concealed holster. Now, with no warning, his fist came up and smashed into Bristow's jaw with devastating power. The blow lifted Bristow off his feet for a second and sent him crashing to the floor, out cold.

"You already work for me," The Hornet said with bitter anger in his voice. "But not any more."

A cool jazz version of "Willow Weep for Me" played softly from hidden speakers in the dimly-lit room. A sleek, handsome man about thirty stood alone behind the bar, counting up the night's receipts. He hummed along with the music as he worked.

"That willow should be weeping for Phil Lockwood, not for you, Duncan."

Lance Duncan's head jerked up in surprise. He hadn't heard anyone come into the after-hours club. His hand started to drop toward a revolver on a shelf underneath the bar.

"Leave it alone," The Green Hornet ordered as he stepped out of the shadows and pointed his gas gun at the club owner. "Get both hands back where I can see them."

Duncan complied with the order. "The Green Hornet," he said. "I recognize you. What does the city's biggest crime boss want with me?"

"You're too modest," The Hornet said as he came closer to the bar. Kato moved up behind him, ready for action if he was needed. The Hornet went on, "I think you're the one who deserves that title, Duncan."

"Me? I'm just a night club owner."

"With a finger in every dirty pie in town," The Hornet snapped. "Including counterfeiting. You blackmailed or bribed a handful of men from the crew that puts out the *Sentinel*'s late edition to print those phony bills for you and hide them in certain copies of the paper. You even got an honest kid like Phil Lockwood to work for you, probably by threatening to hurt his mother if he didn't cooperate, but then his conscience got the best of him. He was going to the cops to spill the whole thing, wasn't he, Duncan? So before he could do that, you sent a triggerman to get rid of him and make it look like a botched robbery."

Duncan shook his head. "I don't have any idea what you're talking about, Hornet. I don't know anything about any counterfeiting, and I'm sure as hell not mixed up with a murder!"

The Hornet smiled. "Oh, no? Your hired killer was careful to carry out his act and leave a witness who'd testify that it was a simple robbery gone wrong, not a rub-out. But then he got too cute and named you."

"That's crazy," Duncan insisted, but The Green Hornet saw the telltale stiffening of the club owner's muscles that told him his shot had found its target.

"Is that right...Lancelot? That *is* your real name, isn't it? Lancelot Keith Duncan? It's easy enough to look up records like that. You should have changed it legally when you decided to go by the nickname The Knight in underworld circles. Of course, with my sources I could have found it out anyway, even if you'd changed it."

Lance "The Knight" Duncan's lips drew back from his teeth in a grimace. "You can't prove any of this."

"The hundred thousand dollars in counterfeit bills that the police and Treasury agents are loading up at your house right now are evidence enough," The Hornet said. "You'll have a lot of questions to answer about how it got there."

"But there were—" Duncan started to say, then stopped short.

"Two hundred thousand dollars?" The Hornet mocked. "That's right. I'm keeping half of it, as a...finder's fee, I suppose you could say."

"You dirty—"

The Hornet gestured with the barrel of the gas gun. "No need for that. It's over, Duncan."

"The hell it is," the boss of the counterfeiting ring snapped. He had moved his toe to an alarm button on the floor under the bar and pressed it as soon as he recognized The Hornet. Now he yelled, "Kill them, Johnny!"

The Hornet went one way, Kato the other. Sub-machine gun slugs chewed through the air between them. As they whirled around, the gunner who had slipped into the room behind them swung the muzzle of his weapon toward The Hornet, probably fooled by Kato's slight figure into thinking that the tall, midnight-green-clad man was more dangerous.

The killer found out just how wrong he was as Kato leaped high and drove a kick into the side of his head.

At the same time, Duncan snatched the revolver from under the bar and fired at the swift-moving figure of The Green Hornet. The bullet whistled past The Hornet's ear as he charged toward Duncan and smashed into the jukebox that was playing, silencing the music with a squawk. Before Duncan could fire again, green gas shot from The Hornet's gas gun at close range and engulfed him. Duncan coughed and staggered and tried to lift his gun again, but his muscles no longer obeyed him. He fell forward, sprawling senseless on top of the bar.

The machine-gunner, who wore a long coat and a fedora, just as Phil Lockwood's killer had done the night before, lay unconscious on the floor. "Good work," The Hornet told Kato. "They'll both still be unconscious when the police get here, but we'll tie them up to make sure they don't get away."

As soon as that task was completed, the two crimefighters slipped out of the club and returned to the Black Beauty. It was early morning, and the sky to the east held a trace of gray light that heralded the approach of dawn.

"What will you do with that fake money we took from Duncan's place, Boss?" Kato asked as he settled behind the wheel.

They had loaded half the counterfeit bills and the newspapers in which they had been concealed back into the truck, leaving half the money behind to serve as evidence against Duncan. With Kato following in the Black Beauty, The Hornet had driven the truck to a hidden warehouse until it and its contents could be disposed of.

"It'll make a nice fire in the *Sentinel*'s incinerator," The Hornet replied in a grim smile, "along with those newspapers." They had left nothing behind that would tie the counterfeiting ring directly to the *Sentinel*, other than an unconscious Neil Bristow.

Britt Reid intended to have a discreet talk with District Attorney Frank P. Scanlon, the only law enforcement official who knew about the publisher's dual identity, and see if it would be possible to keep the newspaper's connection out of the police investigation. The public counted on the *Sentinel* to be unwavering in its pursuit of justice, and their confidence would be shaken if they knew what had been going on in the newspaper's printing plant. Of course, only a few individuals had actually been involved in the counterfeiting ring, and several of them were dead now, but the perception still wouldn't be good.

Being involved in anything that smacked of a cover-up bothered Britt, too, but sometimes compromises were necessary. He made use of the fact that the public believed The Green Hornet to be a crook. Now, maybe Britt Reid had the smallest of stains on his conscience....

But justice would be done, and the flood of counterfeit bills in the city would stop. Maybe not everything was perfect, but it was still a good night's work.

"Let's roll, Kato," The Green Hornet said. "It'll be dawn soon."

"Extry! Extry! Paper! Get yer paper! Police smash counterfeit ring! Nightclub owner arrested for murder! Green Hornet still at large! Extry!"

FLIGHT OF THE YELLOW JACKET

by Howard Hopkins

Britt Reid knew someone had entered the garage that housed the Black Beauty the moment a green light on his desk in the study blinked a silent warning. The alarm had been installed recently, after thieves had broken into the garage and stolen the vehicle.

A glance at the study wall clock told him it was 3 a.m. and normally he wouldn't have been up working this late but, his mind troubled, he'd been unable to sleep. He had a sinking feeling he was not the first man upon whom Laura Cavendish had produced such an effect.

Face grim, he jabbed a button near the blinking indicator on the panel that slid from a concealed niche in the desk. The button activated a similar light accompanied by a soft buzz in Kato's room.

He eased out of his chair, at the same time switching off the small desk lamp, plunging the room into darkness.

With a whisper of movement, Britt turned to the bookshelf behind him and drew three tomes to an outward tilt, which activated a mechanism that sent the blazing fireplace on the far wall whisking upward. Steps fluid, almost ghostly, he crossed the room then entered the revealed compartment, barely discernable in the gloom, to a secret passage leading outside.

Adrenaline made his heart quicken and his senses hyper alert. After exiting the house, he slipped into the garage through the side door. His eyes having adjusted somewhat to the darkness, he could just make out the shape of his white Chrysler 300 convertible, but no human form. He listened, seeking any slight sounds that might pinpoint the position of the intruder. The scuffing of a foot sounded, intentionally stealthy, but he couldn't determine its exact location.

A breeze touched his face and cut through his smoking jacket and he realized the secret garage door opening onto the patio outside his study was open. This should have been impossible to actuate for anyone, save him and Kato. Yet someone had indeed opened it. And that meant someone knew this garage was the lair of The Green Hornet.

He drifted to the work bench flanking the side of the garage, and reached for the switch concealed behind a tool board that would illuminate the garage with green light and slide the garage door shut. The board slid aside and by feel Britt located a metal door to the control panel, opened it.

A hollow click sounded as he flicked the switch.

The garage remained in darkness. Whoever had gained entrance had been smart enough to deactivate the light. That comforted him not in the least, because it meant someone knew far too much about The Hornet's operation. But who? And what did they want?

He got no time to think about it. Something collided with the side of his skull and the next thing he knew the concrete floor was rushing up to meet him. He hit hard, was vaguely conscious of running feet, escaping feet.

Then, seconds later, Kato was kneeling beside him.

"You all right?" Kato asked.

A pounding in his brain like the crashing of a tsunami told him he wasn't, but he said, "Yes," anyway. "Someone...someone ran out..."

Kato nodded, swept upward, and ran after the intruder. Britt doubted his partner would have much luck catching the assailant if the squeal of tires speeding away were any indication.

Six months later...

Even Britt Reid had to admit congressional front runner John Cavendish had a compelling manner about him...and with what he promised in his platform that made him a dangerous man, indeed.

That was one of the reasons Britt had invited the candidate to his home to speak to a select group of Detroit's elite, to determine exactly what the man proposed to do in terms of a certain green vigilante running the streets of the city.

The second was for a more personal reason, one who stood just at the edge of the crowd. She had blonde hair done in a looped bun and curves barely restrained in a cream shantung suit with its hip-length jacket of five large buttons, and small cutaway just above the waist of the knee-length skirt. She clutched a beaded handbag in her slim white fingers. Her pert nose, slightly upturned, fine white skin, and delicate features posed a stark contrast to her candidate father's blocky chin and angular face. She still possessed those emerald eyes, eyes that could pull a man's soul inside out were it not for a particular cold ambition she had always struggled to suppress when they'd spent time together. Those eyes had not once looked his way, and secretly he was glad for that, for if they had he was unsure what emotions they might dredge up. Leaving her had been one of the hardest decisions of his life, yet strangely enough, one without regret.

He got the feeling she was purposely avoiding looking for him or at him, and that she had attended this meeting at all was a marginal surprise. He had half-doubted she would accompany her father to the home of a man she'd once known in an intimate sense. Their separation, at least on her end, had not been the most amicable. Laura Cavendish did not accept rejection and the word "no" was not in her vocabulary.

When she'd walked through the door he hadn't been able to deny a bit of weakness in his knees; like her father she wielded a hypnotic power—especially over men—and Britt Reid, for a few months, had proved no exception. Her power, however, contrary to her father's, focused itself in a different direction, one not always healthy for the object of her desire—or wrath.

Britt glanced to the small bar, gave a slight nod to Kato, whom he had informed of the lady's preference beforehand: pink champagne. Delicate, light, somehow the same as the woman who drank it, yet somehow completely the opposite as well. Kato, keeping to his valet role, poured a glass, set it on a tray, and headed toward the young woman.

Britt had never truly figured out Laura Cavendish, and perhaps that was a blessing of sorts. Some women were better left as mysteries. He sighed. He hadn't arranged this engagement to discover *her* secrets; he had arranged it to determine her father's intent, and his integrity. Candidate Cavendish might be a problem, one The Hornet didn't need. The question was, how serious was the man in his determination to capture the crime fighter the world at large thought to be a criminal? Was it an empty campaign promise or did this man truly intend to clean up the city?

A booming voice from the small podium tore Britt from his thoughts.

"For far too long a criminal has held this city in a grip or terror. Nothing has been beyond his greedy fist—graft, kidnapping, racketeering, the terrorizing of innocent citizens. A criminal called The Green Hornet! And now it appears he has an ally in his deeds, this so called Yellowjacket promising to work with The Hornet to control this city's corrupt officials. I am *not* one of those officials. I am pledging to end these threats, clean up this city through whatever means necessary." Cavendish paused, dark gaze sweeping about the room, mustached face tense. "Just today...I received a threat from this outlaw." John Cavendish reached into his suit coat pocket and pulled out a folded yellow-brown sheet of paper. He set it on the podium, then gazed over the crowd. Britt glanced at Kato, who'd returned to the bar. The manservant frowned.

John Cavendish thumped a fist on the podium, the intensity in his eyes increasing. "My dear friends and fellow citizens, proof of the collusion between The Hornet and Yellowjacket. Yellow paper imprinted with a Hornet seal. I make you this promise—I will bring these criminals to justice! I will see an end to this menace—"

The end came, but it came to Cavendish's speech. The abruptness of the candidate's finish brought Britt Reid's head around. His gaze narrowed as it focused on the podium. A deathly pallor washed over the candidate's face, making his skin appear bloodless, crackled with blue veins. His mouth hung open, and foam bubbled at either corner. His widened eyes froze with a look of death.

A small outline vaguely in the shape of a flying insect appeared on Cavendish's forehead, at first dark green, then quickly blackening; blood dribbled from its pattern and trickled over his brow.

A scream tore through the crowd gathered in Britt's living room, which had previously gawked in shocked silence, followed by the shattering of a champagne glass after it dropped from Laura Cavendish's left hand. As if the scream carried solid substance capable of knocking down a human being, the candidate crumpled to his knees, then pitched forward and slammed into the floor face first.

A great murmuring buzzed through the onlookers and plainclothesmen galvanized into motion, rushed to the stricken politician. District Attorney Frank Scanlon, who'd been quietly observing the proceedings, followed a beat behind.

"Great Scott, he's dead," Scanlon called out, confirming the obvious.

From beyond the living room came a great rumble of an engine, and Reid's ace reporter, Mike Axford, who was covering the event, darted to a window. Despite the darkness of the night, Britt caught a flash of a car tearing away from the townhouse, a long black vehicle of some sort, reminiscent of the Black Beauty.

"Holy crow, it's The Harnet!" Axford yelled, horror on his ruddy face. "He's a killer now! I knew there'd come a day that brigand went too far! He knew Cavendish was just the fella to put him behind bars. He stopped him, that's what he did. Stopped him dead!"

"You sure it was the Black Beauty?" Britt asked.

Axford's brow crinkled. "Well, no, but it was big and black. It sped away too fast for me to get a clean look."

"The Hornet wasn't even in the room!" D.A. Scanlon said, glancing from behind his horn-rimmed glasses from the podium, where he now stood, holding the note Cavendish had left. He glanced at Britt Reid, a puzzled expression on his face. "How could he have killed this man?"

Britt gave him a slight shake of the head. Oh, The Hornet most certainly was in the room, thought Britt Reid. But he most certainly was not responsible for the candidate's death.

Laura Cavendish had stood as if frozen in horror after her scream. Britt Reid couldn't remember the young woman ever showing anything close to that amount of emotion, but, then, her father had just been murdered in front of her.

As if her spell had been snapped by Axford's Hornet proclamation, she ran to her father, dropped down beside his corpse and pulled his head to her chest.

"Please..." she said, a tear coming from her eye and wandering down her pale face. "Please, daddy..."

Scanlon, a grim expression crossing his lips, knelt beside her, touched her shoulder.

"I'm sorry, Miss, but he's gone. And we need to make sure nothing is disturbed."

"No!" she yelled at the older man with gray-peppered brown hair. "No, he's not gone! He's not!" She started to sob uncontrollably.

Britt's eyes narrowed. A certain forced ring laced her emotion, and it brought back flashes of memory as to why he had broken off their engagement.

"Take her out of here." Scanlon motioned to two plainclothesmen. They helped the young woman to her feet then led her towards the door, which had been left open by two other officers who'd charged out after the departing vehicle.

"No one leaves this room!" Scanlon ordered, voice sharp, cutting through the worried murmur. "And we'll be searching all of you."

The decree brought a flash of a look from Kato, and Britt knew what he was thinking. He'd had the same thought himself. He wanted to go after the car that had sped away, but had no way of doing so without exposing certain secrets to Axford and the others.

"Search us for what?" Axford said. "We know who murdered this poor fella. T'was The Harnet. I saw him with me own eyes."

"You think you saw The Hornet's car, but The Hornet's not a murderer, Mike," Britt said, coming up to Scanlon and glancing at the note on the podium, which the D.A. had left unfolded. "And he was nowhere in this room at the time of Cavendish's death. In fact, how the man died is still a mystery. There was no gunshot."

Britt's gaze settled on The Green Hornet seal on the bottom of the note, which informed Cavendish in no uncertain terms he had better suspend his

Hornet/Yellowjacket task force notions or pay the consequences. The seal was one of his own.

Scanlon cast him a look, frowned. "You think this has something to do with those Yellowjacket rumors, Britt?" Scanlon asked, glancing back to the body.

"By god it was The Harnet, I'm telling you! And he's a murderer now, Reid." Axford's ruddy face had grown even ruddier and certainty showed in his eyes. The reporter thought he finally had The Hornet dead to rights.

"Then how did he kill this man?" Britt asked, kneeling beside the body, his eyes taking in every detail. "You've been investigating the Yellowjacket rumors, Mike. He's been looking to control the political arena in this town and using The Green Hornet as a scapegoat. How better to cast blame and build his own reputation than to murder the man threatening to go after them?"

Axford shook his head. "Harnets, Yellowjackets...it's all makin' me buggy!"

Britt's attention focused on the dead man. The insect-like wound on the dead man's forehead trickled blood along its outline. He noticed a slight odor, like sizzled meat.

Something about the method of death seemed...*familiar* and made Britt's stomach sink.

Because it meant that perhaps The Hornet was indeed a murderer after all.

Britt Reid closed the door to his office at the *Daily Sentinel*, then went to his desk, sat, and pulled open a drawer. He fished in the back of the drawer, behind papers, letter opener, and notebooks, locating a small green velvet box. He set the box on his desk, staring at it for long moments, melancholy wandering over him. Along with another feeling that only added to his sour mood: suspicion.

He opened the box, which contained a pair of gold cufflinks. He pried one of the links out of the box, turned it over in his hand, gaze settling on an inscription: "To Britt, Detroit's next congressman."

A sigh of regret escaped his lips and he shook his head. After tucking the link back into the box and snapping it shut, he tossed the box into the drawer and shoved it closed.

He stood, went to the window, stared out at the city. "That was always the problem, wasn't it, Laura?" he said, voice low, sadness bleeding into it. "Your ambitions came before everything, including whatever it was we might have had."

He remembered the night she'd given him those cufflinks, over dinner, when she'd announced she thought he was the best choice for the state's next congressional candidate. If the news had come as a surprise to him, it had come as an even bigger surprise—and annoyance—to her when he refused. She had planned out their future—*his* future—with a peculiar detached surety.

A future he wanted no part of. His duty lay elsewhere, in his mission, which for the time being was written in green.

Laura Cavendish would have none of his refusal, however, and from that night on the writing had been on the wall. And their relationship on the floor.

He glanced at the desk, at the morning edition of the *Daily Sentinel*. Her father's death had brought out some details even he had been unaware of and he supposed that's what had started his mood on its downward turn, as if Axford's blazing headline, GREEN HORNET, MURDERER? hadn't been enough.

"I guess the best laid plans must proceed..." he whispered, then frowned. It was painfully plain, if it hadn't always been, Laura Cavendish arranged her life with replaceable parts and one of those parts had been Britt Reid. For a moment loneliness ached in his heart. Perhaps he was simply meant to be by himself.

A commotion from the outer office broke his reverie and his office door suddenly swung open.

"I'm sorry, Mr. Reid," a young woman with auburn hair piled in a beehive style said, as a second woman shoved past her. "She wouldn't take no for an answer and pushed her way in. I couldn't stop her."

Britt nodded, face tightening. "It's all right, Miss Case," he said to the young woman, who was his secretary. "Miss Cavendish has never been one to take no particularly well."

The young secretary cast Laura Cavendish a look of annoyance mixed with a tinge of jealousy, then backed from the room.

Laura Cavendish dismissed the secretary with a smug expression, then focused on Britt.

Brit couldn't deny a mélange of feelings overtaking him at seeing her again—old emotions of desire, love, irritation, and disappointment formed an orchestra of might-have-beens.

For her part, one might have assumed Laura had just come from a day at a spa instead of having just lost her father. No redness in her eyes from crying, and worse, no grief. Just...coldness.

"My-my, Britt, I see your secretary's still the meek little thing." She punctuated her words with that annoying little chuckle she felt proved her superiority to those she deemed below her. He had to question his own judgment when it came to Laura Cavendish. What had he ever seen in her?

"Lenore Case is anything but meek." His own voice came with a certain chill, though inside the turmoil of emotion still plagued him. There had been good times, he realized, deep conversation and warm moments. He supposed they were warm; they were for him, at least. He had never been quite sure what lurked behind Laura's emerald eyes.

With another haughty chuckle, she stepped deeper into the room.

He remained near the window. Maybe he was for that instant incapable of movement, captured by whatever spell she'd once cast over him. "Why have you come here, Laura? You could have spoken to me yesterday at my home, but I got the distinct impression you were going out of your way to avoid me. I admit, I was surprised you came at all."

She smiled a patronizing little smile. Another affectation he remembered disliking. Any glow of nostalgia he might have felt at seeing her again was quickly dissipating.

"Perhaps I want to give you a second chance, Britt. Maybe I've missed you. Perhaps with my father gone I've come to ask you to reconsider my offer to back you for the congressional seat."

Her tone said otherwise, and he frowned, then went to his desk and flipped open the morning edition of the *Daily Sentinel* resting atop the blotter.

"Perhaps you should have thought about asking me that before you became engaged to the competition."

The smug smile dropped from her full lips, replaced by something much colder. "Good old Axford, I presume? He always was right on the ball...on *most* things."

Britt caught something in her tone he didn't care for, but wasn't sure what it meant. "How long did you think you could keep something like that quiet, especially with your father's death?" The lack of emotion in his own tone surprised him some. He wondered if it weren't a defense mechanism.

"Long enough. Praeton Crandle has a bright future in politics. And it won't stop at congressman."

"Yet he is—*was*—running against your father. You don't see a problem with that?"

The annoying little laugh again. Britt suppressed the urge to cringe.

"No, not at all. Should I?"

Britt shook his head. If anything, the woman had gotten even colder since he knew her last. "What's the real reason you're here, Laura? You didn't come to talk over old times and I assume this visit has nothing to do with your father's death."

Her slim fingers drifted over the top of her beaded handbag. "I came to thank you, Britt."

"For what?"

"For making me see how much of a waste of time it would have been grooming you for a life in politics. I didn't understand then, but I do now. And I understand something else, Britt. I understand I don't like to lose. At anything."

His eyes narrowed. "Hell hath no fury, that it?"

She tilted her head just enough to acknowledge his deduction. She peered at him long and hard, icy lights glittering in her eyes. A causal smile frosted her lips and she turned away, strode to the door. She paused, one hand resting on the jamb, her head lifting a fraction.

"You made a mistake, Britt, the night you let me go. You of all people should have known better."

"I did know better, Laura. It wasn't an easy decision. But it was a necessary one."

She glanced back over her shoulder, and Britt cared little for the chilled expression in her eyes. "Goodbye, Britt Reid. I could have loved you once. A pity."

His gaze locked with hers. "I have my doubts about your ability to love anything completely, Laura."

She laughed her annoying laugh. "Oh, poor Britt, you still don't understand, do you? I love what I love passionately, obsessively."

"There's a difference between loving and controlling."

"Is there? I don't see it. Not when it comes to power..."

He watched her leave, an empty feeling washing through him, nearly the exact feeling he'd experienced the night he broken up with her, though stronger.

"Mr. Reid?" a voice came from the door and he realized Lenore Case was peering in at him and that the clock had jumped ahead five minutes.

"I'm all right, Casey. Get me Kato on the phone, please."

Casey nodded and closed the door behind her. Britt lowered himself into his chair, the light on his phone blinking a moment later.

He plucked the phone from the cradle.

"Anything?"

"Preliminary results from Scanlon," Kato said. "It looks like Cavendish was killed by some sort of electrical or wave device. It instantly stopped all brain activity."

"And couldn't be seen or heard..."

"Had to be at close range, so the killer would have had to be in the same room."

A cinching feeling gripped Britt Reid's belly. "Kato, I need you to check something for me…"

"Mr. Reid?" said the man pushing the mail cart, as Britt closed the door to the office anteroom and stepped out into the hallway.

The man was a gray-haired fellow, heavy about the middle with a face as round and cratered as the moon. "You're working late today, Wagner," Britt said, smiling.

"Not so much, Mr. Reid, Not so much." The man reached to his cart, plucked a yellow-brown envelope free of a stack. He handed it to Britt, who took it with a sudden sensation of dread.

"What's this?" Britt noted the envelope carried no postmark or address. It simply said, *Britt Reid—Important.*

"Don't know, Mr. Reid. I stepped out for me break, I did, and when I comes back there it was. It said important, so I brought it up before I leaved."

"Thanks, Wagner." Britt's tone grew distant as he stared at the envelope. He barely noticed the squeak of Wagner's cart wheels rolling away.

He opened the letter, pulled out the yellow-brown sheet. Dread mixed with gelling suspicion flowed over him.

"Another challenge for The Green Hornet," he whispered. One which for once he had little desire to accept.

"Let's roll, Kato," Britt Reid, now garbed in the costume of The Green Hornet, said from the back seat of the Black Beauty. Behind the green mask his eyes grew intense. His mouth set in a hard line. If ever a time had brought home the point Britt Reid was a lonely man, now was that moment. He saw no way his mission tonight could end well. It reminded him of that night, six months ago, when he'd said goodbye to Laura Cavendish. But this night's goodbyes might prove a lot more permanent.

A moment later double doors slid apart and the Chrysler Crown Imperial slipped out into the back alley.

"Silent running," Britt said, giving his Hornet Sting a final check before shoving it beneath his midnight-green trenchcoat.

"Miss Cavendish's apartment?" Kato asked, guiding the huge car with the finesse of a Nascar driver.

The Hornet nodded. "Yes."

"The note said the Yellowjacket would kill her if Britt Reid didn't come alone. When The Hornet shows up..."

The Hornet gazed out the window. Ahead and about the car the world seemed ablaze with infra-green light, a filter on his mask showing every detail as if it were in emerald daylight, though those outside would have seen only darkness. Somehow, despite the light, the night still appeared embedded with dark loneliness.

"I think The Hornet's expected, Kato. The note said the Yellowjacket wanted to make a deal with Britt Reid. What possible deal could...*he* want to make?"

"I don't follow."

"Britt Reid has nothing this Yellowjacket wants, but The Hornet does. The note sender knows that. The sender had to be in the *Sentinel* building today to leave that note, too; that means somebody who raised no red flags to the staff."

Kato nodded. "Or no yellow flags..."

"I left a lead for Axford. He'll figure it out fast enough to show up and we can hand him the Yellowjacket."

"Then it's a trap?"

"Of sorts. Or a proposition. Yellowjacket wants to work with The Hornet, wants to use his connections. That's why the Yellowjacket used a stolen Hornet seal on the threat to John Cavendish."

"But why threaten Miss Cavendish?"

A bitter laugh escaped The Hornet's lips. "Why threaten Miss Cavendish, indeed."

"But her father..."

"Was murdered right in full view of us and a room full of people.... You remember about six months ago, that night someone broke into the garage?"

"We still don't know who..."

"I think I do. Whoever it was, it was someone who knew I was The Hornet and where to find everything. Perhaps someone who had been in the house before..."

"Or had you followed, like that detective, Oliver Perry."

"Perry's in the clear on this one." The Hornet paused. "At that same time we were working on the miniaturized version of the Hornet Sting."

"But we abandoned that. We couldn't make it small enough without it being lethal to human..." Kato's eyes narrowed as he looked into the review and The Hornet knew his partner had put the pieces together.

"We produced an invisible killing device, soundless. Which made it worthless to us, but invaluable to a criminal."

"And you think…"

"I do, Kato. God help me, I do."

Moments later, the Black Beauty rolled into an alley beside the Trendle Apartments. Doors opened automatically with a flick of switch and The Hornet and Kato slipped from the machine. The doors closed silently behind them.

"Seventh floor," The Hornet said. "I remember picking her up here for dinner all too well. I should have been more careful trusting her in my house, however."

"Perhaps things aren't the way they seem."

The Hornet remained silent. He ghosted down the alley, Kato following. Locating a back door, he slipped the Hornet Sting from beneath his coat, then turned a knob near its top. The end of the sting telescoped and a high-pitched buzz followed. The lock suddenly burst into variegated sparks and the door flew inward.

Returning the Sting to his coat, he entered the building, located a stairwell and took it up to the sixth floor.

"The apartment below hers is vacant," Kato said. "I discovered she rents it when you had me check on her earlier today."

The Hornet nodded. They went to the apartment, but this time he pulled a small round disc from his coat pocket and moved a lever on its edge. A thin rod slid from the disc and he inserted it into the lock. He pressed the top of the disc and the protruding rod turned, probed; a moment later the lock mechanism clicked.

"Let's go," he said, easing open the door as he slipped the disc back into his pocket. Once inside, they closed the door and he listened, hearing nothing. The apartment did indeed appear empty.

In darkness, they moved across the suite to a sliding glass door that led to the balcony. The Hornet opened the door, stepped outside, and looked up.

"We're directly below Miss Cavendish's balcony."

Kato nodded and each pulled a small collapsible grappling hook that looked like hornet wings attached to a slender line from their belts. Kato and Britt had developed the line themselves and it would hold up to 500 pounds without breaking. With a flip of their arms they sent the lines upward. A thin clink sounded as the grapples hooked on the wrought iron railing embedded into the two foot high stone walls surrounding the balcony.

Upward they went, Kato on the left, The Hornet on the right. Hopping over the railing, they left the lines dangling in case they needed a quick egress.

They eased up to either side of the sliding door, and peered into the apartment.

The Hornet's eyes narrowed as he spotted Laura Cavendish and a man in a yellow-brown trenchcoat, mask and fedora, much a copy of hiss own regalia.

"Now I know why you didn't call yourself The Yellow Hornet," Kato said, glancing at his partner.

"Criminals nowadays have no fashion sense," The Hornet said in a bitter tone. His green-gloved hand went to the slider door and he tested the lock. The door was open. "Convenient..."

Kato frowned. "Looks like there's only the two of them."

The Hornet's gaze swept through the apartment, noting the plush white furniture and shag carpet, a beaded purse lying on a mahogany end table. "I wouldn't bet on it." With that, he whisked the door open and stepped into the room.

The man in the Yellowjacket costume grabbed Laura Cavendish and jammed an odd-looking little yellow-brown gun to her temple.

"I see Reid didn't disappoint me," the man in the yellow trenchcoat said. Laura Cavendish looked at The Hornet with pleading, yet oddly cold eyes.

"You were expecting me?" The Hornet asked.

"I was." The man in the yellow mask let a satisfied smile cross his lips. "This was too good for The Hornet to pass up, yes?"

Kato shifted a fraction to the left.

"No, no," the Yellowjacket said, jamming the gun harder against Laura Cavendish's temple. "Stay still. We don't want an accident."

"What *do* we want?" The Hornet asked.

"To work together," the Yellowjacket said. "The underworld in this city fears you; I can use that. And I have money and political ties. Together we can own the city."

"I already own it. Why would I want to share it with you?"

"Because if you don't, I will kill her." He nudged his chin at the young woman.

The Hornet said, "Then kill her and get it over with, then we'll talk."

The man in the yellow mask hesitated, and Britt knew his suspicion was right.

Laura Cavendish started laughing. She stepped away from the Yellowjacket and took the gun from him.

"It's no use, Praeton," she said in a low voice. "Britt's already figured it out."

"Britt?" the man in the Yellowjacket mask said. "Britt Reid? The Green Hornet's Britt Reid?"

She uttered that annoying little laugh Britt had come to loathe and eyed Praeton with a scolding glare. "You're damn lucky I had this room sound-proofed, but, yes, the one and only."

The Hornet moved to his right, closer to the Yellowjacket, his hand starting towards a small green gas gun beneath his trenchcoat. Her mention of sound-proofing the room told him there were others here, somewhere, waiting to attack on some sort of signal from the woman, others who had not heard the revelation of his identity.

"Don't, Britt," Laura said, jabbing the yellow gun at him. "Oh, you might recognize this weapon; I took it from you months ago when I let myself into your garage. I had it modified some, of course."

"And used it to murder your own father for a life insurance policy he took out on you last year," Kato said, eyes hard behind his black mask.

Again she laughed. "You didn't research far enough. My father cancelled that policy a couple months ago, after we had...some words over his clean-up Detroit policy. No, I killed him because he was in my way. I don't like the word 'no'; you know that as well as anyone, don't you, Britt?"

"And you used something you stole from me to do it," Britt said. "How?"

"That purse," she said and Britt's gaze went to the end table. "It has an open middle I kept my hand in. This gun makes no sound, but doesn't have a lot of range. I must thank you for allowing me access to your home, incidentally. I discovered quite a bit about you there, about who you really were. Why do you think I wanted you to run for office so badly?"

"And when I refused and left you..."

"'Hell hath no fury,' isn't that what you said?" She eyed him. "You left me with no choice, Britt. It was either I convince you to work with me... or kill you."

"You're the Yellowjacket, not Praeton Crandle."

"I am, but Praeton is the one with connections and when I marry him... *if* I marry him..." The implication in her words was plain. She was making him an offer and did not expect him to refuse it.

"No deal, Laura. You know who I am, so you know I'm not the criminal this city thinks."

Britt moved, then, diving for the man in the yellow trenchcoat, one hand darting beneath his jacket for his gas gun.

Laura Cavendish shifted towards the sliding doors, jerked up the yellow gun and fired. No sound came from the weapon but a slight odor scorched the air. Britt, still in motion, landed on the couch, bounced back up. Praeton Crandle went rigid, a small insectlike burn mark appearing in his mask. Then he pitched forward, slammed headfirst into the floor, and lay still.

"Whoops," Laura said, shrugging, then jabbed a button on the wall next to the slider.

Doors flew open, the bedroom, a closet. Four men, all large, surged into the room.

Britt lunged as Laura swung the yellow gun towards him.

"Ki-yiii!" Kato said, suddenly airborne, both legs snapping out, connecting with the chest of two of the thugs. He landed, catlike, and delivered a spinning back kick to a third man. The fourth thug lunged at him; he pivoted, jutted out a hip and sent the man over a shoulder onto his back on the floor.

The first two charged him again. He delivered a knifehand to one's throat, and a palm thrust to the other's chin, snapping back the man's head.

At the same time Britt yanked his Hornet Sting from beneath his coat just as Laura Cavendish took a step backward towards the slider and straightened her aim.

He twisted the knob; the end telescoped and he hit a lever; Laura triggered her gun.

An explosive showering of sparks snapped and crackled in mid-air, raining to the floor like dying fireflies. A mule-kick force created by the Sting's ray hitting the gun's emission slammed Britt backward as if by an invisible fist.

For the first time he could remember, a genuine look of shock crossed Laura's face as the same force propelled her backward, in a stumbling gait, out onto the balcony.

"Nooo!" Britt yelled, lurching forward, his balance shaky.

Laura Cavendish continued her backward momentum and went over the low iron railing. The gun flew from her fingers, landing on the balcony with a hollow clack.

Britt heard no scream as she plunged seven floors to the street below.

The Hornet went to the balcony, retrieved the gun, then glanced back at Kato. With a roundhouse kick his partner dispensed with the last of his opponents.

"Let's get out of here," The Hornet said and Kato nodded, crossing the room in a fluid motion. In the distance sirens wailed in the night.

They descended the grappling lines, flipped them loose. In bounds, they took the stairs to the street.

"Hey!" a shout came as they reached the Black Beauty.

The Hornet glanced towards the mouth of the alley to see Mike Axford charging out of his own car.

"I see you, Harnet!" he yelled. "I knew you had to be involved in this."

The Hornet and Kato lunged into the Chrysler. Kato sent the car squealing backward from the alley out onto a back street.

Britt Reid and Kato stood next to the bar in Britt's living room, facing D.A. Scanlon. Casey leaned against the bar, her brown eyes almost glowing, and Britt knew she was all too glad Laura Cavendish was out of his life again—at least for the immediate future.

"You're certain she survived the fall?" Britt asked Scanlon, in one way relieved yet in another strangely empty.

Scanlon nodded. "No sign of a body anywhere. She must have."

"Perhaps she got out the same way we did," Kato said. "She must have guessed we had our lines ready."

"Or just got lucky, because there's no way she expected not to kill me." Britt frowned.

Scanlon sighed. "And you're certain she was the Yellowjacket, not Crandle?"

"*I'm* certain," Casey said, sarcasm lacing her tone. "Yellowjacket males mate once, then die, and only the female stings."

A smile flickered across Kato's lips but Britt didn't see any humor in it. He simply saw tragedy and lost chances.

"She admitted it," he said, voice low.

"She knows your secret..." Scanlon's meaning was obvious.

"And I know hers," Britt said. "But I can't prove it without revealing mine. My guess is she'll be back and with a vengeance. I just hope that prototype Sting gun and Hornet seals were the only things she stole from me."

"She may expose you to Axford..." Kato said, frowning.

As if in answer, the doorbell chimed and Kato went to answer it, returning a moment later with Mike Axford in tow, his face ruddier than usual and a newspaper tucked beneath one arm.

"To what do we owe the pleasure, Mike?" Britt asked, in little mood for Axford's Hornet antics. "Got a lead on the Yellowjacket or Hornet?"

"Pfft," Axford said with a wave of his hand. "I still think The Harnet's responsible for Crandle's death."

"No proof of that, Mike," Britt said.

"No...no, there isn't. But Crandle's body was there, dressed in the Yellowjacket outfit and he was competition for The Harnet. And I saw The Harnet leavin' the scene—say—" Axford's gaze jerked to Kato and Reid's heart sank. He didn't like the look of recognition in the reporter's eyes.

"It's been buggin' me since I met you way back when I was Mr. Reid's bodyguard that you look awfully familiar somehow..." continued Axford.

Worry sparked in Kato's eyes. "I'm sure you're mistaken, Mr. Axford."

Axford's brow arched. "No, no, I'm not. And it finally came to me after seein' a movie on the late show t'other night. You look just like that karate film star, Bruce something or other..."

Kato relaxed, smiled. "I get that a lot."

Axford grinned, pulled the paper from beneath his arm. "There's my lead. But I'll get him, you mark my words." Axford tossed the paper onto the bar. It fell open to reveal the headline:

GREEN HORNET STILL AT LARGE.

BY SCARAB
AND SCORPION

by Mark Ellis

The dead man seemed to be kneeling in prayer. Frozen in a hunched over posture with both hands raised and his head tilted back, he looked as if he sought benediction. Judging by the expression of agony on his face, he had received damnation instead.

Eyeing the man closely, Britt Reid inquired, "Heart attack?"

Charlotte Van Sloan shook her head. "I never knew Fricke to have any health problems." Her English accent held a note of annoyance.

Britt glanced at her with frank appraisal. Dressed in a dark silken gown with a neckline that plunged down between her breasts and cut high on the right thigh, Dr. Van Sloan's warm bronze skin glowed in the lamplight. Her black hair streamed down her back, like a flow of frozen India ink. Straight-cut bangs bisected her high forehead, just above her onyx-dark eyes.

Britt felt a quiver of dismay when he realized there was no concern or worry in those eyes, but there was a quality about them that gave the woman's face the exotic, calculating flair of a Pharaoh's favorite courtesan.

Mike Axford grunted softly. "What's that thing he's holding?"

Britt and Van Sloan leaned forward simultaneously, studying a brown wooden figure gripped in the dead man's hands. Gold gleamed dully from an oblong shape affixed to the statuette's head.

"It's part of the collection," Van Sloan announced. "A carving that represents Queen Nitocris—see her gold scarab insignia? He must have been cleaning it."

Britt nodded, glancing around the huge storage room. Wooden and vinyl crates were arranged in orderly aisles. Styrofoam peanuts, scraps of bubble wrap and strands of straw-like excelsior lay on the floor. On a long shelf above Fricke's head stood a dozen *ushabtis* figures, small wooden statuettes representing laborers in the land of the dead. Moisture glistened on their surfaces.

"He must have been cleaning those, too," Britt pointed out. "Dr. Fricke was very industrious to be doing this at the last minute."

"I'd call it anal retentive," Van Sloan said disdainfully.

Curator Laurence Fricke was a thin, middle-aged man with ash gray hair. Britt Reid knew him only from various museum functions covered by the *Daily Sentinel*. He knew Fricke's assistant, Dr. Charlotte Van Sloan, even less, having met her just an hour before when the museum opened its doors to admit the invitation-only preview party guests.

Axford asked, "Has anybody called an ambulance?"

"I did," announced Nubbar Wanly. "As chief of exhibit security, the job fell to me."

A uniformed man wearing a Sam Browne belt and a .38 Police Positive revolver holstered at his right hip strode in. "The ambulance should be here any minute. As per Dr. Van Sloan's instructions, I told them to come to the loading dock and not to use their siren."

"Thank you, Nubbar," said Van Sloan. "Please return to the ballroom and inform the rest of the security team—tell them not to discuss this incident with any of the guests."

Van Sloan's artistically outlined lips tightened. "This is just brilliant. Half of the city's wealthiest people are in the ballroom, waiting for their sneak peek at the greatest collection of Egyptian artifacts since King Tut's tomb was opened, and the museum's curator drops dead twenty minutes before curtain."

Britt angled an eyebrow at the woman. "Damned inconsiderate of him."

Van Sloan threw him an abashed smile, but it looked forced. "I may sound cold-hearted, but it's my way of coping." She paused and added softly, "Poor Larry. This exhibit was supposed to be the crowning moment of his career. It took a year of negotiations with the Egyptian government to unveil the collection here...the jeweled artifacts alone are priceless. Nubbar and his staff came over from Egypt to guard them."

"Mr. Reid?" Lenore Case's voice floated in from the corridor.

Excusing himself, Britt crossed the storage room and stepped into the dimly-lit hallway. Strains of the overture to *Aïda*, the opera about doomed lovers in ancient Egypt, reached him from the adjacent ballroom. He glimpsed men and women gliding across the marble floor. Like him, all of the men wore tailored tuxedos and the women were attired in the height of formal fashion.

Lenore Case was no exception. The silver gown sheathed every line of her willowy body. Her dark auburn hair, worn in an up-do, accentuated the graceful column of her throat.

She handed him a champagne glass. Swiftly gauging his mood, she whispered, "Is Dr. Fricke really dead?"

"Afraid so. Looks like natural causes."

"But," she interjected, "you have your doubts."

"I do. Dr. Van Sloan is hoping the show will go on. A lot is riding on this exhibit...the future of the museum, maybe."

Lenore's "Uh-huh" was studiedly non-committal.

"You don't think much of her do you, Casey?"

"I don't think much of any egotist—did you notice that the sand sculpture of Queen Nitocris in the ballroom looks like her?"

Britt smiled. "Nitocris is probably the most mysterious of all Egyptian rulers. Until her tomb was unearthed in 1960, she was thought to be a legend. Since there's no visual record of what the queen really looked like, they had to use *some* model."

"You don't think it's a little creepy Van Sloan chose herself?"

"It doesn't matter. Since I'm on the museum's board of directors, I want to see the Treasures of Queen Nitocris exhibit succeed as much as she does."

"Hey, Boss!" called Mike Axford. The broad shoulders of the red-haired reporter strained at the seams of his dinner jacket. "The meat wagon is here."

"Sensitive," Lenore murmured, rolling her eyes ceilingward. "As always."

They walked back into the storage room. Britt placed his full champagne glass on the corner of a crate. At the end of the aisle they saw medics lifting Fricke's body onto the gurney.

Charlotte Van Sloan pried the figurine out of the dead man's fingers. "A tragedy," she murmured, as if by rote. "A terrible tragedy."

Axford snorted out a laugh. "All tragedies are terrible, sweetheart. That's why they're called tragedies."

The look Van Sloan gave him was of pure contempt.

As the medics wheeled the gurney toward the open loading dock, something crunched beneath Britt's right foot. He glanced down at the floor, expecting to see a flattened piece of bubble wrap, but he saw nothing but a dark little speck.

Axford took a sideways step away from the gurney and they heard another crunch, then several more as the rubber wheels rolled over tiny round objects on the floor. The medics paid no attention.

Van Sloan turned away, placing the statuette atop a small table cluttered with notebooks, plastic spray bottles full of cleaning solution, a magnifying glass and various tools. "I've got to get back out there...are you coming, Mr. Reid?"

Britt stared at the specks on the floor. "Soon."

"I don't want to get started without you."

"Don't worry about him," Lenore said wryly. "Everybody out there knows Mr. Reid is always late...except when he doesn't show up at all."

"Mr. Axford is quite capable of representing the *Sentinel* until I get there," Britt stated, gesturing toward the reporter. "Right, Mike?"

The burly reporter hesitated, then nodded. "Guess so."

He joined Charlotte Van Sloan and the two of them left the storage room. As soon as the two people were out in the corridor, Britt grabbed a screwdriver from the table and dropped to one knee. Carefully, he inserted the blade of the tool between the floor and one of the dark, squashed objects. Holding the metal tip up before his eyes, he said, "Hand me that magnifying glass, Casey."

His secretary did so, leaning over his shoulder, squinting through the lens. Her eyes widened. "What is that?"

Britt adjusted the glass, studying the yellow, black-speckled carapace and the tiny, filament-like legs. "An insect of some sort—a very small variety of beetle. Smaller than a ladybug."

Lenore straightened up. "Where did it come from? Look—they're all over the floor."

Standing up, Britt jogged toward the open loading dock door. The medics hadn't yet carried the gurney down the steps to the waiting ambulance.

"Hold it," Britt called.

The medics paused, blinking at him in confusion. Britt lifted the sheet away from Fricke's face. Bending close, Britt nudged Fricke's head to the left, placing the magnifying glass directly above his ear.

"Sir, what are you doing?" demanded a medic.

Britt did not reply. The loose flesh at the hinge of Fricke's jaw was discolored by a livid bruise. The skin bulged slightly, as if an erratic pulse beat there. Then, trailing threads of blood, a line of tiny insects marched out of Fricke's ear canal.

Britt turned Fricke's head to the right. His eyelids twitched and from beneath them oozed droplets of pink fluid, followed by a flow of beetles.

"Holy crap!" cried a medic. "What the hell is going on?"

"Seal this man in a body bag," Britt ordered. "At the hospital, make sure he's isolated in an infectious material container."

Britt turned back toward the storage room. Lenore stood just inside the door, her face taut with fear. "The beetles are inside his body?"

"Appears so."

"How?"

"I have a theory—but for now I want you to get back to the reception.

Tell Mike and Dr. Van Sloan I was called back to the office."

As Lenore walked away, she asked over her shoulder, "What was the curse found inscribed in the tomb of Queen Nitocris? 'Robbers of the dead, look away from this tomb, else my wrath fall upon you by scarab and scorpion'?"

"So far," retorted Britt, "she's been about half right."

Britt stayed in the shadows just inside the door, watching the medics wrestle Fricke's corpse into a vinyl body bag. As they loaded it into the ambulance, he took a gold pocket watch from his vest and flipped open the cover. He adjusted the hands to twelve o'clock and pressed the stem. A faint, tune emanated from it—an electronic rendition of the opening bars of "The Flight of The Bumble Bee."

Britt waited in a pool of darkness outside the museum's delivery entrance. He watched as the Black Beauty rolled to a silent stop. The rear door opened automatically. Britt lunged inside. He removed the long, green-black coat, domino mask and hat from the hidden compartment, and without hesitation assumed the identity of The Green Hornet.

As he changed, Kato spoke from the driver's seat. "I received your signal a few minutes ago...there's not much traffic tonight. I don't think anybody spotted me coming into the lot."

The two men climbed out of the powerful Chrysler Crown Imperial and approached the loading dock. "When I left the storeroom, I closed the door and locked it," said The Green Hornet. "So we can leave signs of forcible entry."

The slender Asian man in the black mask and chauffeur's uniform smiled appreciatively. "Convenient."

The masked men crept up the short flight of concrete steps to the padlocked loading dock door. The Green Hornet took his Sting from a coat pocket, extended it, and focused the ultra-sonic emitter on the lock. A buzzing sound climbed in pitch, the lock quivered, and then broke apart. Kato raised the door halfway, just high enough for them to sidle under it. He lowered it behind them.

They stood quietly, listening to the murmur of voices and music from the ballroom. Kato whispered, "What are we looking for, Boss?"

The Green Hornet stepped over to the small worktable and picked up the figurine Fricke had clutched in his hands. "It's wet."

"Is that important?"

With the magnifying glass, The Green Hornet examined the base of the statuette. "The bottom is riddled with holes. I think when Fricke sprayed it with a cleaning fluid, the liquid interacted with dehydrated beetle eggs that had been laid inside of it."

Kato frowned. "Is that possible?"

"About a hundred years ago when an Egyptian tomb was opened, one of the archeologists dipped some wooden items in a bucket of water to clean them...a few minutes later, he saw that the surface was crawling with tiny bugs, thousands of years old. Once the eggs were rehydrated, they hatched out."

"But *Egyptian* flesh-eating beetles?" Kato's tone was skeptical.

The Green Hornet replaced the carving on the table. "I'd guess this particular species has been extinct for a very long time. They're probably necrotrophs, related to carcass-feeding carpet beetles that are used in taxidermy and museums to clean animal skeletons."

"So you think Fricke was cleaning the statues and beetles crawled out of the wood and into his ears and nose?"

"Yes...but he may have been dead already. Murdered."

Before Kato could reply, a staccato drumming of automatic gunfire crashed in from the direction of the ballroom, followed by screams of terror.

As the two men sprinted toward the door that led to the corridor, a uniformed security guard jogged up, brandishing a distinctly non-regulation Schmeisser M40 subgun.

The guard's eyes widened at the appearance of the two masked men and the weapon swung back and forth to cover them. Simultaneously, Kato's right leg flashed up, the toe of his shoe catching the underside of the barrel, sending the subgun spinning upward. The Green Hornet stretched out an arm and snatched the gun from the air.

The man opened his mouth to shout but The Green Hornet pounded the butt of the M40 into the center of his chest, driving all the air from his lungs. The guard uttered a strangulated cry and Kato chopped him at the base of his neck. He fell senseless to the floor.

They dragged him into the storage room and dumped him into a wooden packing crate, locking the latches. Back out in the corridor, The Green Hornet and Kato moved swiftly to a narrow staircase at the end of the passageway and scaled it, running up the risers on the balls of their feet. They heard a babble of confused, frightened voices.

Reaching a railed gallery overlooking the ballroom, they peered through the bars. The reception area had been laid out around a fifteen foot tall sand sculpture of Queen Nitocris. The track lighting shone down on the flat-topped crown with a scarab above the rim. The queen's features were smoothly contoured, the chin round and firm. She held the Nekhekh, the royal flail, at an angle over her left breast. Her other hand held a short staff tipped by a scorpion.

The sculpture did not hold Kato or The Green Hornet's attention. Nubbar Wanly stood on the raised dais beside Charlotte Van Sloan. He pressed the bore of his revolver against the side of her head. Half a dozen men wearing the uniform of museum security stood at the periphery of the crowd, aiming identical Schmeisser subguns at the people.

"There is no need to panic," Wanly announced loudly. "We are not terrorists, we are Scorpia!"

The Green Hornet and Kato exchanged quick glances. Although Scorpia was not a terrorist organization, they knew it was definitely a criminal one that had begun as a confederation of Persian Gulf pirates centuries before.

"We are here only to reclaim our country's treasures and return them to their rightful owners," Wanly continued. "Since our wishes are not represented by the Egyptian government, we must represent ourselves and take action to restore the majesty of our great Queen. Use the phone to call the police, I have no objection. The negotiations for the return of our relics and your safe release can then begin."

As the man spoke, The Green Hornet scanned the crowd. He breathed a sigh of relief when he saw Lenore and Axford standing at the base the sculpture. He realized that Lenore's assessment was correct—the sand version of Nitocris looked remarkably like Van Sloan.

Gesturing for Kato to follow, he backed away from the railing. He said, "The only Egyptian treasures Scorpia cares about are the ones they can find buyers for."

Kato nodded. "That theater down there is a set-up to cover a standard issue robbery. How do we handle it?"

"Let's get back downstairs…we're going to have take action before the Tact Squad arrives and traps us inside. They're sure to find the Black Beauty and connect us with a hostage situation."

The two men returned to the storage room. Pointing to the packing crate, The Green Hornet said, "Let's check on our prisoner."

Kato raised the lid and uttered a muffled cry of horror. Coming to his side, The Green Hornet gazed down into the container and his stomach roiled with a surge of nausea.

The man's face was covered by an undulating layer of tiny beetles. They seethed in his eye sockets and filled his open mouth. The visible flesh was raw and red.

"Are the beetles multiplying?" Kato demanded. He looked down at the floor and stamped down sharply, bringing forth a series of pops. "This place needs exterminators more than it needs cops."

Voices wafted in from the corridor. The Green Hornet and Kato took up positions on opposite sides of the main aisle, hiding in the shadows between crates. Nubbar Wanly and Charlotte Van Sloan marched in. The man held her by the arm as if he were forcing her along until they were well inside the room.

Releasing her, Wanly demanded, "Where the hell is Hakim? I ordered him to secure the back door."

"Who cares?" snapped Van Sloan. "All I care about is whether the jewels are safely out of the city."

Wanly's teeth flashed. "Sweet little Kepi...little crowned one. Still the same arrogant child-thief you were in the alleys of Cairo. An Oxford education and marrying into British academia has not changed that."

Van Sloan glared at him. "I worked very hard to reach this position, no matter what you think."

Wanly shrugged. "I think the plan is a sound one—with you as my hostage, we'll leave the city while my men hold the prisoners here. Once we're safely away, I'll release you, my men will surrender and the authorities will think I stole the missing relics...and you'll assume your predecessor's position."

The woman's lips curved in a triumphant smile. "It's a shame Larry discovered the theft—I didn't mean to hit him so hard, but his death simplifies things."

Wanly picked up a wooden *ushabtis* figure from the shelf and revolved it absently between both hands. He glanced around. "Hakim should have—"

Charlotte Van Sloan shrieked, bending down to slap at her ankles. "Bugs! Biting me!"

Wanly stared at the woman incredulously as she performed a little dervish dance, crying out and swatting at her legs, smacking the insects away. He started to laugh, then swore explosively in Egyptian, flinging the figurine away from him. His hands were acrawl with beetles.

"They're inside these figures!" he bellowed, shaking his hands furiously, like a cat with wet paws.

The Green Hornet chose that moment to step out into the open, leading with the Sting at full extension. "They're all over the museum by now."

Wanly grabbed his pistol, half-dragging it from the holster before The Green Hornet shot it from his hand with a half-power burst from the Sting. The gun went flying, skittering across the floor to Van Sloan's feet.

She snatched it up, aiming it expertly at The Green Hornet. "I'm glad you're here," she said in a steel-edged voice. "*You* can take the rap."

The Green Hornet shook his head. "You don't have the time for a convincing frame-up. These are flesh-eating beetles and they're multiplying...they'll be eating *your* flesh before you can even start fake negotiations with the police."

Van Sloan hesitated and then she smirked, her finger tightening around the trigger. "All I need is your body to prove you were involved."

Glass shattered behind her. The Green Hornet glimpsed Kato tossing a green-fletched throwing dart at the champagne glass Britt Reid had placed atop a packing crate. She whirled, firing the pistol as she did so. The bullet bit splinters out of the corner of the crate and then she ran. The Green Hornet sprinted after her.

Nubbar Wanly lunged toward the loading dock door, but he jumped directly into Kato's roundhouse kick. Staggering backward, he fell against the shelf holding the *ushabtis* figures. They rained down atop him, the ancient wood splitting open and releasing swarms of the tiny beetles. Instantly, thousands of razor-sharp mandibles sank into his flesh. The man thrashed across the floor in howling agony, clawing at his face.

The Green Hornet pursued Van Sloan only as far as the corridor. As she dashed toward the ballroom, he raced to the staircase. He reached the second floor gallery just as the woman ran in. She brandished the pistol and shouted commands in Egyptian to the Scorpia guards.

The frightened crowd parted for her as she skirted the base of the sand sculpture. Bracing the Sting against his shoulder, The Green Hornet sighted down its length and unleashed a full-power burst.

A webwork of hairline cracks appeared in the effigy of Nitocris. The cracks expanded into splits and the entire figure trembled. Pieces fell away as it swayed from side to side. Crying out in panic, the people milled in all directions.

Charlotte Van Sloan, teetering on her stilt heels, stared up in shock. Lenore reached out from the press of bodies and knocked the pistol from her hand.

Van Sloan stumbled backward just as the entire statue broke apart and collapsed. She managed one short scream before she was swept from view by a torrent of sand. Clouds of eye-stinging grit and dust arose.

The Green Hornet caught a fragmented glimpse of Mike Axford wresting a subgun from the hands of a blinded Scorpia guard and he smiled in satisfaction.

Kato waited for him at the foot of the stairs. "Wanly is alive, but a little chewed up. I think we're done here."

The Green Hornet nodded. "By the wrath of scarab and scorpion."

Kato cocked his head in puzzlement. "Don't get you, Boss."

The wail of sirens in the distance reached them. The Green Hornet said, "Time to roll, Kato."

YOU CAN'T PICK
THE NUMBER

by Rich Harvey

The all night drugstore was slowly fading into obscurity, along with the city's prosperity. A few late-night pharmacies still operated, where a cop on the beat could avoid the rain and make small talk, and perhaps help himself to a free cup of coffee. Most store owners didn't mind, believing that a police presence discouraged robbers. Those that did mind—like Art Levinson—said nothing.

"Well, better get back to me patrol," Officer O'Brien said loudly. Some customers at the counter turned their heads. The regulars patiently waited for him to leave.

Levinson was drying a glass behind the counter. "Good night, Pat." *If I'm ever robbed,* he thought, *I hope you get a shotgun blast to the face.*

O'Brien tipped his hat, carrying his complimentary coffee with the other hand. A gratis copy of the *Daily Sentinel* was folded under one arm when he pulled the door behind him.

Levinson shook his head at the futility of his wish. If a robbery occurred in this establishment, O'Brien wouldn't arrive until long afterward. A generous supply of doughnuts and crullers would probably be confiscated as evidence.

A light rain gave Officer O'Brien pause under a green tarp framing the entrance. He glanced at his pocket watch, a gift from a proud uncle when he became a policeman. Two hours until his shift ended at midnight.

O'Brien grunted. "Little Patty, me boy, you're a fine young lad!" What would Uncle Mike think of him, growing older and grayer and still pounding a beat? It pained him to think that somewhere in that old Irish tavern in the sky, Uncle Mike was crying for him and all those missed opportunities.

"Little Patty" overlooked the ferocious drinking binge that cost him a detective's exam. A handful of investigations stemming from allegations of theft and larceny didn't help, either. But, no...it all came down to poor luck and timing, that's what he told himself. Maybe it just wasn't meant to be.

Begora.

He opened to the *Daily Sentinel* business section. Art Levinson often suggested one of the less popular newspapers, but O'Brien preferred the *Sentinel*. The pharmacist eventually acquiesced and stopped counting the lost sales. O'Brien had taken several hundred gallons of complimentary coffee over the years, anyway.

His thick, meaty lips moved silently. His eyes scanned the columns, rolling to a halt at the market report.

After a strong day of trading, the Dow Jones had closed, and the published daily balance of the United States Treasury was $11,043.03. The ramifications for the world economy meant nothing to him—but the last three digits were significant to a secretive, local economy.

The struggling residents in Chinatown, the Humboldt district, and Cass Corridor were also comparing the Treasury Department's daily balance against small paper tickets. "303" was the "winning" number for that day; thus, thousands of scraps were cascading into wastebaskets across the city. Hundreds of citizens were slumping into chairs, or beds, resigning themselves to another day of working long hours, wrestling with unpaid bills.

O'Brien tossed the remaining coffee in a wastebasket after the newspaper. Only the comics and a brown envelope remained in hand.

The envelope was filled with cash and coded receipts. The pharmacist had dropped it into the *Daily Sentinel*, after suggesting that Officer O'Brien take the lesser selling *Daily Express*. It hadn't worked, since the *Express* didn't carry the *Apartment 3-G* comic strip. He stuffed the envelope into a coat pocket.

Strolling through the residential neighborhood, O'Brien ventured near an alleyway. A gloved hand darted from the shadows and grabbed his shirt, wrenching him away from the main sidewalk. The Irish cop staggered and twirled once, like a Brahma bull attempting ballet. He collided into a carefully aligned set of metal trash cans.

O'Brien quickly scrambled to his feet, leaving his massive impression in a creased metal can. He unholstered his .38 caliber revolver with surprising speed. Even more surprising—more so than finding himself face-to-face with The Green Hornet—was the sudden, stinging pain that radiated from his wrist. His department-issued revolver clattered on the pavement, deep in the shadows behind a wooden staircase.

A black-gloved hand flicked out, so quickly that the wind itself seemed to snap. The stiffened fingers halted within an inch of the policeman's bulbous nose.

"Don't hurt him," The Hornet said. "Yet."

A smaller, younger man in a black chauffeur uniform nodded and stepped back. His stance suggested a familiarity with martial arts—and explained the numbness in Officer O'Brien's wrist. A black mask covered the upper half of his face, giving him a vaguely Asian appearance.

The Green Hornet stepped closer. He was easily six feet tall, garbed in a tastefully subdued midnight green topcoat and fedora. His mask altered the contours of his eyebrows and nose. It was a shade brighter than the rest of his outfit—the only aspect his demeanor that was remotely bright.

O'Brien retreated backward. A brick wall kept him in place. "Saints alive," he stammered. "What do you want?"

The Hornet smirked. "Nothing," he said in a well modulated voice. He held up a brown envelope. "We have what we came for."

O'Brien recognized the envelope. He slapped the breast pocket of his jacket. There was no rectangular bulge.

The cop lunged forward, throwing a round-house punch at the little Asian man. He heard a scream and felt a brick wall collide with his chest. Stars and colors swirled before his eyes. Moments later, he realized that he was flat on his back.

The Green Hornet stood over him, a hand placed against the chauffeur's shoulder. "This should compensate for the receipts I lost today," he said. "Let Mel Hurk know that The Green Hornet doesn't like competition."

The Hornet turned and disappeared into the back alley shadows. The chauffeur followed him, moving like a panther on the hunt.

O'Brien's lungs eagerly filled with oxygen, his breathing gradually returned to normal. He didn't attempt to regain his feet right away. He needed to lie down, allowing the gentle rain to soak him, as he thought of the envelope.

The Hornet had confiscated five-thousand dollars. There would be hell to pay—and there was little doubt that it would be added to his tab.

Marianna Gryzbowski sat quietly on a plush couch, scribbling indecipherable notes in a little pad. She was blonde, wore thick glasses, and was dressed in a blue blouse and skirt. The heels of her black shoes were pressed together. As the stenographer and secretary to Mel Hurk, she recorded conversations, facts and figures, dates and times, and compiled them for Hurk to digest later.

She didn't need the notepad. Her phenomenal memory developed as a little girl in Poland, where her father labored in the fields. He scrounged tiny payments for "sending her to the American." She settled into a little Polish community near the Bricktown section, and searched for "working to pay the bill."

Most employers turned her away, but then she happened upon a classified advertisement placed by "Hurk Investments." The boss, Mel Hurk himself, considered the language barrier an asset. As her command of English improved, she realized that she had chosen the wrong employer.

"Bud" Crocker took a final drag on his cigarette, then ground it unmercifully into a crystal ashtray.

"Five thousand dollars," he muttered.

He was a burly man in his late forties. Gray at the temples denoted age and stress. It also emphasized the darkness of his slicked hair and moustache.

"Christ," replied Hurk. He was seated behind an oak desk. He was younger than Crocker by a few years. His dark brown hair was not styled, it simply was. A sullen expression seemed permanently carved into his solid features.

Everything about Mel Hurk was direct and to the point. The Gotham Hotel had furnished the comfortably-appointed suite—which doubled as an office and an apartment—long before his gang occupied the eighth floor. Hurk would have been satisfied with bare walls and no carpeting.

Two guards sat on opposite sides of the desk. They watched the door, Bud Crocker, the nervous stenographer, and anyone who ventured into Hurk's presence.

"That's just from Levinson's Pharmacy," Crocker added. "The Hornet hit a bagman in Mandarin Park, in the center of Chinatown."

Hurk frowned. "I know where Mandarin Park is," he snarled. He picked up a green betting slip with the numeral "777" scrawled in black felt tip marker. "So, the rumor is true—The Green Hornet really *does* have his own numbers racket."

Crocker swallowed hard. "What do we do, Mel?"

"We won't do anything yet," Hurk said. "Just tell the boys at Detroit Cannery to step up the counting. We need to process the money faster."

Hurk gestured to the door. Everyone scurried into an adjoining room, except for Marianna. Crocker looked at her distastefully before closing the door. She ignored him. As long as Mr. Hurk was in charge, the only thing she had to fear was Hurk himself. One day he might decide that she knew "too much." Whenever someone reached that dubious distinction, it heralded their disappearance.

Hurk scooped up the telephone handset and dialed a number. The eraser end of a pencil tapped the desktop impatiently in his thick fingers.

He identified himself. "The Green Hornet struck one of your men—Officer O'Brien." Hurk paused, nodded, *mmm-hmm*-ed in reply. "Did your informant warn you that this comes out of your payments? Right.... Take care of it."

Hurk hung up and looked over at the Polish secretary. She frantically scribbled stenography symbols. Since Hurk couldn't decipher them, he didn't know that Marianna Gryzbowski was avoiding eye contact, like a small animal immobilized with fear.

Sensing a need to protect herself—or avenge herself from beyond the grave—Marianna began keeping "sidebars" to her notes. It helped her avoid the mistrusting gazes of mobsters trafficking through the Gotham Hotel.

Among other things, she kept notes on Bud Crocker, the second lieutenant. He had muttered statements regarding the inefficiency of Hurk's operation, and things would soon change for the better.

Also, someone "high up" made certain that the "heat" was off the numbers game. Lately, another individual had turned up the "heat."

There were carefully guarded exchanges between Hurk and Crocker regarding a hornet and an exterminator. As they broached the subject of high-powered rifles, car bombs, and police investigations, she decided that this was no ordinary infestation.

She began another notebook, appropriately with a green cover, gathering information regarding the individual code-named The Green Hornet. Someone had described him as a twentieth-century Lone Ranger gone bad.

He demanded protection money from every criminal operating in the city. He rarely collected, since he double-crossed everyone. Once a competitor's business was ripe for take-over, The Green Hornet simply walked away.

Newspaper headlines, especially in the *Daily Sentinel*, demanded his capture. District Attorney Frank Scanlon promised citizens that police would spare no expense to apprehend The Green Hornet—immediately before election day, no doubt.

And yet, The Green Hornet appeared to be helping police. In the past year, he had crippled more criminal enterprises than two dozen undercover operations, wrapped in red tape and billed to the taxpayers. He certainly didn't profit from these ventures—and since when did criminals operate as non-profit organizations?

Men like Bud Crocker only considered the income lost due to The Hornet's interference. They remained oblivious to what Marianna considered an unmistakable pattern—although she didn't voice her opinion for fear of arousing Hurk's temper. She wasn't paid for opinions, he had once told her. The bruise had healed two weeks later.

Now, she gazed longingly at her little green stenography pad. Perhaps the information contained within would be her life insurance policy.

Britt Reid, owner-publisher of the *Daily Sentinel*, signed off on the gallies for the next edition, then returned to his townhouse in Alden Park. It was 9:30 p.m. when he arrived home.

Britt was easily six feet tall, with dark brown hair and piercing gray eyes. He was young, handsome—but he appeared cold and sinister once he donned The Green Hornet's disguise.

"Let's hit the streets," Britt said authoritatively. There was a touch of eagerness in his voice.

Kato led the way to the garage. He climbed behind the steering wheel of an intimidating black automobile. He was again garbed in the black chauffeur uniform and mask. He piloted the vehicle through a hidden garage exit. His driving was swift and precise. The vehicle was large, as formidable as a tank, but Kato maneuvered as though the streets had been built around it.

Twenty minutes later, the chauffeur coasted the vehicle to a halt. From their vantage point, an alley facing the rear of the Gotham Hotel, they witnessed rough-looking men entering and leaving through a steel door. A single, dim bulb above the threshold held back the shadows. Night-vision headlights and a special windshield visor revealed everything to The Green Hornet and Kato.

"Mel Hurk's office is on the eighth floor," said The Hornet. He watched the rear entrance from a closed circuit monitor in the backseat.

Kato glanced over his shoulder. "Last week it was on the sixth floor," he said curiously.

The Hornet nodded. "They move it every week," he said, "as protection against the police. The good cops, that is."

"I've heard that the place is monitored from top to bottom," Kato added. "No one can enter, or leave, without permission."

The Hornet flipped open a pocket in an arm rest. He removed several egg-shaped objects.

"Time to prove them wrong," he said.

The desk intercom buzzed. Mel Hurk impatiently stabbed the button. He sighed. "What is it?" he demanded.

Static answered him. "Mr. Hurk," a voice wheezed. Bud Crocker leaned forward on the couch, removed the cigarette from his lips. "Trouble..." Wheeze. Another burst of static.

Marianna Gryzbowski, the pretty blonde secretary, nibbled at her manicured fingernails.

Hurk and Crocker exchanged glances. Hurk's eyes grew wider. He identified the static bursts—the guard at the rear entrance was coughing.

Hurk stabbed another button. "Charlie, we've got trouble! Take the boys down the back stairs!" Hurk released the transmit button. He sat, fists tensed, glaring at the intercom. *"Charlie!"*

Crocker leapt off the couch. From a tiny utility closet, he distributed machine guns to the three bodyguards. He was reaching for ammunition drums when the secretary gestured wildly and gasped, "Look!"

Wispy green tendrils slithered under the door. Without thinking, the guard closest to the hallway wrenched it open.

A solid wall of green vapor writhed and swirled at the threshold, then collapsed under its own weight. The green wave spread to all corners, rising lazily toward the ceiling.

"Gas!" Crocker shouted. There was a distinct hoarseness to his voice.

Marianna took a feeble breath. An acidic taste flooded her mouth and lungs. She dropped to one knee, then sprawled across the floor.

Two shadowy figures materialized from the foggy depths of the outer corridor. The taller one gestured toward Marianna, the other nodded and moved toward her. He was beside her within the blink of a heavy eyelid. She raised a sluggish arm in a self-defense. The room whirled before her. Before she passed out, she realized that she had been slung over someone's shoulder, and heard an authoritative voice say, "That's her. Let's get her out of here."

She sighed, and spiraled down into a dreamless slumber.

The young Assistant District Attorney's fingertips formed a pyramid as he reclined in his chair. The desk was large enough for his paperwork and an electric typewriter, and his leather chair reached as high as his shoulders. Someday, he mused, his desk would be large enough for a man to sleep, and his leather chair would be a throne.

"Officer O'Brien, you seem quite nervous," the young man said. His blonde hair was combed backward. His face had a fresh quality. He had just returned from the Vale of Eden, an expensive health club he visited once a month. He would patronize the place twice a week, when he was promoted.

Officer O'Brien was gently mangling his police hat in his meaty hands.

He cleared his throat.

"Gosh, Mr. Pierce, I was thinking—"

Pierce raised a manicured hand. "Please, Officer O'Brien, I've told you a hundred times to call me Albert."

O'Brien shrugged. "Sorry," he murmured. "Well, Albert, I been having second thoughts about making me collections. Sure, the money was good, but I got me family to think about, and—"

Pierce leaned forward. "Officer O'Brien," he interrupted, again with a raised hand, "what are you saying? Are you seriously thinking about abandoning your duties?"

"Well, they ain't exactly me duties, Albert. It ain't written into me job description." O'Brien pointed in the general direction of Albert Pierce's future office. "If the District Attorney ever found out, he'd crucify all of us."

Pierce pounded a fist on the desktop. "Frank Scanlon knows nothing!" As Pierce's voice rose, his modulated tones were punctuated with squeaks. "I've gone to great lengths to insure that we can operate securely and safely."

O'Brien leaned backward. "But, Albert, things are becoming riskier. Running the bag and collecting our dough is one thing, but now The Green Hornet is muscling in. I'm just a poor beat cop, not some matinee hero. The Hornet's bodyguard gave me the bruises to prove it."

Pierce stood up and raised the shade on a narrow window. The daylight had been reduced to orange and crimson stains on the horizon.

"Come here, Pat," he said, emphasizing the cop's first name. When O'Brien stood beside him, Pierce placed a hand on his shoulder. "Look out this window." His swept his arm across a view of the city that was slightly obstructed by a neighboring rooftop. Apartment windows were illuminated, whereas the storefronts were growing dark.

"I'm looking."

"No, you're not," Pierce replied. "You're looking with the eyes of a weary cop. You've walked these streets, stood in the rain and braved the snow—and for what?"

O'Brien grimaced. "I don't know," he said softly. "I never get any respect. They never gave me a chance to...to..."

Pierce gripped his shoulder. "It's all right. You do your duty, without any thought of reward. You're not worried about the money.

"Look at that city from *my* point of view. When I see those old brownstones, the crumbling edifices, the decaying streetcars, I think of the people—that's right, the *people*—the heart of this city. People of all incomes—uh, of all different colors and backgrounds. There's the Irish, the British, the American born, the Italians, the Jews, the Chinese guys and the colored people. They make this city what it is, making it their home."

He pressed a thumb against his breast. "My home," he whispered. Then he pressed a finger against O'Brien's badge. "*Your* home."

O'Brien swallowed. "I hadn't thought of it that way."

"They're counting on money from the numbers, to give them hope. They need someone reliable, a strong man, to watch over those betting slips and the money, so that it reaches the right hands. It's a job that can't be entrusted to anyone. Now, you're telling me that you'll turn your back on them?"

O'Brien's gaze lowered to the crimson carpeting. He sighed.

"Well, you may as well turn in your badge, Pat. If you don't care, why should I defend you? Is this how you repay me?"

O'Brien took a deep breath, and lifted his shoulders. "I guess you're right, Albert." He jammed the hat over his thinning red hair.

Pierce slapped his arm, just above the patch bearing one stripe. "Pat, I'm proud of you. If your Uncle Mike...well, I won't forget you when my turn comes."

They shook hands. "I got me a collection to make." O'Brien exited through a skinny door. It trembled when he pulled it shut.

Pierce shook his head. He removed a bottle of scotch and a tumbler from his desk.

The telephone jangled. It was Mel Hurk calling.

Pierce listened, absently nodding his head. "Fine," he replied. "The collection will be picked up, and we'll be in good standing."

"We've had some trouble," Hurk said. "The Green Hornet broke in last night and overpowered everyone. Now my secretary is missing."

"The Pollack? How did The Hornet get inside? I thought—"

"Never mind," Hurk said. "Can you trust that Irish cop?"

Pierce sipped his scotch. "I'll vouch for Officer O'Brien. Tonight I had to give him the 'my city' speech, but he's been co-operative, so far."

"As long as he's loyal, we can worry about The Hornet."

Pierce frowned, pouring himself another drink. "I wouldn't call it loyalty, but O'Brien is on our side. That's why I arranged to transfer him to the sixth precinct. Scanlon wanted him drummed off the force, but I talked him out of it. As for The Hornet, I've got plans for him."

Hurk disconnected the call. Pierce gazed out the window. There was another office, a larger office, with a commanding, unobstructed view of the city. He would occupy that room someday soon.

District Attorney Albert Pierce. He liked the sound of it, and if Frank Scanlon had any objections—well, there was precedent for an untimely death in office.

Marianna Gryzbowski sighed, rolling her head slowly from side to side. Her eyes grew wide when she saw the masked man standing before her. The Green Hornet didn't need to introduce himself, but he did, anyway.

"Miss Gryzbowski," The Hornet said. His voice was authoritative, but lacked Mel Hurk's smoldering abrasiveness. "Are you feeling all right?"

She was seated on a small davenport in a tastefully appointed study. In one corner, a desk was flanked by bookcases. A brick fireplace offered warmth.

"What am I doing here?" she asked.

"Some people call it kidnapping," The Hornet said, "but I'm calling it a second chance. You have an opportunity to break free of Mel Hurk. Tell us everything you know about his numbers racket—from top to bottom."

She gasped. "No," she said. She rose unsteadily to her feet. Kato took her arm, steadying her. "He is bad man. He will kill me if I talk."

The Hornet shook his head. "We won't allow that."

"But, why are you asking me to tell you? I am just his secretary, I only know—"

"Stop it," The Hornet commanded. "A few weeks ago, you considered telling everything to a reporter for the *Daily Sentinel*."

Marianna nibbled on her lower lip. Her eyes glistened. "I was hoping to make money. The newspaper say racket number must go. I think to sell what I know and run. But Hurk would find me and kill me."

The Hornet reached into his topcoat and removed an envelope from the breast pocket. "There's four thousand dollars in this envelope," he said. "That's enough money for you to start over. When things cool off, we'll get you out of the country."

She gasped. "You mean back to Poland?"

The Hornet nodded.

She gently held the envelope, ran her thumb across the crisp bills within. The Hornet returned it to his coat pocket.

"Will you help us?"

She thought of the quiet, solid streets of Gdańsk, and the rolling grasslands of Roztoka. She also imagined Mel Hurk sitting in a federal prison.

"I will tell you everything," she said.

At The Hornet's urging, she donned a blindfold. Kato escorted her to a guest bedroom where she could be safely, and comfortably, contained.

The Hornet walked behind the desk and manipulated a hidden switch. A section of fireplace rolled upward into the ceiling, revealing a hidden alcove. A man in his early fifties, with bulldog features and thinning hair— District Attorney Frank Scanlon—stepped into the room.

"You were right, Britt," he said. "I needed to hear that. But can you trust her?"

The Hornet sat down. He dropped the hat and mask upon the desktop. Britt Reid smoothed his dark brown hair.

"We'll soon find out," he said. "She contacted Ed Lowry, hoping to sell information to the *Sentinel*. Then she backed out. She's afraid of Hurk, but I think she's more frightened by The Green Hornet."

"Luckily for her, she didn't approach the *Daily Express*."

Britt smiled. "The rival newspaper has ignored the illegal lottery." For a moment, a flash of suspicion touched Britt's mind.

Kato's return interrupted his train of thought. Any thoughts regarding the distinguished competition were abandoned.

The young man now wore a white dinner jacket, sans mask and hat. "She's in the guest room," he said. "I gave her a pen and plenty of paper. She's writing up a storm."

Scanlon glanced at his wristwatch. "I've got an appointment at City Hall." He pointed a thick finger at Britt. "I want to be kept informed, Britt, and I want to see her notes. I'll give you three days. Promise me?"

Britt agreed. Scanlon exited via the fireplace elevator. Once the door had secreted itself on hidden, silent hinges, Britt turned to Kato.

"With the exception of Frank, I'm not certain who we can trust."

"You mean," Kato asked, "you won't hand Marianna's notes over to Mr. Scanlon?"

Britt sighed. "We should study them first," he decided. "This goes higher than Officer O'Brien, and it just might lead to somewhere around Frank's office."

Three evenings passed, during which time Marianna ate and slept in the secure guestroom. Kato and Britt Reid would periodically check up on her, garbed in their disguises, but she could not escape. She was, for all intents and purposes, their prisoner.

She committed names, addresses, dates and telephone numbers to paper. She provided detailed information on certain activities and individuals. Others were cryptic references she overhead with no discernable meaning.

Britt had scattered several newspaper clippings—all from the *Daily Sentinel*—across his desk. The clippings bore notations referring back to the secretary's reports.

"She's beginning to worry," Kato said. "Three nights ago, she was prepared to help. Now, she isn't certain that she made the right decision."

Britt sighed. "On the street, she might survive for a few hours."

He read Marianna's list of addresses. There were few surprises, a handful of seedy taverns, and offices where the light of respectability had been eclipsed by suspicion. Some addresses were distinctly low-rent, but others were perfumed with money.

One address intrigued Britt with its notation, "Counting."

He tapped the address with his pencil. He referred to a city map. 1638 St. Maron Street was one block from the Detroit River—the riverfront warehouse district.

Twenty minutes later, The Green Hornet's vehicle—the Black Beauty—was gliding through the designated area.

Prior to sunrise, six days each week, the riverfront was a major hub of activity. Thousands of seamen, dock workers and warehouse employees loaded and unloaded shipments, which were delivered or carried away by large trucks. By nine p.m., the riverfront was largely deserted except for bums and ships' crew members. Veteran watchmen paced the floors of warehouses and factories, counting the long evenings until retirement. The young turks jumped at every sound, eager to shoot someone.

A large warehouse, 1638 St. Maron Street, bore the sign "Detroit Cannery." A corner of the faded wooden sign had chipped off. A river breeze lifted the sign, and slapped it against the building.

Parked between two buildings, The Green Hornet and Kato alighted from the vehicle. The Hornet scanned the area for activity, while Kato removed a rope and steel hooks from the trunk. Confident that they were unobserved, they ascended a steel ladder bolted into the bricks of a building adjacent to the Detroit Cannery.

A chilly breeze whistled across the rooftop. A discarded newspaper flapped and scattered across the sidewalk below. Tiny lights peppered the silhouettes of high-rise buildings in the downtown section. Several blocks away, two pinpoints of light approached, coming down Franklin Street.

The Green Hornet and Kato moved cautiously along the tarmac, pausing at the abutment to watch the truck's approach. The neighboring building, number 1638, was shorter by five feet. Two men opened a wide garage door, permitting the truck to enter.

The street level noise disguised their descent. Kato snared a rooftop fixture with the rope and hook on the first attempt. They slid diagonally to the Detroit Cannery roof.

A dingy skylight overlooked the warehouse floor. The Green Hornet frowned. "This is the counting center," he whispered.

Far below them, people were pouring coins into machines that separated pennies from nickels, dimes from quarters—money squandered by the city's working class. Others were gathering slips of paper from the coin counters and entering numbers into ledgers. Two humorless thugs watched carefully to ensure that money didn't stick to anyone's fingers. The truck driver pushed a flatbed loaded with bags to the nearest coin counting machine.

"One of them, anyway," Kato said. "There may be several more throughout the city."

"I don't think so," The Hornet replied. "I'm betting that we've found the head of the octopus."

"What now?"

A smile tugged at The Hornet's mouth. "I've got a plan." He watched the activity in the warehouse, so Kato's concerned look went unnoticed.

At nine p.m. the following evening, Officer Pat O'Brien had just begun his first complimentary coffee. Art Levinson, the pharmacy owner, hadn't offered it, but O'Brien was too busy sipping and slurping to care. Some of the customers seated at the counter glared at the burly cop. One gentleman was reminded of a brief stint on a Pennsylvania farm.

"Great coffee, Art," said Officer O'Brien. The compliment was preceded by an audible *ahhhh*.

"Yeah," Levinson murmured. "Hey, Pat, I got something for you." Levinson walked around the counter and disappeared behind a curtain at the back of the store.

O'Brien swore softly and followed him. He gulped his coffee, wishing he had remembered his silver flask. What kind of cop forgot his flask, anyway?

A customer glanced over his shoulder. "Must be some kind of trouble?" He sipped his coffee.

His companion alternated his attention between a Reuben sandwich, piled with corned beef, and a crisp pickle. "Naw," he said through a mouthful. "Art's probably gonna give him the cash from the numbers game."

"I thought they kept that under the counter," said coffee man. "He usually hands it to him with a newspaper."

"Maybe Art got tired of arguing about the *Daily Express*."

In the storeroom, Levinson sat at a workbench filling prescriptions.

"Christ, are you trying to give us away?" demanded O'Brien. He peeked at the customers through the curtain. "It's all right. They don't suspect anything."

"Forget them," Levinson snarled. He held up a green envelope.

O'Brien gasped. "Begora."

Levinson held it before him. "It's for you." When O'Brien did not reach out, Levinson mashed the envelope against his chest. "Take it!"

O'Brien tore it open. His lips pursed to a silent whistle. *One Hundred.*

Two hundred. Three...four...five...

"I don't want to know what's inside," Levinson said tersely. "The Green Hornet and his thug were waiting for me. They said to give that to you." He ducked through the curtain and returned to the counter.

Six hundred...seven...eight...nine...one-thousand dollars. Behind the last bill, there nested a stiff business card bearing the image of a winged, angry green insect. O'Brien turned the card over.

TONIGHT. Eleven p.m.

O'Brien looked up at nothing in particular, his mind's eye gazing at the cityscape from Assistant District Attorney Albert Pierce's window. "Those" people were counting on him, but The Green Hornet had just forked over twenty times more than Pierce paid him.

He folded the envelope and stuffed it into his pocket.

One-thousand dollars was a lot of help for "them."

And himself.

O'Brien made his rounds through the neighborhood without enthusiasm. The temperature was dropping. Soon he'd have to wear that heavy coat again. He paid little attention to his environment, his mind preoccupied with his 11 p.m. meeting, which brought him in round-about fashion back to Levinson's Pharmacy.

A shadowy vehicle slid past several parked automobiles, and halted at a "no-parking" sign in front of Levinson's shop. A rear door opened on silent hinges. The Green Hornet beckoned from the interior.

"Get in," he said.

O'Brien looked around cautiously. There were no pedestrians present to witness The Green Hornet's arrival, which both assured him and unnerved him.

"Once around the neighborhood," The Hornet told the chauffeur. The green mask and fedora cast sinister shadows over his eyes.

O'Brien exhaled deeply. "You made me look pretty bad."

"That isn't difficult."

"What's the game, Hornet?" He held up the creased envelope. "You send for me like an errand boy? You think I'll come running just because you tell me to?"

"You just did."

With a snarl, O'Brien clasped the door handle. "Pull over," he told the driver, who glanced in the rear vision mirror for a signal.

"Drive on," The Hornet said. The glow from passing streetlamps flashed intermittently through the interior.

"There's no need to get upset," The Hornet chided. "We all have a job to do—and your job is to round up your fellow policemen, the ones who collect in the poor neighborhoods."

"That would be a stupid thing to do. You want me to rat out me friends?"

The Hornet sneered. "You don't have friends, O'Brien—you have cohorts. If there's money in it, you're willing to look the other way."

O'Brien watched the passing scenery. "Damn it, I'm not gonna be lectured to by some masked hoodlum!"

The Hornet shrugged. "I'm wearing a mask, you're wearing a badge. One disguise for another. I won't stand on ceremony with some dirty cop who works every possible angle. Now I'm offering you a chance to earn real money, a grand a week."

O'Brien's eyes widened. *"Weekly?"*

The Hornet nodded. "You like that?"

O'Brien swallowed hard, moistened his lips. He dabbed at his forehead with a handkerchief.

"Tell the other cops to bring their collections to me," The Hornet said.

"You've got your own numbers racket," O'Brien said, "and now you want the profits from Hurk, as well?"

"Mr. Hurk will soon retire," The Hornet said. "I don't like competition."

"Where do you want me to bring the money?"

"I'll tell you tomorrow night," The Hornet said with a nod. He handed O'Brien a card. "Call this number at 9 p.m. sharp. By 9:03, it'll be out of service."

The driver pulled the vehicle to the curb. On the sidewalk, O'Brien watched the Black Beauty turn a corner and disappear around the block.

He was left standing next to a public telephone outside Pete's Tavern, a friendly place where he often took a complimentary drink while on duty. The interior remained in dusty darkness long after the owner's retirement, and O'Brien had been forced to carry the elusive flask.

He studied his reflection in a large window, a tall, slightly overweight cop with reddish hair that was gradually fading to gray. With each passing year, his waistline was losing its never-ending battle. His feet pained him a little more, and he was still walking a beat.

He entered the phone booth and fished for a coin.

"I won't stand on ceremony with some dirty cop who works every possible angle."

The telephone handset was heavy.

"Little Patty, me boy, you're a fine young lad!"

He deposited a dime. The coin box was cool under his palm.

"Mr. Pierce, I'm sorry to call you at home." O'Brien held the phone away from his ear for a moment. "Right, sorry. Look, I just had a meeting with The Green Hornet. That's right—he wants me to turn over the proceeds from the numbers to him. What should I do?"

O'Brien nodded. A gentle wind was coming in from the northwest, but he was sweating again.

The following evening, a radio-telephone impatiently buzzed. The Green Hornet answered from the rear seat of the Black Beauty.

"I'll signal you when O'Brien and his playmates enter the building," The Hornet said. "Once you show up with your police detail, O'Brien's boss will think that he led you to Hurk's warehouse. He'll probably tell you that they were responding to a disturbance. Don't let on that you know differently."

"I'll have squad cars standing by, Britt," came the gruff voice of D.A. Frank Scanlon. "They'll be out of sight, but ready to surround the building, with the exception of the St. Maron Street exit. That'll be the back door for you and Kato to flee. Make it quick."

The Hornet nodded. "Will do." He broke the connection, then waited for several minutes. The phone buzzed again. "Officer O'Brien? Good... meet us at 1638 St. Maron Street.... One hour." He hung up and leaned back in the plush seat.

Officer O'Brien nodded, gave affirmative answers, then returned the telephone to its cradle. He sighed and looked across the desk at Assistant District Attorney Albert Pierce's satisfied expression.

"Well done, Pat."

O'Brien shrugged. "I hope we're doing the right thing." He looked to three other policemen standing nearby for confirmation, but they remained silent. Officer Harry Braddock crossed his arms.

"Believe me, Pat," Pierce said, "nothing good will come from dealing with The Green Hornet."

"You go in first," Braddock said. "We'll give you two minutes, time for The Hornet to spill the beans. Then we'll come in and make the arrest."

O'Brien and Pierce rose, shook hands over the desk. "You'll be a real hero, Pat." He smiled warmly at the uniformed cop. "There just might be a promotion in this for you—the man who finally arrested The Green Hornet."

"Thanks," O'Brien said softly. He tipped his hat, strode from the room. Officers Maurice and Rogers were on his heels, but Officer Braddock lingered.

"The Green Hornet didn't give us much time," Braddock said. "How do we know he's not baiting a trap for us?"

"Because he has nothing to gain." Pierce looked Braddock in the eyes. "You know what to do, right?"

Braddock frowned and nodded.

Pierce gently slapped his shoulder. "Good man."

Braddock hurried through the door to join his fellow officers. Alone, Pierce glanced at his wristwatch, then studied the paper upon which O'Brien made his near illegible scrawl.

1638 St. Maron Street.

Why had The Hornet chosen this dump in the riverfront warehouse district? Might it be his headquarters? No, The Hornet would never invite anyone, certainly not a shady cop like O'Brien, into his den. In all likelihood, it was a small outpost of his criminal operations.

He wondered if the address held significance for Mel Hurk. He almost telephoned, then promptly reconsidered. Hurk might send a carload of his goons, and bungle everything.

Just then, a cheerful idea distracted him. Perhaps, in the near future, Pierce could use the location for his own transactions—once The Hornet was dead.

The dashboard timepiece read 9:45 when Kato felt the first touch of apprehension.

The entrance to the "cannery" was diagonally across the street from their vantage point, an alley covered with the grime from decades of indifference.

Kato glanced at The Hornet in the rear-vision mirror.

"What's the plan?" he asked. "Why not just sit back and let Scanlon smash his way through the counting center?"

The Hornet shook his head. "We could let Frank handle this, but I want to make sure that O'Brien is present. He'll follow The Green Hornet inside. There's a side door that I can slip out, before Frank's squad gets here."

"You're hoping O'Brien will be discovered in there with the bad guys?"

The Hornet nodded. "He'll admit his involvement to Scanlon," he theorized. "If not, he'll pretend he was responding to a tip. Then Hurk and his boys will think that O'Brien ratted them out."

Kato remained in the vehicle. Britt was always inventing some clever scheme, manipulating criminals—attorneys had taken to calling it "entrapment"—but it didn't always unfold as seamlessly as he intended. Perhaps one day, Kato thought, Britt's plans would go awry, and then The

Green Hornet himself would stand trial for his alleged crimes.

The Green Hornet exited the vehicle and rushed across the deserted street. No parked automobiles were visible. Maybe Hurk's employees were shuttled in and out to avoid detection from police.

At the side entrance, The Hornet pried the lock and gained access to a darkened reception area. The counting center was down a corridor and through a swinging door. No guards were visible, but The Hornet knew they were present—probably keeping vigil over the coin counters and bookkeepers.

Outside, tires coasted to a stop on sand-covered asphalt. A police cruiser had pulled to the curb. Officer O'Brien exited and approached the building.

The Hornet opened the door, beckoned him inside. "You're very punctual, Officer. I appreciate that."

"Uh-huh," O'Brien grunted. "Why am I here?"

The Hornet jabbed a thumb toward the corridor. "Through that door is a counting center," he said. "That's where the boys are tallying up the day's take. I want to show you the operation. Did you bring the money?"

The Hornet turned and walked down the corridor. He had mapped out his escape—coax O'Brien to enter the counting center first, dash down a side hallway and emerge onto St. Maron Street, and escape with Kato. Minutes later, Scanlon would surround the building.

The metallic clicking of a revolver's cylinder halted him.

"I'm sorry, Hornet, but that's as far as you go."

He turned, saw the revolver aimed directly at his heart. O'Brien had lingered for a moment, putting a safe distance between them.

The Hornet's jaw tightened. His gray eyes flared behind his mask. "What are you trying to pull, O'Brien?"

"Dirty cop, eh? Well, maybe they'll pin captain's bars on me after this. I'm the man who's taking The Green Hornet into custody."

"You and what army?"

The policeman suppressed a laugh. "Oh, don't worry. My army will be along soon." O'Brien tilted his head toward the faint approach of engines. "That's probably them, now."

The Hornet slowly sucked in a breath. O'Brien had picked a hell of a time to reclaim his sense of duty.

"Who gave you the order to double-cross me?"

"I don't need an order to do my duty," O'Brien replied.

The Hornet snorted derisively, nearly laughed out loud.

"Don't roll your eyes at me, boy!"

"Come on," The Hornet said. "You've been collecting hush money from the numbers racket for how long? You came running when I offered you more money—and now you expect me to believe that you just recalled the policeman's oath? After all this time, you've actually decided to uphold the law?"

O'Brien's hand tightened on the gun. The gesture was not lost on The Hornet, but he had ventured too far to play it safe.

"Someone is giving you orders, O'Brien," The Hornet continued. "When they say collect the hush money, you hurry out to Levinson's Pharmacy. When they say 'do your duty,' you get self-righteous and pull your gun. But in the end, it's all the same. You're still a lousy cop hiding behind a badge and a sanctimonious speech."

O'Brien gritted his teeth. "Shut up!" The gun trembled in his hammock fist. "You'll be making a speech at your arraignment."

Looking past O'Brien's shoulder, The Hornet saw three uniformed men enter. Their expressions were grim, and their weapons were drawn as they approached.

"It's okay, Braddock!" O'Brien said. "I got him covered."

"Good work," Officer Braddock replied. "Shoot him."

O'Brien hesitated. "What?" Color drained from his face.

"Kill him," Braddock said. "Get it over with."

"But, the boss said—"

"Quiet! We've got our orders, Pat."

The Hornet had involuntarily raised his hands in surrender. The bravado that frustrated Officer O'Brien would be useless, perhaps suicidal, against Braddock and the new arrivals.

"I was never told to kill anyone," O'Brien protested. "I'm not about to start committing murder!"

Don't glance, The Hornet told himself, *to the alcove to the right, with the service door. Be patient. Wait for Kato to make his move.*

Braddock swore. "You're in this just as deep as us, Pat!"

Kato made his move—his arm swung wide. His flattened hand was like a steel bar striking the Adam's Apple of the youngest cop.

The policeman made a sound, a blend of choke and gurgle, before he collapsed. His revolver bounced off the wall and struck the floor with a deafening roar and a gunpowder flash. Everyone was momentarily shocked. For a moment, there was absolute silence. Even the muffled cascading of coins halted.

A pair of nunchakus seemed to materialize from thin air. Kato swung like a professional baseball player, driving one stick into another cop's midsection. The cop exhaled violently before tumbling over a chair.

The Hornet lunged forward, and threw a roundhouse punch. His nose flattened, Officer O'Brien stumbled backward toward Braddock, who raised his revolver in panic. Perhaps he thought he had a clear shot at The Hornet.

His gun roared—and O'Brien dropped to his knees, doubling over.

Braddock stood transfixed, looking to the masked man with confused eyes. His gaze expressed disbelief, fear, and the inevitable declaration of an accident.

The Green Hornet's fierce glare was the last thing he ever saw. Kato answered Braddock with three rapid punches. There was moistness to the last punch. He was kneeling beside O'Brien, before Officer Braddock's forehead smacked the linoleum.

O'Brien was gasping. Kato carefully inspected the wound. His gloved hand came away with crimson stains. O'Brien's shirt was becoming damp.

The Hornet heard a thud, followed by a cascading tinkle. Behind him, twin doors slapped open. Two men with revolvers—the thugs hired to watch the counters—entered the corridor.

Their angry expressions vanished when they saw The Green Hornet. They saw policemen strewn across the lobby. The Hornet's masked bodyguard was kneeling beside a bleeding cop. The Hornet glared at them.

They turned and ran. One of them began screaming.

"Raid! The police are here—and The Green Hornet is killing them!"

The Hornet and Kato heard the stampede for the exits facing Franklin Street. The shriek of police sirens grew closer. Frank Scanlon's flying squad was on the move.

"Let 'em go," The Hornet said. "The police will round them up."

"They'll round us up," Kato said, "if we don't hurry."

The Hornet knelt beside O'Brien. The policeman coughed. Kato shuddered. It sounded like something inside him had come loose.

The policeman lifted his head. "Sorry..." he gasped.

"Get the Black Beauty," The Hornet ordered. "Bring it to the door. I'll carry him out."

The Hornet kicked open the service door. O'Brien had enough strength to shuffle his feet, with The Hornet supporting him. As Kato eased him into the back seat, The Hornet glanced at the blood trail leading from door to curb. The drops were considerably larger nearest The Green Hornet's vehicle.

Kato climbed in behind the steering wheel. Police sirens were practically screaming into their ears.

"We'll have to make a run for it," Kato said. "Hold on."

As he sped the Black Beauty past Franklin Street, two squad cars veered wildly to avoid a collision. They righted themselves, and continued toward the Detroit Cannery.

One police cruiser changed course and followed them for seven blocks, before Kato lost them in the winding network of side streets. He veered right on East Jefferson Avenue, and opened the throttle—Detroit

Riverview Hospital was eighteen blocks away.

"Hurry," The Hornet said. Nothing else seemed appropriate.

O'Brien was muttering beside him. His face had lost its ruddy complexion. Telephone poles blurred past. From the side windows, buildings were colorful streaks.

"...Not such a bad cop," he murmured. "I mean, I done some things..."

"Shut up," The Hornet snapped.

"People...the city...not murder..."

"Shut up."

Kato glanced into the rearview mirror.

"Uncle Mike..."

"Shut up!" The Hornet spoke through clenched teeth, raised a frustrated fist, but the cop could not see it. In his fogged brain, he was no longer in the back seat of the speeding vehicle. He was scampering across a grassy lawn toward a husky man who knelt down and extended his arms for a wide hug.

"Little Patty, me boy, you're a fine young lad!"

As he buried himself in old Uncle Mike's arms, the black limousine lurched slightly to the right. Kato cruised to a swift halt beside a cracked sidewalk.

"Keep going!" The Hornet shouted. "We're almost there!"

Kato pulled open the rear passenger door. He carried the policeman's body and gently laid him on the curb. Finding no pulse, he shook his head at The Green Hornet.

The wail of police sirens drifted up East Jefferson Avenue. A few ambitious cops had taken up the pursuit.

Kato tugged The Hornet's arm. "They'll take care of him," he said. As Kato piloted the vehicle for the sanctity of home, The Hornet watched the passing scenery with disinterest.

"We confiscated over fifty-thousand dollars," Scanlon explained over the telephone. "This will be a real blow to the illegal lottery."

Britt Reid grunted. "Chicken feed," he said. "The illegal lottery brought in thirty million last year. There's more work to be done, Frank."

Scanlon sighed. "Small victories, Britt."

"Well, today I don't feel like celebrating."

Britt glanced over a column submitted by Ed Lowry, discussing the role the illegal lottery played in funding numerous other criminal enterprises.

In his summation of the raid on Detroit Cannery, Lowry singled out the heroic efforts of Officer Pat O'Brien, who went beyond his duty and made the ultimate sacrifice.

Britt grimaced, then scribbled his approval on the article.

EYES OF THE MADONNA

by Ron Fortier

A heavy, wet fog enveloped the city's nighttime docks and kept innocent souls indoors. This was the seediest section of the great metropolis, inhabited by every variety of lowlife and hustler. Through this pea soup thick mist, a strange, sleek mechanical beast moved silently on reinforced rubber wheels. Painted a non-reflective black hue, its headlights shone with an odd, green tint invisible to the naked eye. The eerie green beam was only visible to the car's driver, who watched with intense, inscrutable eyes peering through a black domino mask.

The Black Beauty had her beginnings like millions of sedans rolling off the factory assembly lines. Then, in the hands of her new owners, she evolved; modified with steel plate armor and an engine capable of outrunning the fastest race cars. These were only a few of her added toys. Yet, when cruising the shadowy byways of the city's underbelly, she moved like a graceful panther, quietly seeking her prey, the most dangerous game of all.

"There, Kato! Stop the car!" The voice, cold and direct, came from the back seat and the Asian known as Kato tapped the brakes as he was commanded. "In the alley. Seems Blinky's found some unwelcome attention."

Kato peered into the narrow space between the two decrepit warehouses, the dim light from the corner streetlamp barely illuminating the scene. Two big men wearing dark clothes were in the process of pummeling a smaller man. That would be Blinky Kincaid, the man they had come to meet.

"Take care of it, Kato."

"Yes, sir, Boss," the chauffeur replied matter-of-factly. He shut off the engine and climbed out of the car in one fluid motion. The man in the back seat smiled, knowing his friend would relish the exercise.

"Leave me alone!" Blinky cried out as another fist slammed into his shoulder. "I didn't do nothing to you guys!"

"Shut up, dirtbag," one of the bruisers muttered. "Just hand over your money and we'll let you walk."

"I ain't got any. It's been a slow night!"

"Bullshit," the other tough argued. "You're the best pickpocket on the docks. We seen you coming off the midnight ferry. Figured you were handling the theater crowd from downtown."

Another hard punch connected with the little pickpocket's chest, knocking the wind from his lungs and slamming him into the brick wall. His thick glasses, from which he derived his street-name, were slipping off his thin, pointed nose.

"Look, I'm getting tired of this," the thug-in-charge said. "Either you empty your pockets or we'll strip you right here and now and take what we find."

"That would not be a good idea," the soft, accent-tinged voice spoke from behind them.

Startled, the two muggers turned to see a small man standing before them wearing some silly black leather chauffer outfit complete with a cap. Because he had his back to the streetlamp, the fellow's features, including his mask, were shaded in blackness. He also appeared to be unarmed, his gloved hands held loosely at his side.

"What da hell we got here, some kind of hero?" The taller of the two brawlers asked, sarcasm dripping from each word.

"Beat it," his partner added, pointing a finger at the surprise intruder. "Or you'll get some of the same."

The mysterious stranger shook his head and said, "I guess we'll have to do this the hard way, then."

He took two quick steps and suddenly was airborne as if his feet had wings. A blood curdling scream erupted from his lips and the two muggers were momentarily frozen, totally caught off-guard by what they were seeing. Or not seeing, for at the height of his leap, Kato twisted his body mid-air and shot out both legs, both feet connecting into the heads of his opponents with twin loud slaps. Both men toppled over senseless as he landed squarely on his feet and calmly adjusted his tunic.

Blinky pressed his glasses back along the bridge of his nose, stammering to say something but Kato merely held up a finger and pointed to the parked sedan.

"All right, I'm going," Blinky said, catching his breath. "Give me a second here. Those gorillas banged me up pretty bad."

Unwilling to hear his whining, Kato merely took hold of Blinky's arm and gave him a shove in the right direction. Blinky straightened up and marched quickly with the silent martial artist following behind. As they reached the Black Beauty, the rear passenger side widow slid down.

Blinky blinked. He could just see the green snap-brim hat and outline of the mask beneath it, familiar attire of the criminal mastermind known as The Green Hornet.

"What do you have for me, Blinky?" the deep, commanding voice inquired.

Blinky coughed once to clear his voice. "Something big, Mr. Hornet. Rufus Lord is going to pull a heist tomorrow night at the Trendle Museum of Art."

"How do you know this?"

"Couple of his boys were shooting pool over at Callaghan's Bar earlier tonight. One of them got too many beers in him and started bugging his pals about why their boss would want to stick up an artsy place like Trendle. They thought I was passed out in the back room, but I heard every word of what they said."

"And why bring this to me?"

"Well, hell, Mr. Hornet," Blinky shuffled nervously from one foot to the other. "Everyone knows there ain't no love lost between you and Lord. You two been going at each other for so long, both wanting to be top dog and all. I figured this might be something worth a few bucks to you, is all."

The Hornet's next comment was directed at the Asian. "Pay him and let's roll."

Blinky took a half step back as Kato slapped a folded bill into his dirty hands and then jogged around the front of the long car and climbed back into the driver's seat. Like a purring kitten, it rolled away, back into the fog from whence it had emerged only minutes before.

Blinky held up the fifty dollar bill, kissed it and hurriedly ran off in the opposite direction.

Inside the Black Beauty, The Green Hornet thought about what he had just learned, as Kato easily maneuvered out of the wharf district and back towards the center of the sleeping city.

When his employer didn't comment, the faithful driver spoke up. "Isn't the curator of that museum a friend of yours?"

"Paul Belmont. Yes, we went to college together."

The darkened streets slid past them as the man with the multiple identities contemplated his next move. One that involved a close friend from happier days. The public and the underworld knew him as a cunning, criminal mastermind. Only a handful of loyal allies knew this persona was a sham by which he actually combated crime and villainy. Still, it wasn't often that his outlaw career crossed paths with his personal life, and it was not a matter he took lightly. He could sense Kato's concern.

"I'll pay Paul a visit tomorrow. It's time Britt Reid caught up with his old fraternity brother."

It was mid-morning when Britt Reid parked his convertible in front of the Trendle Museum of Art and trotted briskly up the ten cement steps to the front doors. An old man wearing a guard's uniform told him the museum wasn't open, and Reid explained he was there to visit the curator. The guard made a quick call on his desk phone, spoke a few words, and then told the dapper media mogul he could proceed.

Reid found the main lobby a chaotic maelstrom of activity, as museum personnel moved about pushing dollies carrying crates filled with various artifacts, while others were precariously balanced on ladders mounting new pieces. It was obvious they were in the process of putting up a new exhibition, and orchestrating it from the center of the floor was a gray-haired, attractive woman with a clipboard in one hand and a walkie-talkie in the other. He immediately recognized staff director, Nancy Waldron.

"Hello, Nancy," he said, raising his voice to be heard over the din of busy workers.

"Britt Reid! What a pleasant surprise." She leaned over and gave him a friendly kiss on the cheek. "Care to roll up your sleeves and lend us a hand?"

He held up both hands, palms out. "No thanks, I've been told what a cruel task master you really are."

"Believe every word of it, dear boy. How else can one mount a brand new exhibit with over two hundred paintings in just a week? It's sheer lunacy."

"Why the crunched schedule?"

"Politics, I'm afraid."

"I don't understand."

"Hold on a second, Britt." Waldron stopped a smock-wearing young woman and handed her the clipboard, then instructed her to go to the loading dock and oversee the moving of the next two crates.

"Ah, where was I?" she asked, pushing a strand of loose hair from her forehead.

"You mentioned something about politics?"

"Right, indeed. Three days ago, out of the blue, the museum gets a call from the State Department asking us to drop what we're doing and put up this Cuban show."

"Cuban?"

"Yes, you know? The little island beneath Florida, Cuba. Run by that bearded fellow. What's his name?"

"Castro."

"Thank you. Yes, him. Well, anyway, it seems the current administration in Washington thought it might help improve relations with the bearded one if, in the spirit of good will, we hosted an exhibition of noted Cuban artists, past and present."

"Interesting."

"Not if you're the one chosen to make it happen. Really, Britt, you should check with your own office more often."

"Oh?"

"Your arts and leisure editor, Miss Ducharme, interviewed me yesterday on the whole, madcap affair. Story should run in tonight's *Sentinel*."

Reid chuckled good-naturedly. "Nice to know I employ competent journalists."

"So then, what exactly brings you to our sanctum of organized confusion?"

"I'm here to see Paul."

"Last time I looked, he was in his office buried under tons of legal documents from the State Department, all to be filled out in triplicate. Poor soul."

"Then I'd best go rescue him."

"You do that. I've got to get back to work."

"Thanks, Nancy. Good luck with the show."

Paul Belmont's private office was located in east wing of the building. Britt tapped on the door, heard a muffled acknowledgment from the other side and entered.

Paul Belmont, seated at his desk, looked up, his face a haggard mask of weariness. At the sight of Reid, his entire demeanor brightened and he jumped to his feet. He came around the cluttered desk, hand extended, and they shook like the old friends they were.

"Britt, thank God it's you." Belmont was average height, thin, with wheat colored hair. Reid knew him to be vain regarding his appearance, yet now he was unshaven, his eyes bloodshot and his clothes appearing rumpled as if they had been slept in. "I've been slowly going out of mind."

"What is, Paul? You look in bad shape."

"It's Peggy! She's been kidnapped!" Belmont blurted out, running a hand through his hair as if the mere utterance of those words brought back the horror they implied. Peggy was Belmont's wife.

"You'd better sit down, old man," Reid guided Belmont back to his chair then took the leather straight back chair facing the desk. "Tell me everything from the beginning."

"Well, it happened yesterday. Peggy said she was going to do some shopping downtown and we made a date to meet for lunch at Rennie's. I'd been so strung out about this new Cuban exhibition. It was dumped on us by the State Department..."

"Yes, I know," Reid offered. "Nancy Waldron told me. Go on. You were going to have lunch with Peggy."

"Well, that was the first thing. She never showed up. I sat there for an hour. Finally I used the restaurant's phone and called home but there was no answer there either. Then I thought she must have been preoccupied with her shopping. She's a natural bargain hunter, always trying to save a dollar when she can."

Belmont stopped and tried to collect his thoughts. There was a pitcher of ice water on a side cupboard with a stack of plastic glasses. Reid filled and handed a glass to his distraught friend. "Here, take a drink. Relax. You're doing just fine. Really."

Belmont took a small sip and then another. His shoulders seemed to sag slightly. "Thanks, Britt."

"Go on then, tell me what happened next?"

"Well, I'd already wasted too much time away from the office, so I came back here. As I walked into the room, the phone was ringing and I thought it had to be Peggy calling to tell me what had happened."

"But it wasn't."

"No, it was man. A stranger. A voice I'd never heard before. He said they had taken Peggy and were holding her as a hostage, and that if I ever wanted to see her alive again, I would do exactly what I was told."

Belmont took another drink of water. "Britt, they want me to give them one of the paintings from this Cuban collection."

"A painting? Which one?"

"It's called *The Eyes of the Madonna,* by the late Raphael Sanchez. At midnight I'm to take it to the loading dock and someone will be there to pick it up. If I comply with their instructions, Peggy will be released within the hour. I was warned not to notify the police."

Fear and worry wrestled across Paul Belmont's face, as Britt Reid mentally digested what he had just been told. Remembering his encounter with the pick-pocket, Blinky Kincaid, Reid now had confirmation the snitch's information had been valid. But what to do now?

As if reading his thoughts, Belmont asked, "Britt, what am I going to do now?"

Reid took a breath and then replied, "Exactly what they want. You have no other choice."

He was being honest. Paul Belmont had no options, but The Green Hornet did.

Gus Thorton climbed out of the gray Cadillac along with his cohorts, Dan Parker and Pug-Nose Harry Jakes. Jakes had been a one time professional boxer who had taken one too many falls on his square and homely face, thus the nickname Pug-Nose. He was a towering figure of a man, as he lumbered along behind his companions. All of them worked for the man known as the Crime Lord, Rufus Lord, and they were here, behind the art museum, at his orders.

"What the hell does the boss want with a lousy painting?" Parker, the smallest of three, asked as they walked through the empty parking lot. It was a few minutes before midnight and the place was deserted, lit only by pole lights that surrounded the large, square area used by larger vehicles to load and unload museum cargo. Belmont, the man they were to meet, had been told to send the night watchmen home.

"How the hell would I know?" Thorton snapped back. Parker was always asking stupid questions. It was a bad habit. "And keep it down, will yah!"

"Why?" Parker waved his arms around. "There ain't a soul around to hear us."

"It's still a job." Thornton was the crew chief. "Try to act like a professional, will yah."

"Sure, Gus. Whatever you say."

They were at the wooden steps leading up to the wide loading dock when they heard rollers moving. The big steel bay door slid open and a lone man emerged carrying a bundle wrapped in heavy paper and twine. He spotted them and quickly hurried to the stairs to meet them, all the while nervously glancing around.

"Relax, Belmont," Thornton advised, happy to see everything was going as planned. "You just hand us that painting and soon your wife will be home safe and sound."

Belmont went down the first two steps and began to hand over his package when another voice rang out from the shadows of the building's corner. "I'll take it from here, gentlemen."

Two men came around the corner. One wore a stylish topcoat and fedora, while the other was attired in a chauffeur's livery. Both were masked and the taller of two wielded a strange looking hand gun.

"The Green Hornet!" gasped Parker.

"Move aside," The Hornet ordered, as he approached, using his odd looking weapon to emphasize his wishes.

As Lord's men backed away from Belmont, the curator looked from them to The Green Hornet in confusion. "I don't understand. What's going on here? Is there something wrong?"

"No, Mr. Belmont, nothing at all." The Hornet pointed his pistol and squeezed the trigger. A greenish vapor suddenly washed over the frightened man's face. He tried to brush it away, coughed and then feeling the world begin to spin, he collapsed on the stairs as The Green Hornet relieved him of his package with his free hand. He hated having to use the sleeping gas on Belmont, but it would serve to convince Lord's men of the curator's genuine surprise. The Green Hornet's daring plan depended on Rufus Lord seeing him as an unexpected variable.

Seeing The Hornet was occupied, Pug-Nose rushed forward, his mighty right hand cocked back to deliver a solid knock-out.

It never landed. Just as he was about to let fly, Kato stepped between them and shot a lightning fast knuckle punch into Pug-Nose's jaw. There was a loud crack, and Pug-Nose rocked back on his heels, his eyes rolling in their sockets. Then, with his arm still cocked, he toppled back like a fallen timber.

Thorton and Parker watched him drop and both took a quick step back away from the little man with the lethal fists.

"You ain't gonna get away with this, Hornet!" Thornton felt it his duty to say something to maintain some modicum of his tough-guy reputation. "The boss will make you pay for meddling in his business."

"He's most welcome to try," the green-clad outlaw said. He pointed to the unconscious man at their feet. "Be sure to clean up after yourselves when you leave."

Then, he and his partner were gone again, swallowed by the starless night.

Thirty minutes later the Black Beauty rolled to a stop on a residential side street located near the city's industrial district. Visible down the road two blocks away was an old paper mill known as the Pulp Factory. After the company had gone out of business, the building was purchased by Rufus Lord and converted into his own private headquarters. He left the main floor empty, using it to store ill-gotten contraband or other items of questionable origins. He had the entire second floor made into an opulent penthouse suite where he enjoyed the spoils of his criminal empire.

Lord had begun his career as a mob lawyer. An educated sophisticate, he used his intellect to rise within the criminal underworld until he became the Boss of Bosses. The newspapers christened him the Crime Lord. Now it was he who employed a battery of lawyers and the law couldn't touch him. He fortified his domicile with the latest security equipment and maintained a cadre of gunmen twenty-four hours a day, seven days a week. The Pulp Factory, for all intents and purposes, was an impenetrable fortress.

In the back seat, The Green Hornet picked up his radio-phone and dialed a familiar number.

"Yeah?" The voice was rude and angry.

"Let me speak with Lord."

"Who the hell is this?"

"Tell him it's The Green Hornet." He heard an audible gasp followed by a few minutes of silence and then a shuffling noise as the receiver was swapped from one hand to another.

"This is Lord. With whom am I speaking?" The Hornet smiled. Lord was ever the educated gentlemen.

"This is The Green Hornet. I'm sure you recognize my voice."

"But of course. What is it you want, Hornet?"

"You've been a bad boy, Rufus. Attempting to pull a job without my permission. You hurt my feelings."

"The price of commerce often entails a few ruffled feathers. I would be wary of reckless braggadocio, my verdant-hued friend or it may be more than your feelings that are discomforted. "

"Come, come, Rufus. I didn't call you simply to trade insults and threats."

"No? I thought you enjoyed gloating. Especially after interfering with one of my personal operations."

"Ah, yes, the painting. I was aware of your taste in the arts, but stealing an insignificant work like this is most puzzling."

"Then why did you take it?"

"Because you wanted it. That's reason enough for me."

The line went silent for a few minutes and The Green Hornet knew his nemesis was reevaluating his position. If he had played his cards right, the game was about to shift into the next level.

"Very well, Hornet. I was contracted to steal the painting for another party for an obscene amount of money."

"I see. Then you would be willing to pay for its return?"

"How much do you want?"

"Fifty-thousand dollars."

"What! That's outrageous!"

"Take it or leave it. This is a one time offer."

"All right, you win. I'll pay it. But you must return it to me by tomorrow night. That is imperative."

"Ten o'clock. I will bring it to you. Good night, Rufus. Always fun doing business with you."

Before the other man could say anything further, The Green Hornet hung up. He turned his attention to Kato, who was busy watching the front of the Pulp Factory with special binoculars outfitted with infra-red lenses. They allowed the viewer to see a night scene as clear as if it were midday.

"It's done," he announced. "As of now, Peggy Belmont no longer has any value to him."

"And you believe Lord will simply release her?"

"Yes, Kato. I doubt she was allowed to see him or any of his men. So she poses no real threat to him."

"Hold on," Kato leaned forward, gripping the binoculars tighter. "Someone is exiting the building."

Through the green colored filter, Kato saw two men leading a blindfolded woman to one of the two automobiles parked in front of the building. The woman's hands seemed to be tied together with tape. One of the men climbed into the driver's seat while the other aided their prisoner into the back and joined her there.

"You were right, Boss. Two of Lord's men just escorted her out blindfolded. They're in a car and starting to come this way."

"Good. Let them pass and then follow them. But at a safe distance. They must not see us."

Kato smiled. With the Black Beauty's unique infra-green filtered beams, that would be no problem at all.

Seconds later the sedan bearing the captive Peggy Belmont rolled past them along the main boulevard, which was Kato's cue to start the Black Beauty. He waited a full minute and then pulled away from the curve. Lord's men drove their charge until they came to a downtown intersection. They deposited her on the lonely street corner and drove away quickly.

Kato immediately turned onto a side street as the frantic woman began to pull at the blindfold covering her eyes.

Seeing she was safe, The Green Hornet called the police and anonymously informed them of her location and condition, then quickly ended the call.

"What now, Boss?"

"Now, Kato, we go home and find out what is so important about *The Eyes of the Madonna*."

The next day, Britt Reid and his valet, Hayashi Kato, were having lunch together when Reid's pocket-watch made a familiar buzzing noise.

"It's Scanlon," he said, taking out the expensive time-piece and clicking the top knob.

Kato, dressed in his formal black pants and white jacket, moved across the den area of their apartment and pulled out three books from walnut shelf, instantly activating the secret opening behind ornate fireplace. There was a soft rumbling sound as gears began to shift and the entire front section of the fireplace rose up behind the wall to reveal a hidden space. Gears continued to whir as a small one-person elevator descended into view.

Out stepped District Attorney Frank P. Scanlon, a close friend and the only lawman privy to their secret roles as The Green Hornet and Kato. Scanlon had many times provided them with invaluable information crucial to their never-ending war on crime.

"Hello, Hayashi." Attired in a conservative brown suit, Scanlon was a slim fellow, with gray hair. He wore special horn-rimmed glasses made for him by the Asian, which contained a micro-buzzer used by The Hornet to notify the D.A. when a meeting between them was required. But today's visit was unannounced.

"Good day, sir. Would you like some coffee?"

"Yes, I would. Thank you."

As Kato headed for the townhome's kitchen, Britt put down his own empty cup and looked up at his crime fighting colleague. "What's up, Frank?"

"I hear you boys had a busy night."

"Oh?"

"A patrol car picked up Peggy Belmont on a street corner on the edge of town. It seems she had been kidnapped and then released. When her husband came down to the station, he told us The Green Hornet was behind it all and that he had also stolen some painting."

Reid chuckled. "Well, that's part of it." He indicated the empty chair to his left. "Sit down, Frank, and I'll tell you the whole story."

By the time Kato had returned and poured Scanlon a hot cup of black coffee, Reid had finished his tale. "So we did manage to outfox Lord and save Peggy Belmont, but we still have no idea why on earth anyone would want to steal that painting."

"Well, I think I can answer that one," Scanlon said, surprising his hosts. He took a sip of coffee and then continued. "After the Belmonts gave us their statements and left, I had two rather annoyed visitors from Washington. They were C.I.A. agents. The story they told me was right out of a cloak and dagger paperback thriller."

"We're all ears."

"Okay, here goes. It seems ever since the Russians and Cubans got chummy, the Soviets saw an advantage to using the island as a staging point from which to control a spy operation within the U.S. They set up an extensive joint spy headquarters in Havana. Of course once our boys learned of this facility, they set about infiltrating it.

"A month ago, one of their Cuban people managed to get into this place and photograph the list containing the names of all Russian spies in America and their cover names and whereabouts. All of it was put on a tiny micro-dot no bigger than the eraser tip of a pencil."

"Wow, jackpot!" Reid exclaimed.

"Exactly. But this fellow was afraid he'd be discovered before he could get the information out of Cuba and into our hands, so he broke into a local art gallery and hid that micro-dot somewhere on a painting called *The Eyes of the Madonna.* Then he vamoosed back into the country and radioed his contact in Miami as to where the information was hidden."

Reid snapped his fingers. "Which explains why the State Department became involved in putting this cultural exchange program together so quickly."

"Right again. The C.I.A. went to the State Department, explained their dilemma, and between the two agencies they came up with this ploy to get the painting here where they could retrieve the stolen data."

"And we upset the apple cart by stealing it."

Scanlon finished his coffee and nodded. "That's pretty much it. Those two agents in my office were really riled up about the theft. It's a matter of national security that the painting be recovered."

Reid pushed his chair away from the table and rose to his feet. "Then I think we'd better re-examine *The Madonna* and see what we can find. Hayashi."

"Coming right up." Kato left the room and returned only minutes later carrying the painting. He rested it on the sofa so that they could all see it clearly from a standing position.

The image displayed by the artist was of a young peasant in her garden. Done portrait style, it was a close up of her upper torso showing her in a white cotton blouse, her dusky skin off-setting the sterility of the shirt. She was young and beautiful, and energy seeming to radiate from her skin, yet there was a distinct mystery of age about her eyes, which seemed to look back at the viewer with a startling openness. Long jet-black hair with blue highlights framed her face and fell to her bare shoulders. Behind her, barely visible, was a garden, lush with vines and flowers.

"It's a beautiful piece," Scanlon felt compelled to say, his admiration genuine.

"Yes," Reid agreed. "From what Belmont told me yesterday, critics believe Sanchez, the painter, was inspired by DaVinci's *Mona Lisa* while in art school, and wanted to paint a similar woman of mystery. Like the other, the emphasis is clearly on her eyes, thus the title."

"We looked over every inch of it," Kato told the D.A. "But last night we had no idea what we were looking for."

Reid, arms folded over his chest and tugging at his chin, studying the painting. "Hayashi, in my desk drawer. Please get a magnifying lens and pair of stamp tweezers."

"You see something?" Scanlon asked as the valet went to comply with his employer's request.

"Not yet. But I think I may have figured out why the C.I.A.'s man chose this particular painting."

"I don't follow you."

Kato reappeared with the requested tools and handed them to Reid, who approached the canvas and then knelt before it on one knee. He brought the round lens up to the face of the Madonna and centered it over her eyes.

"Aha," he exclaimed leaning his head closer. "Brilliant." Holding the magnifying lens steady, he brought the small steel tweezers into play. Carefully he used them to touch the woman's left eye. "*Eyes of the Madonna.* Our man didn't choose this painting at random, he chose it because of its title, to tell us where he hid the micro-dot."

"In the eyes!" Scanlon clapped his hands. "But of course!"

"And here it is." Reid pulled back the tweezers, put the magnifying lens down and held up his open hand to catch the tiny black dot of film.

"Amazing."

Kato reached into his jacket for small plastic envelope used for stamp collecting. Reid took it, squeezed the top open and slid the micro-dot into it safely. Then he handed it to the city's top lawman. "Voila."

"Thanks, Britt. This is a huge load off my mind, believe me. And those boys from D.C. are going to be very relieved."

"Maybe you shouldn't be so quick to notify them, Frank."

"Why not?"

"Because this case isn't over yet."

"I don't understand. What am I missing?"

Reid's face became all business. "You're forgetting the unknown person who hired Rufus Lord to steal the painting in the first place."

"Oh."

Kato picked up the thread of Reid's topic. "That someone had to have known there was something hidden on that particular painting in the first place."

Scanlon finally realized what his friends were on to. "Meaning someone on our end is a Russian spy!"

"Exactly," Reid continued grimly. "When he learned the painting with the micro-dot was coming here, he set about having it stolen before our people could retrieve it. Meaning he is still at large and planning to pick it up from Lord later tonight after The Green Hornet has returned it.

"Only this time he's going to get much more than he bargained for."

At exactly ten minutes to ten, the Black Beauty appeared in front of the Pulp Factory under another starless night. Storm clouds were threatening, and area meteorologists were predicting showers before the night was over. The sleek automobile's yellow headlights bathed the front entrance of the old brick and mortar structure, and revealed two men armed with shotguns awaiting their arrival.

"The rockets are primed?"

"Yes," Kato replied as he handed The Green Hornet a small black box studded with six red buttons. "Number one has the reduced charge."

"Understood. Let's not keep Lord waiting."

The two masked men exited the car. Kato carried the painting, once again covered with paper and twine. As they approached the louvered loading doors, one of the guards tapped a button and the door silently folded up and away. The building's interior was brightly lit with florescent fixtures set high among the old, heavy timbers. The renovators had kept those stout beams intact.

As The Green Hornet and Kato proceeded down a wide corridor between stacks of wooden crates and other assorted paraphernalia, they heard the gate closing behind them.

Welcome to the spider's web, The Hornet reflected. He and Kato were once again putting themselves at risk. It was an occupational hazard when one's goal was preserving justice and defeating those with no respect for the laws of society.

Fifty yards into the cavernous building they finally entered a wide open space and confronted the Crime Lord. He stood surrounded by a half dozen men, including a seven-foot-tall black behemoth named Moose Malone. Malone was a one time Wrestling Federation star until his sadistic lust for violence brought about the deaths of several opponents and he was banned from the ring. Lord was only too happy to recruit Malone as his personal bodyguard. He had another, but she was nowhere in sight, a fact not lost on The Hornet and Kato, who had crossed path with Lord and his people before.

Rufus Lord was a big man, almost rotund, a result of his unquenchable love of gourmet food. He employed a famous French chef who prepared rich, full course meals five to six times a day. Still, Lord wore expensive tailor-made suits, like the dark blue three piece suit he now had on. His beefy face was topped with thinning gray hair and he wore horn-rimmed glasses, which he now pushed up over the bridge of his nose.

"I am always amazed, Hornet, by the sheer audacity you display."

"I'm glad I amuse you so much," The Green Hornet smiled wickedly.

Lord took a few steps and waved his right hand to indicate their surroundings and all his armed soldiers. "You walk into this place as if without a care in the world. Surrounded on every side. Now I ask you, is that courage or foolish bravado?"

There was a soft swishing noise and suddenly Kato whipped off his hat and swung it up into the air in front of The Hornet's face. There was a ripping sound and he yanked it back to reveal a tiny feathered dart snagged in the fabric. Both The Hornet and Kato looked to their right. Standing deep in the shadows of two massive crates was a lone female figure, barely visible.

No one had noticed the small box in The Hornet's gloved right hand. Now he held it up and pressed the first red stud. A loud explosion followed, rocking the building's foundations, and a cloud of dust and debris flowed into the room from behind them. Seconds later a dazed guard came stumbling forth. "They blew the front door. Some kind of miniature missile came out of their car!"

A subtle look of anger swept over Lord's face.

"That rocket had a diluted charge," The Hornet explained, now holding up his hand to reveal the remote control unit. "The Black Beauty is equipped with another five, all containing maximum charges. Try something like that again and I'll bring this little factory castle of yours down around your ears."

"That's preposterous," the crime boss retorted, his face clearly reddening. "You would die with us!"

"True enough." The Green Hornet took a step forward keeping the remote box in everyone's sight. "Shall we go together then? On the count of three. One...."

Rufus Lord studied his masked rival and cursed softly. Even with his green mask, there was something about The Hornet's stance and the forcefulness of his words that convinced Lord he would carry out his threat.

"Two."

The Crime Lord had no intentions of dying any time soon.

"Very well, then. Let's get on with our primary purpose and end this silliness."

"I brought the painting. Do you have the cash?"

Lord snapped his fingers and a thin-faced mobster appeared from behind him carrying a black brief case. Lord nodded his head and the man brought it to The Green Hornet.

The Hornet held up the case, snapped open the lock, and saw it was filled with banded stacks of hundred dollar bills.

"Fifty thousand dollars," Lord confirmed. "I believe that was the stated price?"

The Hornet closed the briefcase and nodded to Kato. The wiry chauffeur handed the framed portrait to Lord's man, who immediately returned it to his boss. He quickly ripped off the covering paper and held it up for Lord's inspection. "Very well, Hornet. You have delivered what I desired."

As Lord's man returned to his former position, still grasping the painting, the stout criminal boss folded his hands together over his considerable middle and uttered a final word. "Our business is concluded. Good night, sir."

The Green Hornet turned and started to make his exit. Kato walked backwards behind him. As they passed the slot between the two tall crates, the Asian pulled the tiny dart free of his torn cap and spinning, hurled it with one easy motion. At the end of the aisle, the young female martial artist screamed as the dart caught her dangling pony-tail and nailed it to the wall directly behind her. Kato held up his cap, a finger poking through the tear the dart had made. The gesture was self-explanatory.

He raced after The Green Hornet and together they drove away in the Black Beauty, just as a peel of thunder cracked through the skies.

As they had done the previous night, The Green Hornet and Kato parked the Black Beauty a few blocks away from the Pulp Factory and waited. Rain started to fall and every few minutes the darkness was ripped apart by glaring bolts of white lightning.

In the front seat, a hatless Kato flicked a small screen open on the dash panel. A tiny red light winked at him indicating the bug he had planted on the painting's frame was active.

"The locator is getting a clear signal from the micro-transmitter," he said, satisfied The Hornet's plan was going smoothly.

"Excellent. I'm guessing our spy was sequestered in Lord's private rooms and they are conducting their exchange right now. Keep a sharp look out, Kato. Once that light starts to move, it will be our target on the run."

"Right, Boss." Despite the booming thunder and steady downpour, Kato remained focused on the small monitor. Five minutes later he sat up straight and gripped the steering wheel tighter. "It's moving!"

"In which direction?"

"South. Going to pass us just about...now!"

The Green Hornet leaned forward to look over Kato's right shoulder just as a sleek, foreign sports car went racing past them through the intersection.

"That's it, Kato! Get him!"

Kato popped the clutch and slammed the gas peddle to the floorboards, the Black Beauty responding like a well bread thoroughbred coming out of the gate at the Kentucky Derby. Her reinforced tires gripped the rain-slicked road and pulled her after the receding tail-lights in the distance.

The Black Beauty's speed increased as she wove her way through the empty streets. Steadily she began to shorten the gap between herself and the speeding sports car. Kato wondered if the fleeing driver had any idea he was being pursued. As they approached another intersection and the light turned red, the other car suddenly shot forward ignoring the signal.

"He's spotted us," Kato told The Hornet, as he too ran the red light. He was grateful for the lateness of the night and the empty streets.

"All right, Kato. Stop him before he reaches the city proper."

As Kato pushed the Black Beauty ever faster, the little car made a sharp turn onto an adjoining street, taking the corner on two wheels. The driver was desperate to elude them. Through the slapping windshield wipers, Kato kept his eyes on the escaping vehicle and skillfully navigated the turn without losing any ground.

Seeing they were on a flat stretch of road surrounded by woods, Kato unleashed the Black Beauty's full complement of horsepower and she rocketed forward.   Within seconds they were moving up alongside the other car. Frantic, the other driver tried to cut them off by veering into the center of the road. Kato refused to budge and drove the Black Beauty into the smaller car's driver's side. There was a jarring impact and the expensive foreign racer, unable to match the Beauty's weight and velocity, was propelled off the road and over a grassy mount. It careened into a gulley, where its front end buried itself into the muddy gravel.

Kato hit the brakes, brought the Black Beauty around in a doughnut spin, and pulled up to the edge of the road, capturing the stalled car in its headlight beams. He and The Green Hornet were climbing out when suddenly the sports car driver pushed open his door and staggered out into the pouring rain, a pistol in hand. He shaded his eyes with his left hand, firing a quick shot at them. The Hornet ducked behind his open door, while Kato, realizing the man couldn't see clearly, took off at a run. Coming up over the small rise, he jumped into the air, twisting his body as he did so and yelling to the top of his lungs, "KIAAAA!"

The startled spy tried to find the source of the cry and looked up in time to see something big move across the glaring lights before his eyes. Then it was too late. He tried to shoot, but Kato was flying through the air, his right foot smacking into the man's chest. The fellow fell back into the car, the back of his head hitting the roof, and he collapsed senseless to the ground.

Landing in a crouch beside the unconscious man, Kato stuck his head into the small car and saw the painting snug on the floor of the passenger side. He looked back towards the Black Beauty and called out, "The painting is here, Boss!"

At that The Green Hornet returned to the back seat of the Black Beauty and using his portable phone, called Frank Scanlon as he had planned. The District Attorney had been waiting only a few blocks away from the Pulp Factory in an unmarked police cruiser, awaiting their call. By the time he drove up ten minutes later, Kato had dragged the comatose agent up on to the road and handcuffed him. To ensure he wouldn't awake any time soon, The Hornet had given him a dose of the gas-gun's spray.

"My God, that's Agent Schiavino!" Scanlon exclaimed, as he looked down at the trussed up man. The Hornet and Kato looked at him perplexed. "He's one of the two C.I.A. men who came to see me this morning."

"Obviously a double-agent," The Green Hornet surmised. "No wonder he was so desperate to retrieve that list on the micro-dot. I'll bet his name was at the top of it."

"You're right. I'll bet it is. Well, the two of you have really done your country a tremendous service. One I'm afraid you'll never receive credit for."

"You know that's not why we do this, Frank. Now, let's get this Commie spy into your car. We need to get home and go buy Kato a new hat..."

Scanlon looked at his masked friend and then at Kato, his wet hair plastered down over his forehead, and started to laugh. The other two joined in.

"Why, she's so beautiful," Lenore Case said, gazing at the painting called *The Eyes of the Madonna*, as she and her boss, Britt Reid, examined it. The Trendle Museum of Art was packed with people, as the Cuban Art Exhibition was officially open to the public. Reid had suggested the date to his lovely, auburn haired-secretary and she was delighted to attend with him.

"Mesmerizing," he agreed, as they, and others stood looking up at the framed masterpiece on the museum wall. "Those eyes are truly special."

"I keep looking into them," Case said, "and I can believe she is hiding a secret in them."

"Casey, truer words were never spoken."

STORMY WEATHER

by Patricia Weakley

Let me introduce myself. My name's Stormy Weather. Yeah, that's my real name. Sister's Sunny and brother's got Winter, so you can get the drift of what Mom and Pop had in mind. They got themselves a serious humor problem, if you ask me. I kind of wish though that they had passed my name by, but after a while things tend to stick, especially since I'm the first to admit that I do have a bit of a temper problem.

As to my looks, well, folks like to call my hair dishwater blonde, but personally I'm kind of partial to ash blonde. That's what the Revlon box calls it, and I think that's a mite better than comparing my hair to the water that's been left over after you're done doing the dishes. And my figure, well, I don't like to brag none, but I do tend to stop traffic especially when I fit my size ten into a size six. Like I'm doing now.

Now, my folks never did like me leaving Texas to join Uncle Jesse's detective agency in LA. But a girl's got to break away from the nest some time, and I figured being a private detective was the way to go. Except things haven't quite worked out the way I planned. I figured I'd be trailing famous movie stars and rubbing elbows with Liz and Richard within a few days of hitting sunny California, but instead all I'm getting are the worst jobs in the agency: divorces between people who I can't imagine anybody wanting to marry in the first place, never mind cheating with, and serving papers to people who skip out as soon as I knock on the door. Anything nobody else in place the wants to do. That is, when I'm not making coffee or answering the phones. You know, real big important stuff like that.

That's why I'm in Detroit City. I heard that some local newspaper called the *Daily Sentinel* would give fifty big ones to the lucky man, or woman, who manages to bring The Green Hornet in. I figure if I bag me a Hornet, my reputation would be set. I'd be famous. Everybody would be knocking my door down just for the chance to have the P.I. who captured The Green

Hornet work for them. No more would I be getting the worst jobs in the agency. No more divorces, no more serving papers. No more disrespect from the other guys in the agency with their icky cigars and the ickier haircuts.

Now I heard that The Green Hornet has himself a mighty big curiosity bone and being a man, I'm sure has a weak spot when it comes to women, so I put a little, old classified in the local newspaper saying that I had an interesting message for him. I said for him to look for a short blonde dressed like a cowgirl in the local red light district downtown around midnight. That's where all the local ladies of the night congregate to find themselves a gentleman, or two, for a night, an hour, whichever. So here I am a-swinging and a-swaying my hips with the best of them. Not that there's much of a best to the ones that I'm working the corner with. One of them's got a butt that's wider than mine and an afro I swear she could hide a tommy gun in.

The other, well.... She looks at me and sneers, "You ain't gonna get no damn man dressed like that." Not that she's a winner herself. She's got no butt to speak of, her voice is a lot deeper than I ever heard on any lady, and I swear that she's packing extra equipment, if you know what I mean.

Besides what's wrong with the way I look? I'm dressed in a tight little white halter top that barely manages to hold my boobs in, and short shorts that barely cover the cheeks of my hiney, and the fringes of my vest do nothing to cover anything up either. A big ten gallon cowboy hat tops off hair that's been teased within an inch of its life. Hell, I see girls dressed like this every day in Dallas.

Anyways, to catch the wrong kind of man, you got to use the right kind of bait, that's what I say. But all the bites I've been getting have been way wrong. None of the guys who cruise by are even remotely what I'm looking for. No wonder they gotta pay for a little nookie. But, hell, I wouldn't give any one of those guys the time of day even if I got paid a million bucks for a minute of it.

There's a heart-stopping minute when a police cruiser slips by, and I think I'm going to be spending the rest of the night in the slammer, but the car never stops. It just keeps on going, minding its own business while I keep on minding mine. I start thinking that this has been a whole waste of my time.

All I'm looking for is two masked men in a long black car. How hard can that be? Damn hard.

Suddenly an old blue Chevy comes screeching up to the curb and a scrawny dude jumps out of the car. "Get in the car!" he hollers at me.

Well, now I don't take to hollering too well, so I holler right back him, "Hell, no. I don't know you from nobody, and there's no way I'm getting in that there car."

Unfortunately he's got an equalizer the size of Texas, so I decide it's better if I do as he says. You can never say that I disrespect the great state of Texas.

"Let's get out of here!" he hollers at the guy in the front seat. Dude is too damn fond of hollering, if you ask me. The other dude in the passenger seat seems to think so too and gives him a sour look. Could be indigestion, though. All of them's got that same sour look. Must have ate themselves some bad food.

The guy in the back seat with me starts digging around in my purse. "Where is it?" he hollers. Damn, like I said. Here I am in the back seat right next to him and he got to holler. He pulls out *my* equalizer from my purse. Except it's the size of Rhode Island. Did I happen to mention that purse is a tad on the small side? With a sneer, he tosses my gun to the floor. I guess he don't have any respect for the great state of Rhode Island.

"You dumb broad!" he hollers, "Where is it?" He reaches a hand out to slap me. To teach me a lesson, or two, I guess.

I haven't the foggiest notion what he's talking about. I just put that ad in to see what would happen. Not that I'm going to explain that to ol' pimple face here. Still, I'm not going to sit still and let that guy think he can slap me around. Daddy didn't raise me to be a punching bag, and neither did my Momma. My gun's lost somewhere on the floor, so I yank off one of the stilettos that I'm wearing, and start whaling away at him. Since they were doing so much damage to my feet, I figure they ought to do some to back seat Charley here.

Well, now he starts to howl, and the dude in the front seat reaches over and grabs me by the hair, just like my folks used to do when us kids would start to beat on each other. Well, I start to wailing as I'm trying to pull my hair out of the guy's grip. I drop the damn shoe and Mr. Charley here thinks it's his opening. He dives for my legs, trying to hold them still, so I let my feet do the talking all over his ugly face.

So here we all are, a-screaming, and a-hollering and a-wailing, when it suddenly it feels like the bottom of the car drops out.

I poke my head up over the edge of the back seat and there's this big, beautiful black car. My, my, my...

The Chevy isn't going anywhere; The Green Hornet's car done taken care of that. It feels like the two back wheels hit a land mine and I can see the bumper throwing off sparks as the car comes to a screeching halt.

The dudes scramble out of the car, tumbling me onto the concrete with them—none too gently either. Being of sound mind, of course, I dive back into the car for Rhode Island, because you never know when you'll need a pea-shooter. Just as I'm managing to squeeze it into my purse, the driver pulls me out by the neck of my top. Thank God I believe in wearing a bra, and that I picked out the pretty lacey one instead of the Eighteen Hour.

"Stand back, Hornet!" he hollers, "Or I'm going to put a bullet in her head."

And then he steps out in all his glory. The Green Hornet. So calm and steady there, like a pillar of green marble. And Fred, his driver, hell, his name could be George, who knows, but anyways, he steps out too, all eager, like some Rottweiler ready to tear somebody's throat out.

And you know what The Green Hornet does? You know what that man does? He shrugs! Dammit! He shrugs!

"What exactly is she to me?"

"You blasted the back out of my car!" the driver screams. "Why'd you do that if she isn't anything to you?"

"I was curious," The Green Hornet says. "It looked like you were up to something and I wanted to find out what."

"So you blew my car to smithereens because you were curious?"

"Yes."

Vibrating with frustration, the driver shoves me right at The Green Hornet. "Have her!" he hollers, "You deserve the little hell-cat!

Then, like the coward he is, he runs off, trying to catch up with his buddies who are long gone. Hell-cat. Little hell-cat. I like that. Especially the 'little' part.

The Green Hornet picks me up in those nice strong arms of his. Nice aftershave, too. Mmm, heaven, I think I'm in heaven.

"Do you have something for me?" he asks.

My heart, my body, my life, anything.... I pull out Rhode Island. "I'm taking you prisoner." Of my heart...

He smiles. Oh gawd, what a beautiful smile. He gently takes Rhode Island out of my hand. I guess he doesn't respect Rhode Island either. "Be careful," he murmurs. He murmurs! "You might hurt yourself."

So what do I do?

What could I do?

I'm from Texas.

And the great state of California.

I toss him on his ass with the neatest little old flip you ever did see.

Fred's just standing there staring at me, his mouth wide enough to catch flies while tall, dark, and green is staying down.

"Uh, you okay?" I ask. I'd sure hate to have hurt a nice looking man like that.

The Green Hornet gets to his feet and brushes himself off. "Fine," he bites out. I think I might've hurt his feelings.

"Well, I'll be going, now, if you don't mind."

Fred moves toward me, but The Green Hornet stops him with a shake of his head and a disgusted look his face.

So what do I do?

Well, I sashay my way into the night. I got me a pair of stilettos in one hand and Rhode Island in the other. Just to protect myself. After all, you never know.

"Next time, Tiger," I promise The Hornet to myself, "Next time, I'll getcha."

I'm kicking myself right now. I should have waited until I got into that car of The Green Hornet's before I pulled out my gun. I don't think it would have much worked, but at least I would've gotten my foot in the door. But no, I had to let my pride get a hold of me, and I had to toss him on his ass. Yet, you know, it was satisfying in its own way.

Now what am I going to do, though? I don't much think The Green Hornet is going to fall for the same trick, but I can't for the life of me figure out how I'm going to get that man out into the open. That's a problem with a guy wearing a mask. He can hide in plain sight and you'd never know it.

So here I am in a bar nursing a bottle of cheap beer, wishing I was back home, but not too sure if it's the hill country of Texas or the California coast. Hank Williams is on the jukebox singing about the lonesome whippoorwill, and somewhere in a backroom I can hear the sound of billiard balls clacking against each other. I've got to get moving before I start crying along with poor old Hank.

I slide off the bar stool, making sure that I find the floor. Amazing how cheap beer can make you as unsteady as expensive champagne. I follow the sound and find a bunch of guys watching another dance the balls along the green felt of the billiard table. He's a tall man, big but not heavy. White shirtsleeves rolled up show muscular forearms, powerful; yet he finesses the balls like a magician, making them go exactly where he wants them to.

Fast Eddie moves, Paul Newman eyes. He looks up at me and the ball he hits skips and jumps up into the air. A big whoosh comes out of the guys around the table. Then they start laughing all embarrassed-like at realizing that they had been holding their collective breaths as the master worked his magic. Fast Eddie shrugs his broad shoulders and cocks an eye toward me. Shaking their heads, the other guys laugh a little harder. Dames, I hear one or two mutter. Something too about balls. Men.

Suddenly I feel shy as Fast Eddie walks toward me. Eyes like arctic ice, black hair, nice tan, looks that make my toes curl.

He tosses the ball into the nearest pocket as he grabs up a suit jacket, and slings it over his shoulder. "So," he says to me, "You come here often?"

Now that's one of the oldest lines in the book and I've heard it a million times, but coming from Fast Eddie, I don't mind it so much. Black velvet voice with a hint of West Texas in it. I feel a bit more homesick.

"How about I buy you a beer?" I ask.

He smiles, a nice broad smile, friendly, not fresh, a real surprise there. "First time I've been asked that question by a lady," he says, not disapproving.

I return his grin. "Who says I'm a lady?" I say, all kidding-like.

He laughs. I love that laugh. He looks at the beer in my hand. "How about I buy you a real beer instead. Something from my private reserve," he suggests.

So after he orders a pair of Lone Stars we sit down at a table. "Sounds like you're a long way from home," he says after pouring his drink into a frosted mug.

I shrug a bit, introduce myself, and tell him a little bit of my life story. "Sounds like you're far from home, too," I say afterwards.

He shakes his head, "No," he says, "This city's my home."

"Oh? I don't think anybody'd get a taste for Lone Star, here."

Again the bright smile, but this time a little wistful. "My family's got a little ranch in Texas. I spent a lot of my childhood there. Probably the best time of my life. So what brings you out here?" he asks, changing the subject.

So I tell him the whole long story including my dumping The Green Hornet on his butt.

He smiles and shakes his head. "So are you heading back to California, now?"

"Nope. I'm not leaving until I bring him in. It's a matter of honor, you know?"

"And the bounty?"

"The bounty and the reputation."

He frowns and says with a sigh, "Stay away from The Hornet. He's nothing but trouble."

"Do you how many times the hero in detective stories get warned off?" I ask.

"Too many."

"And you know how often it works?"

A wry smile appears on his lips. "Never. But," he adds, "this isn't a detective story. This is real life. When people get hurt, the blood's real."

"Still..."

He sighs again and shakes his head. "Don't think The Green Hornet is some kind of clown because he decides to wear a mask. He's far from harmless. He had his man put a bullet in me because I wrote an editorial he didn't like."

"Oh," I say. For once in my life I'm at a loss for words. Although the little devil in me is asking for a peek at the scar, hoping it's below the belt line, I pay her no mind.

He glances up when the bar's door opens and a guy slouches in. His eyes meet Fast Eddie's and they lock. Fast Eddie is suddenly all business. He pulls out a business card, writes a phone number on it and hands it to me. "This is my private number. Give me a call me if you need any help."

I look at it and all it says is, "Britt Reid, *Daily Sentinel*."

"Thanks," I say. I glance at the other guy who's hanging around near the bar. "Work?"

"Something like that," Fast Eddie, uh, Britt, that is, answers. He pauses, "Go home, Stormy, before you get hurt." Then he's gone, walking purposefully to the guy at the bar.

I know when I've been dismissed and I don't like it one bit. For a moment I just sit there watching the two men talk. The smart thing would for me to head back to the motel, call Pan Am, and head back to LA tomorrow morning. Admitting defeat sticks in my craw though, especially when it comes to admitting it to Uncle Jesse.

I decide to hang in there a little while longer.

The cold air nearly knocks me over when I step outside the bar. It reminds me that fall is almost over and that winter is fast approaching. There is no way I am going to let winter catch me here in this damn city. I most definitely have got to get a leg on.

Across the street I spot the familiar shape of The Green Hornet's long black car. I walk across to see what he's doing there, but the car pulls away from the curb without a sound. For a minute I wonder if it had only been my imagination, but decide it's better to hit the sack and leave the wondering for another day when I'm a little fresher and my head isn't feeling so fuzzy.

My motel's only a short walk away, but the cold makes me wish I'd driven instead. Three guys jump me just as I open the door to my room, the same three who messed up my trap for The Green Hornet. To tell you the truth, I didn't much want to see them again, and at the end of a long night, they are the last men I'd want in my motel room. Of course, that Britt fella, that'd be another story, but here I'm stuck with these three jokers instead.

"Where's the stuff you have for The Green Hornet?" the ugliest of the three demands, shoving an even uglier gun in my face while the other two grab my arms.

"I have no idea what you're talking about, you flippin' idiot," I scream at the guy.

"We saw the classified ad. And The Green Hornet was interested enough to show up for it!"

"Hell, I don't know what was going on in his head. All I was tryin' to do is catch the guy by getting him out into the open."

"What're you, a cop?"

"No, I'm a private detective."

"Lousy one, if you ask me."

"I ain't asking you. Now let me go!" With that I dig the heel of my boot into the instep of one of the guys holding my arms. Did I happen to mention that I'd slipped into my Tony Lamas when I'd changed into my jeans? Two-inch stacked heels will do a lot of damage, I tell you.

So anyway, the guy starts hopping around on one foot, a-screaming and a-cursing. I pull my other arm free from the other guy and shove him into the gunman, sending them both to the ground. I grab up a lamp and smack the hopping guy in the head, intending to put him out of his misery. Instead he dodges and grabs a hold of me. We both fall to the ground. I'm kicking and biting and scratching and he's trying to grab my hands, my arms, anything to stop me. Well, he winds up getting a handful of my right boob and that's just too much. So, I put a knee into his nuts and he is most definitely out of commission.

Just as I'm pushing myself off the floor, the other two jokers dump the bedspread on top of me. I'm screaming my lungs out as I'm trying to grab a hold of something useful but that damn bedspread has me all covered up. I can't do nothin'. I'm trapped and I figure that this time I'm in for a solid come-to-Jesus meeting with these bozos.

But instead of being beaten on like I expected, there's total silence. The bedspread's lifted from me and who do I see but The Green Hornet.

"Don't you think this is getting a bit repetitious?" he comments as Fred folds up the bedspread. Guy must be a neat freak.

"Not at all," I answer. "I was just getting started."

"Started doing what?" he asks, coming close.

I pull on his tie, pulling him down so that we're eye to eye. Then I lay a big wet one on him, a nice long one. The world stops as he's enjoying it as much I am, at least until he hears the click on my handcuffs around his wrist. Before he can react I snap the other cuff around my own wrist.

"What's this?" he asks.

"You're under arrest. I'm taking you in."

"Really? You know I have something that will take care of this in minutes."

"Boss," says Fred, "They're coming to."

"Good," The Green Hornet says, and he makes for the door, dragging me with him.

"Now wait a damn minute," I say, digging my feet in.

The Green Hornet shakes his head and then, without another word, slings me over his shoulder like I'm a sack of potatoes.

After escorting us to the car parked several doors from my room, Fred opens the car door and The Green Hornet dumps me into the backseat before sliding in himself.

"Where's the key?" he asks, lifting up his handcuffed wrist, bringing mine up with it.

"In my room, inside the nightstand."

He sighs peevishly, "I don't have time for this..."

"Honest," I answer, "You can search me if you want."

"Don't tempt me..."

I give him a big grin. "Wouldn't think of it," meaning the exact opposite.

He shakes his head.

"Boss." Fred. Again. That man must have the worst timing in the world.

"I see," The Green Hornet says and so do I, as the three jokers head out of my room and get into their car.

"Follow them."

"What's going on?" I ask.

The Green Hornet looks at me, and I know he's trying to decide whether or not to satisfy my curiosity.

"Please?" I ask all sweet-like.

He sighs. Again. I must be getting on his nerves.

"The man in the blue suit is Terry Smutz," he says, meaning the ugliest one of the three. "He's the youngest son of the leader of a gang that hijacks semis for their freight. He's been trying for years to get on the good side of the old man. His older brothers are in prison, so he figures it's now his time to shine. I've been tracking him for days trying to figure out where Old Man Smutz is hidden, but it seems like he's become obsessed with you."

"I wonder why," I say innocently, fluttering my eyelashes at him.

He glares at me. "Must be your stunning beauty," he says, not meaning a single word of it.

"All I did was put in a simple classified ad in the newspaper. I don't have anything. It was just a way to get you out into the open. That's what I explained to him."

"I see."

"So what are we doing now?"

"There's no *we* in this, Stormy."

Interesting, I don't rightly remember introducing myself to him. "Okay," I say, "So, what are *you* doing now?"

"The police are making this city too hot for Old Man Smutz to continue his operations. I just got word that he's going to skip town tonight. This will be our last chance to find him before he disappears into another city or even state."

"Why would you care?" I ask.

"Why I do anything is none of your business."

"Oh." Screech, shut down. Could he have been any blunter? Should've kissed him longer.

"So you think Terry there is going to lead you to his old man?"

"You have him so flustered he's not making any effort to hide his trail. I'm sure he'll lead us directly to the Old Man."

"None too bright is he?"

The part of town we are driving through is definitely off the tourist trail. High gray warehouses merge into the gray sky so that it's hard to see where one begins and the other leaves off. Blank windows look down on us as if they disapprove of us being there. There is no one on the street, no people, no cars, nothing. Except for the car that we are following, we could be the only ones alive in this whole wide world. Gives me the creeps. I look over at The Green Hornet and he looks all calm and steady, like this happens everyday to him. Maybe it does. I sidle a little closer and I feel his hand close over mine. Suddenly I don't feel so scared.

In a narrow alleyway of a road, the car ahead of us finally stops and we stop well behind it out of sight. The Green Hornet regards the handcuffs still on our wrists. "You sure you don't have the key?"

"Positive."

He shakes his head. He pulls out a longish black rod, and hands it over to Fred. "I'm going to need your help with this," he says, "There's no way I'm going to drag her along with us."

Suddenly all hell breaks out. We're caught in a firestorm of flying lead. I'm about to pee in my pants when I realize that the bullets are bouncing off the car. Bullet-proof! Thank God!

Out of nowhere a big semi comes barreling in our direction. Fred throws the car into reverse and we're backing up faster than I usually drive forwards. Then in a space barely wide enough to turn a Volkswagen, Fred slams the massive car around. I swear for a few minutes we're nearly airborne or at least on only two wheels and I'm not too sure which two they are.

"Hold her steady," The Green Hornet says to his man as he pulls out a panel from behind the front seat. "Steady," he says again, while we're being peppered by bullets from the semi.

He presses some buttons and I see the flash of fire as a pair of rockets blast out of the car. They fly along the asphalt low and fast, like a Saturn V. Then, kerblooey, they hit the front wheels of the semi. The cab rocks and the trailer starts swinging around, shooting up sparks as it hits the sides of the buildings around it.

"Got 'em, Boss," Fred says.

You think? Fire is licking up from the truck's saddle tanks and men are scattering from it like rats on a sinking ship.

Loud sirens split the air as cops start collecting from everywhere.

"Boss?"

"Back to the warehouse."

"Why?" I ask, "You don't think the Smutzes were with the truck?"

"What do you think, lady detective?"

"Ohhh, it's a diversion."

So we drive sedately around to the other side of the building as cop cars and fire trucks go screaming past us. They're too busy chasing the fire to spot our little old black car.

We park and slip quietly into the warehouse. I'm still attached to The Green Hornet, but I'm starting to have a few doubts about the whole thing. Everything's quiet. Inside it looks like every other warehouse I've ever seen, including the movies and TV. Boxes of stuff stacked nearly to the roof. Dusty, musty. A forklift is idling next to an open door. A toad-like old man is swearing his head off at the guy The Green Hornet called Terry. Terry's two minions are hanging their heads like bad little boys.

"Going somewhere?" The Green Hornet asks, all polite-like, coming up from behind them.

"Damn it, Hornet!" the old man screams, "Why the Hell can't you keep your nose out of other people's business?"

"All I asked for was sixty percent."

"Sixty? You said it was fifty!"

"That was before you decided to skip town without notifying me. I'm thinking about upping it up to seventy."

"Are you nuts?"

Probably, I think.

"So, it's either you or the cops?"

Now I'm thinking there's something screwy going on around here. Fred has dropped out of sight and I have the feeling that there's somebody else in the warehouse.

"I found the papers," Fred says, from an office high up on the catwalk.

214 The Green Hornet Chronicles

"Papers? Is that what you were looking for?" the old man croaks.

"Of course," The Green Hornet said. "Now I have everything I need. I have no more use for you." He aims the green gun in his hand at the men.

I go ballistic. I'm not about to let him murder unarmed men, no matter how unlikable they are. I slam my shoulder into his, spoiling his aim. We both stumble into the boxes behind us. I feel the zing of a bullet crease through my hair just moments before I hear the crack of a rifle. The Green Hornet rolls me over out of the way and pulls me into cover. Another crack of a rifle and a hole appears in a box over our heads.

I see Fred slipping along the catwalk to where the shooter is firing down on us. The man sees Fred at the same time and starts firing at him. The Smutzes are fast making their getaway. The Green Hornet has no choice but to pull me along with him as he tries to stop them. I tag along because it's a lot easier than trying to stop him. Being handcuffed to somebody will do that to you.

"Wait a minute!" I shout, pulling The Green Hornet to a stop. "Where's the old guy?"

"Right here," the old man says from behind us. The gun in his hand looks like a cannon. "At least this way no one can say I shot you in the back," he says to The Green Hornet.

"Look," I say pitifully, holding up our wrists, "I'm handcuffed to this guy, could you at least give me a chance to unlock the cuffs? I'd much appreciate it, you know. I'd be ever so much grateful," I add with a long wink.

"Dad," Terry says, "Don't. She's nuts."

"You're just jealous," I answer, "You just don't know how to deal with a real woman." I make a kissy face at him and a long promising look to the old man.

"All right. Do it," the old man says.

I reach into my bra and pull out the key with my free hand. "See, you should have searched me," I say to The Green Hornet as I unlock the handcuffs. He glares at me. If looks could kill, I'd be one dead lady.

I lazily sashay my way over to the old man. I swear he's drooling. Draping myself over his shoulder, I whisper into his ear, "Put the cannon down sweetheart, before I put a nice little old hole into your dried up old balls."

He looks down to see my little old pea-shooter aimed directly at his crotch. Needless to say, he lowers his gun. There is something to be said about the great state of Rhode Island.

Fred comes up behind me with a big box of papers in his hands. "I've taken care of the shooter," he says to The Green Hornet. He looks at me and Rhode Island with a grin. Must've been watching the whole drama.

The Green Hornet pulls out that green gun of his and I start to say to something.

"Sleeping gas," he explains.

Ohhh.

He gives a whiff to the old man, Terry, and his minions.

Back in The Green Hornet's car, he makes a phone call, "They're ready. You'll find a box with all the bills of lading and everything else you'll need on the loading dock."

I don't bother asking who he's talking to. I already know it's none of my business.

"So, where shall I drop you off?" The Green Hornet asks when he gets off the phone. I have got to get myself one of those car phones. They are so handy.

"My room at the motel is trashed..."

"It certainly is."

"I've always wanted to stay at one of those ritzy hotels, but you know..."

"The Sheraton-Cadillac is considered one of the best."

"But the cost..." I wiggle a little closer to The Green Hornet, such nice strong arms...

He smiles. Nice smile. "I don't think you'll need to worry about the bill."

"That's nice..."

"I'll have the bill at the motel taken care of as well, and your things will be brought over to the Cadillac in the morning."

I snuggle in a little closer. And stifle a yawn.

"Late night for you."

"Yep. Could use a bubble bath." I grin up at him. "How about you?"

He grins the kind of grin that makes me think of silk sheets, wine and a crackling fire.

Ohhh, the bubble bath. Never got to it. The bed was so big and soft that I never got around to taking that bath. At least not that night.

I met up with Britt Reid the next afternoon. Had a nice talk and told him the whole story, although I think he already knew most of it. I cut out the story when it appeared in his newspaper. It even hit the *LA Times* and the papers back in Texas. The folks back home had a great time talking to all their friends about their daughter, the detective.

As for The Green Hornet, who is he?

Well...

That's for me to know, and for you to find out.

Adios, for now.

THE AUCTION

by Terry Alexander

"Gunnigan, this is Axford. I just got a hot tip. A drunk saw the Black Beauty racing away from Merriman's Furriers, about four this morning. He said The Hornet's dead. He watched a street thug run out of the alley carrying his hat and mask." The words ran together, nearly incoherent in their urgency. "Get Britt on the phone. I've got tomorrow's front page story. Maybe the story of the year"

"Mike, settle down. Your witness doesn't sound very credible." Gunnigan's voice held an edge. He and Axford mixed like oil and water. "Get your story; bring it in. If it's good enough, you'll get the second or third page. The front page is reserved for the President; he announced it last night on nationwide television. He's backing out of the presidential race; he's not running for re-election. Maybe you should watch a little TV."

"Those guys aren't real reporters. Why is LBJ backing out? What's going on? Is it the war?"

"I don't know. But a presidential announcement is news and that's our business."

"Get Britt on the line; let me talk to the boss."

"Britt's not here. He called in sick this morning. I think he has the flu."

"Britt's sick." A note of concern entered Mike's voice. He had been Britt's body guard for many years after leaving the police force, prior to becoming the *Daily Sentinel*'s ace reporter. "How bad is he?"

"I don't know. Miss Case is at his house now. She took some papers for him to look over. Now excuse me, but I've got a newspaper to run." Gunnigan expelled a deep breath. "Bring in that story and I'll give it a good look."

"You're just like The Hornet, Gunnigan." Mike slammed the receiver down. "You're a bum."

Britt Reid's eyelids fluttered open, his vision hazy, his eyes mere slits as he stared at his surroundings. Familiar shapes slowly swam into focus; he recognized his bedroom and the trio waiting anxiously at his side.

"How did I get here?" he mumbled.

"Hayashi brought you home. You've got a nasty head wound Britt." Lenore Case's chestnut eyes appeared puffy and red.

Britt reached up, patting his bandage covered head. "How bad is it?"

"It could have been far worse, another inch and Mike Axford would have the story of the century." Frank Scanlon stepped closer to the bed. "You'll heal in a few days."

"I need to get back to the office." Lenore Case wiped her eyes with a crumpled tissue. "Take care of him, Hayashi." She squeezed Britt's hand before leaving.

"Don't worry, Casey. I'll be fine." He flashed a thumb up.

Frank Scanlon immediately moved to the chair. "Tell me what happened." He removed his thick glasses, placing the ear piece in his mouth.

"Hayashi may have a clearer memory than I have."

"We were coming up the alley behind Merriman's warehouse." Hayashi's soft voice filled the room. "Three thieves were carrying furs out the back door, loading them into a van. They wanted to fight, but lacked the skills. We thought it was over when a man on the roof sprayed the alley with an automatic weapon."

"We missed the lookout." Britt added. "I'm not sure if I got hit by a direct round or a ricochet."

Frank returned his glasses to his nose and opened a pocket notebook. "Your shooter killed two of his partners; the third man is in custody. A three time loser named Larry Miles, a graduate of the Kansas Department of Corrections."

The Asian averted his eyes away from the bed. "I dragged The Hornet behind the van and used it for cover while I dragged him around the corner and back to the Black Beauty."

"I'm going downtown; see if we have any information on Miles. We'll find out who the shooter is, I promise you. We'll find him." Frank stood, patting Hayashi on the shoulder. "Make sure he gets some rest."

"There's something you're not telling me," Britt said, after the District Attorney departed. "What is it?"

"We lost your mask and hat." Hayashi refused to make eye contact.

An uneasy silence filled the bed chamber. "Did he see my face?" The words echoed in the still room.

"No, you landed face down away from the shooter. He couldn't see you."

"We need to find this man quickly." Britt threw the bedcovers away, swinging his feet over the edge of the bed. A wave of dizziness overcame him as his feet touched the floor. He fell back into the comfortable embrace of the silk sheets.

"Don't worry, Britt, I'll find him." Hayashi closed the door; his silent footsteps carried him down the hall.

"Mr. Diamond." Louie 'The Weasel' Parks, a short balding man with a bad overbite, rushed in to the elegant dining room. From the expensive draperies covering the windows to the beautiful hand made chairs and table, the Windsor-Ontario estate screamed money.

Nick Diamond paused, a slice of buttered toast held in his right hand. He turned his head, staring at the intruder with his good eye. A large vivid scar ran the length of Diamond's head from hairline to chin. Jim Kirby ruined his face ten years ago. Being young and foolish, he crossed the Tony Galliano mob, paying dearly for the experience. He remembered Kirby every time he looked in the mirror; revenge is a wonderful thing. Kirby died a very painful death at his hands six years ago.

"Louie, why are you interrupting my meal? I sent you across the river to Detroit." The toast crunched between his teeth.

"Mr. Diamond, I've got big news. The Green Hornet was shot last night. He may be dead."

"What?" The toast dropped to the plate. "What did you say?"

"The rumor is circulating across the river. The Hornet's dead."

"Who did it? How did they pull it off?"

"I don't know, sir. My contacts at the police department haven't been able to verify anything. They are questioning a man they found at the scene."

"Find out." Diamond lifted the cup of coffee to his lips, blowing the steam away from the surface. "Don't come back until you do."

"Yes, Mr. Diamond." He licked his lips. "There may be an opportunity to make a profit here."

"Always the dollars, huh, Louie? If you can make money on this deal, you make it." Nick Diamond tipped the cup to his lips, slurping the contents.

Hunger drove Billy Flagg, a large hulking man, to the streets after three days. He left his small apartment, after hiding the bloody hat and mask in a safe place. He kept to the side streets, glancing over his shoulder constantly, jumping at the slightest noise. The small sign above Little Mae's diner seemed like an oasis in the desert. A dingy place for a select clientele, to anyone on the dodge it served as a safe haven. The bell above the door jingled as he entered. An open stool beckoned at the counter.

"Billy, haven't seen you here in a long time." A portly woman, her gray hair held back in a tight bun, braced her palms on the counter.

"Been laying low, Mae, give me a cup of java and a couple of scrambled eggs."

"Got any cash?"

"Down to my last sawbuck."

"I heard the job didn't go well the other night. The cops have Miles on ice downtown. Collins and Tracy are dead. Who dropped the hammer on em'?"

"The Hornet showed up. I barely got away with my life." He shook a cigarette from the open pack Mae kept on the counter.

"You got The Hornet," she winked. "No one's seen him in days and word is his bodyguard's been driving all over town looking for you."

"I got him? I nailed The Hornet?"

"That fella by the door wants to talk to you about it. You listen to what he has to say, and I'll get your breakfast." She patted his hand. "Pay me when your ship comes in."

"Mr. Flagg, may I have a word with you?" A balding man with a noticeable overbite took the empty stool to his left. "My name is Louie Parks, and I have a proposition for you."

Britt blinked his eyes several times; a small tendril of light entered the room from the eastern window. He rubbed the whiskers along his jaw. A blurry figure at his bedside slowly became clear.

"Casey." The fuzzy image became solid. "How long have I been sleeping?"

"Three days." She said her complexion ashen.

"How long have you been here? Where's Hayashi?"

"Hayashi is asleep. He's been out every night looking for the shooter.

I've been here every day." She gazed at the folded hands on her lap. "Britt, I need to say something. It needs to be said, now."

"Casey, you can say anything to me."

Casey's back stiffened; her cat eyes locked with Britt's. "I want you to stop. I want you to stop risking your life as The Green Hornet." Her upheld hand silenced a response.

"You know how I feel about you, and I know you feel the same. But we can't have any life together with The Green Hornet standing between us." She turned her head, a tissue pressed against her eyes.

"Casey, I..."

"Please, Britt." She interrupted. "If I don't say this now I never will. You were nearly killed the other night, gunned down in a filthy back alley." She stopped to staunch the flow of tears streaming down her face.

"Lenore." Britt dropped the nickname. "My father, Henry Reid, died in an eight-by-eight prison cell for a murder he didn't commit. He believed in justice. It was that belief that put him in that cell. He was framed for murder and died in disgrace."

"I know, Britt. I know."

"He started the *Daily Sentinel*, used it as a weapon against the mob, the crooked politicians, the corrupt police officers who looked the other way. He wanted to make a difference." He paused to take a breath. "If some one like The Green Hornet had helped my father, he'd be alive today."

She nodded. "I know, but is it worth the price?"

"The Green Hornet is needed. He protects those who can't protect themselves, and that's worth any price."

"Next time, you may get killed."

"This is Detroit. I could get killed crossing the street. Justice is for everyone, no one is above it, but no one is beneath it. The Hornet does good things for the people justice has forgotten; let him continue to do good."

"Britt, there are other ways; The Hornet can't last forever."

"No innocent will suffer because I've turned my back on my beliefs. I won't do that. I can't."

"I understand and I love that part of you, but I hate it at the same time."

"Hello." Nick Diamond's morning quickly soured. His eggs were undercooked and the coffee bitter. "What do you want?"

"It's Louie, Mr. Diamond. I've found our man, Billy Flagg; they call him the Bull, from Kansas City."

"Never heard of him, and I know the boys in K.C. really well. What's he trying to do, build a rep on the back of someone else?"

"He is the man who killed The Green Hornet. He watched his Oriental bodyguard carry The Hornet's limp body from the alley. He also has certain items of The Hornet's wardrobe he recovered from that alley." Louie paused, savoring the moment. "He has the bloody hat and mask as proof."

"Is this on the square? This nobody really killed The Green Hornet?"

"Indeed it is. The Bull and I have arranged for an auction at the Iverson Warehouse on the Detroit River, three a.m. on Saturday morning. I hope you plan to attend and bid for these once in a lifetime items."

"You're moving into freelancing now? Don't forget you still work for me."

"Of course, Mr. Diamond, but you said to make a profit if one was to be made."

"So I did. When is this auction again?"

"Saturday morning, three a.m."

"I'll be there"

"And, Mr. Diamond, please bring cash."

Britt's bare feet touched the carpeted floor; a mild buzz filled his ears. "That's the easy part." He smiled at Casey. "Now it gets more difficult."

"Don't push yourself too hard." Casey grabbed his arm to steady his balance.

"I've been in bed for three days; I need to work out the kinks."

She brushed a stray lock of auburn hair from her eyes. "Where to first?"

"The kitchen, I'm famished."

"That's a good sign. Let's go eat."

Britt clutched the staircase handrail, negotiating one step at a time. A light film of perspiration covered his forehead as he reached the bottom step. Hayashi stepped from the kitchen.

"I heard you coming. You two make enough noise to wake the dead."

"Hayashi, I'd like bacon and eggs for breakfast and a large cup of coffee."

"Anything you say, Britt." The Asian's grin grew into a wide smile.

The door bell rang, followed immediately by a loud banging. "Britt, Kato, is anyone home." Mike Axford's brassy voice penetrated through the wood and glass.

"It's Mike." Casey nervously licked her lips.

"I could tell him you're asleep." Hayashi glanced at the door.

"No, show him in. Casey and I will be in the kitchen." Britt eased himself through the entryway and into a large wooden chair. Mike rushed into the room; his ill fitting suit stained at the elbows and knees. He gripped his hat tightly in his fist, taking the chair next to Britt.

"What happened to you?" He pointed at the large bandage.

"I had an accident; I passed out and fell down the stairs."

"He was lucky, Mike. It could have been much worse." Casey added quickly.

"You need to get well quick. We need you at the paper. Gunnigan's going to ruin it." He glanced up as Hayashi placed a cup of coffee on the table. "Man that looks good."

"Pour Mike a cup, please, Kato."

"Yes, Mr. Reid." Kato nodded.

"I've been working this Hornet thing for three days." Mike sipped the steaming liquid.

"Have you turned up anything?" Casey leaned toward the aged reporter.

"Everybody's buzzing about the LBJ announcement; but I got wind of an auction."

"Hold on Mike, what announcement did LBJ make?" Britt's eyes lost their dull appearance.

"You didn't hear? Man, you've really been out of touch. Johnson's not running for re-election, he's bowing out." Mike took another sip of coffee. "I would have loved to have gotten the scoop on that one."

"That is strange." Britt shook his head. "Now what's this about an auction?"

"A street punk named Billy Flagg is popping up all over town, bragging about putting The Hornet down. He's got this sleazy guy, Louie Parks; I think that's his name, planning things for him. They're having an auction for The Hornet's mask and hat." Mike drained his cup and walked over to the counter top and poured another.

"An auction?" Britt's mouth hung open. "They're planning an auction?"

"Yeah." Mike shook his finger at Britt. "You know, I've went to all the hospitals, clinics and morgues in Detroit and I can't find anyone who could be The Hornet. I don't think he's dead. He may be hurt, but I don't believe he's dead."

"Any idea when this auction is scheduled?" Britt lifted the cup to his lips.

"Friday, sometime Friday."

"Keep digging, Mike. Keep me informed."

"I'm going back out and hit the bricks; I'll call if I hear anything." Mike placed the half-filled cup on the counter. "You need to get better, we need you at the paper," he repeated.

Britt watched as Hayashi walked him to the door. Only when he heard the door close did he speak. "We have to get the location and time of that auction."

"Britt, you're hurt. Don't take a chance like this, not now." Casey grasped his arm, shaking her head. "Wait for a few days, until you're recovered."

"If I let this auction go on, The Hornet will lose control of the city. The underworld will lose all fear of him." He looked up at Hayashi. "We have to find Bennie Chapman."

Hayashi nodded. "I've looked for him; I couldn't find Bennie the Book."

"Who's Bennie the Book?" Casey asked.

"A Vietnam veteran, he wanders the streets, carries a dog eared paperback in his pocket. He favors westerns."

"He sounds like a strange man." Casey shook her head.

"He is." Hayashi nodded in agreement. "But he knows what's going on in the city."

The Black Beauty cruised silently through the night. The Green Hornet sat in his customary place in the rear seat, his face covered by his original cloth mask with a hornet emblem over the mouth.

"Where do we look first?" Kato glanced in the rear view mirror.

"We search the parks, they're his favorite spots."

Two hours and three parks later, they found their man. Bennie the Book stood in the shadow of the Hurlbut Memorial Gate at the entrance to Water Works Park, one of the oldest in Detroit. The Green Hornet approached him slowly, his hands open and held away from his sides.

"Bennie." He kept his voice low. "I need some information."

"I've been expecting you; I knew that zero couldn't kill you." The Book glanced at him through his thick wire-rimmed glasses, his old field jacket zipped up tight against the night's chill wind. "I see you took the old reliable out of mothballs."

"You know what they say about desperate times." He reached into his coat and withdrew a fifty dollar bill. "Where's the auction?"

Bennie plucked the greenback from his fingers. "It's at Iverson's warehouse, three o'clock. This guy Flagg has invited people from all over to bid on your mask and hat. Naturally, he's gonna tell everyone how he killed you; there'll be a lot of heavy hitters there, a lot of muscle."

"What about this man Parks?"

Bennie shrugged. "The weasel, he smells money. Guy works for Nick Diamond across the river. Keeps track of the books, plans the operations, and counts the money."

"Diamond's running this operation?"

"Naw, the weasel is free-lancing this one."

"Buy yourself some food, and get some more reading material."

"Thanks, Hornet. Watch yourself, you're walking into a den of vipers."

The masked man nodded, trotting back to the Black Beauty. "Iverson's warehouse, three a.m., can we get there in time?"

"Of course we can, Boss. Sit back and enjoy the ride."

"Let's roll, Kato."

"How many guards do they have?" The Green Hornet stared out the specially treated windows. The ride to the warehouse had taken thirty minutes. The illuminated clock in the dash showed two-thirty.

"I count five," Kato answered.

"Go around the building. I'll take the sentry at the main door. Then meet me inside."

"Boss, are you sure you're up to this?"

"No time like the present to find out." The rear door opened, the weak glow of the streetlamp highlighted a masked man in midnight green.

"I'll meet you at the front door in ten minutes." Kato disappeared into the shadows.

The Green Hornet climbed from the modified Chrysler. A wave of dizziness blurred his vision, leaving him disorientated. The feeling passed quickly. He walked over the uneven concrete in slow measured steps. The guard altered the position of his weapon, an M-16 capable of spraying out a hail of bullets in seconds. The single bulb above the doorway provided scant illumination against the darkness.

"Stop where you are," he shouted. "Don't come any closer."

The Hornet kept his measured pace.

"Didn't you hear me? I said stop."

The Hornet stopped in a pocket of deep shadow twenty feet away.

"Don't you move." The voice held a hint of fear. "What do you want?"

The shadowy figure slowly lifted his hands above his head.

The sentry drew closer. "What do you want?" He repeated, approaching two more paces and pointing the assault rife toward the ground. His eyes widened, as he recognized the midnight green hat and coat. "You're supposed to be dead."

The Hornet leaped, closing the distance quickly. A sharp left connected on the hood's jaw. His head snapped back from the impact. A hard right followed, downing the crook before he could utter another sound.

"You can come out of the shadows now." A gloved hand slipped into the overcoat pocket, withdrawing the Hornet Sting. "Did you think I couldn't handle it?"

Kato emerged from the darkness. "The others didn't put up much of a fight. I thought you might need some help." He shrugged. "You are hurt, after all."

The Hornet nodded, He pointed the extended weapon at the door. "Let's crash the party."

"Ladies and gentlemen." Louie Parks stood before a microphone on a makeshift platform. "The auction will begin in a few moments." He loved being the center of attention. "We even have Mike Axford of the *Daily Sentinel* here to document this historic event." He gestured to the far end of the stage, a blindfolded, gagged man in a grimy suit sat bound to a chair. "But first a few words from Billy 'The Bull' Flagg, the man who killed The Green Hornet."

"I don't believe it." Nick Diamond's distinctive voice filled the large warehouse. "I don't believe this two bit heel killed The Hornet."

Billy Flagg tugged at his collar; a coating of perspiration covered his face. Louie leaned in close to his ear. "Remember now, just the way I told you."

Billy nodded, taking his place before the microphone. "Lou Collins, Kevin Tracy, Larry Miles and I were knocking over Merriman's Furriers. I was the lookout. The Hornet came out of nowhere and killed Lou and Kevin, shot them down like they were nothing. The Chinese guy took Larry out or The Hornet would have killed him too. I've got to give Larry credit cause he kept the gook busy long enough for me to get the drop on The Hornet." He paused to pour himself a glass of water from a pitcher on the table behind him, chugging it down.

"He was down on his knees, my .45 pressed to his forehead. The man was begging for his life. I ripped this mask from his face and blasted him right between the eyes." He lifted the blood stained mask above his head.

"Fat chance." Diamond jumped to his feet. "I dealt with The Hornet before. The man's tough. He wouldn't beg, if he could live another thousand years."

The street entry door began to vibrate. The shaking grew more violent, rattling the door from the hinges. The audience drew in a collective breath as The Green Hornet walked through the fog of dust hanging in the air. Nick Diamond reclined back in his chair, a smug look on his face.

"You're dead. I shot you; you're dead." Billy Flagg stood riveted, unable to move away from the microphone.

"The reports of my death are grossly inaccurate." The Green Hornet walked slowly into the warehouse, followed closely by Kato. "You have property that belongs to me." He pointed at Flagg. "I've come to reclaim it."

A dozen hoods reached for concealed heaters. "Sit down, you lugs," Nick Diamond stood, placing himself between The Hornet and the advancing goons. "The Hornet has the floor." Reluctantly they returned their seats.

"You're not The Hornet. The Hornet's dead." Louie rushed to the mike. "You're an impostor, trying to get the hat and mask to sell later."

"I want my property, weasel." The Hornet collapsed the Sting and returned it to his pocket. Kato positioned himself to The Hornet's right, anticipating a possible attack.

Louie drew in a deep breath and swallowed, sweat reflected from his bald dome, his eyes scanning the room. "If you're really The Hornet, you can take it from the Bull. If you're able."

"Yeah, Hornet." Diamond walked toward the masked man. "If you can beat Billy. You win your hat and mask."

"Just you, Hornet, not your bodyguard," Louie shouted. "You alone."

Silently he shrugged the overcoat from his shoulders, passing it, his jacket and hat to Kato. "I'm ready."

Billy Flagg dropped his double-breasted jacket to the floor. He unbuttoned his shirt sleeves, cuffing them back to the elbows as he jumped from the platform. "Anything goes?'

The Hornet nodded. "Anything goes."

The Green Hornet watched Billy's approach; the large man tended to lead with his right foot, his fists held away from his body, ready to throw a punch or grip. He wanted to grapple. He wanted to get in close and get the advantage on the floor.

Billy closed the distance quickly, his hands outstretched to clamp down on the masked man's white shirt. The Hornet pumped two swift left jabs into his face. Billy's teeth clacked together. A hard right cross knocked the thug down.

Flagg crashed through a table. Spilled wine and brandy drenched his shirt. His face a red mask of rage, he jumped to his feet, kicking the wreckage aside. He gripped the thin neck of a champagne bottle in his right hand. He rushed The Hornet.

The Hornet focused on the bottle, ignoring the clenched fist. A wide looping left smashed against his jaw. The bottle followed, smashing to pieces just above the bullet wound. Stars exploded behind The Hornet's eyes. A line of blood stained the mask, threading down his neck.

The masked man gave ground waiting for his vision to clear. He used the classic boxer's defense to shield his face. Flagg pressed his advantage, landing several blows on The Hornet's arms. A wicked right flew in over his guard and The Hornet fell to one knee. His defenses shattered, The Green Hornet appeared helpless. Flagg moved in for the kill lashing out a devastating kick for The Hornet's bloody head.

The Hornet moved at the last possible moment and the leather shoe sailed over him harmlessly. He landed on his back and lashed out with his legs, sweeping the larger man from his feet. The Bull hit the floor awkwardly; a string of blood flowed from his nose and circled his mouth, his arms trembled with strain as he pushed himself up from the floor.

A gloved fist slammed down on Flagg's granite jaw. He went down flat on his face. He gained his knees, shaking his head, only to be met by a series of rock hard blows. The Hornet interlocked his fingers, driving a double handed smash to the big man's head. Billy the Bull's eyes rolled back in their sockets. He collapsed on his face and lay still.

The Green Hornet gulped air through his mouth; he limped across the room, climbed onto the makeshift stage. His deep breaths sounded through the microphone and echoed through the warehouse.

"This is my city. It belongs to me. To do business here you deal with me. I'm the man that rules Detroit. If anyone present wants to do business on my terms, arrangements can be made. To all others you have twenty-four hours to leave. Now I advise everyone to depart, the police are on their way here." He hopped to the floor, slowly making his way through the crowd. "Get Axford, he's going to write this story."

An ill-suited hood pulled his pistol, only to receive several martial art blows and a savage kick to the face. "Anyone else want to try?" Kato asked. Dozens of weapons leveled at the masked intruders.

"Put 'em down boys." Nick Diamond waved his arms in the air. He moved into The Hornet's path. "I knew a lowlife like that couldn't put you down. You're too good to die so easy. The privilege of killing you is gonna be mine. I could do it right now, but I want you at your best when I lay you low. You remember what I did to Jim Kirby." He turned to his men. "Come on boys; let's get back across the river."

The masked man nodded, and he lifted the bloody hat and mask. "Take care of these." He passed the items to Kato. "They're very valuable."

"What about Axford?" Kato led the blindfolded reporter through the crowd.

"We'll take him home, but leave the gag in."

GO GO GONE

by Robert Greenberger

Ed Lowery had trouble focusing on Lenore Case's words, preferring to admire her legs. He prided himself on having a sharp eye for detail and he knew the rising hemlines of the day were something to be applauded. The shapely, younger woman had approached his mess of a desk mere minutes ago, concerned about a missing friend. If the absent girl was as attractive as Case, Lowery suspected she was likely out on a prolonged date, but he wasn't really paying attention. His mind had been focused solely on a political corruption story he had been investigating for two weeks. Case's arrival was just a welcome respite.

"So what do you think?" she asked, a plaintive tone in her soft voice.

Lowery had to quickly reconstruct what she had been babbling on about, when something began to stir in the recesses of his mind, tucked in a dented metal file cabinet along with other tips and tidbits he'd been collecting during his storied career as the *Daily Sentinel*'s best reporter.

"Let me make certain I have the facts straight," he began, using a mnemonic trick he taught himself years before. "Your pal…"

"Marie," she said with exasperation.

"Right, Marie," he continued. "She's a regular gossip, calls every morning during your coffee break to chat. Didn't call yesterday or today and won't answer her phone. And she goes out most nights, but you don't think she went home with anyone."

"She's not the type," Case repeated. Lowery suspected Marie *was* the type but just didn't tell her best friend. One of the growing trends the last few years had been more sexually permissive attitudes among younger people, meeting up at bars or the discothèques, and being more willing to get cozy after a few drinks. He considered himself a generation too late to take advantage of the new attitudes. "Have you checked at her office?"

"All I was told was that she hadn't come in the last two days," Case said.

Lowery frowned, earning him a mirror look from the far more attractive Case. "What is it?" she prompted.

"Been a rise in missing persons stories," Lowery said, grabbing for a pack of cigarettes. He lit up and exhaled before continuing, allowing his mind to gather the facts. "Axford first noticed it, truth be told. Police usually can predict the number of missing cases month by month, but this time something's been off. Haven't really looked into it."

"Where's Axford?" she asked.

Lowery craned his neck towards Axford's emptier, and far neater, desk. He returned his gaze to Case and shrugged. He felt sorry for the girl, perhaps now another statistic, but something was beginning to bother him about the whole thing. His instincts were now alert and he suspected there was a story brewing. Right after the current hot story....

"What does Gunnigan say?"

"No idea," he admitted, thinking about the gruff city editor. "Axford may never have mentioned it."

Case fumed and stalked away from the desk, not at all happy with the conversation. He watched her shapely posterior swivel in the distance then took a drag and flipped open his notebook, beginning to jot down notes.

"Where's Casey?"

Lowery looked up from his typewriter to see the immaculately dressed owner of the *Sentinel* standing in the middle of the newsroom. Conversations drifted off and typing immediately stopped, so the only sound in the room was the steady clacking of the teletypes delivering wire stories from out of town.

All eyes were on Britt Reid except for the reporter's, who studied the reactions of his colleagues, seeking telltale signs someone knew something. Not a single face betrayed a useful clue, frustrating the suddenly anxious man. If she hadn't reported to work or called in sick, then something was most definitely amiss.

Several murmurs confirmed this, much to Reid's obvious displeasure. Lowery glanced at the huge wall clock hanging over the teletypes and noted that it was well past eleven in the morning.

His mind instantly replayed the conversation he and Case had the previous day. Rather than say anything out loud, he caught Reid's eye and gestured. A subtle nod indicated the sharply intelligent millionaire had received the message.

"If anyone hears from her, let me know," he declared. With that, everyone returned to their work, no doubt anxiously waiting for their employer to depart so the speculation could begin. While everyone liked Lenore Case, they loved gossip.

Lowery casually rose from his desk, hand automatically going to tighten his stained tie, and made a direct path towards the publisher's office on the other side of the floor. Reid had left the door open, and without Case to act as his guardian, the reporter strolled right in. The handsome boss was already behind his modern style desk, which was highly polished and relatively empty of paper, making Lowery wonder what Reid did all day. Reid, who inherited the paper from his gutsier father, was a fine leader and allowed the paper to tackle the hard stuff. Many a time, Lowery was proud to see the paper's headlines change public opinion or expose political corruption, making Detroit a somewhat safer place to live.

"You know something," Reid said, making it a statement.

Lowery nodded, waited to be invited into a chair and then recounted the conversation he had just a day earlier. Reid's brow furrowed and his expression grew darker. The guy really cared for Case, beyond being a top-notch secretary. He doubted there was any hanky panky going on, but wouldn't be surprised if Reid wished it were otherwise.

"What does Axford know?"

"I'm not certain, sir," Lowery admitted. "We never really talked about it except that one time."

Reid reached to his intercom, depressed a toggle and practically barked for the city editor to come in. The publisher visibly fumed and Lowery could hear the rapid patter of shoes on the linoleum hallway. Gunnigan rushed into the doorway, his right hand catching on the doorknob to slow himself down. Gunnigan's dark eyes were wide and afraid.

"We have missing people in Detroit, did you know that?" Reid demanded without preamble. To Lowery, the words seemed cold and harsh, not at all like the boss. Casey's absence was really eating at him and poor Gunnigan was bearing the brunt of Reid's fears.

It took Gunnigan a moment to process the comment, and clear his mind of the imaginary errors he thought earned him the boss' uncharacteristic anger. "We have people going missing all the time," he said in a soft voice.

Reid leaned back in his leather chair and fixed his gaze on his trusted news editor.

"Axford thinks the numbers are going up. I want to know why."

The other man blinked as he processed the information, clearly dredging his memory to see if there was something he missed. "I sure don't know why," Gunnigan began before being cut off.

"I didn't think *you* would," Reid began in a cold voice. He stopped himself and sat still. Lowery watched the man's eyes soften a bit, the deep breathing seeming to expel the cold fear that was clearly gripping his keen mind.

"It's a big city," Reid said in a different tone of voice. He was speaking at Gunnigan, not to the veteran reporter. "Lot happens and it takes time to hear enough to force you to look. You begin connecting the dots and then the story presents itself. Axford never had time to find all the dots, let alone connect them."

"Casey found a new dot," Lowery interjected, helpfully guiding the conversation back to something Gunnigan could follow. "Her friend went missing. She told me about it yesterday."

"Do tell," Gunnigan said to fill the uncomfortable silence. Everyone liked Casey, Lowery knew, including the news editor, so this was tough news.

"Has Axford begun digging into this?" Reid's voice sounded normal, but a peek at the man's clouded eyes told Lowery he was controlling his concerns.

The editor finally shook his head and said, "No, sir, he's been looking into the racial violence angle."

The answer caught Reid by surprise, the reporter noted. He seemed ready to jump down the city editor's throat for missing out on the missing persons matter, but clearly recognized that the growing racial tensions across the country, and here in Detroit, were straining the police departments. It was newsworthy as well, in some ways more so given how explosive things were getting. He merely nodded and held his tongue.

"Okay," he replied after a moment. "That's important, too. Keep him on that. Thanks, Gunnigan, sorry to jump down your throat."

"We'll find Casey, Mr. Reid," the editor said as he got out of his chair.

Reid eyed the man, then he swiveled his head to look at Lowery and rose.

"We're going out to find her," he said with finality.

Lowery rose and nodded in confirmation. Reid buttoned his suit coat and followed.

Britt Reid thought the world of Lenore Case. She was smart and highly competent, the perfect secretary. Better yet, she shared his secret and that made her an invaluable ally in his fight on crime. That she was gorgeous and flirtatious was not lost on him, but right now he was more concerned with her well-being.

As he and Lowery drove away from the *Sentinel* offices, he berated himself for jumping down everyone's throats when it was clear she was gone. True, Gunnigan missed a lead, but in Detroit there were countless stories to research and the cadre of reporters could chase only so many. Still, something got Casey worried and if it tied in with the missing persons matter, then this made it personal and that had him acting out. He needed to get control over his emotions, lest they trip him up when things got dicey, and he just *knew* that would happen.

Since he began his dual career—publisher of the great metropolitan newspaper and costumed crimefighter—Reid had to walk a fine line, constantly on the alert so the roles wouldn't be blurred. The last thing he needed was for people to realize The Green Hornet was anything but the criminal the police and press made him out to be. That the general populace, including the police and his own reporting staff, believed The Hornet a criminal mastermind allowed him to work within the underworld with great ease. His very silhouette tended to open doors and loosen tongues these days, and he relished that advantage.

But right now, his reporter and public face would have to do the initial legwork, hopeful that Casey would be easily found with a good excuse.

He doubted it, but hoped for a positive outcome regardless.

"Where to?" Reid asked as he directed his white Chrysler 300 convertible away from the office building.

"Casey said her missing pal liked to go to the hottest clubs," Lowery began.

"Arthur's then?" Reid tried to make certain he paid as much attention his society pages as the rest of the paper, so The Hornet would know where the action was likely to be on any given evening.

"Nah," Lowery said casually, as if he and Reid were drinking buddies. "Arthur's is over. The hot new place is The Raven down from the Maccabees Building on Woodward Avenue."

Reid looked over quizzically. Lowery shrugged and said, "You know how it is. Word of mouth travels fastest."

The problem with the nightclub scene was that hot clubs proved so trendy that just as a place started to get written up, the "hip" crowd had already found somewhere new. It made it hard for many, including the national chain Arthur's, to remain both relevant and profitable. Reid had never heard of The Raven.

Being lunchtime, the streets were busy, but the curb by the downtown club was actually fairly empty, and Reid had no trouble finding a place to smoothly glide to a halt. The Raven had a large orange neon sign with a picture of the bird above the door, and in the sunlight, it looked like every other discotheque that had opened in the last few years. There wasn't even a doorman on duty since the club didn't officially open for a few more hours.

Still, the door was unlocked and the two eased in, adjusting their eyes for the low lighting. Most of the overhead lights were off and the red emergency signs by the exits cast the most illumination. Two burly men were working at the lengthy bar, stacking clean glasses on shelves.

"We're closed," one said in a gruff voice, ignoring them. He was dressed in a wife-beater and jeans, clearly not ready for the public. The well-muscled arms seemed better suited for leg breaking than mixing Manhattans. Reid scanned him, concluding the swarthy man was unarmed.

Reid and Lowery drew closer and the other man, smaller and less muscled, with a droopy mustache and sheen of sweat on his lined brow, looked up and noticed them. He recognized the man: a three-time loser The Green Hornet had apprehended on at least two other occasions. For the crusading vigilante, it took a mere moment to conjure up the name: Willie "Two Finger" Watowski.

"He said we're closed," Watowski asserted, waving his two-fingered right hand in the air.

"We're looking for a woman," Reid began.

"Ain't we all," Willie said, receiving a chuckle from his partner.

Reid withdrew a picture of Case, one he collected from her personnel file as they exited the offices. Willie gave it a long, admiring look then showed it to his silent partner, who tried to whistle but couldn't seem to manage.

"She's a looker, all right, but we get hundreds of them every night. Can't say I know her," Willie said amiably enough.

The other man shook his head in agreement.

Lowery had been studying the interior décor while Reid asked some other questions about the club. Reid was satisfied that neither man recognized Casey, but the very idea that a known thug worked at the club raised his suspicions. While driving on to the next hot spot, Reid made up his mind that he'd be back that evening, but in a different outfit.

The dashing millionaire dropped Lowery off at the Police Commissioner's office, ordering his reporter to begin compiling statistics on the missing people to confirm Axford's gut impression. The political corruption story could wait; there was always a political corruption story.

Hours later, just as most of the day staff had departed for home, the bedraggled looking reporter returned. Without bothering to adjust his rumpled appearance, he marched into Reid's office and tossed his pad on the desk. Sure enough, the numbers over the last three months had shown a marked increase. More interesting was the demographic breakdown. A disproportionate number of woman, aged between eighteen and thirty-five, were the ones reported missing. Since that fit Casey and her friend, Reid was now convinced there was danger.

Reid also knew that in cases like these, timing was essential. He had a day or two at best to find her or there would be little hope of a happy ending. As it was, her friend Marie was already three days or more gone and likely out of the city, or the state. Whether or not she was still alive was actually a fifty-fifty proposition.

He ordered Lowery home and then to do nothing but cover this story starting first thing in the morning. Once the office was empty, Reid called for his friend Kato to get their nighttime clothes ready. It was to be a working evening.

Clad in his heavy green overcoat and matching fedora, The Green Hornet studied Woodward Avenue as Kato drove the Black Beauty through the refuse-strewn streets. It was a calculated risk to be merely cruising down a fairly popular street in the evening hours. Still, the police night shift was sparse and more spread out, giving them greater leeway. To the general public, the little photographed vehicle was the stuff of legend, so there remained little chance it would be immediately recognized.

"What else did Lowery learn?" Kato asked as they drove.

His long-time friend and partner explained the afternoon's events as the sleek vehicle rounded another corner. The Hornet noticed that The Raven, at night, was obscured by the even brighter neon coming from the flanking the State Theater and the Fox Theatre. The sidewalks were heavy with people seeking a night's entertainment. Still, his trained eye noticed that the younger people were lined up the discothèque, not the stage performance or feature film offering. He indicated that Kato should circle around to see what was behind them.

Woodward Avenue, also known as US-10, was one of the major streets in the industrial city, carrying goods in and out of the metropolis. As a result, warehouses dotted the area and The Hornet coldly smiled when he realized that several dark warehouses were directly behind the bustling business.

"What are you thinking," Kato asked, his concern obvious.

"Missing people have to go somewhere," The Hornet said. "Why not a warehouse?"

His friend and fellow adventurer nodded in agreement, but as they turned the corner, he continued, "Aren't you making a leap here? Two girls go missing and you think they're taken from a nightclub, then stored next door?"

"When you put it that way, sure," The Hornet admitted. "But, add in Two Fingers Watowski and a rising tide of missing people and I get the idea it's all connected."

Kato nodded just once, accepting his friend's conclusion. "We corralled Watowski when we stopped Johnny the Tree's import-export business. He likes to jab with his right."

The Hornet nodded in agreement, smiling at his friend's incredible memory for opponents and their fighting tendencies.

"What do we do now?" Kato asked.

"I'll take a walk back there while you keep an eye on the club. Let's see if Willie is trying to go straight or he has more colleagues also working for The Raven."

Kato nodded again and pulled over, double-parking just long enough for the other man to slide out of the car and into the shadows. Few would notice him in his dark green coat, fedora, and form-fitting mask that wrapped around his eyes and nose, obscuring his features.

He was the only person walking along the asphalt, street lights and a stray cat the sole other companions. Dumpsters were stuffed with garbage to be collected and the air was filled with rotting odors in the summer heat. In fact, he wished he had the full-face gas mask to avoid the stench.

A sound made him freeze in place,. The groan of a metal door on rusty hinges briefly drowned out the sounds of partygoers from the adjoining buildings. Out here in the back, in the narrow alley for service vehicles, The Hornet was the only person exposed. A hulking shape emerged, framed in the dim light. The Green Hornet saw a flare of yellow and a glowing red-tipped cigarette. As he adjusted his eyes, the adventurer realized this was a guard coming on duty but one who did not expect trouble. That was sloppy, but he counted on such advantages.

Of course, a guard meant there was something to protect and it had to be something other than commercial goods.

As quietly as possible, he moved deeper into the shadows, his black leather glove-covered hand reaching into a pocket to withdraw his Hornet Gun. The forest green pistol was loaded with Kato's specially-designed knockout gas.

Moving with sure steps, he inched towards the doorway, remaining in the shadows until he had no choice but to step forward to reach the door and its burly protector.

"You!" The guard's eyes went wide with recognition of the feared gangster. As his hand reached to the holstered gun, hampered by his ample gut, The Hornet rushed forward, holding the gun in his right hand. He lashed out with his left fist, a solid strike at the man's solar plexus, knocking the air from his lungs. Then he followed with an upper cut to the jaw, dislodging the cigarette and forcing the man into the metal door.

The next thing the stunned guard knew, a deadly looking gun was angled under his jaw and the emerald-masked man was leaning in close.

"What's inside?" The Hornet asked in a voice that normally made others' blood run cold.

"N-nothing," the guard replied.

The gun pressed against the fleshy wattle.

"Women."

The first thing Lenore Case realized was that she was very thirsty.

The next thing she realized was that she was not at home. The handkerchief stuffed between her teeth and drying her mouth confirmed she was in danger. Her mind tried to resurrect memories while she repeatedly blinked, clearing her vision to study her surroundings.

Whatever she was riding in hit a bump in the road and she was jostled, alerting her to the fact she was far from alone. At least six other women were in the vehicle, a van of some sort, and all were bound. Most had their wrists and ankles tied with rope plus handkerchiefs, keeping them quiet. She managed to spit out her oily handkerchief, despite the incredibly dry mouth, but no doubt yelling would do little good while the van was moving. Straining her ears, she heard other cars rushing by at high speed and presumed they were on a highway, meaning they weren't in Detroit anymore. Traffic never moved this fast downtown. Lenore feared they had crossed the border and were in Canada already, far from home.

All of the others were still out or slowly coming around. Those awake were bug-eyed with panic, screaming to no avail. Since her movements were restricted, she decided to focus on how she wound up in this dangerous predicament.

Lowery's tip about missing people led her to go out after work, hitting several of the clubs Marie had been talking up. Her friend was most certainly the bigger party girl, enjoying hopping from one trendy place to another. While Lenore liked going out, she was nowhere near as avid as Marie was, preferring to living vicariously through the after-action reports during their morning phone chats.

Dressing in her shortest and tightest evening clothes, she was ready for action. Lenore felt out of place in the first two clubs she visited, refusing drink offers and lewd suggestions from men twice her age, but then remembered Marie had been excited about trying The Raven, which clearly was the "It" disco this week.

A dry swallow reminded her of her intense thirst, which she suspected had something to do with the drugs that knocked her out. Looking down, she saw her clothes were in place and her body did not feel as if it had been mishandled. Instead, she seemed to recall going to the bar and talking with a bartender who spoke in one syllable words.

Frustrated, she lingered and ordered a soda.

Then…nothing. Something must have been added to the drink and now she had been trussed up. What happened in between was difficult to determine since she had no sense of how long she had been out. Everyone else was dressed as if they were out for the evening, so it had to be at least the following morning or more likely, the afternoon.

Her mind felt clearer and her body was shaking off the drug's soporific effects. There was still the matter of the ropes holding her tight. While she may not have known which places were the most popular, she did know other important facts, lessons taught her by her employer, who just happened to be The Green Hornet.

"I smell opportunity," The Green Hornet said as he walked into the warehouse. A small dose of the gun's gas took out the guard so he was able to stroll inside unmolested. He carefully surveyed the space, its wide hallways devoid of signage leading into the main area. Before coming into clear view, he studied the storage area and spotted row after row of army surplus cots along with several boxes filled with purses, hats and other accessories.

Four men were playing cards at a folding table at the far side of the empty cots and he recognized the pencil-thin mustache on one man, recalling he was a regular employee of the city's mob leaders. He quickly deduced that women were being abducted, held here, and then taken somewhere else. With the night's festivities just getting underway, snatches were not yet happening—if they occurred nightly, then it would be later. By now, the goons were merely doing reconnaissance. The actual snatching probably took place nearer closing time when the women were likely tipsy, if not outright drunk.

He cursed to himself that the empty area meant Casey was not here. Learning her whereabouts became his primary goal, figuring he had time to come back and dismantle the operation later.

The card players looked up at the unfamiliar voice; when they saw it was the infamous Green Hornet, they shoved their chairs back, all reaching for guns.

The Hornet was faster, already brandishing his Hornet Sting, the metal baton extended to its three-foot length. Being infamous came with certain advantages, including having a reputation. That meant the men knew what the Sting could do, even from that distance.

"What do you want?" asked the mustached man.

Being the best dressed of the lot, The Hornet presumed him to be in charge.

"Stewie Stutz," The Hornet said in recognition. Stutz was a Detroit player but also answered to someone in the national crime syndicate. He was a thread to follow, but not tonight. Instead, the empty warehouse told him he was in a race against time, so he needed information.

"I heard you had some action going on," he said casually. "I want a piece of it."

That earned him a nervous laugh as Stutz clearly tried to figure out an angle. The Green Hornet posed as a dangerous criminal, playing one gang against the other to maintain his control over the criminal doings in Detroit. While far from the truth, it was an effective story and one he supported whenever possible.

"You have a way to collect the women that few have noticed...so far," The Hornet continued. "I can ensure they leave the city undetected. I can even find you alternate transportation to get over the border."

"In exchange," Stutz prompted, his eyes indicating he was still looking for an advantage. The other three stood, keeping their hands loose, preparing for a firefight if it came to that.

"I'll take fifteen percent of whatever you're getting, a more than fair deal, don't you agree?"

"Actually, I don't," Stutz said, walking towards the costumed figure, gesturing like they were old friends. The others hung back, their hands not far from their still-holstered pistols. "We've got a smooth machine, why add an insect to gum up the works?"

The Green Hornet stood still, refusing to rise to the jibe.

"I can distract the police; lead them on a merry chase, giving you any number of other routes to take. Patterns get noticed eventually," he said. "I can vary that and prolong your business."

Stutz, tall, somewhat muscular and looking well-dressed in shirt sleeves and wool pants, paused in his approach. Clearly he was considering the matter, and that emboldened The Hornet.

Stepping closer to his adversary, The Hornet spread his arms, making certain the Sting was not pointed at any of the men. After all, they were about to become business associates.

"I suppose the cut would come off the top," Stutz said slowly, still pondering the offer.

"Of course," The Hornet said, pushing the point. "I run this town and a business like this must generate lots of profit. Tell me, what do you do with the girls?"

"You know, I have an out-of-town partner," Stutz continued, warming up to the entire notion. After all, allying oneself with the notorious Green Hornet was good for business; it meant he was no longer a potential rival. "We built a nice little network. I collect women here and send them on for…processing."

The Hornet imagined some underground railroad north, into Canada where police pursuit would be hampered by international law. A nice pipeline and one he would crush.

"We dope the skirts, let them sleep it off here, then take them to the airport, using four different carpet installation company vans. See, we do try and vary things."

"And they go to Toronto?"

Stutz shook his head with a broad grin. "Too obvious, pally," he said, feeling expansive. "We've got some nicely designed cargo containers and they go south, to Honduras. My contact has got them coming from six different cities, almost ready to take custom orders…but not yet. Maybe you can help with that."

This was worse than The Hornet expected. If this was a true pattern, then Casey and last night's catch were en route to the airport or worse. He suspected Casey's friend Marie was a lost cause. It was time to bring the negotiations to a close.

Moving closer, to make sure all four men were within range, he tapped the Sting against his gloved palm.

"Nice set up and a good move to use four different companies. It shows initiative," The Hornet admitted.

Stutz smiled at that, clearly taking credit for the minor innovation.

"I can see where I can make the best contribution by keeping the police busy away from the airport. I'll start making plans and we can get started next," he said, slowly beginning to aim the Sting at the card table. "But first, I have to run."

Activating the powerful high-frequency sonic cutting device, it shattered the table, sending playing cards, chips, and dollar bills flying. Two of the men covered their ears, while Stutz covered his eyes. The fourth man, though, was reaching for his gun.

Leaping forward, The Hornet reached out and struck the man in the gut with the tip of the Sting. Coming closer, he sent the man flying backward with a sharp jab. Moving quickly, he collapsed the Sting, pocketed it, and withdrew The Hornet Gun. Holding his breath, he depressed the trigger, letting the dark pistol emit a thick plume of jade smoke.

Quickly, the men gasped, inhaling the fumes whether they wanted to or not, and they collapsed, unconscious.

They were essentially small fry in the bigger picture of the international slave trade, so The Hornet couldn't bothered wasting time tying them up for the police. They'd be out for hours but he might only have minutes to rescue Casey.

He rushed out of the warehouse and sprinted for Kato and the waiting Black Beauty.

The van slowed and made a series of twists and turns which nauseated Casey. The other women were finally all awake and on the verge of panic. Since none of them could speak, their muffled groans and screams filled the small area.

While they were rousing themselves, she had loosened her bonds, using tricks Kato had taught her not too long ago. Her calmness seemed to radiate across the others and as the women gathered their wits, they watched in fascination.

It didn't take her long to free one hand and then it seemed a mere instant before she had hands and feet free. The gag finally was unknotted and she tried to spit but had no saliva to work with. Whatever drug was used left her dehydrated and she had to keep that in mind. It would not do to faint while escaping. Britt Reid would never let her hear the end of it.

She massaged her wrists and felt the circulation returning to her hands. Ignoring the tingle that came with the returning blood flow, she addressed the other women, already pleading with their eyes for freedom.

"I'm Lenore Case. We've been kidnapped, that much is clear. By whom and why I don't know. But I can assure you, we won't go quietly. Now, stay silent and I'll free you all."

With that, she set to work, hoping everyone could be freed before the sickening ride came to an end.

The Black Beauty raced past red lights and merged on to the Edsel Ford Freeway, heading east toward the airport. The Hornet could tell Kato shared his apprehension, given how tightly his hands were wrapped around the steering wheel.

Once The Hornet scrambled into the backseat, Kato automatically gunned the engine to life and pulled away from Woodward Avenue. As they moved, the two men shared notes. Once The Hornet explained about the slavery ring, Kato confirmed his fears, having recognized the two bouncers at the door as members of a mob they previously decimated a year before. Whoever ran The Raven in conjunction with Stutz was using it as a front for the operation, but that was something Britt Reid would investigate later. Now was the time to stop the current shipment.

"International departures may be tricky," Kato warned.

"I'm not interested in being tricky," The Green Hornet grimly replied. "Speed is all I want right now. Cargo planes are far enough away from the passenger terminals that we should be out of sight."

The trip normally would have been just over half an hour, but Kato made certain the Beauty effortlessly got there in just under twenty minutes. The speedy vehicle cut corners, ignored traffic lights and moved with purpose. As a result, they cruised into the airport's maze of roads, which were well-lit given the evening hour. With practiced ease, Kato found an access road to the tarmac and the hangars where international cargo flights were based.

Only one had the massive door up and some semblance of activity, rare for business at night. Kato slowed just enough so the two men could study the situation. They spotted several cargo containers on the ground and three men standing by each one. In the background was an older looking plane, a twin propeller job, but dark. A windowless van was coming from a different angle and was being met by four more men. That meant there were at least ten criminals ready to pack the women away as cargo.

Ten men who were about to get stung.

"Target those containers," The Hornet commanded.

"The women may be in there."

"Too many women, too small a space," he replied in a confident tone.

Kato nodded once and activated the sixteen rocket tubes, concealed beneath the headlights, which were able to fire rockets capable of blasting through the containers. It would also cause chaos, allowing the two men to fight.

When the targeting was complete, a black-gloved finger hit the red fire button and four powerful missiles were released. It took only seconds for them to cross the distance and strike their targets with perfect accuracy.

The resulting explosion tore the metal containers to shreds, sending shrapnel in every direction. Two of the men went down with clear injuries while the others scattered. The flash and shockwave of the twin explosions caused the van to veer away from the hangar, nearly falling on its side. It did, though, screech to a halt.

By then, The Green Hornet and Kato had burst from the Black Beauty and were ready to take down the men.

Gun shots rang out but missed their targets. The shooter was greeted with one of Kato's patented hornet-shaped darts, causing him to drop the gun and writhe in pain.

Two other men withdrew their guns and tried to take aim, but Kato executed a flip high in the air, landing feet first into one shooter. The Hornet's fists took out the other man before a shot went off.

While three of the men were incapacitated, the duo was still outnumbered by three to one, plus whoever was in the van, which had come to a stop.

One man charged Kato, who sidestepped him, delivering an open-handed slap to the next nearest man. His arms moved at a blur, landing a series of successive blows with precision. The man could not mount any sort of defense and fell to the hard ground, senseless.

A different man grabbed The Hornet from behind, knocking his fedora from his head. Holding him in a tight bear hug, a second man neared and began delivering a series of blows to the stomach. The heavy coat absorbed some of the powerful blows, but each one still made The Hornet wince. He gritted his teeth and braced himself, stomping hard on the right foot of the man behind him. As the foot came off the ground in reaction, The Hornet twisted his entire body, lifting the man into the air. He was then slammed into the ground, breaking the grip.

Free, The Green Hornet stalked the other man, who decided running away made more sense than trying to win.

One of the other men had hung back, taking refuge behind the melted and twisted debris. He now aimed his gun at Kato; in a flash The Hornet withdrew his Sting, extended it, and fired at the container's remains. As the metal shrieked, it was joined in a horrible chorus by the man's own screams.

Kato seemed able to mop up the remaining conscious thugs, so The Green Hornet ran for the van. He was surprised its occupants had yet to emerge. As he approached, he heard sirens in the distance and knew he was running out of time. Then he saw the van rock back and forth.

The rear double doors were padlocked but the Sting made quick work of the lock and he yanked the double-doors open. As he did, one man came tumbling backwards out of the van. A quick kick from Kato saw to it the thug would remain down for the count.

The Hornet peered into the van, just in time to see Casey rear back and deliver a two-handed blow to the chest of the sole conscious guard in the van. He tripped over the legs of two other women and fell to the tattered carpet. Suddenly, he was being pummeled by sharp and pointy heels from several of the women.

"About time you showed up," Casey said, her voice worn and thick.

"Casey," was all he managed before catching himself, realizing he shouldn't reveal their relationship. They shared a look and then he heard the tires of the Black Beauty. Looking over his shoulder, he saw the car pull around. In the distance, the red lights atop police and fire vehicles approached.

Certain the job was done, The Hornet dashed for the car and he and Kato sped off.

The following morning, Casey arrived for work, attractively attired, her hair perfectly in place, her makeup expertly applied. Strolling through the newsroom, she grinned a bit, pleased that not a single reporter had a clue she was sitting on a story more spectacular than the one Axford had written for the morning edition.

While she had desperately wanted to leave with the Black Beauty, Casey chose to remain with the other women, protecting her connection to the elusive Green Hornet. Instead, the women looked to her to act as their leader, their spokesperson. They were all checked over by paramedics and gave their statements to the flock of police that showed up moments after the Black Beauty vanished from sight. Once the police arrived, they busied themselves with handcuffing the criminals, and tending to various wounds. The first fire truck doused the remains of the metal containers. Hysteria was more prevalent than serious injury among the seven women, all of whom looked much the same. Attractive, young, and single.

News crews and reporters from the competition had arrived soon after, but Casey wouldn't speak with them. All she wanted was a long, hot bath. While it felt like days, she was actually home only two hours later. She fell asleep before she could even run water into the tub.

As it was, she was bone tired but refused to take the day off. Britt Reid had called her first thing in the morning and suggested it, but Casey wanted to resume her life.

Casey didn't want to be the center of attention so actually managed to get in early enough to avoid most of the morning staff. She took the fastest route from the elevator to the Publisher's offices. Placing her handbag in the bottom left drawer of her desk, Lenore quickly visited the break room, filled a mug with fresh coffee, added some cream, and then delivered it to Reid's plush inner office.

He was at his desk, looking over the morning edition of the *Sentinel*, and raised his eyebrows as she glided in and placed the still-steaming mug on a coaster. She stood as she always did, ready to take instructions for the next task.

Reid put the paper down and gestured toward one of the guest chairs. She hesitated but lowered herself, smoothing out her fuchsia skirt in the process.

"Thank you," she said in a soft voice.

He raised a hand to stop her.

"I have news." She gave him a quizzical look.

"Your report last night has already made it to the FBI and from there to Interpol. I got a call from Frank Scanlon a little while ago and they have a lead on the Honduran running the ring. But, from what they can figure out, finding any of the taken women will be next to impossible."

Her fingers flew to her mouth as she whispered, "Marie."

Reid patiently waited for her to either cry or ask a question. Casey had been through enough in the last two days and was unwilling to show weakness.

"That could have been me," she did manage to say.

"You did what my reporters failed to do. You followed a lead and uncovered a criminal conspiracy that will have major international implications. This is big, Casey."

"But all those girls..." she said, her mind whirling with memories of her friend, a woman she would likely never see again.

"That's over. The Raven has been shut down, it's employees all being questioned this morning. You did good work, Casey."

She stared at him, his words meaningless to her.

"You showed some real courage and strength," he added and that caught her ear.

She nodded once and then fell silent. Her mind replayed the struggle in the van and how she channeled her rage into useful action. It made her feel good and she wanted more.

"Any chance Kato can train me to defend myself? Life around you is anything but safe."

Reid stared for a moment, then grinned and gave her an affirmative nod.

MUTUAL ASSURED DESTRUCTION

by Bill Spangler

The wail of sirens split the night. A second, then a third unit of the Detroit fire department arrived at the scene. The red of the flames was reflected by the flashers of the emergency vehicles. Neighbors and students from nearby Wayne State University started to join the reporters at the police barricades.

"Hey, Ed!" Clicker Binny shouted. "Look who I found!"

Ed Lowery, reporter for the *Daily Sentinel,* turned at the sound of the young woman's voice. The photographer was accompanied by a handsome, dark-haired man dressed like he had just left a formal party. It was Britt Reid, the *Sentinel's* publisher.

"Evening, sir," Lowery said. "What brings you out tonight?" This wasn't the first time his employer had appeared at the scene of a breaking story. Although he had inherited the newspaper from his father, Britt Reid had always taken an active role in the operation of the *Sentinel*, and its affiliated television station. On the one hand, Lowery thought, Reid's surprise appearances demonstrated his commitment to journalism. On the other hand, he didn't like the feeling that the boss was looking over his shoulder while he was working.

"Saw all the emergency vehicles headed this way and I thought I'd check it out," the publisher said. He gestured towards the burning building on the other side of the barricades. "What've you got?"

"It's a shop, with an apartment above it. There are a lot of them in this neighborhood. This particular shop was owned by a man named Lawrence Zell. He's an antiques dealer; specializes in rare books and coins. And it looks like he lived above the store."

"Damn," Reid said softly, almost to himself. "I was afraid of that."

"Did you know him, sir?"

"He located some things for me. Is he all right?"

"Nobody's sure, sir," Binny answered. "No one's been able to get inside the building yet. The fire's just too hot."

Lowery added, "I talked to some of the neighbors, and they say the building went up fast. Nobody knew for sure that Zell was there, but..."

Reid stared at the blaze for a few moments. Then he said: "Clicker, do you have all the art you need?"

"I never have all the art I need," the blonde-haired photographer replied. "But, yeah, I've got enough."

"Ed, is the fire marshal going to investigate this?"

"That's what I'm being told. But he's not here yet. I'll get a quote from him as soon as I can."

"One of the neighbors says he saw The Green Hornet leaving the scene," Binny added. "But there's always one, isn't there?"

"There always seems to be," Reid said.

"You never know with The Hornet," Lowery added, "but arson doesn't seem like his sort of thing."

"No, it doesn't, does it? Go ahead and call in the story, Ed. And, when you get a chance, see what you can dig up about Zell's background. I've got a feeling we've got more work to do here. A lot more work."

"I was hoping Zell had left town, after the last time we talked," Britt Reid said. "But I guess it was too much to ask for. Lowery said the fire department found a body around 4 a.m. and it's definitely him."

"Sorry to hear that," Hayashi Kato replied. "Any idea of what caused the fire?" The two men were sitting in the living room of Reid's townhome, in an elite neighborhood in the center of Detroit. It was late in the afternoon, the day after Lawrence Zell's shop burned down.

"No, not yet," Reid replied, taking a drink of coffee. "Mike Axford would like to pin it on The Green Hornet, but he doesn't have anything to go on."

Kato chuckled, then said, "That's never stopped him in the past." The Green Hornet and Kato had, in fact, just settled a dispute between two warring gangs, when they heard the fire alarms over the emergency band scanner installed in the Black Beauty. Rather than get too close to a scene where there would be a significant number of police officers, The Hornet changed back to Britt Reid and Kato dropped him off several blocks away from the fire.

"That's true," Britt admitted. "But Mike has so much work right now, all he can do is nag Ed and Lowery's gotten pretty good at pretending to listen to him. Anyway, I think we need to focus on finding Zell's killer, not how it happened." He put his cup down on a side table and picked up a hardcover book. "And so far, this is the best clue we've got."

"So far, it's the only clue," Kato said. "Exactly what did he tell you again?"

"Well, you remember how it started: I was looking for someone to help us find some of the dime novels that were written about Great-Uncle John." He smiled at the memory of John Reid, the first member of the Reid family to put on a mask and fight crime. "Glenn Valkenburg suggested that I try Zell, and Zell said he had some sources he could check for me. But when I went to his shop on Tuesday, he said I had to find another dealer. He said he had just gotten some bad medical news that required him to move south immediately, for his health."

"And he didn't say what the bad news was."

"No, he kept it pretty vague. He gave me my retainer back, and he gave me this." Britt held up the book again. "A collection of Edgar Allan Poe short stories from a hundred years ago. He said it would compensate me for my inconvenience, particularly if I read it closely.

"I told Zell that I didn't want anything, but he said he was going to liquidate his inventory anyway. He said he wanted to give the book a good home. He was trying to hide it, but I could see he was upset. So I took the book and said I that I hoped things would work out for him." Britt sighed, then added: "Not the smartest thing I've said recently. But I do think he was trying to send us a message with the book. We just have to figure out what it is."

"Let me see that 'bookmark' again," Kato said. As he was on duty as Reid's valet, the Asian was dressed in a white jacket, with a bowtie and black slacks.

In response, Britt opened the book and took out a dollar bill, which he handed to his associate. Kato studied it for a few moments then said, "I thought I might have missed something, but I really don't think I did. As far as I can tell, this is a real dollar bill."

"I agree, Kato. And we've both seen enough funny money to be able to tell the difference. But look at the date on this bill: 1955, more than ten years ago. But it doesn't look like it's seen a lot of wear."

Kato added, "Never mind the question of why someone would use a dollar bill as bookmark. Where was it in the book again?"

"At the title page of 'The Purloined Letter.'"

"A story about hiding things in plain sight."

"Exactly," Britt said. "That's why I think Zell was trying to send us a message. Or he left something for us."

"Something in plain sight," Kato said. "But where would he put it? If it was in his shop, we're already too late."

Britt started to pace around the room. "Well, let's assume, at least for now, that Zell knew his house wouldn't be safe. Where would he put something that he wanted somebody to find?"

"In another book, maybe? Taking it to the public library would qualify as hiding it in plain sight."

"I suppose so. But we wouldn't have a chance of finding it. Wait a minute!" Britt snapped his fingers. "Glenn Valkenburg told me that Zell was evaluating his collection when he announced he was quitting. Sounds to me like he should get a visit from The Green Hornet."

The Hornet's Sting emitted a high-pitched note. A moment later, the back door of the Valkenburg home popped open. After one last glance around the property, a midnight green figure entered the structure, followed by a second figure, dressed in what, at first glance, appeared to be a chauffeur's uniform.

"Do you think the Valkenburgs will miss seeing Britt Reid at the fundraiser?" Kato asked softly

"They might," The Green Hornet replied, as he swept the beam of a small flashlight around the hallway. "But it'll be easier to explain that, than it will be to encounter them here. I think the library is on the right."

The intruders found the library in disarray, with partially empty shelves and stacks of books piled on the floor in no perceptible order. Kato said, "Haystack, comma, needle in a. I don't suppose Zell gave Valkenburg a book too?"

"Not as far as I know. Good thing we have some time to look."

"Too bad we don't know what we're looking for."

"Look for anything out of the ordinary," The Hornet replied.

"Some comic books? Romance novels, maybe?"

"Well, that would be out of the ordinary, all right. But I don't imagine we're going to get that lucky."

The two men worked silently for a few minutes, their lights gliding through the darkened room. Then The Hornet's attention was drawn to what appeared to be a duplicate of the Poe collection that Zell had given him. The book didn't stand out from the other volumes on the shelf, but the coincidence was enough to prod The Hornet into opening it.

One of Lawrence Zell's business cards was inside the book. Written on the back of the card was: KEEP DIGGING. YOUR TREASURE IS NOT OLD. The Hornet showed the card to his partner, who replied, "Interesting. Digging. Treasure...buried treasure?"

"Treasure Island!" The Hornet completed. "Look for a copy of *Treasure Island.*"

After another minute of searching, Kato said, "Got it!" He took a book from a stack sitting on the floor. "A copy of *Treasure Island*—and it's a new one too. At least it's new compared to the other books here." As he opened the hardcover volume, he added, "And here's our treasure."

"What?"

Kato let the book drop. He held a key in one hand and some folded sheets of typewriter paper in the other.

The Hornet smiled. "Of course. Zell wouldn't damage an old book—not even in these circumstances. Good job, Kato. Let's roll."

Once inside the Black Beauty, The Green Hornet glanced at the sheaf of paper. It turned out to be a long letter, addressed to Britt Reid. He recognized the handwriting as Lawrence Zell's. But he didn't read the letter until they were safely back home, and had switched back to their civilian clothes.

Britt:

I'm not sure whether this is an act of desperation or an act of arrogance. To be honest, I suppose it's both. I know I am guilty of...well, as you'll see, I'm guilty of quite a few things. So, really, I have no right to ask you for help.

But that's exactly what I'm going to do.

As Valkenburg may have told you, I have not been an antiques dealer for a long time. Before that, I held a very different job. I was an intelligence analyst for the Central Intelligence Agency. It was not glamorous job, by any stretch of the imagination. I studied news reports and scholarly papers, looked at what was said and what wasn't said, and decided what to pass on to my superiors. I never found out which items were important... or if any of them were.

That changed when I met Stan Foley.

You've probably met Foley; I'm sure you know him. He represented this district in Congress for years.

"We've heard some rumors about Foley taking bribes and kickbacks," Britt said. "But we were never able to make anything stick. He actually seemed cleaner than some of the politicians around here." The publisher was seated at his desk, in his home office.

"Maybe we've underestimated him," Kato said.

But you didn't know him the way I knew him. I met him at a party in Washington D.C. When I told him what I did for a living, he told me a story that changed my life. A few years earlier, he learned about a strange project that the President had approved. The President had ordered that secure vaults be built in various secret locations around the world. Large amounts of money, in cash, were placed in these vaults. This money would be used, somehow, to restart the American economy after an atomic war.

Foley asked me whether I had ever heard of these vaults, or whether I had ever seen anything in my readings that suggested where they were located.

Even now, I'm not sure what shocked me more: the revelation itself, or the fact that Foley had shared the information with me. I told him I had never heard of the program, which was true. I asked Foley why he was asking me about it. He said it was more curiosity than anything else. He and a few other congressmen had been briefed about the project, but they weren't told where any of the vaults were located. But I was fascinated by the idea, this glimpse into the world of nuclear paranoia, and, God save me, I think Foley knew I would be.

I started searching for information about Foley's mysterious vaults. I pushed my security clearance as far as I could, then I pushed it a little farther. It took me months of late nights and traded favors, but I determined—to my satisfaction, anyway—that there was one of these vaults in northern Ontario, Canada. I went to Foley with the information, telling him that if I could locate the vault, others could too. He replied that he wasn't concerned about national security. He was more interested in our security.

Ever since he had learned about the program, Foley said he thought that these vaults, stuffed with money that no longer officially existed, would be a great target for what he called "ambitious entrepreneurs." If World War III actually did occur, no one would be able to find these caches. And, even if someone did, the money would be worthless. It would be just paper—toilet paper, he said. The money wasn't doing anyone any good, sitting in the ground. And no one would notice if it was gone.

It was a chilling thought, even more chilling than learning about the vaults' existence. And yet...

I thought about having my own business. I thought about actually holding a rare first edition in my hands. I thought about seeing the world, not just reading about it.

I told Foley that he had a partner. But we still had work to do. I had three potential locations for the Ontario vault, and the only way to find the right one would be for someone to check out the areas in person. And neither of us were exactly outdoorsmen.

Foley just smiled. It would mean taking on another partner, he said, but he knew someone who could do the job: Wayne Travers. When I asked Foley who Travers was, he replied "Let's just say he's a retired police detective." What was important, Foley said, was that Travers, was an avid hunter and knew that part of Canada well.

"Why does that name sound familiar?" Britt said. He took a drink of coffee, then answered his own question. "Oh, I remember now, there were reports that Travers was shaking down some local businesses, but Internal Affairs didn't find anything, and he retired shortly after that. Medical reasons, he said."

About six weeks later, I met Travers for the first time. He had spent the intervening time in Canada, studying the areas I had identified, and he believed that he had found the vault. If he was going to break into it, though, we had to accompany him. All three of us had to get our hands dirty.

Travers took us to what seemed to be an ordinary-looking farm: a small house, a barn, a silo. The house was in good shape, but we quickly established that it was abandoned. My research had given us a good idea of what to look for, but it took us a day's worth of searching to find it: a box containing three deceptively normal looking keys.

Inside the silo was an elevator that led down to the vault. All three keys had to be inserted simultaneously into a control panel in order to make the elevator work. More importantly, all three keys had to be used at the same time, in order to open the vault.

We weren't disappointed by the contents of the vault: one million dollars, in bills of various denominations.

"Maybe that dollar bill is from the vault," Kato suggested. "That would explain why there's so little wear." Although they were back at the townhome, Kato had not put his valet uniform on again. He was wearing a short-sleeved, black turtleneck t-shirt with his slacks.

"And Zell gave it to us as proof that the vault was real," his employer continued.

Despite our success in locating the vault, we were still cautious. We decided that each of us would take a key and each of us would take $100,000 from the vault. Each year, we would come up come together and make a similar withdrawal.

I moved to Detroit and established my business. I told myself that I was living the life I always wanted. Deep down, though, I knew things would turn sour. The only question was: how fast would it happen?

Two years ago, a hunter stumbled over the farm while we were there. Travers worked him over, thinking he knew about the money too. And we watched. God help us, we watched him do it. And I helped Travers dig the hunter's grave.

Then there was the question of the money itself. What would we do when it ran out? The three of us wouldn't just shake hands and walk away. Could I find another vault, particularly since I no longer had the resources of the company to draw on? The idea seemed insane, and yet...I couldn't rule it out, not entirely.

If World War III actually happened, and if someone actually found one of the vaults, wouldn't the builders want that person to have access to the other caches, if necessary? It made a sort of sense, as much sense as the vaults themselves did. But that information would have to be somewhere on the site.

Three months ago, on our last trip north, I proposed my theory to Foley and Travers. They agreed it was worth investigating, and they helped me search. We didn't find anything, but they encouraged me to do what research I could. I felt like we were still business partners, if not necessarily a team.

I was, of course, wrong.

Two weeks ago, someone broke into my shop and confronted me. I didn't know him, but he knew all about me. He wanted to know where I had hidden the map. At first, I couldn't figure out what he was talking about, but then I realized it could only be one thing: the locations of the other vaults. I told him that I didn't have any map, that I wasn't even sure that there was one. He destroyed several of my rarest books, and said my memory had better improve—and fast. All I can do now is run—run as fast and as far as I can. I don't know who's behind the break-in; both Foley and Travers are capable or sending someone after me. If I'm lucky, maybe I can find a place to hide. If not, maybe you can find a way to stop them. I've lived in Detroit long enough that I know how you and the Sentinel stand up against the bad guys in the world, how you've risked your own life sometimes to do it. And, frankly, I don't have anyone else to turn to. We may not be friends in any traditional sense, but I feel like you're the only one I can trust.

Kato shook his head. "Thieves falling out, I understand. But secret government vaults? World War III? I feel like we've seen something we were never meant to see."

"I know how you feel, Hayashi-san" Britt replied. "But I think we need to concentrate on the things we can change, like finding Zell's killer."

"And you have something in mind?"

"Of course I do. First, we need to make a courtesy call to Foley and Travers..."

Growling and snarling, two German Shepherds charged across the carefully tended lawn. The Green Hornet respected the dogs' strength and their ferocity, but he had encountered similar security precautions before. He held his ground until the dogs got close enough to enable him to fire his Hornet gun.

Billows of emerald gas enveloped the dogs. In the space of heartbeats, the canines sank to the ground, unconscious. The Hornet, protected by his gas mask, muttered, "Good night, boys," then glanced around. His next opponent was human, a well-muscled man with a blonde crew cut, dressed in jeans and a t-shirt. He was pointing a pistol at The Hornet, and he was chuckling.

"I don't believe it!" he said. "The Green Hornet! I should shoot you right now, and collect the reward myself."

"But you're not going to do that, are you?" The Hornet replied, after taking off his gas mask. "The senator wouldn't like that, would he? I want to see Foley right now. Wake him up, if you have to. Tell him it's The Green Hornet, and tell him it's about Lawrence Zell."

The man with the crew cut studied The Hornet for a few seconds. "Yeah, the senator'll want to see you," he said. "But you better give me that zap gun of yours first."

"How about if I meet you half way?" the green-clad figure replied. He took a cartridge out of the gas gun and pocketed it, while he handed the weapon to the newcomer. He looked puzzled for a few seconds, then motioned with his pistol. The two men walked towards the Grosse Pointe estate of retired senator Stanley Foley.

Once inside the mansion, The Hornet's captor used an intercom on a nearby wall to contact his employer. The conversation started with the voice on the other end saying, "This had better be good." However, it ended with the voice saying, "Take him to my office." When they arrived at that room, Foley was waiting for them, seated at his desk.

"Thank you, Carson," he began." Good work." The man with the crew cut took a position by the open door, while Foley turned his attention to the figure in green.

"I've always admired your nerve, Hornet," he began. "But I never expected that we'd meet under these circumstances." Foley was in his early sixties, heavy-set, with steel-gray hair. He was wearing an expensive-looking dressing gown, over his pajamas. "To what do I owe the pleasure?"

"Your man Carson told you why I'm here. It's about Lawrence Zell."

"That's what he told me, but I'm afraid you're mistaken. I don't know any Lawrence Zell."

The Hornet replied, "Don't waste my time, Senator. I know all about you and Zell and Wayne Travers. And I can prove it, if you'll let me take something from my pocket."

Foley smiled. "Go ahead. You've aroused my curiosity." His smile vanished, though, when he saw the key that The Green Hornet produced. "I see. Well, that certainly puts a different complexion on things."

"Yes, doesn't it? I know that Zell is dead, and I know that either you or Travers had him killed."

The older man said, "Dead? Wh—what're you talking about? I didn't have anything to do with—"

The Hornet slammed a fist against the desk. "Don't waste my time! I don't care which of you killed Zell! All that matters is that there's going to be a new arrangement now. I'm going to be taking his place."

"What?"

"I'm your new partner. I know everything Zell knew about your little piggy bank so there won't be any on-the-job training. Travers already knows about the new deal. Now you do too."

Foley chuckled. "Now I know, you're bluffing. If you had talked to Travers, I would have heard about it by now."

"I'm sure Travers will confirm my story...once the Hornet gas wears off."

"I see," the older man said slowly. "Do we get any say in this matter?"

"Oh, you get a say," The Hornet replied, with a feral smile. "You can decide whether I have you killed, or whether I have you charged with treason."

"Treason?"

"Disrupting a top secret project qualifies as treason, don't you think?"

The two men stared at each other for a few seconds. Then Foley said, "Even you don't have that kind of clout."

"Are you willing to take that chance?"

More silence.

"No," The Hornet said. "I didn't think so. I want to have a meeting with you and Travers. I'll let you know when it's going to take place. Now, if Mr. Carson would be kind enough to give me my gun back..."

Carson glanced at his employer. After a moment, Foley said, "Do what the...um, distinguished gentleman asks." Carson gave the exotic looking pistol back to The Green Hornet, who quickly left. The Black Beauty was waiting for him on the street nearest the mansion.

As he slipped into the back seat, The Hornet asked, "Any problems, Kato?"

"We should be fine. I planted the homing devices on both of Foley's cars, just like I did with Travers' car."

"Good job," The Hornet said. "With a little bit of luck, one or both of them will decide that they have to check the vault. And when they do, we'll be able to follow them."

Back at the townhome, the two men spent several hours preparing for their next outing. In addition to monitoring the homing devices, they both took short naps. They also transferred some equipment from the Black Beauty to secret compartments in Britt Reid's white Chrysler convertible.

"I feel like we're going into battle half-dressed," Kato said.

"Frankly, I do too. But it's going to be easier to get into Canada this way. I know we could outrun any pursuers in the Black Beauty, but this gives us one less thing to worry about."

After dark the next day, the duo learned that Wayne Travers was going to make the first move. They were able to follow the car easily, with only a short delay at a customs station. When Travers finally stopped, Reid told Kato to pull off the road roughly a half-mile away from the signal. The two men changed into their costumes and walked through a wooded area to reach their destination. There were no lights on in the farmhouse, but Travers' car was parked near it.

Kato said, "He's probably preparing a reception for us. The question is: where?"

"Only one way to find out." The Green Hornet took a few steps forward. That action produced a gunshot that he dropped to the ground to avoid. The Hornet quickly regained his feet, though, and said, "You're making a big mistake, Travers! It doesn't have to go down this way!"

A second shot raised a puff of dirt near The Hornet's feet. That shot, however, enabled him to determine that Travers was hiding in the barn. He signaled Kato to go around the far side of the barn while he approached the structure. "Put the gun down, Travers. We can still be partners."

"Bull!" the former detective replied. His voice was muffled but still audible. "I know why you're really here. Foley hired you to kill me!"

"You've got it all wrong! I don't work for Foley. I just want a—" The masked figure was interrupted by a third shot, which he easily avoided. However, before Travers could fire again, there was the sound of breaking glass and a distinctive *whump*. The Green Hornet recognized the noise as one of Kato's gas darts exploding. After waiting for the gas to dissipate, they entered the barn. Travers was lying unconscious on the floor, a rifle lying next to him. They quickly found his key to the vault, then tied him up.

"Once he wakes up," The Hornet said, "I want to talk to him again about Zell's death. I know he denied being involved before, but circumstances have changed. We've got him and the vault."

"But we've only got two keys."

"Two keys and the Sting."

"The Sting can't open the vault...can it?" Kato asked.

"I doubt it, but he doesn't know that."

The next few minutes passed in silence, while they waited for their captive to regain consciousness. However, Travers was still out when they heard the growl of another car engine, approaching the farm.

"That can't be Foley," Kato said. "There was only one signal on the monitor for the entire trip up."

"For a place in the middle of nowhere, we seem to be awfully popular. Why don't you hide in the stall over there, until we get a fix on what's going on?"

Shortly after Kato took his position, a new voice said, "Looks like I'm going to collect that reward after all."

The Green Hornet studied the source of the voice. "Still doing Foley's dirty work, I see."

Carson laughed. "You think you got it all figured, don't you, Hornet? Well, you're wrong. I'm running the show now. Foley's dead and I've got his key." With the pistol he was holding, the bodyguard pointed at The Hornet and the still-unconscious Travers. "And it looks like I'm going to get the other two keys real soon now."

"'How long have you known about the vault?" The Hornet asked, hoping to keep the newcomer talking.

"Long enough. I didn't put it together at first, but the senator tended to forget when I was in the room. Pretty funny, really."

"It's hysterical. Did you kill Lawrence Zell?"

"Nah, Zell knew me, so I hired a guy. When you spend twenty years on the force, you make all sorts of connections. The fire was his idea, but I told him to make sure that nothing—yaah!" One of Kato's darts struck Carson's hand and he dropped his pistol. The Green Hornet took advantage of the diversion by running forward and landing a solid punch in Carson's stomach.

The blonde man recovered instantly and swung at The Hornet. The blow landed on his shoulder, knocking him back a step. Before The Hornet could respond, Kato sprang out of the stall, ready to join the fight.

"Another one?" Carson muttered. He threw a punch at Kato, but the martial artist blocked it with a left-handed, downward block. He grabbed Carson's wrist with his left hand, then twisted his body so he was standing beside his opponent. Kato struck the side of Carson's head with his elbow. Two more quick hits left Carson unconscious on the ground.

"I think that's our last visitor for tonight," The Hornet said. He plucked the third key from Carson's trouser pocket. "Ah, here's what I was looking for."

"So what are we going to do with these guys?" Kato asked. "We can't exactly take them back over the border."

"We can't, but we can arrange for them to be picked up here. Once we find a phone, I can call Scanlon back in Detroit. He can arrange for Foley's body to be picked up and for someone to get these two."

"We're not going to have to stay and guard them, are we?"

"I don't think so," The Hornet replied. "Now that we've got all three keys, I thought we'd take Carson and Travers underground and leave them by the vault. We'll leave the keys here in the barn, and make sure the officials find them."

"What happens if our playmates implicate us?" Kato asked, gesturing towards the two unconscious men.

"I doubt they'll be able to find anyone who'll take them seriously. They won't have any evidence to back up their claim."

"I guess so," Kato said. "But we could be in trouble if someone does believe them. The government's not going to like the idea of a master criminal knowing about the vaults."

"I suppose not, but any government agency is going to know that we can make the existence of the vaults public, before they can find us. I don't think they're going to take that risk."

"You're assuming that everyone in the government thinks rationally. After learning about these vaults, I'm not sure that's a good assumption to make."

"Maybe, but if The Green Hornet's going to keep going, it's only one we can make. Now let's take these guys underground. They may not see World War III, but they're definitely going to see the end of the world... their world."

THE CRIMSON DRAGON

by Mark Justice

The Green Hornet was in trouble.

In the dark and the fog, he'd become separated from Kato. The struggle with two of the Crimson Dragon's men had carried the fight to this alley. The first thug, a tall thin Asian with long hair and a goatee, had managed to knock The Hornet Gun away in the darkness. The Green Hornet quickly dispatched the man with a knife-hand strike to the throat, a move he'd perfected thanks to the hours spent training with Kato.

But even as the drug dealer collapsed to the pavement, his comrade, a short, wide fireplug of a man, stepped in swinging at The Hornet's head. The Green Hornet twisted away, and the tip of the lead-weighted sap glanced off the back of his skull. It was enough to stagger him and set off a pinwheel of lights before his eyes. He allowed himself to fall down, grasping for his opponent's legs as he dropped.

He missed. The Green Hornet heard the man shuffling closer, edging in for a killing blow. He raised his gloved hands to protect his skull from further damage.

The blow never fell. The thug exhaled a low moan and fell next to The Green Hornet. He lay still. In the dim light from the mouth of the alley, The Hornet saw the tiny hornet-shaped dart protruding from the short man's neck. He raised his head, ignoring the throbbing headache from the sap, and saw a familiar silhouette at the alley's entrance.

Kato seemed to glide soundlessly to his side. With a strength The Green Hornet always found surprising, the smaller man pulled his partner to his feet.

"You okay?"

"Got my bell rung," The Green Hornet said. "Thankfully, I've got a hard head."

The wail of multiple sirens pierced the night. They sounded close.

"We have to go now."

The Green Hornet found his gas gun propped up against a brick wall. He slipped it into his pocket. "I want to take one of the Dragon's men with us for questioning."

"No time, Boss," Kato said.

The Green Hornet knew his friend was right. The last thing they needed tonight was a battle with the police. The pair of crime fighters hurried to the massive black car parked at the curb.

Four men were sprawled near the vehicle. All were unconscious and all four Asians sported a small tattoo of a red dragon on their left hands, signifying their allegiance to the newest crime lord in the city, a man The Green Hornet vowed to bring down.

As the Black Beauty pulled away from the curb, a pair of police cars squealed around the corner. The passenger in the first car reached out the window and fired his weapon. As far as the cops were concerned, The Green Hornet was just another criminal, as bad as or worse than the Crimson Dragon. It was an image The Green Hornet had worked tirelessly to cultivate. It allowed him to operate more freely within the city's underworld.

But it was damned inconvenient when it came to escaping the police.

The bullets bounced harmlessly from the Black Beauty's armored frame. With a chuckle, Kato mashed the accelerator and the heavy vehicle pulled away from the pursuit. A quick turn down one alley, then another, put The Green Hornet's powerful car safely out of the path of the cops. Kato took a series of residential streets away from downtown. The Black Beauty's unique infra-green headlights and the special glass in the windshield allowed Kato to navigate at top speed while remaining nearly invisible to any nocturnal observers.

"How's the head, Boss?"

"Get me a couple of bottles of aspirin and I'll be right as rain," The Green Hornet said. "I just wish we had some solid information on the Crimson Dragon."

He saw the shrug of Kato's shoulders. "We'll have better luck next time. Meanwhile, six of the Dragon's men are being picked up by Detroit's finest even as we speak."

The Green Hornet closed his eyes, trying to ignore the pain in his skull. *Not good enough*, he thought. *Not nearly good enough.*

The next morning, Britt Reid settled in behind his desk in the publisher's office of the *Daily Sentinel* and reached for the intercom switch. Before he could press it, the intercom buzzed and the voice of Lenore Case came through the speaker.

"You have a visitor, Mr. Reid."

Reid frowned. His head hurt and he had a busy morning. He would have Lenore send whoever it was away.

As he was about to respond, his secretary added, "It's Patricia Redmond. She says she's an…old friend."

There was the tiniest note of disapproval in Lenore's voice, so slight no one else would have caught it.

Patricia Redmond. Reid sighed. "Old friend" was putting it mildly.

At one time she had been everything to Reid. Long ago, when he was just starting college and still unsure of his place in the world and in his father's newspaper business, he thought Patricia was the woman he would spend his life with.

But that was before he changed. Before he saw what crime was doing to his hometown and the people he cared about. Before his father died.

Before he became The Green Hornet.

What could she possibly want? His time with Patricia seemed a lifetime ago.

He cleared his throat, pressed the intercom button, and tried to sound pleased. "By all means, Miss Case, send her in."

Seconds later, the door opened and Patricia Redmond entered his office. As she pulled the door closed from the outside, Lenore paused to offer Reid a mischievous smile.

Patricia looked just as she had when they were at school. She was dressed in a simple yet expensive dress. Her golden hair was pulled back in a youthful ponytail.

Reid noticed the diamond-encrusted wedding ring she wore and the puffiness around her eyes.

He stood up and offered her his hand. Patricia stepped forward to embrace him.

As he reluctantly returned the hug, he felt an unexpected wave of emotions. Holding her felt familiar and right. Once he thought Patricia would be in his life forever. And he also recalled the night he told her he could no longer be with her.

As he pulled away, she took his hand. "Still not married?"

"Only to the job," Reid said. "And you?" He guided her to the leather sofa. They sat, separated by a safe distance.

Patricia touched her wedding ring absently. "He's a good man, Britt. A doctor. A fine provider. He just patented a type of artificial heart, which will save thousands of lives, and make us very comfortable. But...he's not..."

"What can I help you with?" Reid steered the conversation away from the past. From what could never be.

"Do you remember Cassie?"

Reid recalled a skinny little girl with braces. Full of boundless energy, a real tomboy. When he had visited Patricia at her parent's home, Cassie had always been underfoot.

"Your little sister," he said. "What happened?"

Patricia stared at the floor. "She got mixed up with a bad crowd. She ended up on drugs. David— my husband—and I tried to help her, but she always went back to that life. Before she disappeared she...she was even arrested for prostitution." Patricia reached into her expensive purse for a tissue. She dabbed at her eyes.

"Disappeared? When?"

"Two months ago. She ran off with some drug dealer named Johnny Ng. The police back home said he has family here. Of course, I've heard the news about Detroit's drug problems, and I thought..."

Reid grasped both of her hands. "I'll do everything I can, Pat. Between the staffs of the *Sentinel* and the TV station, I have the best investigators in the city working for me. If Cassie's out there, we'll find her."

Patricia nodded. When she tried to speak, her lower lip quivered. Then the sob broke from her throat and she collapsed against Reid's chest. He held her tightly as she cried.

When she could finally speak, she whispered. "I knew you would help. Thank you."

Less than an hour later, Reid was in the *Sentinel*'s newsroom, perched on the edge of the desk of Gunnigan, the paper's tough city editor. The man behind the desk was a medium-sized leathery guy with the bearing, build, and haircut of a Marine drill instructor. He was studying a thin notebook filled with tiny, neat handwriting.

"We don't know much about this Crimson Dragon, Mr. Reid," Gunnigan rumbled. "Cops started hearing the name a few months ago, about the same time drug overdose statistics went through the ceiling and gang violence exploded, particularly in the Asian community. He might be a refugee from Vietnam. Maybe had a nice little trafficking business going there until the bombs started falling."

"Any proof of that, Gunnigan?"

The city editor dropped the notebook on his cluttered desk. "Speculation. Nobody has a thing on this guy. The cops will occasionally bust one of his boys with the tattoos on their hands, but the punks never talk. The Green Hornet left a few of those lowlifes on the sidewalk last night. My buddy down at police headquarters says none of 'em would talk, not even after getting a little, ah, tune-up in the interrogation room."

"Okay. I want a full-court press on the Crimson Dragon. As of today, this is your number one priority," Reid said.

"I figured. That's why I had Cannon sit in on this."

The smiling man who leaned back in a chair next to Gunnigan's desk looked like a kid. But Greg Cannon had won the Pulitzer while reporting from Vietnam for the *Chicago Tribune*. When he got out of the jungle Cannon wanted a change of scenery and Reid had leapt at the chance to hire him for the *Sentinel*. In his short time at the paper, Cannon had already exposed a corrupt city councilman who was doing business with the mob, thanks to a key piece of evidence supplied anonymously by The Green Hornet.

"I think Gunnigan's refugee theory is solid," Cannon said. "The drug warlords are a dime a dozen in Southeast Asia. It's not a stretch to think one of them has set up shop in Motor City."

"Find him," Reid said.

"You got it." Cannon stood up. "Save the front page, chief," he said to Gunnigan before he walked away.

The city editor chuckled. "Cocky kid, but one of the best reporters I've ever seen."

"Better than you?" Reid said.

"Don't get carried away," Gunnigan growled.

"So we're going to comb the city looking for one particular junkie hooker?"

Kato kicked at Reid's head. Reid blocked it with his forearm. It was easy, because Kato was moving at half-speed. Maybe less. Reid feinted with his left, then unleashed a powerful roundhouse with his right. Kato dodged. One second he was right there, the next he had moved two feet to the left.

"You know that it's going to be next to impossible, right?" The smaller man's fists lashed out, a blur in the harsh light of Reid's basement gym. Despite the speed, Kato's fists barely tapped Reid's chest. Kato danced away, breathing lightly.

Reid felt like a lumbering old man. He was breathing hard and his head still ached. He had also felt a little disoriented since Patricia Redmond walked into his office. She had opened a door he wanted to keep locked.

"We didn't sign on for the easy stuff," Reid said. "This one...is important to me."

Kato picked up a couple of towels from a rack on the wall. He really didn't need one. The other he tossed to Reid. "Where do you want to start?"

"The usual spot. We'll talk to Frenchy."

Kato smiled. "After that I want to find more of the Crimson Dragon's goons."

"You think one of them might be in a talkative mood?"

"I guarantee it."

It's was Reid's turn to smile.

"Let's roll, Kato."

Harrigan's was a dark, damp bar about a block from the river. Frenchy felt right at home there. He was in his usual booth at the back. On the dirty, scarred table were the tools of his trade: the racing form, the sports page from the *Sentinel*, a small black notebook with a pencil rubber-banded around it, and a schooner of beer.

As he studied the racing form, someone slid into the booth across from him.

"Sorry, bub. The book closed on the Pistons already," Frenchy said without looking up.

"Hello, Frenchy."

The voice was low and friendly. And it sent a chill through his guts.

His head snapped up. It was dark at the back of Harrigan's but Frenchy could still make out the color of his visitor's fedora and coat.

And the color of his mask.

"H–hornet! What, uh, can I do for you, old friend?"

The Green Hornet smiled, and a squeak escaped Frenchy's constricted throat.

"You remember our arrangement, Frenchy?"

"Sure, Hornet. Sure! I, uh, occasionally provide you with a stray bit of information that I may run across, and in exchange–"

"I don't kill you in a very slow and painful manner." The Hornet leaned forward. One gloved hand patted Frenchy's arm. The bookie jumped like he'd been shocked by a live wire.

"R-right. So, what do you need from me?"

The Green Hornet pulled a photograph from his coat and slid it across the table to Frenchy. The girl was young and pretty. A little too skinny for Frenchy, though. She was smiling at the camera while she sat on a perfectly manicured lawn in front of a big house.

"Who is she?"

"Her name's Cassie," The Green Hornet said. He wasn't smiling anymore.

"Rich girl get lost? She'd stand out like a sore thumb down—Ow!"

The Green Hornet squeezed Frenchy's arm. "I need you to listen, Frenchy. Not run your mouth. Can you do that?"

Frenchy nodded rapidly.

"The girl is somewhere in town. She won't look like that anyway. She'll be thinner. Her hair and makeup won't be as nice. Neither will her clothes. I need to know if anybody's seen her."

Frenchy raised his eyebrows, afraid to speak. The Green Hornet nodded.

"Will she...I mean, that is, would she be a, uh, working girl?" He flinched back against the seat of the booth.

The Green Hornet clenched his jaw. He nodded, then said, "Or she'll be scoring."

"Sure. I got it. She's one of yours, ain't she? Got hooked on the junk and ran off."

Everybody knew The Hornet had his fingers in everything. If it was dirty and it made money, you knew he got a piece.

The Green Hornet smiled again.

"Right, Frenchy. You're a smart guy. I knew I came to the right place."

Frenchy relaxed a bit. He picked up the schooner of beer.

"Sure, Hornet. Ol' Frenchy'll find her."

"I want her back. In one piece."

Sheesh, Frenchy thought. The Hornet must have a sweet spot for this little tail. Must be his favorite. That made Frenchy chuckle. In one swift move The Green Hornet snatched the glass from Frenchy's hand and broke it against the bookie's head. Warm beer and tiny pieces of glass slid down Frenchy's face and neck.

One gloved hand grabbed the collar of Frenchy's shirt and hauled him across the table until his face was a couple of inches from The Hornet's. When The Hornet spoke again, his voice was barely above a whisper.

"I will find this girl, Frenchy. And if she has been harmed, I will hurt a lot of people. Guess where I will start."

The Green Hornet released the bookie. He fell back against the cracked linoleum of the seat.

"I hear ya, Hornet. I'll be discreet, you bet. Nobody —"

He looked up. The other side of the booth was empty.

"Son of a ..."

Frenchy took a moment to get his breathing under control before he leaned from the booth and shouted at the bartender.

"Hey, Pepper! Get me another beer, will ya? And a towel."

The rest of the night was fruitless for The Green Hornet and Kato. It started snowing before midnight and soon the streets were icing up. If the Crimson Dragon and his minions were working tonight, they were indoors. After another hour of useless searching, The Green Hornet instructed Kato to return home.

The telephone rang a little past three in the morning. Reid was at the desk in his home office, unable to sleep. He lifted the receiver before the first ring had ended. His city editor was on the other end, calling from one of the city's hospitals.

"It's Greg Cannon," Gunnigan said. "He was attacked."

"How bad?"

"They don't know yet. The docs are checking him out now."

"Did you see him?" Reid said.

"Yeah. He looked like he lost a fight with a dump truck."

"Where did it happen, Gunny?"

"He was in and out when I talked to him, but it sounded like he said Chene Park. Close to where The Green Hornet mixed it up with those Crimson Dragon punks the other night."

It was nearly four when Reid arrived at the hospital on East Jefferson. Gunnigan was standing by a window in the lobby, sipping coffee out of a paper cup and watching the snow fall. Despite being up most of the night, the *Sentinel*'s city editor was dressed in a crisply pressed white shirt and tie. The creases in his pants were razor-sharp.

"Good morning, Mr. Reid."

"We'll see," Reid said. "Anything yet?"

Gunnigan shook his head. "Cannon told me he was working on the Crimson Dragon thing. Poking around. Asking questions. Guess he asked the wrong ones."

Reid sat down in an uncomfortable chair and sorted through a pile of outdated magazines.

Whatever happened to his reporter, Reid silently vowed that this was one more thing for which he would make certain the Crimson Dragon paid in full.

Within a half hour, a doctor in a white coat came to the lobby. He had met Gunnigan earlier in the night, and headed straight for the editor.

"This is my boss, Britt Reid," Gunnigan said.

"How's Cannon?" Reid said.

"Badly bruised. Shaken up, with a slight concussion. But nothing's broken. He's a lucky man, Mr. Reid."

"Can we see him, Doctor?"

Greg Cannon was sitting on the edge of a narrow bed in an alcove of the emergency room, slowly buttoning his shirt. He had two black eyes, a cut on his forehead and nose, and a swollen lip. There was a roadmap of bruises and abrasions on his exposed chest.

"What are you doing?" the doctor said.

"Going back to work," Cannon said. He forced a smile, then winced.

"No, you're not," Reid said. "You're taking some time off. And when you do go back out there, you'll go with some protection."

Cannon gingerly stood and slipped into his coat. "No offense, Boss. But it's not the first time I've been smacked around for following a story. When you do this work, you can't hide and you can't back down. And a bodyguard would only make the job twice as hard." Cannon shoved his hands in his coat pockets. "You can fire me but you can't make me quit this story. Excuse me."

Just past ten, Gunnigan came into Reid's office with two men. One was a uniformed cop that Reid had never met. The other was a detective, an old friend of the city editor.

"You heard of a bookie named Frenchy Cooke?" Gunnigan said. "His body was dumped in front of police headquarters an hour ago."

Reid kept his expression neutral. "So?"

"This was found on him," the detective said. He placed a photograph on Reid's desk.

The black and white photo showed an emaciated woman sitting in a chair. Her eyes were open wide in fear because of the knife held to her throat. She was holding a copy of yesterday's *Daily Sentinel*.

"It's the same girl in the picture you gave me yesterday, isn't it?" Gunnigan said. "Cassie Redmond. What do you think it means?"

Reid knew what it meant. It was a warning for The Green Hornet.

Johnny Ng was hanging by his feet in the empty warehouse.

Hours earlier in Reid's office, the detective mentioned that Ng, the last of the Crimson's Dragon's men, had made bail. He turned out to be the boyfriend of Cassie Redmond. Kato followed Ng to a derelict apartment building near the corner of Third and Bagley. After dark, The Green Hornet and Kato went in and found Johnny Ng sleeping on a stained mattress. They convinced him to take a ride in the Black Beauty.

This warehouse was owned by Reid. In a few months it would become the home of the *Sentinel*'s new state of the art press. Tonight, it was the interrogation room of The Green Hornet.

Ng twisted from the shove Kato had administered. The Asian man's face was red from hanging upside down. The only sounds in the warehouse were the creaking of the rope and Ng's frantic breathing.

The Green Hornet stepped into a small circle of light near Ng's swinging form.

"Do you know who I am?"

Ng swallowed before answering. "Yeah, and I'm not scared."

"Good. That means this will be fun for my partner."

Standing in the shadows being the man, Kato shoved Ng again.

"Your boss has moved into my turf. That ends tonight," The Green Hornet said.

As he swung past The Hornet's head, Ng said, "He'll kill you."

"Maybe. Maybe not. Either way, you won't be around to see it unless you tell me where he is."

"You're gonna kill me anyway," Ng said. "Why should I be a rat?"

"To save yourself a lot of pain," The Green Hornet said.

"I'm not scared," Ng repeated. His shaky voice said otherwise.

"I'm tired of looking at that dragon tattoo," The Green Hornet said. "Get rid of it."

Kato jerked Ng's left arm behind his back. Ng grunted in surprise.

The Green Hornet smiled. "We have to remove any identifying marks. As a fellow professional, I'm sure you understand."

Kato went to work. Ng began to scream.

The Green Hornet knew that Kato had removed an ice cube from the cooler on the floor and run it across Ng's hand. A squeeze bottle of syrup simulated blood flowing from a deep cut. Ng's imagination filled in the rest. "This is taking too long," The Green Hornet said. "Just cut off the whole hand."

Kato pulled Ng's arm a little harder. The punk screamed.

"Stop! Stop! I'll talk! Please!" Ng began to sob.

The Green Hornet asked his questions.

Johnny Ng directed them to a dilapidated three-story apartment building less than a mile from Chene Park. After cutting him down, they left Ng tied up and gagged in the warehouse.

The Black Beauty was parked three blocks away. The car's heater kept the windshield free of the snow that was piling up on the street.

Ng said the Crimson Dragon owned the building, and that he kept his stock of heroin there under heavy guard. He was sure to be there tonight.

He expected a huge delivery from his supplier, the biggest yet. Ng told them the Crimson Dragon was always masked and must be an Asian since he spoke Vietnamese, Thai, Burmese, and a smattering of both Mandarin and Cantonese.

The Green Hornet knew that if Cassie was still alive she would be held here where she could be guarded.

Over the next few hours, they witnessed several Asian men arriving. Nobody left. Finally, around one, a white panel truck slowed in front of the building and turned down the alley.

"That's the delivery. Everybody will be there now," The Green Hornet said.

"It's not the only delivery they're getting tonight," Kato said.

A white guy, likely the driver, leaned against the truck and smoked while four Asians with Crimson Dragon tattoos carried boxes from the truck through a door in the side of the building.

With a silent squeeze of the trigger, The Hornet Gun dispensed a cloud of gas that quickly encompassed the small crowd. The effect was instantaneous. After the men had slumped to the ground, The Green Hornet stepped from concealment. The sound of gunfire from deep inside the building told him Kato had cleared the front door.

The Green Hornet stepped through the side door, prepared to encounter gang members. One man was on his way out, probably to grab another box. The Green Hornet hit him with a solid left, putting his shoulder into it. The thug fell back into the arms of a second gang member who suddenly appeared from around a corner. The Green Hornet swung the Hornet Gun into the side of the second man's head. Both hoods dropped to the floor. The barrel of the Hornet Gun was bent. The Green Hornet muttered an oath, shoved the Hornet Gun into a coat pocket and continued up the hallway.

He heard pounding footsteps and two more gunshots from the floor above him. He entered the foyer of the building, immediately spying Kato's handiwork. Two men were lying motionless at the foot of a narrow staircase. Two more gang members were sprawled on the steps. The Green Hornet stepped over them as he quickly climbed to the next floor. At the second floor landing more bodies were piled up. One of them had a Japanese throwing star embedded in his neck. The Green Hornet continued to the top floor.

The stairway opened up to a large room that occupied the entire floor. Two men lay unconscious near the landing. The Green Hornet was separated from the room by a half-wall about four feet high. He crouched behind it and listened to the sounds of combat. Kato was fighting two of the gang members at once, circling them like a tornado.

A single man stood against the far wall. His face was concealed by a red hood. Holes had been cut out for his eyes. The entire hood was embroidered in gold with exquisitely rendered dragons. The man held a gun, waiting for an opening to fire at Kato. Tied to a wooden chair next to him was Cassie Redmond.

The Green Hornet estimated the Crimson Dragon was twenty feet away. The Hornet Sting—a device which emitted a devastating sonic blast—could pulverize the wall or floor near the drug lord, but there was a risk to Cassie, if he wasn't careful.

The Green Hornet took careful aim with the sting, targeting the center of the hooded man's body, then pulled the trigger—

At the same instant, something slammed into his knees. As he fell, The Green Hornet saw his shot go wide. The wall above the Crimson Dragon exploded. Then he was on the floor and another of the Crimson Dragon's thugs was on top of him, battering him with fists and knees and elbows.

Kato saw The Green Hornet go down, but he was too busy to help.

The two members of the Crimson Dragon's gang were skilled fighters. Both employed a form of *Bokator*, the ancient Cambodian fighting art. One of the thugs was short and squat. He stayed low to the floor and worked at sweeping Kato's legs from under him. The other opponent was thin and possessed freakishly long arms. He was able throw jarring punches then dance away. His last blow had opened a cut on Kato's forehead.

Kato knew he had to end this. Despite the fighters he had already faced, his breathing was still steady and even. But if he let his focus falter for even an instant, the two henchmen would take advantage of it.

He could hear the heavy breaths of the shorter man; he was becoming winded. When he made his next attempt to grab Kato's legs, Kato leapt into the air and drew his knees up. As he descended, he uncoiled his legs like a powerful spring. Both feet landed on the back of the squat man's head, driving the man's face into the floor.

At the same instant, Long Arms threw another punch. Kato caught his wrist and jerked the tall man forward and down. Kato's knee struck the point of Long Arms' chin with a satisfying crunch. Kato stepped aside as the tall man collapsed onto the body of his fellow gang member.

He meant to rush to the aid of The Green Hornet. As he turned, though, The Hornet landed a fist in the center of the face of his opponent. The man slumped to the floor. The Green Hornet reached for the Hornet Sting. The weapon had fallen a few feet away. But Kato saw a danger The Hornet had missed.

The Crimson Dragon now had a clear line of fire. He aimed a large automatic at The Green Hornet.

Kato's hand was a blur as it darted into his jacket and came out with a *shuriken*. Continuing his lightning-fast movement, Kato launched the metal throwing star. The ninja weapon seemed to hiss through the air as it flew to its target. One sharp metal point sliced into the Crimson Dragon's gun hand. The gang leader gasped in pain. Though he didn't drop the automatic, the weapon hung loosely in his wounded hand.

One second after Kato threw the *shuriken*, The Green Hornet was on his feet, running toward the Crimson Dragon. It took the hooded man precious seconds to fight through the pain and raise his gun. By the time he squeezed the trigger, The Green Hornet was close enough to launch a flying kick at the drug lord.

The Green Hornet's right foot hit the Crimson Dragon's chest like a sledgehammer. The gun shot went wide. The Crimson Dragon was thrown against the wall. The Green Hornet landed in a crouch. He quickly stood, just as the Crimson Dragon, breath wheezing in ragged gasps, straightened up, raising the automatic yet again.

The Green Hornet blocked the man's gun hand with his left arm while driving his right fist into the center of the red hood. Cartilage collapsed beneath The Green Hornet's knuckles. The Crimson Dragon pulled back to try to free his gun hand. The Green Hornet's gloved right fist landed again, this time on the drug lord's jaw. The criminal lost his balance, falling against the wall. The Green Hornet reached for the gun, but the Crimson Dragon dropped to a prone position on the floor, rolled, then jumped to his feet. He swung the gun into position. The Green Hornet grabbed the Dragon's wrist with both hands. Pivoting on his left leg, The Green Hornet drove his right foot into the drug kingpin's midsection in a powerful side kick. The Crimson Dragon collapsed on the floor, with the gun under him. There was a muffled pop, like a firecracker exploding a block away. The Crimson Dragon did not move.

"Boss, you okay?"

The Green Hornet turned around. Kato was next to him. The Green Hornet rushed to Cassie's chair. The girl was unconscious. He removed a glove and felt her pulse. It was strong. She had fainted. Did the Crimson Dragon hope for ransom from the good fortune Cassie's brother-in-law was due to receive, thanks to his artificial heart? Or did the drug lord take her for another, darker reason? Perhaps the girl could clear matters up when she regained consciousness. Ultimately, it didn't matter.

Kato took another throwing star from a pocket inside his jacket. He used it to saw through the ropes. Kato picked the girl up as if she were a child.

"Who was that guy?" he said, nodding to the body of the hooded man.

The Green Hornet rolled the body over and pulled off the hood. He stared at the battered face of Greg Cannon. He imagined the drug lord ordering a couple of his most trusted men to work him over. Beat him up without doing any lasting damage. Just enough to be convincing until the Crimson Dragon could close this last deal. Then he would disappear or move on to another city, plying the trade he'd discovered half a world away.

He thought the mild beating would fool everybody. It almost did.

"He was nobody. Just another lowlife." The Green Hornet dropped the hood over Cannon's face.

Within minutes, the Black Beauty rolled through the snow-covered streets toward home.

Britt Reid had an important call to make.

FANG AND STING

by Win Scott Eckert

Detroit, Summer 1964

Like a small insect, the dark figure deftly skittered up toward the twenty-second floor of the Lafayette Pavilion Apartments. Quite a feat, considering the building's walls were aluminum and glass, with few or no handholds.

At the summit, the shadowy figure slipped over the ledge and padded silently across the rooftop terrace to a large set of modern glass panes. A cutter efficiently removed a circle of glass. A brown hand reached inside to unlock the sliding patio door. Inside, shoeless feet crept unerringly for the bedroom, from which deep snores rumbled.

Had the slumbering man been awake, white moonlight would have revealed the dark form standing over him, dripping a viscous liquid down a silken cord and onto his upper lip. The victim stirred, but did not awaken.

The brown-skinned man took a small jar from a pocket in his robes and quietly unscrewed the cap, releasing the buzzing fury within. The hornets swarmed and attacked the helpless man in his bed.

The intruder bolted, exited back onto the rooftop terrace, and sealed the circle in the glass with a spray foam substance from a small can, so that the hornets could not escape.

He descended the building as easily as he had come up, ignoring the penthouse resident's screaming death-throes.

GREEN HORNET MURDERS THIRD CITY COUNCILMAN IN AS MANY NIGHTS

By Mike Axford

City Councilman Earl Hayden was murdered in his bed last night, another victim of The Green Hornet. As with previous killings, Hayden was surrounded by the corpses of countless hornets—green hornets—which swarmed and stung him to death before he could react. The Coroner's report showed traces of a strong pheromone on Hayden's upper lip. The pheromones are known stir up hornets, causing them to swarm and attack the victim.

*Scientific tests indicate the hornets are a mutated version of the Asian giant hornet (*Vespa mandarinia*), known to have potentially toxic stings. Unlike ordinary hornets, these green hornets die after they sting, leaving a trail of evidence at the scene of the crime.*

The murder of Hayden comes on the heels of the recent slayings of several other councilmen, high ranking automobile executives, and union leaders.

Asked about the connection between the gruesome hornet killings and the notorious underworld figure, "The Green Hornet," District Attorney Frank Scanlon had no immediate comment.

Scanlon also refused to discuss recent rumors that The Green Hornet is now operating in partnership with the mysterious Doctor Fang, under whom the gangs of Chinatown are being organized, and who last terrorized Detroit back in 1935.

In fact, this reporter was present and witnessed when Warner Lester, the famed "Manhunter," took on Doctor Fang. It was thought that both perished in the resultant conflagration, but unfortunately it seems the scourge of Chinatown has returned to plague our honest citizens...

"Come now, Mike," Britt Reid said, tossing the copy on his modernistic desk. "You know I can't print such an unbalanced piece."

"Now see here, Britt, of course the presence of green harnets as murder weapons has the city stirred up, so to speak, and all blame rests upon The Green Harnet himself." Axford's Irish brogue usually wasn't too noticeable, but when he was excited the word "Hornet" invariably came out as "Harnet."

"The papers are all editorializing," Mike continued, "demanding police protection for other political figures, and massive law enforcement mobilization to bring The Harnet to justice. If not, he'll end up controlling the city, through the remaining councilmen who will buckle under to his demands in exchange for their lives."

"It's not just the green hornets as murder weapons," the *Sentinel* owner replied. "Your article goes off on a speculative tangent about a connection between The Green Hornet and some historical master criminal. Where's your evidence? The *Sentinel* prints facts, not conjecture."

"But Britt, the *Express* is running with it. I heard it straight from Dan Scully. Rumors are spreading like wildfire in the underworld that Doctor Fang has returned, and that the Harnet and Fang are in league, planning the run the city together. After all, isn't the Harnet's bodyguard supposed to be Oriental? The Harnet probably got him from Fang's ranks."

"No buts. The piece is about the murder of Earl Hayden, period. Rewrite it to stick to the known facts, or I'll have to kill it."

Reid's secretary, Lenore Case, entered the office with the latest batch of paperwork. She wore a stylish shift dress that came just below the knees and showed off her legs to great effect.

"Talk some sense into him, Casey," the grizzled reporter growled on his way out. "If only his father were here to see things run right."

Britt's father, Henry Reid, had died in prison two years earlier after being framed by the syndicate for a crime he didn't commit. The truth was finally known, but too late to save the elder Reid. In the intervening years, Britt had taken over the reins at the *Sentinel* and had come into his own, making a name for himself as an upright and crusading publisher.

Britt shook his head as Axford slammed the door behind him. "He just doesn't get it," he said to Casey.

"Mr. Reid, if you don't mind me saying so, in one sense I think Mike is right."

Britt was very interested in his secretary's response. In fact, Lenore Case intrigued him. He found her intelligent and resourceful, with an impish sense of humor. He wanted to hear what she had to say. "Is that so? Please, do tell."

"Well, Mr. Reid, it's like this. I know you've never quite believed that The Green Hornet is as bad as others make him out to be, but if the *Sentinel* doesn't join in the calls to at least investigate The Hornet's role in the killings, people are going to start asking why."

Britt Reid, of course, knew that he was not behind the nefarious murders, but Casey had a point. He couldn't singlehandedly fight the tide of public opinion, and if he didn't speak up, it might look suspicious.

"I see your point, Miss Case, but such opinions belong on the editorial page, not in a hard news story about a councilman's murder."

"Precisely, Mr. Reid." Lenore Case smiled. "And from a purely business perspective, you know that the competition isn't shying away from such editorializing. Sabrina Bradley over at the *Daily Express* is really playing up the Fang-Hornet rumors. You know she covets the number one spot, and her editorials are playing on fear, creating an even greater atmosphere of terror than already exists. If you wrote your own editorial, you could mention the possible Hornet connection that Mike can't touch in his story, but provide a more balanced perspective than the *Express*."

Britt sighed. He'd been out-maneuvered and he knew it.

"Shall I get my notepad?" Miss Case asked.

Britt grinned. "That, and two steaming mugs of coffee. Pronto."

Casey nodded and went out.

Chinatown, a mile or so in from the Detroit River.

Mike Axford looked up and down Cass Avenue. It was a hot, muggy day, and he fanned himself with his hat.

Near the corner of Cass and Charlotte Street was the Golden Lotus Café. Next to that was the Golden City Club. An eight-sided marker, about ten feet tall with various red-painted Chinese characters, and topped by what looked like a large red Chinese hat, stood down the block from the Café at the corner of Peterboro and Cass. The marker's few signs in English welcomed Mike to Chinatown and advertised antiques. Mike knew that a similar marker was erected a couple blocks away, at the corner of 2nd and Peterboro, denoting the other border of Chinatown.

He took a deep breath, then ambled past the Gold Dollar Show Bar. He stopped for a few moments window-browsing at Sai Woo's Curios, and checked his watch again.

It was time. Mike marched further down the street and entered Chin Tiki's Chinese Restaurant. He took a seat in the corner of the tiny dining room and doffed his fedora. It was the middle of the afternoon and he was the sole customer. Mike tapped his fingers impatiently as he took a gander at the usual trappings: gilt dragons on the walls, hanging lanterns, and Chinese watercolors. Strong sandalwood incense smoke wafted gently from several Buddha-shaped urns placed on the dining tables, and Mike began to relax.

Moments later, a striking Chinese girl slipped through a curtained alcove, bowed, and took Mike's order for tea. She bowed again and left.

A few minutes later, the diminutive waitress returned with Mike's tea. She poured the steaming, reddish liquid into a small cup from a laughing Buddha teapot and began to withdraw.

"Hold on a moment, please, Miss," Mike asked.

The girl stopped and watched Mike silently. She had green eyes, and Mike figured she must have some Western blood far back in her heritage.

"What's your name, please?"

"Isabella, sir," the girl replied.

"Isabella? That's not much of a Chinese name now, is it?"

She shook her head nervously and said nothing.

"Can you help me? I was supposed to meet someone, but there's no one else here. Has anyone been here, or perhaps left a message?"

Isabella looked terrorized. "I am not the one you seek, sir," she said quickly. "Perhaps he will come later." Then she scurried behind the emerald silk curtains before Mike could utter another word.

Can't say I blame her, Mike thought, *everyone in Chinatown's running scared right now.*

He lifted the teacup to his lips and took a sip.

The Buddha incense burners writhed and danced on the tables, and the room spun, and everything went dark.

Drake Matson, copy boy at the *Sentinel*, knocked at the door leading to the suite of Britt Reid's offices. At the call to enter, he crossed the threshold tentatively.

"Well, hello Drake, what can I do for you?" Miss Case asked.

"I have a telegram for Mr. Reid, Miss Case," he said, teenage nervousness evident in his voice. Like all the copy boys, Drake had a crush on Britt Reid's lovely secretary. It wasn't hard to understand why. Lenore Case's auburn hair, exotic brown eyes, and girl-next-door friendliness were an unbeatable combination.

"Thank you, Drake, I'll give it to him." Miss Case held out her hand.

"Well, Miss Case," Drake said, with increasing awkwardness, "it's like this. The telegram came to the City Room and Mr. Gunnigan sent me up with it. I'm to deliver it to Mr. Reid, and no one else."

"Drake, that's fine, I understand. But Mr. Reid is extremely busy, and I am his confidential secretary, after all." Miss Case smiled at Drake and held out her hand. "I promise to take it straight to Mr. Reid. No one else will read it before he does."

Drake thought about it a moment, then handed over the slip of paper.

TO: Britt Reid, Publisher, *Daily Sentinel*
           Sabrina Bradley, Managing Editor, *Daily Express*
Very unhappy with your recent stories and editorials. Stop. Mike Axford captive. Stop. No more stories or editorials on partnership between Doctor Fang and Green Hornet, or Axford pays price. Stop. Signed, Fang and Hornet.

Britt Reid hadn't looked this grim since his father had been wrongfully convicted. He handed the telegram to Casey. She scanned it quickly and handed it back to him when his office line rang.

She picked up the phone, spoke briefly, then said to Britt, "Sabrina Bradley on the line, sir."

"Tell her I'm unavailable. Tell her I don't expect her to cave in to Fang's threats, and the *Sentinel* won't either. That's all."

"That's all? But Mr. Reid, what about Mike—"

"Mike will understand, Casey. I've got a paper to run. Please have my car brought around. I'll be working from home the rest of the day."

Miss Case nodded, passed on the message to Sabrina Bradley, hung up, and left Britt's inner office.

As the door closed behind her, Britt pulled out his gold pocket watch, a Reid family heirloom, and turned the hands to 1:50 on the dial. He pressed the stud at the top of the watch and a miniature antenna sprang out of a hidden aperture. Satisfied that the necessary signal had been delivered, Britt put the watch away, grabbed his coat, and left.

As he passed through the outer office, Miss Case called out, "Good afternoon, Mr. Reid," to his swiftly retreating back.

District Attorney Frank Scanlon leaned back in his office chair, dictating a legal brief. His impeccable gray suit was perfectly pressed. Black horn-rimmed glasses, in conjunction with a slightly receding hairline, gave Scanlon a somewhat academic look which belied his reputation as a fierce advocate for justice.

He paused, took a sip of coffee, and was about to resume when the miniature transistor-receiver embedded in his glasses activated with a signal so low only he could hear it.

Scanlon turned off his Dictaphone, bookmarked his legal research, and grabbed his hat and coat. He picked up the phone and told his secretary, Miss Hewitt, to hold his calls. Then he left his office via the private entrance.

Hayashi Kato began to bow to his opponent, in preparation for their next bout, when he saw the red light blinking unobtrusively in the upper corner of the basement gymnasium in Britt Reid's townhome.

"I regret, Miss Patricia," he said gravely, coming out of his stance, "that I am obliged to cut today's lesson short."

Kato's student smiled slightly. Although only fourteen, she was well-proportioned and a few inches taller than her teacher. Her eyes swirled with pools of gold flecks as she released a shock of bronze-colored hair from the ponytail. "Finally saw the blinking red light, huh?"

"How long—"

"Only thirty seconds. Don't worry, although my father has officially retired, he's still interested in crimefighting and approves of your and Mr. Reid's work. Otherwise, rather than sending me here for training, you'd both be undergoing rehabilitation at his Crime College."

Kato nodded. "I think such conversations are better left between your father and Mr. Reid. I've signaled for your car. It should be here to pick you up in five minutes."

The girl bowed. "Thank you, Mr. Kato. I will look forward to next week's lesson."

"As will I, Miss Patricia. Good day."

Lenore Case pulled over to the curb a few cars down from Britt Reid's townhome. She watched as he expertly slid the white convertible into the garage at number 312 and the door automatically swung down behind him.

She killed the engine and sat. Reid's townhome, tall and narrow, was near downtown, in Alden Park, and sandwiched between other townhouses and shops. It was fronted by pale bricks in a modern style. There were no signs of life, no open windows or stirring curtains.

Five minutes ticked by and still she sat. Should she go knock? If she did, would Britt let her in? Though no one else would have observed the signs of strain in Britt Reid's stoic exterior, she could see through the façade and knew Mike's kidnapping had hit him hard. The last time she'd seen him like this, his father had been on trial. She'd wanted to reach out to him then, and hadn't, leaving the barrier of their professional relationship in place.

She chewed on the tip of her forefinger, ruining a perfect French manicure, and continued to sit, undecided.

That's when Casey spied Frank Scanlon pulling into a parking place on the street near Britt's house. She watched as he slammed the car door shut, looked up and down the street, and strode up to the townhome next to Britt's. She recalled it had been listed as "For Sale" for what seemed like forever. Scanlon unlocked the door and went inside.

What the hell?

Britt Reid pulled the three books slightly out of their slots in the bookcase, and the fireplace slid upward into the ceiling. Simultaneously, a metal platform behind the fireplace descended and steps unfolded. Frank Scanlon stepped off the platform.

Scanlon extended a hand and greeted Britt's valet, Kato, who was decked out in a white jacket and black bow-tie, then firmly shook Britt's hand. The fireplace slid back down in place behind Scanlon.

The three men took seats around the coffee table, and Britt handed the telegram to Scanlon.

"Of course, this has the effect of making The Hornet look guiltier than ever," Scanlon said, handing the slip of paper back to Britt.

"I know that, Frank."

"What do you want me to do?"

"Buy The Hornet some time to get to the bottom of this."

Scanlon took off his glasses. "That won't be easy, Britt. Fang, whoever he is, has got this set up against you pretty well. He's already framed you for the murders of three councilmen: Martin Powell, Alan Burke, and now Earl Hayden. If Fang keeps up this pace, planting evidence and rumors against you, the calls for a citywide manhunt will be beyond my control. Capture and exposure will become inevitable."

"I understand, Frank, but just try to stave off that manhunt as long as you can."

"Will do. What's Fang's goal in all this?"

Britt shrugged. "Draw out The Hornet, then coerce him into a partnership? With the evidence he's manufactured thus far, The Hornet would have little choice in the matter. Disagree, and Fang will continue to frame him, planting evidence and fanning rumors. Agree, and they can control and manipulate the city's political leaders together. That's just a guess, of course."

"What's The Green Hornet's next move?"

Britt took a moment to answer. He stared at the painting hanging next to the fireplace. It depicted his ancestor atop a magnificent white stallion, six-guns drawn, the brim of the white cowboy hat pulled low and masking the eyes.

Then he said, with resolve, "The last entry in Axford's appointment book showed he was meeting a contact at the Chin Tiki in Chinatown. We'll pay a little visit."

"Keep me updated." Scanlon stood and shook Britt's hand again. "And be careful, Britt, you're playing with fire this time."

"I will, thanks for your help, Frank."

The older man nodded curtly, then departed through the fireplace, which had opened again on Kato's manipulation of the books. Scanlon had a choice of exit routes. One would take him back through the tunnel from which he had come. It had a hidden egress in the empty townhouse next door, which was also secretly owned by Britt. However, this time Scanlon choose the other exit, which would deposit him in the alley behind Britt's townhouse. He'd circle the block to retrieve his car.

As the D.A. departed, Britt looked at Kato. "Please get the Beauty ready. Let's pay a little visit to Chinatown."

Casey was getting restless, sitting in her car for over an hour.

Then she saw Scanlon walk around the corner, get in his Chrysler, and drive away. It was odd, very odd, that he hadn't come out of the empty house which he'd entered an hour earlier. He must have exited from a back door and walked around the block. His behavior was furtive. Was he visiting a woman?

Dusk was settling over the city. She couldn't sit here into the night.

Casey gathered her nerve and got out of the car. She strode up to Britt's front door and rang the bell.

And rang, and rang.

She was alternately puzzled and miffed that neither Britt nor Kato answered the door. They must be at home. She'd been watching the house and no one had left.

Growing even angrier, Casey marched back to her car and got in. She slammed the door, gunned the motor, and took off.

"Let's roll, Kato."

The false back wall of Britt Reid's garage elevated and the Beauty thrust forward into the enclosed backyard patio area of his townhome. The car accelerated straight at the back brick wall. Tiny cameras embedded in the other side of the wall transmitted to small television screens set in the front dashboard and the control panel in the back seat.

All was clear.

The brick wall split in two, each side moving horizontally away from the other. The Beauty sped into the alleyway behind Britt's townhome, and the two sides of the wall came back together, reuniting the two lovers on the large advertisement covering the side of the wall facing the alley: "Kissin' Candy Mints. How Sweet They Are."

The Black Beauty raced toward Chinatown.

The Green Hornet and Kato had decided to forgo guile and burst through the front entrance at Chin Tiki's, startling the restaurant's few customers.

"Everyone stay quiet and seated, and no one will get hurt. Our business is with the manager." The Hornet brandished his gas gun for emphasis.

At the commotion, the back curtains parted and a stunning Chinese girl came out, decked out in traditional Chinese silks and slippers. She bowed calmly and respectfully to The Hornet and Kato, and then beckoned them into the back.

The two followed her, warily, through the tiny kitchen. The three made an odd procession, but the two Chinese cooks, hot and sweaty in the enclosed space, studiously ignored them. She led The Hornet and his bodyguard into a storeroom at the back of the restaurant and closed the door.

Kato scanned the room for traps or other occupants, while The Hornet spoke.

"That's far enough. You seem to be expecting us."

"We are honored by your presence, Green Hornet."

"'We'? We're not going any further until you explain."

"Then you will go no further, and you will learn nothing more." The girl bowed politely again. "Please excuse me. And please leave by the back alley. You've already disturbed our customers enough."

She made to leave, daintily gathering up the red silks of her gown in her hands so as not to dirty them on the dust-covered floor. The Hornet and Kato made eye contact. They functioned so well as a team that no words were required, and together they decided.

"All right," The Hornet said, "we'll play it your way. Do you at least have a name?"

The girl looked at him with an odd smile. "Of course I have a name. You may call me Madame Isabella."

She went to a small hanging Chinese lantern and tugged the cord. In response, a stack of boxes in the corner of the dingy storeroom moved aside, revealing a dark stone stairwell cut into the ground.

She led the way and the two crimefighters cautiously followed. The boxes slid back into place above them.

They continued to descend, the stairway doubling back and forth. The air became progressively cooler and more damp. When the tunnels finally leveled out, Britt estimated they were four to five stories underground.

They followed Madame Isabella into a narrow tunnel cut into the stone. Dim light came from dragon-mouthed braziers mounted in the walls at infrequent intervals. Finally they entered a larger domed chamber that was better lit. Orange and yellow shadows flickered and the scent of jasmine permeated the air.

The girl walked to one end of the hollow and tugged on a brazier. The spot of ground she stood upon began to rise until she was about six feet above The Hornet and Kato.

"This," Isabella said, "is where we part ways for now. When you awake, I assure you you'll be entirely unharmed, but Doctor Fang, of course, cannot allow you to know the precise path to his location."

The room turned a deeper shade of orange as the flames in the wall braziers extinguished and a soft, unearthly light emanated from them.

The Green Hornet and Kato were immediately hit with a profound drowsiness. "Visors," The Hornet clipped out, before they lost consciousness altogether. A quick touch to each of their masks caused green-tinged translucent shades to slide over the eye-slits, and both men rapidly recovered. The strange orange light must have been intended to somehow stimulate the brain's sleep center.

"Unacceptable," The Green Hornet called to the girl above them. "We cannot, of course, allow Doctor Fang to unmask us while we're unconscious."

Madame Isabella shook her head ruefully. "Too bad, Green Hornet. This calls for more conventional methods." Her platform began to rise again, delivering her through an aperture in the cavern's ceiling, and taking her from their sight.

Around them, six panels in the grotto walls slid upward, each revealing a brown-skinned man of Eastern descent. All wore loincloths and tightly wound turbans. They were poised and ready for combat.

Kato leaped in a flash, flying through the air with a kick that connected soundly with one man's jaw, rendering him unconscious. He landed, pivoted on one foot, and was in the air again like a ballet dancer, removing a second opponent with a hard kick to the gut. As the man doubled over in pain, Kato dispatched him with a fast chop to the back of the neck.

The Hornet, in the meantime, had telescoped out his Sting and held it in two hands, blocking a swinging scimitar. He kicked the sword out of the dacoit's grip and drove a hammer-fist to the side of the head, laying his opponent out cold.

Another challenger came at him from behind, and The Hornet ducked as the sword cut a wide swath where he'd been standing. Before the man regrouped, The Hornet sprang up and smashed the man in the face with a double-fisted punch, the Sting still held in one fist.

In the interim Kato had rendered a fifth man almost senseless with a blur of flying fists, and now held their final opponent pinned to the ground, clutching him by the neck.

The Green Hornet came over, crouched down next to Kato, and prepared to question their captive. At the sound of padding feet, The Hornet and Kato turned to see the other five men disappearing back into the tunnels from which they'd come, false cavern walls sliding back into place.

Turning their attention back to their prisoner, they heard a crunching sound. The man's eyes went white as they rolled back up into his head, and a bubbly froth spilled out of his mouth, covering his suddenly blue lips.

He jerked a little in Kato's hands and died.

Kato released his grip.

"Quite a nice group of bodyguards Madame Isabella has down here," The Hornet said. "And loyal enough to commit suicide."

Kato nodded. "Burmese dacoits. A warrior sect, and absolutely devoted to any cause they join." He paused, then asked, "What now?"

"Time to call it a night, I think. Let's find a way out of here."

"Right." Kato pulled a small device of his own design from an inner pocket. He clicked a button and an antenna extended while a small view screen activated. The sonar monitor displayed a myriad of underground tunnels and warrens, and Britt wondered just how extensive was this underground complex? Further exploration was called for, but not tonight.

Using the sonar scanner, Kato led them upward through the channels and caverns, finally arriving at a small room with a wooden trapdoor in the ceiling. Kato jumped up, caught the latch, and the door swung down, along with a ladder.

The men climbed up and closed the trap behind them. It fit seamlessly into a wooden floor and was invisible unless one knew it was there.

They were in a low, narrow corridor. A cone of light cast from a lone bulb in the ceiling split the darkness. Along the passageway were several doors marked with cheaply gilt stars. Dance hall music came faintly from somewhere above them.

"Nice masks."

The Hornet and Kato whirled, confronting a woman in a burlesque costume.

"I said," came the distinctly male voice, "nice masks." They were obviously in the bowels of the Gold Dollar Show Bar.

"Thanks," The Hornet said. "What's the fastest way out?"

The performer pointed behind them. "Alley door's that way."

"Thanks."

The Green Hornet and Kato exited into the alley, turned onto Cass Avenue, and walked past the Show Bar's front entrance. They passed Sai Woo's Curios, then darted across the darkness of Cass Park, known to the locals as Mandarin Park. From there they cut through Half Moon Alley, racing past the back entrance of Mao Tze's store.

When they arrived at the Black Beauty, the motor was already purring, as if the car were a living machine that had been waiting for them.

The Green Hornet sighed.

"Home, Kato."

Britt Reid slapped the paper down on his desk.

"Well, that's that." His second editorial decrying Doctor Fang's activities had just gone to print. Despite Fang's warning, the editorial exposed Fang's kidnapping of Mike Axford.

Lenore Case rested a hand on her boss' shoulder. "Mike will understand, Mr. Reid. You can't knuckle under to these threats, and compromise the journalistic integrity of the *Sentinel*."

"I know, Miss Case. Thank you." He patted her hand lightly, then stood up.

"Mr. Reid," Casey began tentatively, "I'm worried about you."

At Britt's raised eyebrows and a slight gesture, she continued. "I followed you home last night to speak with you—"

The floor-to-ceiling plate glass window of Reid's office exploded inward in a shower of glass, which was remarkable since his office was on the 28th floor of the city's latest modernistic skyscraper. Scaling the building would have been well-nigh impossible, although of course the same was said of the late Earl Hayden's residence.

In this case, though, it was very clear how the intruder arrived, crouched amidst the shards of glass littering the plush carpet in Britt Reid's office.

The dacoit wore a harness attached to a rope which trailed out the window and curved upward. The sound of rotor blades and the whipping wind indicated a helicopter hovering just out of Britt's line of sight.

In an instant, the intruder whipped a scimitar from a scabbard on his back and pressed it against Casey's throat, the other arm tight around her neck.

She screamed and tore at the man's arm, but he only tightened his grip.

"Don't struggle, Casey!" Britt yelled.

"Sound advice, Mr. Reid," a voice boomed from a loudspeaker on the copter floating outside. Britt wondered how the speaker had heard him. Then he realized the henchman with the long curving blade at Casey's throat must be miked.

The dacoit swiftly sheathed his sword and pulled a small transparent container from the folds of his robes, thrusting it out aggressively toward Britt.

The jar contained a swarm of Asian giant hornets.

Green hornets.

"Do not interfere, Mr. Reid," the voice thundered from outside, "or face a very painful death. Now. Listen carefully. I know that Miss Case is your personal secretary. She was followed to your home last night. I make no moral judgment about your relationship with her. I care not one way or the other. But you must care for her. So understand this. Miss Case will not be harmed—unless you feel the need to further editorialize. Now, back up to the door of your office and stand there."

Britt did as instructed.

"Very good."

The interloper gripped Casey tight about the waist. The rope connected to his harness went taut, and suddenly the dacoit and Casey flew backward through the window, Casey's screams diminishing as she receded.

Britt lunged forward, catching a glimpse of the copter hovering outside, but as the dacoit crossed the threshold of the destroyed window, he lobbed the jar of hornets against the wall, smashing it.

Britt turned and dived for his office door, slamming it behind him and shutting the buzzing death-swarm on the other side. He ripped off his suit jacket and stuffed it against the narrow opening under the door, just in case.

Breathing hard, he turned and saw Drake Matson and a junior reporter, Pat Allen, staring at him wide-eyed.

"Holy cow, Mr. Reid!" the boy shouted.

Britt knelt and caught the boy tightly in his arms. "Don't go in there, Drake. Don't go in there."

He shook his head to himself, grim fury etching his features.

The copter had been glossy black all over, with midnight green running lights, search lamps, and rotors.

A flying arsenal to complement The Green Hornet's Black Beauty.

Forty minutes later, Doctor Fang's statement hit the wires and news services, bragging that he and The Green Hornet had kidnapped Lenore Case in response to Britt Reid's editorial. Perhaps now the publishers and owners of the city's papers and television news stations would learn their place and refrain from any further persecution of Fang and The Hornet.

If not...then Mike Axford and Lenore Case would die horribly, stung to death by The Green Hornet's Asian giant hornets.

The Black Beauty rolled through deepest night. Pedestrians out late noticed only an ominous buzzing before the infamous car was upon them and past, headlamps showing the faintest green glow.

Passing streetlamps caused a bizarre flickering effect across the immobile mask worn by the man in the back seat of the racing vehicle.

The portable telephone buzzed, and The Green Hornet reached over his shoulder to pick up the handset.

"Yes."

"I can't do much more." Neither party identified himself, but The Hornet knew that the person who spoke was Frank Scanlon, voice altered by a scrambler Kato had invented. On the other end of the line, Scanlon heard a similarly altered voice.

"I know."

"Fang has succeeded at laying more blame at your feet."

"Yes."

"What's your plan?"

"Find Axford and Casey," The Hornet said. "Eliminate Fang's threat."

"That will end the threat against the city's political machine. But you also need evidence that Fang has been solely responsible for all this. Otherwise the police will mobilize in such numbers that you'll never avoid capture; you'll have to give all this up."

"I know."

"Then beware. They're already out in force tonight."

"I understand," The Hornet said, and hung up. "Go to silent running," he instructed Kato.

As if in response to Scanlon's warning, a cop car fell in behind them, sirens blaring, spotlight blazing on the Beauty's cryptic license plate, V194.

In the front seat, Kato tapped the accelerator and the over-powered engine responded. It wouldn't be long before more patrol cars joined the chase and the Beauty was trapped.

Their plan had been to return to the Gold Dollar Show Bar and re-enter the underground warrens via the secret trapdoor. In the battle last night, the dacoits had seemingly come from nowhere. There must be more secret entrances and tunnels, and the idea was to find the way to Fang's secret headquarters using the sonar scanner.

The police chase changed all that.

As they headed for Chinatown, Britt tuned into the police scanner frequency and learned that another cruiser was on its way, aiming to cut them off at Cass and Temple Street.

"Turn left on Ledyard," The Green Hornet ordered.

"Boss, that's the wrong way on a one-way street."

"I know."

Kato swung the Beauty hard and the back end slung around. The car screamed as the special tires gave way and then re-gripped the asphalt, caught, and the vehicle thrust forward. The revolutionary suspension Kato had designed gave the Beauty performance and handling unexpected in an automobile so large and heavy. The patrol car trailing them was unable to make the turn and blazed past Ledyard, braking hard to make a U-turn and resume the pursuit.

"Hard right on 2nd Avenue—"

Kato nodded in satisfaction. Another wrong way. "Then onto 2nd, circle the Park, and right onto Temple?"

"You read my mind."

Kato spun the wheel again and the Beauty responded, racing down Temple Street with Mandarin Park on their right. At this point the first police cruiser was only now turning from Ledyard onto 2nd, attempting to catch up.

The second police cruiser had been lured away from its waiting spot at Cass and Temple and had fallen in far behind the first two cars. If it had stayed put, The Hornet and Kato would be approaching it now, from Temple Street.

The Black Beauty sped by the huge gothic structure of the Detroit Masonic Temple on the left. Knowing from the police scanner that the second patrol car had given up its position, Britt ordered Kato to make a hard left into a narrow alleyway dividing the Masonic Temple complex.

Kato braked to a swift halt. The car was still on silent running so that no others could hear the engine.

"Smoke," The Green Hornet instructed.

Kato flipped a switch on the control panel, and an inky black smoke poured forth from the tailpipe, blending the alley entrance with the rest of the deep night and camouflaging the Beauty.

Kato threw the car in reverse, in preparation for a quick escape after the cop cars passed. As he did so, however, a garage door sized panel in the Temple wall slid in and upward.

"Take it Kato, fast," The Green Hornet said.

"Boss, it's a trap."

"Yes. But the cops know we're in Chinatown tonight and they'll be sure to cordon off the area. Our original plan to get to the Gold Dollar is scratched. Casey and Axford are running out of time. We need to ditch the cops and get to Fang. This is the most direct path."

Kato shrugged and yanked the wheel, and the Beauty tore into the secret opening. The panel slid shut and the patrol cars raced past, none the wiser.

Kato navigated down a spiral driveway that seemed to take them even deeper underground than they had been last night. The vehicle's infra-green headlamps were activated. Surely their enemy had cameras in the corkscrew tunnel, but there was no point in providing the watchers with extra light to track their progress.

Finally the curving drive ended in a circular stone chamber. The cavern appeared to be a dead end. The Hornet and Kato exited the car in search of hidden tunnel entrances, when the half of the circular floor upon which they stood began to sink.

They watched the Beauty rise above their eye level and disappear from sight. Kato pressed a button on his watch which ensured their rolling arsenal was remotely armed and protected against any intruders.

The elevator platform finally slowed and came to a halt in another stone chamber, where The Hornet and Kato were greeted by three men of East Indian extraction. The men were robed and wore elaborate moustaches. One of them suffered from gigantism, standing almost eight feet tall. The Hornet recognized them as Thuggee, or Phansigars, Indian assassins supposedly wiped out by the British in the last century.

This time, however, the men did not attack, but beckoned the two masked men to follow.

The Hornet and Kato exchanged glances, then fell in behind the men. In for a penny...

After several more tunnels, they arrived at a set of massive wooden doors, framed with emerald silks and bookended with two massive Siamese cat shaped braziers, each of the cat's eyes alight with flames. Two dacoits stood guard.

The doors swung open automatically, and the dacoits stood aside, gesturing the two newcomers to enter. The Hornet and Kato did so, and the doors closed behind them with a whisper.

The underground den was lavishly furnished with velvet settees, oversized silk-embroidered pillows, and Persian rugs. Candles hung from brass lanterns. Cloying incense filled the room. Gilt-edges screens set off different areas of the chamber.

Inset in one wall was a massive computer console with television monitor screens, and microphones. Three Chinese men, heads shaven, sat abreast wearing headsets with earphones. Each was assigned a station consisting of one screen, console, and mike.

On one screen was the Black Beauty in the chamber where they had left it. That image rotated with the dining room of the Chin Tiki restaurant. The next screen displayed the outside of the *Daily Sentinel* building at One Woodward Avenue, circling to show the Art Deco Guardian Building and the aerial bridge connecting the two structures. The view then shifted to the exterior of police headquarters. The third screen showed Mike Axford lying on a cot in a dark cubicle, looking dejected. It alternated with a display of Casey in her own cell, sitting on a thin mattress and staring at the ceiling.

The Green Hornet and Kato displayed no emotion. They were too professional, and too ensconced in their criminal personas, for that. But The Hornet was secretly elated that his friends were unharmed, and he was sure Kato was as well.

This was marred, however, by sobering thoughts which had been growing since events involving Fang had begun to unfold: just how extensive was the mastermind's organization, anyway? Dacoits and Thugs were in its employ. It was headquartered in a secret underground complex of immense proportions. It had vast technological resources at its disposal, as evidenced by the helicopter and advanced surveillance equipment. Britt wondered if it could be on the order of SPECTRE, which a few years back had used two hijacked nuclear bombs to hold the world hostage to the tune of a hundred million pounds.

Perhaps it *was* a revived SPECTRE, although Britt couldn't imagine what would bring such an outfit to Detroit—other than the automobile industry, the center of American manufacturing and production.

"Well, what do you think?"

The men whirled.

Through a semi-transparent dressing screen, they saw the silhouette of a nude woman draping a robe around her well-proportioned figure and stepping into high-heeled slippers.

The Chinese girl from last night slunk out from behind the screen and stood before them.

Tonight she was dressed much less demurely. An emerald gown of the best Chinese silks clung to every curve. The negligee was cut low and the silky material met in a V at her navel, exposing a liberal amount of cleavage and leaving nothing to the imagination. The gown had equally generous slits up to the waist, displaying perfect legs as the girl—the woman—padded toward them.

Her hair was cut in a straight bang across her forehead. The rest of the silky black hair, held in place by an ornate headband topped by a jade orchid, spilled across her shoulders and down her back.

The woman halted in front of them and smiled. There was a wicked gleam in her green eyes.

"Madame Isabella," The Hornet said.

"Isabella?" the Chinese woman laughed.

"We're here," The Hornet replied. "No more games. When do we meet Doctor Fang?"

"When do you meet Doctor Fang? When?" She laughed again. "My poor, poor dear. You just met her."

Doctor Fang and The Green Hornet reclined on oversized pillows on a purple velvet settee, bathing in the orange glow of burnt embers from the small firepot at their feet.

She pulled away from a deep kiss and held his face between her delicate hands. Her eyes glittered with a magnetic energy. "Is there anything for which you take off the mask?"

"Just one thing," The Hornet said.

Doctor Fang traced one long scarlet nail down his cheek along the border of his mask. "Will I find out some time?"

"Perhaps."

"Not now?" she pouted.

"Not now."

She pulled back a little further and cinched up her robe, covering her breasts. Matching The Hornet's more businesslike tone, she said, "I am so glad you've seen things my way."

"Don't get me wrong. Your frame-up job has angered me."

"And yet...?"

"I make a habit of cutting myself in on others' rackets. Those tactics have been turned against me. Whoever's smart enough to do that intrigues me."

"Is intrigue enough to solidify our partnership?"

"Business is business and I'm a pragmatist. You've been very... persuasive."

"I was taught well," she responded.

"By whom?"

"Those who raised me."

"That's not much of an answer," The Hornet said.

"They were members of a larger organization to which my late father belonged."

Earlier in the evening, Doctor Fang had insisted on speaking to The

Hornet privately, and he had agreed. Upon her assurances Kato would not be harmed, The Hornet had instructed him to accompany her men.

Now he was probing, searching for a crack in her defenses.

"A tong?" he asked.

She shook her head in disdain. "Tongs are mere street gangs in comparison. Do I—*we*—wish to rule a street, a neighborhood? Of course not. You and I are better than that. We shall rule the city, control its industry, and extend our influence from there."

"This is my city," The Hornet replied. "Many have crossed me; some have even lived to regret it. Others...did not. You'd do well to remember that."

Doctor Fang nodded with a slight smile, and he sensed a deep ruthlessness within her. "Yes, I'll remember," she said, her voice like honey. "Partners?"

"Partners," The Hornet responded after a pause, as if still thinking it over.

"There must be no secrets among partners. You must unmask," Doctor Fang said.

"Of course. But later...when we have complete privacy." He nodded toward the men at the far end of the chamber sitting at the monitor screens. "First, I want to see that my aide is unharmed, and bring him up to speed on our alliance."

Doctor Fang snapped her fingers, and a hulking East Indian appeared from the shadows. Britt recognized him as one of the three Phansigars who escorted him and Kato earlier.

"This is Behram," she said.

The man glared at The Hornet and said nothing.

"Behram," she ordered, "escort Mr. Hornet to his assistant and allow them to confer privately for ten minutes. Then bring them back here."

Doctor Fang glided over to the computer bank at the opposite end of her den. She stood behind the workers manning the television monitors. The men at the screens did not turn or acknowledge her presence. To do so unless spoken to first, or to raise an alarm, meant instant death.

She observed the monitor screens as Behram and The Hornet navigated the warrens. The two passed out of site of one camera and the screen switched to another, and then another, keeping The Hornet under constant surveillance.

She watched Behram and The Hornet pass through the dungeon. The gigantic oak doors had small cutout windows with iron bars. Mike Axford was in a cell around the corner and couldn't see The Hornet's passage.

But the path Behram took led them right past Lenore Case's cell. Doctor Fang saw Britt Reid's secretary press her face against the bars, gripping them in supplication.

Doctor Fang nodded with satisfaction as The Green Hornet strode by her cell door, ignoring her pleas for release.

The Hornet must know he was under observation. Still, he had passed the test, at least provisionally.

She continued to watch as Behram and The Hornet arrived at Kato's holding room. The Thug dismissed Kato's guards and left the two masked men alone, as his mistress had instructed.

Doctor Fang listened as The Green Hornet explained the situation.

Of course the two men understood they were being watched on Fang's camera system. Nonetheless, she could detect nothing untoward in their demeanor as The Hornet explained their new partnership to his bodyguard. The man did not question his chief, and she grew more satisfied. The Hornet's aide knew his place was to obey orders.

The Council would be pleased.

The Green Hornet's fingers tapped out a nervous tattoo as he described the alliance with Doctor Fang.

The Hornet's fingers, hidden from the camera which must be concealed in the room's sole ornament, a laughing Buddha statue, told Kato a different story.

Casey was being held in a cell about two minutes away. Take the tunnel to the left and three right turns. Presumably Axford was close by.

A power substation—albeit a very strange one and clearly not built by the city utility company—was four tunnels further back, near Fang's den. The Hornet had glimpsed it through a crevice in the rock wall. The underground complex was apparently drawing on a power source, perhaps the Masonic Temple's independent power plant.

Kato responded, also tapping, with a suggestion that a powerful enough jolt from The Hornet's Sting, delivered through the camera watching them, might cause a feedback loop which would short out the whole system.

The plan, then, was straightforward. Disable Fang's surveillance system. Immobilize the guards outside Kato's holding room. Rescue Casey and Axford. Destroy the power sub-station and hopefully bring Fang's operation to a halt. Capture Fang.

The Green Hornet whipped the Hornet Sting from the sheath on the inside of his left forearm. The Sting itself had a very narrow circumference.

This fact, in conjunction with the soft padding of the sheath, was enough to cause Fang's men to miss it in their search, although they had located and confiscated his gas gun.

He extended the Sting with a flick of the wrist, and set it to the highest power level. He aimed it at the hollowed eyes of the laughing Buddha statue and activated the switch. A high-pitched whine filled the space, accompanied by a brief but blinding light.

The Buddha's head exploded.

In Doctor Fang's den, the television monitors flickered and went dark.

Enraged, Fang circled the room like a trapped feline and screamed, spittle flying from her mouth.

She took a deep breath and stalked back towards the dark monitors.

"Mr. Hsu, come here."

A small man in a technician's coverall came and stood before her, shaking.

In a flash, she whipped a small *keris*, an asymmetrical dagger, from its scabbard on her inner thigh and ripped it across Hsu's throat. Blood splattered her face, hair, and torso. She licked her lips, reveling in the taste, as Hsu collapsed and bled out over the Persian rugs. She massaged the dead man's blood into her abdomen and breasts, and felt a pop and a wave of warmth within her.

Calmed by the violence, and the pleasurable release, she ordered the rest of the men sitting at the now useless television monitors to get after The Hornet and his bodyguard.

She went to another corner of the cavern and activated a device which resembled a sophisticated radio apparatus. She spoke into a microphone. Her voice was a sibilant hiss.

"Huan Tsung Chao, come in. Come in. Connect me with Shan Ming Fu."

Kato slammed the door outward, right into the giant Phansigar's face.

Blood blossomed from Behram's nose in a geyser, which didn't stop him from twisting his *rumāl* head scarf—used by Thuggee as a noose—and attempting to swing it around Kato's neck to strangle him.

Kato ducked the garrote and jack-hammered a hardened fist into the man's gut. Behram doubled over and Kato kicked out, his black boot connecting sharply with the Thuggee's chin.

The Hornet, meantime, had removed his miniature backup gas gun from his heel and dispatched Kato's former guards.

He turned to find that Behram had turned the tables on Kato, who was on his knees, tearing at the *rumāl* wrapped around his neck. The Thuggee stood over and behind Kato, tightening his grasp.

The Hornet couldn't use his gas gun without also knocking out Kato. He adjusted the Sting to the lowest setting to deliver a stunning blast. Using the Sting on humans was risky, but necessary in this case. He aimed at Kato's adversary and pulled the trigger.

And was shocked when it barely fazed the giant Indian.

The blast did cause, however, a momentary lapse in Behram's grip, providing the brief respite Kato needed.

The Hornet's bodyguard used his enemy's weight and size against him, tossing him over his shoulder. Kato pounced forward, and landed a quick one-two punch, finally rendering his foe unconscious. He pulled the deadly yellow scarf from around his neck and tossed it aside. The two crimefighters took off at a dead run for the dungeon.

Outside Mike Axford's cell, The Green Hornet aimed his gas gun through the window and pulled the trigger.

He let a moment pass for the gas to dissipate, then risked a glance in through the iron bars to confirm Axford was out. He was.

The Hornet activated the Sting and disintegrated the lock. Kato rushed in and hefted the Irishman over his shoulder in a fireman's carry.

The two masked men rounded the corner. Casey's face was pressed against the metal bars, roused by the commotion, when The Green Hornet stepped into her field of view.

"What's—"

He brandished the Sting. "Please step away from the door and shield your face," he said politely.

She did as instructed and he blasted the cell door open.

Casey rushed out and confronted him.

"The Green Hornet," she breathed.

"Who are you?" The Hornet asked. He did his best to disguise his voice, as he always did when meeting those he knew well as Britt Reid.

"Lenore Case. Britt Reid's secretary."

"I see. Miss Case, please accompany my man here." He gestured at Kato. "He'll escort you out and to safety."

"What about you?" she asked.

"I won't be far behind. I have a few things to clean up around here first."

"Not a chance," Casey protested. "I'm sticking with you."

"Why?"

"He's got his hands full carrying Mike Axford, whom you conveniently gassed. I assume you didn't gas me because he can't carry two." Casey crossed her arms. "Now you're stuck with me."

"Miss Case, please—"

Casey stepped forward and got up in his face. "I'll stick with you, thank you, and there's not much you can do about it. You're wasting time."

The Hornet glanced at Kato, who only shrugged. No help there.

He waved Kato on and the bodyguard dashed off at a fast trot, carrying Axford. Then The Hornet gestured for Casey to come with him.

They sprinted for the power sub-station he had seen earlier. Along the way they were confronted by a few more dacoits, whom he easily dispatched with the gas gun. One last dacoit flashed around a corner and The Hornet slugged him with a vicious uppercut that left the man's jaw at a nasty angle.

The Hornet knew, however, that although Fang's guards must be having some trouble tracking them due to the destruction of the surveillance system, the respite wouldn't last. Doctor Fang's men would recover from their temporary disarray and converge on them.

They needed to act quickly.

They reached the crevice in the rock tunnel and peered through it at the power station. Then he ordered her to stand aside and shield her eyes. He aimed the Hornet Sting once more.

The edges of the gap in the rock glowed, and expanded. Bits and shards of stone flew in all directions until the opening was wide enough to accommodate them.

They stepped through, taking care not to touch the super-hot borders of the gap in the rock wall, and alighted on a vast metal grilled catwalk which ringed the upper circumference of a gigantic hollow.

Below them stood several buildings resembling concrete bunkers. Pipes and power conduits ran in a metallic spider web around the buildings and the cavern walls.

On a low platform he saw the helicopter version of the Black Beauty. Presumably the platform would rise into the ceiling and give forth somewhere above ground, similar to the large elevator which had delivered him and Kato deep into the bowels beneath Chinatown.

The centerpiece of the complex was a colossal transparent cylinder which extended from the roof of the center building up to and into the ceiling of the cave. Fluorescent green and yellow gases sparked and swirled inside the tube, throbbing with lambent energy.

Workers below, in hard hats and jumpsuits, were pointing up at The

Hornet and Casey, raising the alarm. Behind them, in the tunnel from which they had just exited, the sounds of running feet indicated the approach of more of Doctor Fang's guards.

The Hornet grabbed Casey's elbow and guided her about twenty feet along the catwalk. He stopped, turned back, and blasted the area of the catwalk on which they'd just been standing into smithereens.

No way Fang's dacoits could get to them through the gap in the tunnel wall now.

A klaxon sounded and the men below took up machine guns, spattering gunfire at The Hornet and Casey. He shoved her down in the corner of the catwalk, out of the line of fire, and crawled toward the edge.

Rather than bring any of his arsenal to bear against the men below, however, he aimed the Hornet Sting at the pulsating cylinder of energized gases. He'd never seen anything like it, and deduced it must have special significance to the operation of the power station.

He was right.

Under the Sting's assault, the tube fractured, leaking out gases which, heavier than air, rolled down the sides and across the sub-station floor like a flood of seawater through a broken levy.

The men threw down their weapons and ran for their lives. The Hornet heard roiling explosions inside the concrete buildings, and the lights flickered and dimmed.

He turned back to Casey, elated at his bit of good luck in so quickly putting the power plant out of commission.

Doctor Fang held his secretary from behind. A dagger which The Hornet recognized as a *keris* was pressed against Casey's throat, drawing a bead of blood.

Faster than thought, The Hornet whipped out his gas gun and fired at the two women.

Casey gasped out "Britt," and then fell forward unconscious, while Doctor Fang, surprised by her captive's sudden deadweight, accidentally let the other woman slip to the ground.

The Green Hornet was stock still at the double shock: Casey uttering his name, and Doctor Fang unaffected by the gas.

He came out of it and dove at Fang, wrestling her to the ground. She kneed him in the stomach and he doubled up with a *woosh*, rolling toward the catwalk's edge. He scrambled to his feet as she lunged toward him, dagger outthrust, and managed to grab her wrist before the deadly blade gutted him. Fang kicked at him and clawed with her free hand while they struggled back and forth for the *keris*, until finally his greater weight and strength overcame her and they fell back to the catwalk floor.

He held her pinned down, face above hers, and smelled the iron scent of the blood coating her skin and soaking her robes. He looked down.

The *keris* was buried, up to the hilt, in her abdomen.

She reached up, pulled his mouth down toward her red lips, and kissed him, passionately. He pulled away.

"You will serve the Council of Seven yet, Green Hornet. Or as I've just learned, Britt Reid. The *Si-Fan* will not allow you to turn away from them so easily. And the Doctor is accustomed to getting his way."

"The Doctor? Who do you mean? I thought you were a doctor? Or a scientist, to create all this?" he asked, indicating the immense underground headquarters and power plant.

"I am as nothing compared to *him*."

"Who is *he*?" The Hornet demanded.

"*He* has been known by many names," she whispered. "Shan Ming Fu, Doctor Natas, Hanoi Shan, Li Chang Yen, it matters not. He is a genius of the highest order, a scientist and a medical doctor. You Westerners will yet shake with fear of the legions at his command."

"Did he create the killer hornets?"

"Of course..." Her voice was fading.

"And designed this underground complex and power converter? And an antidote to my gas?"

"Yes. And devised the scheme to encourage you to join us. *He* wishes to expand his power base in this city, with you as his local representative. And he will, one way or another."

"Why me? Why not just try to eliminate me?" The Hornet asked.

"You effectively control the city's underworld—or could, if you just went a few steps further. He will control you, and thus the city, its industry, and the workers. Beyond that, it is not for us to question the desires of the Great One."

The Hornet wondered how much the mysterious Doctor knew about him, or thought he knew. But there wasn't much time—the light in her eyes was rapidly dwindling—and instead he asked: "What about the original Doctor Fang?"

"He served Shan Ming Fu as well," said Fang's daughter.

"But that was thirty years ago!" The Hornet said.

"Indeed it was. The Doctor will still lead the Council in another thirty years, and more, until long after you and I are dust." Fang sighed and looked almost beatific, at peace with her failure and her fate.

The sour stench of blood pumping from her stomach was sickening.

"Doctor Fang, where is Shan Ming Fu?"

It was too late. Bloody froth foamed from her cold purple lips. "Shan

Ming Fu," she gasped. "Grandfather..."

Doctor Fang was dead.

The Green Hornet took off, hoisting Casey over his shoulder, as the power sub-station went up in flames. He imagined Kato would want to get a look at the strange power converter, but that was a thought for the future. If they survived, perhaps they could return and investigate the remains of Doctor Shan Ming Fu's advanced technology.

For now, though, it was a race through the corridors and tunnels, finally leaving the reverberating destruction behind.

Every so often The Hornet stopped to utilize Kato's sonar scanner, then kept going. In thirty minutes of trudging uphill through the dank warrens, he never encountered any more of Fang's men. They must have been under orders to evacuate the complex in certain circumstances.

He finally came upon a set of tunnels that looked familiar, leading to the exit below the Gold Dollar Show Bar, only to find the way blocked by rubble and debris. The whole place was starting to come down.

He turned and raced back to an intersection, checked the scanner and saw another potential egress. He pulled out the pocket watch communicator and tried it.

"Kato, come in. Kato."

Was there too much rock between The Hornet's location and the surface, blocking communication? Or had his friend not made it out?

He put the thought aside and plowed onward and upward, finally arriving at a claustrophobic storeroom with a trapdoor in the ceiling. It was similar to the arrangement at the Gold Dollar. He pulled down the ladder and somehow got Casey up it. He rolled her away from the trapdoor, flung the heavy door shut, and collapsed in exhaustion, chest heaving.

The Green Hornet was in excellent shape, or at least he had thought he was before this escapade. When this was all over, he'd institute an even more vigorous training and exercise regimen with Kato.

Kato...

A mammoth underground explosion rocked like an earthquake. The walls shimmied and shook. He scooped up Casey again and raced past shelves of knick-knacks and bric-à-brac in a darkened store. He reached the front entrance and kicked the door open, smashing the lock.

The Green Hornet burst onto the street, still carrying Casey over his shoulder, and found himself outside Sai Woo's Curios. He scanned desperately one way, then the other. The ground under Chinatown was shaking, rocking the Chin Tiki, the Golden Lotus, the Gold Dollar, and other surrounding structures.

The buildings' inhabitants poured out, seeking the relative safety of the open streets.

The Hornet peered around again. He was conspicuous, wearing a mask in the middle of the night, with a woman's dead weight hefted over his shoulder. People started to point.

Where the hell was Kato?

He turned around again, then back, and there was the Black Beauty, engine humming almost silently. He rushed to the car, gently set Casey in the back, and climbed in after her.

Axford was snoring in another corner of the back seat.

Kato smiled. "Where to, Boss?"

Lenore Case stirred as the Black Beauty approached her apartment.

She sat up and rubbed her eyes, then looked around the back seat, alarmed.

"Where's Mike?"

"Don't worry about him," The Green Hornet replied. "We unloaded him on the sidewalk outside the *Sentinel* to sleep it off. In fact, he's probably awake and inside by now."

"Raising the alarm about the dastardly 'Green Harnet,' no doubt," Casey said.

The Hornet smiled. "No doubt." He pressed a button, and the barrier between the back seat and front rose, affording them a moment of privacy.

"Well?" Britt asked.

"Well what?"

"Are you going to raise the alarm about the dastardly 'Green Harnet'?"

"Not unless you don't allow me to help you wherever I can," Casey replied. "I'm certainly not going to just sit on the sidelines after this."

"You mean," he said, "you're cutting yourself in for a piece of The Green Hornet's action."

Casey smiled. "Bingo."

"Good, I think I can live with that split." He lowered the barrier and continued to speak to Casey. "You can start by huddling with Mike Axford tomorrow morning. Chat him up about your time in captivity, reminding him that neither of you ever saw The Green Hornet, only Fang and her minions."

Casey nodded and Britt continued. "There's no proof at all The Hornet was ever in league with Fang, and in fact you're convinced The Hornet had a part in your rescue. Now, why would The Hornet do that if he was in on it with Fang? It must have been an elaborate frame-up. Your job is to convince Mike to take that angle with his story."

"Got it," Casey said. "Eventually Mike's take on it will spread and the public furor against The Hornet will die down—at least for the time being."

"For the time being."

The Beauty pulled up in front of Casey's apartment house. He pulled off his mask, tossed his hat on the seat next to it, and walked her to the front door.

Casey turned and grabbed him by the back of the head. She kissed him goodnight.

He returned the kiss, and then asked her, "How did you know?"

"Two things. First, tell Mr. Scanlon to be more careful in the future that he isn't watched coming in and out of your house, or rather the house next door. Speaking of which, you probably want to ditch that set-up with the 'for sale' house next to yours.

"Second, don't wear the cologne your secretary bought you last Christmas, when you're out and about as The Hornet, and expect your secretary not to notice."

Britt Reid nodded. "I'll see you bright and early at the office, Miss Case. You've had your day off, now it's back to work, we have a paper to run. And a Green Hornet to clear."

Casey shook her head, kissed him again, and went inside.

The Green Hornet and Kato rolled homeward.

They had won this round, but the shadow of Doctor Shan Ming Fu hung over them, and the city.

THE INSIDE MAN

by Matthew Baugh

The big, black car hardly made any noise as it slid through the warehouse entrance. I watched as it pulled to a stop, straining to see through the tinted windows.

Nothing. The man on the inside was notorious about his privacy. Nobody even knew his real name, only that he was an independent operator in a Syndicate town, but his operation ran so smoothly that even the big boys didn't want to give him a hard time.

He was exactly what I needed.

The driver's door opened and a guy dressed in black chauffeur's livery and matching mask stepped out. From the look of his lower face, I guessed he was Asian. From the hint of a smirk I knew he was confident, maybe even cocky. I filed that away as potentially useful information.

He opened the rear door and a taller man stepped out wrapped in a long coat that was such a dark green it blended with the shadows. He wore a mask too, and a fedora that matched the coat. I had to admit, it gave him a stylish look.

"You wanted a meeting with The Green Hornet," he said. "Tell me why I'm talking to you."

I noticed that my palms were sweating, but managed not to wipe them on my pants. I didn't want my nerves to show, not to someone like this. He radiated even more confidence than the driver.

"I've got a business opportunity for you," I said. "It's gonna make you a pile of money. My name is—"

"Timothy Nektosha," the chauffeur interrupted, "age twenty-four, graduated high school before serving one tour in Vietnam with the Army Rangers, decorated twice, discharged three months ago."

"You do your homework," I said. This time I couldn't help wiping my palms.

"So," The Hornet said. "Why does a war hero want to work for me?"

"Same reason anybody wants to work for anybody: money."

"You don't seem too particular about how you make it."

"What the hell do you care?" I said. He didn't react to the sudden anger in my voice, but it scared me. I needed to be more in control than that.

"Makes no difference at all," The Hornet said. "Not if you're telling the truth. The police have tried to plant men in my organization before. If a good citizen with no criminal record wants to work for me, I need to be sure of him."

"I'm no cop."

"Convince me."

"Look." I paused for a moment. I didn't want to be here and this guy had me rattled.

"Well?"

"I was a good soldier," I said. "I did what I was told and I got a medal for it. That seemed like it meant a lot at the time, but when I came back I was just one more Indian looking for work. You know where I live?"

"Ojibwe-Pottawatomi Reservation," the driver said. "You don't have a street address, but your PO Box number is 1268."

"Yeah," I said, wishing that I could smack that smirk off of his face. I didn't like men like this knowing so much about me.

"The Rez is a tough place to get by," I continued. "It's poverty like you don't even see in the worst part of the city. I got a job at the new casino, but my dad got sick with cancer. They say he needs more expensive treatments, but the bills he's already got are killing me."

The Green Hornet crossed his arms and leaned back against the car. "So you thought you'd get a nice advance from the casino?"

I shrugged. "It's not like that place does anything for my people anyway. The DiMara Family runs everything behind the scenes."

"They've got a nice racket going," The Hornet said. "I've been wanting a cut of that for myself."

"That's what I heard," I shifted from foot to foot and wished I could be as still as these two. "Look, I work security there so I know where the money is counted, the routine for shipping it to the bank, everything. With that info, plus your organization, we can take it all."

"Maybe," he said, "but I like to know about the people I work with. For example, I don't know how you are under pressure."

"The Army thought I did okay."

"I'd like to see for myself." The Hornet nodded and his driver moved in on me. I had four inches and at least thirty pounds on him, but the cat-like way he moved made me nervous. I tried to beat him to the punch with a left jab but he landed a kick to the side of my knee first. While I caught my balance, he was on me with a flurry of punches.

I bent into a boxing stance and covered up, but the blows came so fast that some of them got through. They hurt like the devil. This guy looked like a junior welterweight at best, but he hit as hard as anyone I'd ever fought. He left me an opening; it wasn't much, but I managed to land a right cross to his solar plexus. The punch wasn't solid enough to stun him, but it broke his rhythm enough for me to start my own attack.

I threw everything I had at him but it was like trying to grab water. He was quick and seemed to know what I was going to do before I did it. He trapped one of my punches and countered with a backhanded blow to my temple that made my knees want to fold. Then he planted a kick in the center of my chest that staggered me backward three steps.

I decided to try my own kick as he moved in. I spun my body around, lashing my heel in a deadly arc.

It didn't work. Somehow the chauffeur dropped under the kick and swept my other leg out from under me. I landed hard but managed to get right back up.

The little guy was backing away. Apparently the fight was over; I hoped my chances with The Green Hornet weren't over also.

"So he wins round one," I said. "I can still take him."

"Relax," The Hornet replied. "You don't realize how impressed I am that you're still standing."

"He's tough and fast," the driver said. "Most important, he's a smart fighter, keeps his head even when he's getting hit."

He turned his attention to me with a look of what might have been approval. "You know boxing, and that kick—was that Taekwondo?"

I nodded. "One of my sergeants in 'Nam knew a lot of that stuff. He taught me."

"You'll hear from me soon," The Hornet said. Without any ceremony the two of them got into the big car and glided into the night. I stood watching the darkness for a while before I followed.

The sky was overcast and a light drizzle had chased the people from the streets, not that there was much foot traffic at the docks at two in the morning anyway. I walked four blocks to a pay phone and fished in my jeans for a dime. As I did, my fingers brushed something small and round that I didn't recognize. It was the size of a quarter but thicker, and the texture was different—more like plastic than metal. I pulled it out and studied it under the phone booth's light.

The disc was a dark green and there were holes on one side that made me think of the mouthpiece of a phone.

A listening device.

The driver must have slipped it into my pocket during the fight. These guys didn't leave anything to chance. I dropped it on the sidewalk and ground my heel on it. When I moved my foot, I saw something white in the crushed plastic and wires; a piece of folded paper. I opened it and read the tiny script.

CONGRATULATIONS. IF YOU'RE READING THIS, YOU HAVE PASSED THE SECOND TEST.

It was signed with a circle around an angry-looking hornet. Green, of course.

I stuffed the paper in my pocket and made my call. The phone picked up after two rings.

"Yeah?" said a voice that sounded both tough and bored.

"This is Tim Nektosha. Tell Big Joe that I met the man tonight."

"Just a minute." The phone went silent. A moment later another voice answered; this one deep and refined, like someone who'd been trained to give speeches. Even if I hadn't seen him a couple of times at the casino, I'd have known it was Big Joe DiMara.

"He trusts you?" the voice said.

"Probably not, but he's interested in the bait."

"Good. He's probably going to put you through your paces to make sure of you. Keep me posted."

"Yes sir."

"I'm looking forward to stepping on that insect," he said and laughed softly.

I hung up the phone and absently wiped my hand on my pants. I pictured Joe, a heavy man whose soft belly was offset by eyes as hard as quartz crystal. He loved expensive new suits and always looked neat and clean as if he'd just stepped out of the bath.

I always felt dirty after talking to him.

My drive home took me east to Chelsea, a little town of century-old brick buildings and nearly three thousand salt-of-the-earth types. There was a bit of tension between the locals and the Pottawatomi—it always seems to be that way in the biggest town near a reservation—but I liked the place pretty well.

I turned north onto the crumbling blacktop of the Reservation Highway and switched on my headlights. It was nearly eight by the time I pulled onto the side lane that led to home. Like most roads on the Rez it was unpaved, a single lane, and the summer rains had made its surface into a long series of bumps and jolts.

I saw the headlights of a pickup truck coming from the other direction and pulled over to let it pass. It stopped alongside me and the driver—a small woman with her dark hair worn in two braids—leaned out of her window. I recognized Hahnoma Return, the new intern at the Health Services Clinic.

"Tim Nektosha. Hi."

"Hi," I said. My first thought, always my first thought these days, was that something had happened to Dad. But the doc wouldn't be smiling if that was the case.

"I came by to check on your father," she said.

"Kind of late for a house call, isn't it?"

"He invited me to stay to dinner," she said with another smile. "He's a hard man to say no to."

I knew that too well. His stubbornness had led to a lot of arguments between us over the years. That was something I hadn't missed when I was in the Army.

"Thanks for checking on him," I said.

She nodded. "Give me a call and let me know how he's doing later in the week, okay?"

I grunted and put the car into drive. I felt like a rat being that rude, but I didn't feel like conversation. Maybe I was afraid that the dirtiness from talking to Big Joe would rub off on her somehow.

Home was a small clapboard farmhouse with a rundown red barn and a twenty-five-year-old tractor. I found Dad inside sitting in the easy chair that he always kept draped with a green sheet to hide all the holes in the upholstery. He was watching *Hogan's Heroes* on the little black and white TV.

"Hi Dad," I said.

"You just missed the new lady doctor," he said.

"I passed her on the road. She said you asked her to stay to dinner."

He chuckled, which brought on a long and painful fit of coughing. I sat and waited in silence until it passed.

"That was her idea," he finally said. "She even cooked."

"That was nice of her."

"I think she was hoping you'd show up."

I grunted.

"She's a good cook," he continued. "Nice looking too."

"She's too skinny."

"You think you'll do better at that place you work? Maybe catch one of those flashy '*cmokmankwe*'?" Dad didn't usually use the Pottawatomi epithet for white women, but he thought that the girls who came to the Three Fires Casino were floozies.

"I'm not looking for a woman, Dad. I just work there."

"I don't like that place," he said.

"The pay's good."

"I don't like you taking money from crooks."

"If I don't work for crooks, who does that leave?" I said, trying to keep the heat out of my voice. He always did this to me, turned the simplest conversation into a criticism. We locked eyes for a moment, then he used a cough as an excuse to look away.

"So, what were you doing in Detroit today?" he said.

"I was meeting with crooks."

"What crooks?" His tone was suspicious, not certain whether I was putting him on.

"The Green Hornet."

"Hah!" The exclamation almost sent him into another coughing spasm, but he managed to stifle it. "You had me worried for a minute."

"I saw a movie," I lied. *Bonnie and Clyde*."

He shook his head. "I remember when they were in the news all the time. That Clyde was a vicious little punk. At least The Green Hornet doesn't kill people like that; he's got a little style."

"Are you kidding?" I said. "The only difference between him and Big Joe DiMara is that he's crazy, running around in a mask."

"That's something I like about him," my father said. "It's like the paint our people used to use. You put on the face you need for war, then you can take it off when it's time to come home and live in peace. Men like Clyde Barrow or Big Joe DiMara don't understand that. They wear their war-mask so much it's the only face they have. Not even their friends or family are safe."

"The Green Hornet named himself after a bug," I said.

"Hornet's not a bad totem. It's fierce and relentless when it's protecting its nest."

"Totem? Dad, this guy's no Indian. He's just some crook with a screw loose."

"Probably," he said. "You never know with a masked man."

I didn't respond and, after a moment, Dad turned his attention back to his program.

Dad and I were eating breakfast when the phone rang. I left him to his Cheerios and picked it up.

"Hello?"

"We have a final test for you," said the accented voice of The Green Hornet's driver.

"Okay."

"Have you heard of Britt Reid?"

"Yeah," I said. "The guy with the newspaper and the TV station."

Dad glanced up, his eyes curious, a little milk dribbling down his chin.

"Mr. Reid has been campaigning against The Green Hornet recently; the Boss wants him to back off. Your job will be to take that message to him."

"Me?"

"Be persuasive. As a sign of good faith, The Hornet wants him to make a donation to our organization. He keeps about ten thousand in his wall safe."

My mouth went so dry that I barely managed to get out an affirmative grunt. Selling one crook to another was bad enough; shaking down a straight-arrow citizen was not something I'd planned on.

"There's an envelope waiting in your post office box," the driver continued. "You'll find instructions there."

I opened my mouth, wanting to say something, but not knowing what. It didn't matter; the line was already dead.

"Hi Tim!" Hahnoma Return called as I stepped out of the Rez post office. I stuffed the blank envelope into the back pocket of my jeans and returned her greeting.

"How's your father?"

"About the same," I said. "He still thinks he's going to be strong enough to get out and fix up that old tractor."

"Yeah," she said, her smile turning sad. "I wish we could do more for him here."

"You do a lot. You do more than you know."

She didn't meet my eyes when I said that, but the warmth crept back into her smile. It made me feel good.

"I heard there's going to be a big rent party in Chelsea tonight," she said. "They've had some really good musicians staying there recently. Maybe I'll see you there?"

"No," I said. "I have to be in Detroit. Look, I've got a call to make and then I need to get going."

"Okay," she said. The disappointment in her eyes made me want to kick myself.

When Hahnoma left I crossed the street to the Trading Post to use the pay phone. I couldn't get her out of my mind as I dialed. Dad told me that her name meant 'honeybee,' which really seemed to suit someone so little, and such a busy worker. I frowned, reflecting that people named after small stinging insects were making my life complicated.

Tough-but-bored answered the phone and put me through to Big Joe.

"Britt Reid, huh?" He laughed. Unlike his voice, the laugh sounded crude, vulgar.

"Yeah," I said.

"That's pretty smart. The Hornet figures he'll have the goods on you for that so you can't ever betray him."

"I guess."

"He tell you to rough him up?"

"No, just to scare him."

"A man like Reid doesn't scare," Joe said, "He's one of those silver-spoon types who thinks no one can touch him. A little honest pain is the only thing to make that kind see reality."

"That's not what The Hornet—"

"That's what *I'm* telling you," Big Joe's interrupted. "Reid's been a thorn in my side too, and I want to see the job done right."

I crouched in the bushes outside Britt Reid's townhouse. The place was nice, but smaller than I would have expected, and in an older neighborhood. You'd think a millionaire would be in a penthouse or something.

The letter had told me that Reid lived alone, except for a valet, who was out of town tonight. The letter said he'd be alone, working on an editorial series for his news program. It told me what kind of burglar alarm he had and how to get past it. I didn't know where The Hornet got his information, but more and more I was learning he was a very dangerous man.

There had also been a key in the envelope, and instructions to pick up a package from a locker at Michigan Central Station. The package held clothing, a black suit, mask and fedora that fit like they'd been tailored for me. I was glad that he hadn't dressed me like a butler...or a French maid.

Under the clothes I'd found a flashlight and a gun: a new .45 automatic with the serial number missing.

I slipped into a back bedroom. The little flash showed a room that was decorated nicely but very simply. The only art was a black and white landscape on one wall, signed with Chinese characters. The foreground held a gnarled tree—or the suggestion of a tree. In the back I could make out the hint of tall, jagged rocks, dimly seen, as if in a fog. It was simply done but I really liked it.

I switched off the flash and moved into the hall. There was light ahead and the sound of a typewriter. I peeked through the entryway into a spacious living room. Reid was at his desk, less than a dozen feet from me, framed against a large bookcase. He glanced up as I entered, blue eyes narrowing, his hand moved toward the desk drawer.

"Don't do that," I said, raising my pistol.

"Who are you?" he said. "What is this about?"

If he was afraid, I couldn't hear it in his voice. There was a little bravado there, but mostly it was composure, more than I had expected from a rich man facing a bullet.

"I work for The Green Hornet."

"How do I know that?" he said. "He's only ever had one man working for him."

"Believe me or don't," I replied. "Just as long as you lay off the editorials."

"Or he'll have me killed, is that it?"

By the look in his eyes, I guessed that Big Joe was wrong. A beating, even one that put him in the hospital for a few weeks, wouldn't stop Reid. If anything it would make him more determined. I asked myself again what I was doing here; I liked The Hornet more than Big Joe and was starting to like Reid better than either of them. How had I gotten myself involved in this?

"Back away from the desk," I said.

He complied without a word. I opened the drawer he had been reaching for and pocketed the little pistol he kept there. Keeping my gun on him, I gathered all of his notes from the desktop. The wall next to the entrance I'd used was flagstone with a fireplace set into it. He had one of those perpetual gas flames going, providing decoration but nothing much in the way of heat. I would have had the thing turned off on a mild summer's evening like this, but that's just me.

I stuffed the papers into the fireplace and watched Reid as they flared up. He gave me a crooked smile.

"That's only a few hours' work to replace."

"I'm surprised that you do your own typing, Mr. Reid," I said. "I'd think a guy like you would have a pretty secretary to do it for him."

"I gave her the evening off."

"And your valet too? Good thing, because it would have been bad if they'd been here."

By the way his jaw tightened, I guessed I'd hit a nerve.

"You seem like a brave man," I continued. "That's good, but you should remember that it's not just you that'll be in danger if you push The

Green Hornet too far."

I had a creepy feeling as I spoke. Maybe it was just Reid's eyes burning a hole in me, but I had the sense of being watched. That didn't make sense with just the two of us in the room, but the Army taught me to trust my instincts.

"Is there anyone else here?"

"No," he said.

"That's good, but if there was, I hope you know that I can drill you before they could do anything about it."

He didn't speak, just kept staring me down.

"You've got the message," I said. "Just give me your money as a good faith gesture and I'll be on my way."

"I don't keep any money in the—"

"Ten thousand in the wall safe," I interrupted. "The Hornet knows a lot about you, Mr. Reid, including how to get to you any time he wants."

"All right," he said. "There's a button on the underside of the desk."

I found the button and hesitated a moment. I didn't think he was stupid enough to tell me to press an alarm, but I wasn't sure what to do if I was wrong.

The hell with The Green Hornet, I thought, *and the hell with Big Joe too.* If I was wrong I'd get out, fast, but I wasn't shooting a man for anyone. I'd wash my hands of the whole business and take whatever consequences came.

It wasn't an alarm.

When I pressed the button a painting on the wall slid aside, revealing a small safe. I observed Reid closely as he turned the dial. The feeling of being watched still bothered me, and I risked a glance over my shoulder. There was nothing but stone wall and burning paper. That's the problem with instincts, sometimes they tell you things that can't possibly be true. I decided to ignore them and focus on Reid.

The safe yielded some papers, which I ignored, and a thick stack of green with Ben Franklin's chubby face beaming at me. I stashed the money in my jacket, handcuffed Reid to an iron stair rail and left by the front door. I walked for three blocks before the big black car pulled up alongside me and the rear door opened.

Climbing in, I noticed that, aside from the driver, the vehicle was empty.

"Where's The Hornet?" I asked.

"That's not your concern," he said. "Did things go as planned?"

I considered telling him that was 'none of his concern' but decided the timing was bad for that. I pulled out the wad of bills.

"It went pretty good."

"Keep the money," the driver said. "The Boss says it's a down payment on our arrangement. Write down all the information on the Casino and send it to PO Box 4952. We will contact you when we're ready to move."

I didn't call Big Joe; I just changed my clothes, hid the money under my truck seat and headed home. Every time I saw a patrol car on the highway, I could feel myself go cold all over. My mind came up with a thousand different scenarios in which they knew what I had done and were just waiting for the right moment to descend.

As I came through Chelsea, I saw crowds of people at the base of the old brick clock tower. This must be the rent party that Hahnoma mentioned; I wondered if she was there and that made me feel worse. I had no business thinking about someone like her with the stuff I was wrapped up in.

Dad was asleep by the time I got home. I stuffed the cash in an old shoebox and placed it as far as I could reach into the heating register in my bedroom. Then I sat up the rest of the night imagining everything that could go wrong.

I called Big Joe from the Trading Post pay phone the next morning.

"I saw the papers," he said, sounding pleased. "Good job. Just let me know The Hornet's plan as soon as he tells you."

"Okay."

I hadn't seen the papers and didn't have a clue what he was talking about, but didn't want to tell him that. After I hung up, I went inside and picked up a copy of the *Daily Sentinel*.

Britt Reid was in the hospital.

According to the front-page story, Reid had been assaulted by a prowler in his home last night. His condition was listed as 'serious,' but he was expected to make a full recovery.

What the hell?

"It's simple," The Green Hornet said. "After you left Reid's place, I decided that it would be useful if he was out of action for a few days."

We were meeting in the back of a dive on the outskirts of the city. The Hornet was smart enough not to use the same rendezvous twice.

"So your man went back and roughed him up?"

"I took care of it myself," he said. "Does that bother you?"

"Just that the police are going to think that I did it," I lied.

"Don't worry," he said. "Reid will tell them that it was me. Now, here's how we're going to hit the Casino. We'll do it tomorrow at midnight, just as they're starting to count the evening's take. You still have the gun I gave you?"

"Yes."

"Make sure you're carrying it tomorrow."

I field-stripped the gun when I got home that evening. Everything looked fine until I checked the clip. The first bullet came out okay, but what slid into place behind it was no bullet. He had rigged my gun to do something, but what?

I stared at the device for over an hour before I decided what to do about it. If The Green Hornet thought he'd pull something on me, he'd have a real surprise.

At 11:55 p.m. the following evening I slipped away from my post and made my way to the rear entrance of the Three Fires Casino to meet The Green Hornet and his man. The door had a crash bar on it and the fire inspector said it was to be unobstructed at all times. The thing was, Big Joe DiMara said he didn't want the back entrance open in case the Feds ever came calling. The heavy chain and padlock said that, given the choice between being trapped in a burning building and facing an angry Big Joe, the employees would take the flames.

I didn't blame them.

I'd told The Hornet that I didn't have a key for the lock, but he didn't seem worried. As I reached the door I could see why. A shrill buzz cut through the air, not loud but painful anyway. As it intensified the door latch and the chain seemed to melt away. It was like seeing them cut with a very hot welding torch, but there was no light.

The Hornet pushed through the door holding a yard-long metal wand in his hands. He collapsed it like a telescope and tucked it in his coat.

"My 'Sting'," he said with a crooked smile. "It uses ultrasonics to cut through almost anything."

The driver entered after him.

"Change of plan," The Hornet said. "We're not going after the money."

"What?" I said.

"I want Big Joe's books, the real ones. The ones that the District Attorney's been wanting to read."

"What?"

"Why settle for taking one night's haul when I can move him out and have the whole thing?"

So that was it, and it meant that there *was* no difference between The

Green Hornet and Big Joe after all.

"We might as well do both," I said. "They keep the books down in the safe, where no one can get them."

I pulled out my gun but The Hornet signaled me to put it away. He produced his own, a sleek Buck Rogers-looking thing. The driver didn't appear to have a weapon.

We moved through the building quietly. Once we happened on another security guard, but The Hornet shot a spurt of thick green gas at him and the man collapsed.

"He'll be out for a couple of hours," he said. "By then we'll be long gone."

We reached the counting room where two big security men guarded a steel door. The Hornet's gas gun took one down and the driver took care of the other with a kick to the gut, followed by a chopping blow to the base of the neck. It happened so fast that the man never had a chance to draw his weapon.

I found the door key on the sleeping guard's belt, so there was no reason for The Hornet to use the sting again. Then we were in, with only half a dozen frightened counters to oppose us. We sat them against the wall and The Hornet gassed them into slumber.

"Where are the books?" he said.

"Books?" said a cultured voice from the door. "What's he talking about, Tim?"

Big Joe stood there, flanked by half a dozen gunmen. I drew my own weapon, pointed it at The Green Hornet and backed toward Joe and his men.

"Set-up," the driver said through clenched teeth. It was the first time I'd seen him look anxious. He didn't look worried the way other people do, just less cocky than usual.

"I made Tim an offer before you did," Joe said. "He sets you up, and I set him up for life." He chuckled, and the ugly sound of it made me sick.

A lot went through my mind then; that there really was a difference between these two. The Hornet was tough and shrewd, but he wasn't a sadist. Dad was right; what was behind that mask had to be more human than Big Joe DiMara.

"Why don't you let your spy do it?" The Hornet said. "Let Tim shoot us, then he's one of you for real."

"No," Joe said. "This pleasure's going to be all mine."

"Wait a second, Joe," I said. "I know what he's trying to do."

"He's just playing for time."

"No, he wants me to shoot because he gimmicked my gun."

"What?"

"He didn't think I'd be smart enough to inspect it, but I did. I found that he'd put this in place of a regular ammo clip." I held up the clip I'd removed earlier and replaced with one filled with real bullets.

"What is it?" Joe said. "What does it do?"

"I think it does *this*!"

I threw the clip as hard as I could to the ground at Big Joe's feet. It shattered, releasing a thick cloud of green gas. Joe took two steps then collapsed and two of his gunsels followed.

The other four men weren't affected much, but the gas plus the confusion let me tackle one of them to the ground. I pinned his gun hand with my left and hammered him with hard rights until he stopped moving.

The Hornet and his man moved quickly as well. He went for one of the gunmen with a series of boxing combinations, softening him up with jabs. Then he drove a right cross to the solar plexus followed by a punishing left hook to the point of his chin. The man sank to his knees and made no attempt to rise.

The driver had already taken one of his two guys out, I didn't see how. The remaining man threw a punch, but the driver blocked it and drove a sidekick to the gunman's belly. As the man staggered back, the driver leaped high and came down with an elbow to the top of the head.

And then it was over.

"I'm glad you came around, Tim," The Hornet said after we loaded DiMara and his men in the vault and sealed the door.

"What now?" I said.

"Now we give Joe's books to the D.A. By the time they open the vault tomorrow morning, there will be warrants waiting for every one of them."

It wasn't hard to get the books from Big Joe's office. All of his boys were in the vault with him, and Casino security didn't want to mess with The Green Hornet. Ten minutes later, we were speeding south in the big black car.

"What was the idea with the gun?" I said.

"It was my last test. If you shot me, I'd know you were one of DiMara's men at heart. If you'd shot him, I'd know your better instincts had won out. Either way, the gas would have given us the distraction we wanted."

"That was a big risk."

"I had a back-up plan."

After what I'd seen, I believed him.

"So," I said. "What now?"

"Now DiMara goes to prison and I control the casino. I'd like you to run the operation for me."

"Just like before?" The anger started to rise in my voice.

"Just like before, except you'll see that the money goes where it needs to go. You can see that Reservation roads get paved, schools get built... maybe refurbish that clinic."

"I don't get it."

The Green Hornet gazed out the window at the passing shapes of pine and oak trees in the moonlight.

"Let's just say I hate the DiMaras of the world, and I have a strong interest in seeing your people do well. There's a connection I have with them that goes back a long way."

"What sort of connection?"

"Boss, this guy is awfully curious," the driver said.

The Hornet smirked. "Wise words," he said. "Curiosity is a sign of intelligence, but so is knowing when something isn't your business."

I nodded, not wanting to provoke him. Still, there was one more thing I just *couldn't* let go.

"What about that business with Reid?" I said.

"He's fine. I thought it would look better to Joe if we planted that story."

"He was in it with you?"

"He wanted DiMara as much as I did, more than he wanted me. We set up the robbery; if you'd tried to shoot Reid the trick gun would have gassed you."

"But, the money..." I was at a loss by this time.

"Keep it. Reid hasn't reported it missing because it was my fee for helping him with Big Joe."

"Keep it?"

"I'm not some small-timer to worry over ten large. Besides, you earned it."

The car slowed to a stop. I peered out, recognizing the side road that led to my home.

The Hornet pressed a card into my hand. On one side was his seal—The Hornet in the green circle—on the other a phone number was written.

"That Casino is The Green Hornet's operation," he said. "If anyone else tries to muscle in, call that number."

"And you'll handle it?"

"And *we'll* handle it."

They left me there, still dazed by things. I thought of Dad, and Hahnoma, and of all the things that a mask can hide. For the first time, it felt good to be the inside man.

The Green Hornet Meets the Phantom
in
The Soul of Solomon
by Harlan Ellison®

What Is, Is;
Sometimes, Perhaps, What Ain't
Shouldn't Be

"Wisdom come late, is wisdom nonetheless."
Paul Selvin, Attorney

I curse the lesson, and bless the knowledge. An old man sits at a manual typewriter as the midwinter sun sighs beyond the horizon. He seeks what he has always sought, the right path through the story. The correct and only way to weave the spell, sense and mordant wit, adventure and recurring surprise. As with each time, all the way back to the very first one, it calls its name, finally revealing its true self, and he follows where it leads. He trusts those tiny voices. They always give up their name and their hiding place. The story tells itself.

An old man practices his craft.

But this time he hears only his own heartbeat and the empty cavern of his mind. The story hides. But he goes on, because this is the work, the work he has done all his life, and one does not leave the plough in the unfinished furrow.

It used to be so effortless, a glide, a slalom; now, there is heaviness, and the voice out there is barely audible. Time and gravity are no man's friends.

But he said he would do it, and the plough stands waiting, so he goes on. And how little the younger ones know. How shallowly they confront the work to come. A tsunami is coming toward them, and they perceive of it merely as a new season of American Idol.

Arrogance will not suffice. Nor will putting the shoulder to the wheel. No amount of dithering will shorten the heavily-trod pathway to the abyss. Nonetheless, dammit, the work must be done. How did I ever get into this? the old man muses. Who got me into this one?

His name is Ruben Procopio. I curse the lesson and bless the knowledge.

It is possible that the cover of this very book may sport a painting by Ruben Procopio. He is an excellent artist.

He is also a gracious and great-hearted man, and his friendship manifested itself one day last year in the manner of his arriving at my home bearing gifts. Sumptuous gifts. Sculptures by Ruben. The Phantom. The Green Hornet. (And Andy Panda, but he doesn't make any more than this cameo reference.) Ruben had come to tell me how much he

admired <u>my</u> work, and we stood around like two seven-year-
olds, praising each other's toys. And as I stared at the
magnificent double-statue of The Green Hornet and Kato,
back to back and radiating all the grandeur I'd known through
    radio
their exploits as a little boy in the early 1940s, the
beginning of the lesson Ruben was to drag me into learning,
began.

I said, "Boy, wouldn't it be wonderful if there were
a story in which The Green Hornet actually <u>met</u> The Phantom?!"

The old man pauses. He needs to explain a theory.
Because the theory lies at the heart of the trouble, of
the lesson, of the anguish.

#

Sometimes, what is...simply <u>is</u>. It is that way because
the universe has decreed it so. No larger, no smaller, no
more blue, not patterned with stripes. Just because we <u>can</u>,
doesn't mean we <u>should</u>. What an arrogant, transitory little
species we are. Change, always change; just for the sake of
spewing NEW! on the carton. No better, no richer, no more
profound...just <u>other</u>. The great French poet Mallarmé
wisely pointed out, "To define is to kill. To suggest is
to create." The old man smiles and concurs.

Besotted with technology, but no greater of heart or
innovation, the world goes a-whirling, onward ever onward,
but loses its shadow. The moment is suffused with a cobalt
blue miasma, and a kind of cultural hypnosis takes us all.
We stare at the unreal, creating nothing of our own, providing

willing customers for the Company Store. And all that was,
is lost, unremembered, ridiculed and discarded.

Because we <u>can</u>, we do.

No better, no nobler, merely one more pony added to
that dog-and-pony show that recycles the old ideas, but
leaches from them their freshness.

For instance, the old man points out, we <u>had</u> one
<u>King</u> <u>Kong</u>. A perfectly good one. We never needed five or
six others, just because we had the ability to articulate
the great beast a little better.

One still goes back to that crampy, stop-motion
black and white artifact, and the wonder is not dimmed.
One watches for a while all "re-imaginings"—theft is too
harsh a word—and after a time there is a nasty buzzing
between the ears. Just because they could, well, they
needn't have. The universe created that first, miraculous
<u>King</u> <u>Kong</u> and said, "Never again." But we are a duplicitous
little species. Give us a knife, and we can whittle a
flute to charm a child, or to cut our meat to survive. But
because they <u>can</u>, some use the knife to bury the blade in
someone's skull, to build the bomb, to strap the death
onto an old woman and send her into a marketplace. The
knife makes no flutes, quarters no loin of beef: it kills.

Because we are capable, if we can, we do. Even though
the universe makes it clear: sometimes, what is, <u>is</u>; and
sometimes what <u>ain't</u>, shouldn't be.

The old man looks back on the theory, and sighs. It
seems diffuse. Does it parse at all? What all this of
a universe of IEDs and fat people losing weight on

teelvision? If one were just encountering such maunderings,
if one were younger and had no idea who, say, Willis O'Brien
was, or Christy Mathewson, or Ma Rainey, or Jim Tully,
would this theory make any sense? Or would it merely
resonate with a great and deep, heartfelt sense of loss?

#

The world is run by the geek-boys. Anything they
can think of, is ooo <u>awesome</u>! Kewwwwwl!

And the geek-boy said to Ruben Procopio, "Woooo,
wouldn't it be neato keeno kewwwwl if The Phantom met The
Green Hornet?!" And Ruben Procopio said, "I am seven
years old, too. And I'd <u>love</u> to illustrate that!" And
the geek-boy, overcome with gratitude and respect for the
great gifts the artist had given him, being only seven
years old himself, let Ruben Procopio take it to his
publisher. And the geek-boy did nothing to stop the
publisher from making it all real, asking permission of
two elegant gentlemen--David Grace of the firm of Loeb &
Loeb, that represents the Trendle holding of The Green
Hornet, Inc.--and Brendan Burford of King Features
Syndication--and the seven-year-old geek-boy cozzened
them, and chatted with them, and told them of the sublime
story that could be written. Not knowing that this was
a lesson brutal in the learning, defying the universe
and its message: what is...just <u>is</u>. Let it lie, old man.

And so, arrogant and naive, even after all these
years, after chasing down and capturing every one of
those fleeing little creatures, and gaining power over

them by uncasting the runes and learning their true
names...

I could easily lie, and say it was the fault of
Britt Reid and The Ghost Who Walks. I could lie and say
I held sway over them, that they were just fictions
and so many hundreds of others had done with them as
they chose...why not I? I could lie, but I won't.

It was arrogance. A fool's pride and refusal to bend
to the will of the universe. I had to learn that lesson,
finally, after all the years I had pulled that plough.

Yes, it was Procopio who abetted my fecklessness.
He had no way of knowing that's what he was doing, but
if I lie and attempt to blame Ruben, I might get away with
it, oh poor sad old man, he didn't know what he was doing,
and I might get away with it. But always, inevitably,
the fault is mine. More than sixty years at this typewriter,
I should've known what the hell I was getting into.

But I was arrogant. No other word for it.

It is an explanation, but not an excuse.

I have to eat that rotting, redolent fish, head
and bones and all.

#

That was April 5th 2009. It is now nearly ten months later.

So I began to write. And here is the beginning of
that story. It is all you'll EVER get of "The Soul of Solomon."

MY name is Kato.

At one time or another, I have been asked thus: "Ah, well and good. Kato. Yes, we know that name. But what is the full of it? Kato "Who?""

The asking is simple. Unsullied and clear, without twist or turn. The answering is much more difficult; and never fully satisfying. Kato Kikigaki, the faithful Japanese house boy. Kato Aguinaldo, the staunch Filipino aide; Kato Tung hu, of what you might call "royal" Manchurian lineage. Kato Yutang, who was definitely Chinese; and Kato Nguyen, who might have been Korean, Vietnamese, even Laotian, there is no certainty.

My name is Kato.

Let that suffice for the duration of this narration.

I would tell you of two men I knew: Mr. Reid, for whom I worked many many years, until he committed suicide and this telling will disclose the reason for his final act of life and Mr. Walker, who said to me, "When the devil is your landlord, you had best begin humming "The End of the World Blues." Immediately after the events of which I will treat here, Mr. Walker shunned his other self, and turned what you might call the "family business" over to his son. He then became hermitic, as one with aramites; and sequestered, let the ashes of his final days disappear on the winds of the years.

My name is Kato, and I worked for the man who

was known as The Green Hornet, and once, just once, I was of avail to The Ghost Who Walks, he who called himself both Mr. Walker and The Phantom. Beside them in the most terrible moments of their lives, on the path that forced them to cut trail with each other as I say, once, just once.

The beginning, if you believe, was long before the birth of Christ. If you believe, it was long before the Neolithic peoples of Middle and Lower Egypt, more than a thousand years before Mentuhotep II reigned in the Middle Kingdom. Perhaps even before, as one has said, "the oceans drank Atlantis," if you believe. Again, the asking is simple, any fool can play in that field. Not even belief, not even faith, suggests that the beginning occurred at the same moment most life on Earth succumbed to the flaming cudgel that snuffed out the saurians. No ... no one can believe that.

It has been said that the second beginning was during the excavation for the Temple of Jerusalem. Not the Haram al Sharif, not Herod's Temple on the Mount, not the temple of Zerubbabel, but the first Temple, the one called Solomon's. It was erected based on plans given to Solomon by his father, David; and decades before Solomon completed his father's dream, ground was first broken, the soil was first turned, in 959 Before the Common Era.

Beneath the blade of one such exploratory spade, an Israelite laborer struck something that rang with the sonority of a carillon. When it was unearthed, it was carried to the overseer, who held it away from himself as he rubbed it clean. And he took it to the Master Builder Hiram, who had been sent to Solomon by the ruler of the Phoenicians, and Hiram was dazzled by it, and he took it to Solomon, and the King held it, staring into its abyssal depths for a very long time. It was neither stone nor gem, neither coral nor petrified wood, neither scoria nor glass. It was exquisite; and it rang sonorously; and it gave back the sunlight and starlight in colors and shadows whose hues could not be named.

They came to call it The Soul of Solomon, and it was put in the inner sanctuary, the Holy of Holies, the *debir*, nearby the Torah and the Ark of the Covenant and the twin cherubim covered with gold that were fifteen feet tall, each with a fifteen foot wingspread and there, for three millennia, it lay waiting, there atop Mount Moriah, on the threshing floor of Araunah where (if you believe) not only had Abraham sacrificed, but so had Adam, Cain, Abel, and Noah.

There it remained, for almost four hundred years, till the First Temple was burned and plundered by the Babylonians of Nebuchadnezzer.

And so vanished from men's eyes, The Soul of Solomon. If you believe.

Night had dropped its tonnage...

I wrote in a frenzy, all of that opening in one sitting.
I was so drunk on it, I called Josh and read it to him. And
he was knocked out by it. Then I read it to Susan and <u>she</u>
was knocked out by it, but she loves me, so I can't trust
that. Then I called Joe Gentile, and <u>he</u> said, "Britt Reid
commits <u>suicide</u>?! You can't do that!" And I, arrogant and
puffed up like a pouter pigeon, replied, "Trust me. I'm
the fuckin' king of the universe; you'll only <u>love</u> it when
you see where I'm going with this." And Joe trusted me,
because he didn't know he was talking to a seven-year-old
geek-boy.

Goshwow, wouldn't it be so kewwwl if Godzilla battled
The Creature from the Black Lagoon while Flash Gordon and
The Bowery Boys joined forces to bring down The Red Skull
who travels around in the Tardis! There is a balance in
the universe, dear friends. Trifle with it at your peril.
I sat and stared at Ruben Procopio's magnificent sculptures
of The Phantom and The Green Hornet, and I wrote as well as
I could write--Josh said so, Susan said so, even Ruben
said so--but I didn't realize, till the white heat of my
beginning cooled, and I had to contemplate how I was
going to run down that fleeing creature called story, and
gain the power of its name. Then I began to learn that
lesson, and began to fear the knowledge.

What happened was this...

I knew <u>how</u> I was going to tell the story: from Kato's
viewpoint.

But why had Britt Reid killed himself? Why had The
Phantom passed over his active life to his son, the <u>next</u>

Walker, after the affair of The Soul of Solomon. And
what was the Soul? I knew! It is no less than the conscience
of god; the ability to know, and to do, good or evil.

It would have a powerful, possibly deleterious effect
on anyone who possessed it. For instance, on Mount Moriah,
Abraham would have sacrificed his son; Solomon would have
cut the baby in half. Cain did slay Abel, there on Mount
Moriah, because the Soul lay just beneath.

What a great concept. Bigger than I'd planned, more
complex and ethereal than I'd intended, but what a kewwwwl
idea. In pursuing the Soul, for whatever reason, The
Phantom comes to Chicago, where he and The Hornet cut trail,
and this happens, and that happens, all of it written with
all the skill and imagination of a lifetime of unraveling
storylines and creating characters.

I even went so far as to seek out a pseudoscientific
reason for that stellar object to possess the qualities
I needed to move the plot. And I called my friend, the
(also) stellar science fiction writer, Jack McDevitt,
and shared my plot-problem with him. And Jack, good friend,
went to a prestigious reference source with geek-boy's
conundrum.

"Michael," Jack wrote, "Harlan Ellison is working on
a story. He has a meteorite which puts out radiation that
effectively bifurcates the nature of an observer, causing
him to go to one extreme or the other. Think the Lone
Ranger deciding he has had enough and shooting the bad guy.
Or an individual who is normally extremely selfish
sacrificing himself to save someone else. What he needs is

an explanation--something that can be encapsulated in three lines or so; how might this happen?"

Already, the universe was trying to tell me...what is, simply _is_. If it were condign for The Phantom to meet The Green Hornet, it would not require this convoluted, cobbled-up <u>Lara</u> <u>Croft</u>, <u>Tomb</u> <u>Raider</u> jiggery-pokery. You are suddenly in the middle of doing what only the crappiest kind of Michael Bay filmmakers do...you are twisting and corrupting your own story to achieve an artificial end. I was doing exactly what I'd spent a lifetime avoiding -- I was lying.

And the "Michael" whom Jack had asked to intercede on my behalf, Michael Fossel, MD, PhD, MA, FACEP, wrote back and said, "...the quantum nature of consciousness. It goes something like this: consciousness is absolutely dependant upon the quantum nature of reality and its inherent unpredictability (hence free will). The radiation (it immediately makes me think of 'Bizarro' from <u>Superman</u>) inverts the relationship between normal neuronal function and consciousness by producing a mirror image of the normal quantum connection (and here a great deal of hand waving occurs)..."

The Green Hornet possesses the Soul. He does something so tenebrous, so impossible to live with, that he kills himself, even though what he did was sunk to the roots in the greater good.

<u>What</u> "greater good?" What am I talking about here? What sort of nebulous Judeo-Christian morality am I trying to sell? Why didn't I just do a simple, silly story about gangsters and goons in the jungle and Chicago back'o'the'yards?

What the hell have I gotten myself into here?

And that was in May. Then June. Then year-end. And now I come to the end of my tale.

The old man sits hunched as he has been for decades, tapping out line after line. He has learned a terrible lesson, and it may be the very last one of his life:

Ruben responded to the geek-boy. Wouldn't it be kewwwl if...

If what? If worms had wings? If monkeys bit the heads off every lubricating vampire-loving teen? If a thought got lost and found its way into Sarah Palin's arid Sahara of a skull? If this and if that; it is a terrible lesson finally to learn that just because we <u>can</u>, it doesn't mean we <u>should</u>.

I spent a year near the end of my life, trying to write what should never be written. The Phantom stands, The Green Hornet stands, they need never meet. They have nothing in common, ultimately, save the arrogance of an old man who has learned at the last doorway that sometimes what ain't, shouldn't be.

Wisdom come late, is wisdom nonetheless.

HARLAN ELLISON, a Grand Master Lauerate of the Science Fiction and Fantasy Writers of America, was recently characterized by *The New York Times Book Review* as having "the spellbinding quality of a great nonstop talker, with a cultural warehouse for a mind." And the *Washington Post Book World* said simply, "One of the great living American short story writers." In 2009 a best-selling documentary of his life, "Dreams with Sharp Teeth" premiered at Lincoln Center, and is currently high on Amazon's "Best" list.

He has written or edited 75 books; more than 1700 stories, essays, articles, and newspaper columns; two dozen teleplays, for which he received the Writers Guild of America most outstanding teleplay award for solo work an unprecedented **four** times; and a dozen movies. He won the Mystery Writers of America Edgar Allan Poe award twice, the Horror Writers Association Bram Stoker award six times (including The Lifetime Achievement Award in 1996), the Nebula three times, the Hugo 8½ times, and received the Silver Pen for Journalism from P.E.N. Not to mention The World Fantasy Award, the British Fantasy Award, the American Mystery Award, two Audie Awards, the Ray Bradbury Award, and two Grammy nominations for Spoken Word recordings, the latest being this year!

He created great fantasies for *The Twilight Zone* (including Danny Kaye's final performance) and *The Outer Limits*; traveled with The Rolling Stones; marched with Martin Luther King from Selma to Montgomery; once stood off the son of a Mafia kingpin with a Remington XP-100, while wearing nothing but a bath towel; sued Paramount three times and ABC-TV for plagiarism and won $337,000—(among his perfect score of legal wins, including AOL and hundreds of internet pirates) and probably *is* the most contentious person now walking the Earth. But the bottom line, as voiced by *Booklist* last year, is this: "One thing for sure: the man can write."

In 1990, Ellison was honored by P.E.N. for his continuing commitment to artistic freedom and the battle against censorship. He lives with his wife, Susan, inside the Lost Aztec Temple of Mars, in Los Angeles.

DEAN JEFFRIES: LIFE AT 90 MPH

by Rubén Procopio

**An interview with Dean Jeffries,
creator of TV's Black Beauty**

Interview May 3, 2010, at Dean Jeffries' shop, Hollywood, CA, conducted by Rubén Procopio

Rubén: I'm here with the man himself, Dean Jeffries!

Dean: Thank you much.

Rubén: Let's jump in with our first question, how were you approached to do the Black Beauty?

Dean: I met with the folks at 20th Century Fox and Greenway Productions, Producer William Dozier and Maureen O'Hara's brother, Charles Fitzsimons. I sat there and made a drawing, that quick, and I started on it right away.

Rubén: Were they specific in what they wanted? Did they ask you to use a Chrysler or was it all your creation?

Dean: They didn't discuss any specifics or say what car or nothing like that, the object was to come up with something unique that would fit as The Green Hornet car.

Rubén: Had you known of The Green Hornet?

Dean: Oh yes, from way back.

Rubén: Whose idea was it to use a Chrysler Imperial Crown?

Dean: That was mine. I got ahold of the right people at Chrysler to get the cars, and they said no problem. It was TV, so there wasn't too much money to invest and until the show was done they didn't know if it was

going to be a moneymaker, so they came to me and trusted what I would come up with.

Rubén: What was your inspiration for the design?

Dean: Well, to tell you the truth I don't remember a hundred percent, but I looked at it from a design standpoint, what would make it a unique type of a car.

Rubén: I consider you an artist as well as a builder of these incredible cars. We're surrounded here in your shop with all these wonderful designs that you've drawn on paper. How do you envision the design? Do you see it in your mind's eye before you start, or is it a process that develops as you go along?

Dean: Well in the case of the Black Beauty I was picturing kids looking at this car and thinking "this is neat." I didn't look at any of the old comics. So, I didn't see it in my mind, rather I started by thinking what are they going to do with The Green Hornet's story in the TV show. From there I thought of the design and items to go on the car. Then I start doing drawings, that's the way I approach all cars. I did the Monkeemobile the same way.

Rubén: Did they tell you they wanted the car to have gadgets like the James Bond car, you know, like shoot rockets and have little brooms come down from the rear to cover up the tire tracks?

Dean: No, those were things that I came up with. They wanted the car to do things, so I knew I could make things like guns come out the front, or have it squirt oil and flames and shoot rockets. What they did want was it to be clean and a design that was streamlined and different from any other car, so you couldn't tell what make it was. Also at that time cars had big chrome bumpers, I took those off. Same with the rear view mirror, and no car handles. I got rid of all that so it was clean and sleek. Even the doors opened by themselves. We even had a little model made for the turnaround garage floor sequence.

Rubén: That's a clever unique design element to get rid of the bumpers.

Dean: What was neat about that is that no one else had done that before.

Rubén: Tell me more about the little scaled model of the Black Beauty?

Dean: Well I told them that for the garage sequence I would have to build another car, but it would have to be gutted. They said no, let's use a model instead.

Rubén: What timeframe did they give you?

Dean: We had to have the whole thing done in a month. It's TV. For features it's a different story, you have more time and money. I've always known this, heard this even from my wife Rosalie, who worked in the financial side of things at Warner Bros. We had to build two cars at the same time. Things work fast in TV, so we had to go 90 miles an hour to get it done in 30 days.

Rubén: Did you have a team of people helping you?

Dean: Yes, I always had people here, sometimes one or two, other times up to fifteen to twenty. Depends on how quick the project needed to be done.

Rubén: You hear that the glossy black paint was a problem. Could you tell us about that?

Dean: We did a super nice job making it highly glossy black, but they had to matte one of them down because of the glare the camera picked up. So one was used on the show and the other one, the shiny one, toured the car shows. Only one time did both cars appear in an episode of The Green Hornet, and they dusted down the shiny one so the camera wouldn't pick up the glare.

Rubén: There's no fiberglass on there, is there?

Dean: No, it's all metal and handmade.

Rubén: So if both cars were built at the same time, why is one called the number 1 car and the other the number 2 car?

Dean: When I started building it, I started with the first car, that's the number 1 car. The other one sat next to it for several days until I'd get to that one. Simultaneously someone at the shop was making the same part for the second one. That number 1 car was used inside and out for all the scenes. As an example, when I did the cars for the movie *Romancing the Stone* I did three of them, with three different engines that were used on the set. One was quiet and they were able to shoot dialogue scenes in it, the other ones they wanted it to sound like a big racing car.

Rubén: Did both of them have all the gadgets?

Dean: Yes, they both were the same.

Rubén: The show and the car have made an impression on so many and have lived on all these years. What does the Black Beauty mean to you today?

Dean: Well, you know at the time to me the Mantaray and the GT40 were important one of a kind cars. When I built the Black Beauty I didn't think it was something spectacular and now it's became a world wide famous car. That doesn't happen to very many cars, so that's special.

Rubén: You were at a great time and place in the history of TV and movie making because you had all these requests to do all these cars, and the cars themselves became stars, as you said, they became world famous. Not only does The Green Hornet show have fans, but the Black Beauty itself has a fan base. Are you happy with how it came out?

Dean: Oh yeah… extremely. I'm surprised that to this day it's still popular. They still do stories on it and people want to know things about it. Like the Monkeemobile, they both have been a great personal satisfaction.

Rubén: How did the Black Beauty affect your career at the time?

Dean: It kept getting me recognition up until this day. It helped me crawl up the ladder. It's like a top-notch movie actor that we all admire, they're always good and talked about forever, from now until doomsday. That's the way it works. That's a really nice thing to happen in one's life. But if you're no good, no one talks about you, they don't want to.

Rubén: To this day you still get visitors because of the Black Beauty?

Dean: Yes, it's strange, people come and I'm not aware of if, but they tell me my name is known across the country and everywhere. I even used to keep the gate closed because I would never get anything done. I'm not one to say I did this or that, I'm just glad that I did it. All of it is good. It's been great!

Rubén: Wonderful. So, are there any behind the scenes stories you can tell us?

Dean: It's pretty much all been all said. I'm just happy to have been part of this big thing called the motion picture industry. It's the best.

Rubén: In your opinion what are the top cars you've created?

Dean: The Mantaray, it's a one of kind non-symmetrical design, it's offset, but people still admire it. I did that in 1962. Then, the other one that I feel was really neat was the Landmaster from the movie *Damnation Alley*, it had to do a lot of neat things nobody had done before. It was a 12-wheel drive unit, and to top it off, it had to float in water! That was a tough one. I would have to say, I'm really proud of the Monkeemobile and the Black Beauty, those two cars have kept nicely. I didn't look at them as a real zoomy design, but people to this day still tell me nice things about the Black Beauty, which is now in the Peterson Museum. It sold for almost $200,000. I got $10,000 back in the 60's when I made it, and that was good money back then! It was great, just to think, I was happy to get $10 a day way back when!

Rubén: So what are your thoughts all these years later about what you've done?

Dean: To this day I don't feel any different from when I was 18 years old or how I feel today. I still feel the same. It's all how you feel in your mind and like what you've done in life. And I'm extremely happy with myself. It's not about what other people say, that I did this or that. You can look back and say I should've done this or that, but you can't win them all, that's for sure. There are more and more talented people out there, you just try to do the best you can.

Rubén: Is there anything you want to say to The Green Hornet fans and those reading this book who are Black Beauty fans?

Dean: I want to thank them very much. I'm extremely thankful that people still know and remember me. I still like what I do. I'm just happy to see the sun every morning.

Rubén: Well Dino, thank you very much.

Dean: Okay… I'm off and running!

Rubén Procopio is a longtime Black Beauty fan, friend and neighbor to the Legendary Car Customizer.

DAILY SENTINEL MORGUE: AUTHOR BIOGRAPHIES

Terry Alexander and his wife Phyllis live on a small farm in Oklahoma. He is a relative newcomer to the writing world. His most recent work has been published in *Night of the Wolf* and *End of Days III* by Living Dead Press and on Frontiertales.com. Contact him at terryale@crosstel.net.

Matthew Baugh has been a fan of The Green Hornet since seeing the TV series as a kindergartner. He never got to own one of the cool die-cast Black Beauty toys with the firing rockets, or even one of the fedoras with a mask and Green Hornet sticker like all the other kids did, but he's over that now. He lives and works in the greater Chicago area and has previously contributed to *The Phantom Chronicles 2*, *Tales of Zorro*, *High Seas Cthulhu*, and other anthologies. When not writing about heroes, monsters and such he works as a pastor.

Thom Brannan (est. 1976) is a former submariner, radiation worker, electrician and dabbler in unemployment and is now an offshore oilfield technician with questionable intent. He currently lives in Austin, Texas with his lovely wife Kitty, his boy Bobby and a pair of dogs that might or might not be escapees from an extraterrestrial zoo of some sort. He's frantically trying to prepare for a newborn and hopes that the little girl will be easier on him than he was on his parents. You can find his work in *Robots Beyond* (Permuted Press) and at www.DarkTomorrow.net.

James Chambers' short story collection, *Resurrection House*, was published by Dark Regions Press in 2009. His tales of horror, fantasy, and science fiction have appeared in *Bad-Ass Faeries*, *Bad Cop No Donut*, *Breach the Hull*, *The Dead Walk*, *Domino Lady: Sex as a Weapon*, *Dragon's Lure*, *Hardboiled Cthulhu*, *So It Begins*, and the magazines *Bare Bone*,

Cthulhu Sex, and *Allen K's Inhuman*. He is also the author of *The Midnight Hour: Saint Lawn Hill and Other Tales*. His collection of novellas, *The Engines of Sacrifice*, will be published by Dark Regions Press in 2010. His website is www.jameschambersonline.com.

Greg Cox is the *New York Times* bestselling author of numerous books and short stories. He has written books and stories based on such popular series as *Alias, Batman, Buffy, CSI, Daredevil, Iron Man, Fantastic Four, Farscape, The 4400, Ghost Rider, The Phantom, Roswell, Star Trek, Terminator, Underworld, X-Men,* and *Zorro*. His official website is www. gregcox-author.com.

Win Scott Eckert's *Myths for the Modern Age: Philip José Farmer's Wold Newton Universe* (MonkeyBrain Books) was a 2007 Locus Award Finalist for Best Non-Fiction book. His credits include stories about adventurous characters such as The Avenger, The Phantom, The Scarlet Pimpernel, Doc Ardan, Sexton Blake, Hareton Ironcastle, Captain Midnight, and Zorro; as a longtime Green Hornet aficionado, he's gotten quite a buzz—*ahem*— from co-editing and writing a tale for the present volume. In keeping with the Green theme, he (along with co-author Eric Fein) is writing the Green Ghost for Moonstone's Originals comic pulp project. Win's latest books are *Crossovers: A Secret Chronology of the World 1 & 2* (Black Coat Press, 2010), and the novel *The Evil in Pemberley House*, about Patricia Wildman, the daughter of a certain bronze-skinned pulp hero (co-authored with Philip José Farmer, Subterranean Press, 2009). Find Win on the web at www.winscotteckert.com.

Mark Ellis is a novelist and comics creator whose credentials include *Doc Savage, The Wild, Wild West, The Justice Machine, Death Hawk* (with Adam Hughes) and *The Miskatonic Project*. The author of 50 books, he created the best-selling *Outlanders* novel series for Harlequin Enterprises' Gold Eagle imprint and co-wrote *The Everything Guide to Writing Graphic Novels* with his wife, writer/photographer Melissa Martin-Ellis. He has been featured in *Starlog, Comics Scene* and *Fangoria* magazines. He has been interviewed by Robert Siegel for NPR's *All Things Considered*. His latest book, *Cryptozoica*, is on sale now. www.MarkEllisink.com. www.Cryptozoica.com.

Ron Fortier For the past thirty-five years Ron has worked for most of the major comic companies. He's best known for writing The *Green Hornet* and *Terminator: Burning Earth*, with Alex Ross, for Now Comics back in the '80s. Today, he keeps busy writing and editing new pulp anthologies and novels via his Airship 27 Productions (www.gopulp.info) and contributing to Moonstone's Originals with brand new I.V. Frost adventures in both prose and comics. Visit him at www.airship27.com.

Robert Greenberger is a writer of fiction and non-fiction, largely involving the world of pop culture. He has worked for Starlog Press, DC Comics, Gist Communications, Marvel Comics, and *Weekly World News*. His numerous credits include numerous *Star Trek* novels and the Scribe Award-winning novelization of *Hellboy II: The Golden Army*. His most recent works include *The Batman Vault*, *The Essential Superman Encyclopedia*, and *Iron Man: Femme Fatales*. Bob continues to write news and reviews for ComicMix.com. He makes his home in Connecticut with his wife Deb. Find out more at www.bobgreenberger.com.

Rich Harvey is a New Jersey-based writer and designer. He edits and publishes material pertaining to the pulp magazine era under his Bold Venture Press imprint. www.boldventurepress.com.

CJ Henderson is the creator of the Jack Hagee hardboiled PI series, the Piers Knight supernatural investigator series, and many more. Author of some seventy books, as well as hundreds and hundreds of short stories and comics, as well as thousands of non-fiction pieces, this prolific writer is known for action, adventure, comedy, horror, fantasy, sci fi, and for being able to assemble the best BLT this side of the Pecos. For more info on this truly wonderful fellow, to comment on his story in this volume, or to read more of his fiction, simply hop over to www.cjhenderson.com.

Howard Hopkins (www.howardhopkins.com) is the author of thirty-two westerns under the penname Lance Howard, six horror novels, three young adult horror novels and numerous short stories under his own name. His most recent western, *Dead Man Riding*, is an August 2010 release and his most recent horror series novel, *The Chloe Files #2: Sliver of Darkness*, is available now. He's written widescreen comic books and graphic novels for Moonstone, along with co-editing and writing for *The Avenger Chronicles*, and will soon bring The Golden Amazon back for a new generation of readers in Moonstone's Originals comic book pulp line.

Mark Justice lives in Kentucky with his wife and cats. *The Dead Sheriff*, his prose and comics series, is forthcoming from Evil Eye Books.

Will Murray first heard the ominous buzz of The Green Hornet over Boston's WORL circa 1963, and never forgot it. When the ABC TV show premiered in 1966, he was front and center, audio taping the incidental music. With the dawn of video tape, he acquired the complete series, and it was while running comic book conventions in the 1980s that he first talked about his vision of creating a second-generation Hornet with a female Kato. When NOW Comics sought to revive the character, Murray was instrumental in helping acquire the rights. "The Night Car" is his first Green Hornet story.

Rubén Procopio is a multi-tasking artist with more than twenty-five years of experience. Rubén is a credited animation artist on dozens of Disney feature films, including *The Little Mermaid, Beauty and the Beast, Aladdin,* and *The Lion King.* In 2003 Rubén founded Masked Avenger Studios, reflecting his lifelong love for the masked heroes of yesteryear and providing animation, sculpting, comics, and illustration services to many entertainment clients. Highlights include Rubén's sculpts of such legendary characters as The Lone Ranger, Zorro, The Phantom, and The Green Hornet & Kato for Electric Tiki's Classic Heroes Line, and the publication of Rubén's original character Chameleon Man™ stories. Other Moonstone Books projects include illustrating *The Phantom Chronicles* anthology and its accompanying *Artist's Annex, Tales of Zorro* and *Captain Action* books, and collaborating on *Phantom Generations* covers. Rubén became a Green Hornet devotee after giving a Disney Studios tour to Van Williams and befriending car designer Dean Jeffries. See more of Rubén's work at: http://www.maskedavenger.com and http://www.maskedavengerstudios.blogspot.com.

A lifelong Texan, **James Reasoner** has been a professional writer for more than thirty years, authoring several hundred novels and short stories in numerous genres. Writing under his own name and various pseudonyms, his novels have garnered praise from *Publishers Weekly, Booklist,* and the *Los Angeles Times,* as well as appearing on the *New York Times* and *USA Today* bestseller lists. He lives in a small town in Texas with his wife, award-winning fellow author Livia J. Washburn, and blogs at jamesreasoner.blogspot.com.

A professional writer since he was sixteen years old, **Bill Spangler** has contributed to *Star Wars on Trial, Farscape Forever,* and *Getting Lost,* all volumes in the Smart Pop series published by BenBella Books. He scripted the recent *Tom Corbett, Space Cadet* revival from Bluewater

Comics and wrote a short story based on the classic serial hero Commando Cody. Before that, he wrote comics for several independent publishers, with both original and licensed characters. Bill and his wife, Joyce, live in Bucks County, Pennsylvania.

Richard Dean Starr has published more than 200 books, graphic novels, articles, columns and stories in magazines and newspapers including *Starlog*, *Twilight Zone*, *Science Fiction Chronicle*, and the *Tribune-Georgian*, just to name a few. His fiction and non-fiction has appeared in *Hellboy: Odder Jobs*, *Tales of Zorro* and *More Tales of Zorro*, *Kolchak: the Night Stalker Chronicles*, *Kolchak: The Night Stalker Case Book*, *The Avenger Chronicles*, and the 2005 Stephen King Halloween issue of *Cemetery Dance*. He is also the author of the graphic novel *Wyatt Earp: The Justice Riders*, the editor of *Tales of Zorro* and *Sex, Lies and Private Eyes*, and co-editor, with Matthew Baugh, of the *Captain Action* comic and prose line.

Patricia Weakley — I am a Libra. That just about sums it all for me. Balance is the byword of my life. I believe that while there is much bad in this world, there is also a great deal of good. People every day are doing small and large acts of "heroism." I see the tales that I write as mental experiments on the nature of heroism. In my attempt to answer the question: "Why are there no real masked vigilantes like in books and TV?" I put together characters of different personalities and backgrounds, and then let them tell me their stories. For my Green Hornet stories see www.fanfiction.net/~patweakley.

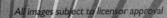

THe GReeN HOrNeT

Classic TV Figures
COMING 2011

www.factoryent.com **FACTORY**
ENTERTAINMENT

A History of Radio,
Motion Pictures,
Comics, and
Television

THE GREEN HORNET

by Martin Grams &
Terry Salomonson

Documents the entire history of the radio series,
comic books, movie serials and television series-
816 pages thick, over 100 photographs.

Includes complete episode guide for all 1,000 plus radio episodes
and all 26 TV episodes. Fully indexed. $29.95 plus $6 postage:
OTR Publishing, Po Box 252, Churchville, MD 21160